THE HALFLIFE

Tor books by Sharon Webb

The Halflife
Pestis 18

THE HALFLIFE

by

Sharon Webb

A TOM DOHERTY ASSOCIATES BOOK
NEW YORK

This is a work of fiction. All the characters and events portrayed in this book are fictitious, and any resemblance to real people or events is purely coincidental.

THE HALFLIFE

A TOR BOOK
Published by Tom Doherty Associates, Inc.
49 West 24 Street
New York, NY 10010

First edition: August 1989
0 9 8 7 6 5 4 3 2 1

This book is dedicated to the many professionals of the Central Intelligence Agency, past and present, my cousin among them, who refused to compromise their innate morality and decency in the name of covert action or expediency.

And to the coffee-drinking cops in emergency rooms everywhere, who, when the moon is full and things get crazy, make every nurse feel a little safer.

And especially to Diane Hughes, who helped make much of this book possible.

Acknowledgments

I would like to thank the following people who have been so generous with their time and advice:

Denver Adams for his mechanical advice and his technical suggestions.

Jerry and Sharon Ahern for their "ode" on a D-string.

Diane Hughes, LCSW, doctoral candidate in clinical psychology, for the many notes she shared, for the hours of helpful speculation, and for her invaluable insight into the mind of the multiple personality.

Robert Jordan for his suggestions and engineering expertise.

All the librarians at the Mountain Regional Library for their patience with my pesky interlibrary loan requests.

Harriet McDougal, my editor, for her patience, moral support, and advice.

Wendy Neshelm, R.N., M.Ed., and Jerri Thompson, R.N., for their medical error checking.

Marybeth Wiles, M.D., for her advice on trauma and drugs.

Bryan Webb—for being there.

And to the person whom I can only refer to as The Nameless Source: you know who you are. Thanks.

Finally, let me stress that any errors in this book are solely my own and not the responsibility of anyone listed above.

Sharon Webb

THE HALFLIFE

PROLOGUE

Orange light from the crackling fire danced across the faces of the eight boys clustered around it. Below them, along the dark winding path that led to the cabins, a half-dozen other campfires spit red sparks into the clear June night.

Tim Monahan skewered a pair of marshmallows onto a sharpened birch stick and held them over the fire. The heat felt good. Just after sunset, a cool wind sweeping down from Thunder Mountain had dropped the temperature twenty degrees in as many minutes and the boys had pulled on gray Camp Challenge sweatshirts. The Grays were the best. Better than the Blues. And the Gray Foxes were the best of all. They were going to win the canoe trophy for sure, and probably archery too.

Tim stuck the end of the stick into the ground and angled it over a rock in the fire ring. The trick was to get the marshmallows as fat and gooey as you could without letting them melt all the way through and fall in the fire. Murphy wouldn't give you seconds if you burned yours up. Compared to the other counselors, he was okay, only sometimes he was a pain in the butt.

Murphy was passing out chocolate-covered graham crackers to go with the marshmallows. Tim balanced his on his knees and stared down at the lake glimmering like black ice in the pale light of the moon. He could make out the tiny tree-covered island near the shore. That's where they said it had happened.

Murphy pulled a half-pint carton of chocolate milk from the cooler and shook it. "Heads up." Feinting at Tim, he tossed the milk in the opposite direction. Aiming a sharp elbow to hold off The Wolfman's lunge, Razorback caught it, and with a quick guffaw ripped it open and began to drink greedily.

Murphy, shaking another carton of milk, looked up. "You're gonna lose it, Pig."

Pig's sneaker whacked Tim in the knee as the boy scrambled to rescue his dangerously elongated marshmallows.

"Watch it, lard ass." He wasn't afraid of Pig, even if he was almost a head taller. Pig was older too. Going on thirteen. But he couldn't get out of his own way.

"You watch it, Money-man," said Murphy, and sailed a carton of milk in Tim's direction. Money-man was his camp name, a corruption of Monahan. The only one that went by a real name was Wolfman, except his was spelled with two "n"s.

Tim caught the carton with one hand. More than Pig could do. Old Pig probably couldn't catch a cold. He watched Murphy shaking the milk cartons, shaking, shaking. What kind of gunk in there needed all that shaking? He turned his attention to the marshmallows, sandwiching them between two chocolate grahams, pinching down, sliding the stick out. Hot marshmallow goo began to melt the chocolate. He gave it a swipe with his tongue, relishing the sweet hot candy.

Murphy dangled the bait. "Who's got a story?"

Mark Shad—The Shadow—poked Tim in the ribs, but he didn't mind. The Shadow was his friend, a Wallenski kid like he was.

"Lookit."

Across the campfire, The Wolfman had scrambled to his knees. Elaborate movements of his hands cast fluttering shadows across his face. Suddenly he threw back his head and gave a blood-curdling howl.

Murphy grinned. "Let's have it."

The Wolfman settled back on his haunches with a satisfied grin. "Bet you never heard what happened to the Blues. These guys over in Cabin Three were sitting around just like us when all of a sudden they heard this noise." The Wolfman's mouth made a little O and out came a low-pitched "oodle-oodle-oodle-ooh" that sounded like an owl, only different, eerier.

Tim stuffed the rest of the chocolate grahams into his mouth and stared at The Wolfman in frank envy. Everybody was watching him, taking it all in. Why couldn't he ever tell stories like that? The stories that crowded Tim's head never came out right when he tried to tell them out loud. Somehow, the only way they turned out right was when he got them down on paper. He had a couple of good ones; he had scribbled them down on the notepad he kept under his pillow while everybody was supposed to be writing letters home.

Maybe he could tell the one about the UFO—about the aliens that came down and changed so they looked like humans, only if you looked at them just right, with your face kind of squinched up, their eyes got transparent and you could see through their disguise. And what you saw was really disgusting—like the slugs down in the shower house that made silvery goo on the concrete.

But every time he tried to tell his stories out loud, he'd get something wrong, leave out something important. Then he'd have to backtrack and say, "I forgot to tell you there was this spaceship." Stuff like that. The Wolfman never had to do that; The Wolfman could make his eyes all dark and mysterious, and the next thing you knew, you believed everything he said without half trying.

Dark streaks of chocolate smeared Tim's fingers. He sucked them clean and picked up his milk carton. It was cool in his hands. He started to open it when he noticed a little drop welling out near the top. He wiped it off with an index finger. Underneath was a tiny, barely noticeable hole as if someone had stuck a needle through the wax container. Tim gave the carton a shake, and another drop oozed through the pinhole. He licked it off. Chocolate milk all right.

Or was it?

He imagined an alien proboscis spearing into his milk, dribbling poisoned gunk inside. A thin alien proboscis—sharp as the stinger on a bee.

Tim shivered at the thought and stared down at the shadowy little island near the edge of the lake. That's what they said happened to the Blue. What was his name? Jerry or Jimmy, something like that. They said it happened Monday after supper. The Blue was messing around on the island when a bee got him. Right on the throat.

They called it anaphylaxis. He repeated it under his breath: "Anna-fuh-lax-us." It could happen to anybody. If you're allergic, one little bee sting, and zap, you're dead.

He pried open the carton and took a swig, then another. Saving some for later, he set the milk down and leaned forward. The Wolfman pulled his lips back in a hideous grimace and curled his hands into claws. In spite of himself, Tim was sucked into the story.

The Wolfman's arms were swooping bat wings. "OODLE-OODLE-OODLE-OOH!"

Tim glanced uneasily over his shoulder. Anything could be back there. Anything.

The Wolfman was swaying now in the low light of the dying fire, bat wings out, fangs dripping blood. Swaying closer and closer toward Razorback, who was grinning a silly you-can't-scare-me grin.

Then suddenly The Wolfman changed direction and pounced on Billy-the-Kid.

"GOTCHA!"

Billy-the-Kid, who was about as brave as a rabbit, hollered like he was killed, and everyone laughed fit to be tied. Billy-the-Kid was really stupid not to see that one coming, thought Tim. Not that he wasn't smart; he was a Wallenski kid too, but that didn't mean he had any common sense.

Out of the corner of his eye, Tim caught a movement. Pig, swiping his milk. He lunged for the carton, but he wasn't quick enough. Pig straight-armed him and slugged down the rest of the milk in two gulps. Then he was grinning this stupid grin—and chocolate milk smeared all over his mouth.

"You shit." Tim's gaze darted toward Murphy. Did he see? But the counselor had turned away and was pulling out a green garbage bag.

"Snitcher. You gonna go snitch?" Pig crushed the carton in a freckled fist, and a thin trickle of chocolate milk dribbled over his fingers. "You know what happens to snitchers."

Tim narrowed his eyes. "I don't need to, see. I'm gonna get you tonight when you're sleeping."

"Sure," sneered Pig. But a flicker of doubt crossed his face.

"Okay, Foxes. Butts up." Murphy handed the plastic bag to Razorback. "Able team, police the area. Baker team, secure the fire ring. I don't want to see a single live coal." He passed out entrenching tools.

Tim dug a spadeful of dirt and heaped it on the coals. "Gee, Murphy. This is too much like work. Can't we just pee on it?"

"You and the Jolly Green Giant? Dig. You've got ten minutes until taps."

From below them came the sound of the Blues' fight song. Instantly the eight began to sing the Grays'. A third squad joined in, then another, and the hillside was a cacophony of raucous voices. But then the songs died away and the sweet sound of a bugle echoed across the lake.

Day is done . . . Gone the sun . . .

As the little fires on the hillside went out, flashlights came on, flickering like fireflies through the trees, bobbing along the curving path toward the cabins waiting in the dark.

Tim hitched up on one elbow and stared out of the window. From his upper bunk, he could see all the way to the counselors' cabin. Murphy was halfway there, flashlight playing along the path.

He was probably going to drink booze, he thought. That's what they did after lights out. They sat around outside and sipped out of paper cups. The counselors' cabin sat fifty yards up the hill just above the campers' cabins. That way they could keep an eye on everybody. And an ear. It was amazing how they could hear the littlest sound. Then, the next thing you knew, here would come Murphy and maybe one of the other guys wearing big scowls and threatening to take away swimming privileges or something.

Outside the counselors' cabin, a match flared as someone lit a cigarette. "Betcha they're drinking booze," Tim whispered. The Shadow had the upper bunk next to his, but he didn't answer like he usually did. "Betcha they're drinking booze," he repeated a little louder.

No answer.

Tim squinted through the dark at the stripe of moonlight on the next bed. The light fell across The Shadow's open mouth. Sleeping.

Tim ducked his head off the side of the bunk. "Hey, Razorback. You awake?"

A faint snore.

"Wolfman?"

But no one answered.

How come everybody was asleep already? Wolfman was always the last one up. It seemed strange. But before Tim could ponder the reason, a sudden drowsiness overwhelmed him, and his eyes dragged shut.

During the night, Tim thought he heard Murphy's voice, low and indistinct in the darkness. He tried to pop his head up to see, but somehow he could not lift it.

He was in a deep sleep when the voice came again. "This one."

A hand touched his shoulder. Then someone was lifting him, plucking him from the bunk. He tried to pull away, but he did not have the strength.

"Come on, buddy. Lie still."

His eyes popped open, and he tried to focus, but all he could see was a blurry light moving in the dark.

A whisper. "Go back to sleep."

He slept. . . .

* * *

Red.

Red in front of his eyes.

His eyelids fluttered, squeezed shut. He lay on his back on something hard. A light bright as the sun was overhead. He tried to fling a hand over his eyes, but it felt heavy as stone.

Something cold splashed against his throat, and his nostrils filled with the sharp odor of alcohol. He tried to wriggle away.

"Lie still."

Hands grasped his chin, tilting it sharply, turning his head. "Just a little bee sting."

Hot pain speared his throat just beneath the angle of his jaw.

A bee! Like the Blue. Anaphylaxis, like the Blue.

A voice: "Don't screw up this time."

Voices. A thousand whispering voices humming in his brain.

Pictures. Flashing, flickering, blurring.

Blackness. . . .

The first light of dawn crept through the window, waking him. He lay staring at the dark tree branches outlined against the gray sky and tried to remember the odd dream he had had. But the more he woke up, the dimmer the dream became.

His stomach suddenly felt strange, and he interpreted the empty feeling as hunger. Pig probably had candy bars in his duffel. It wouldn't hurt to check it out. But first, he had to pee.

Tim struggled up and sat on the edge of the bunk and looked around the dim cabin. Everybody was still asleep. He was swinging down when a sudden dizziness struck and he clung to the bed for support. In a moment, it passed, and he found his shoes and went to the door.

The path to the latrine twisted downhill through a thick stand of wild rhododendron. Pushing the wooden door open, he tried not to breathe in the smell. Inside, the acrid sewer odor laced with disinfectant made his stomach churn, and instantly he was thoroughly, wretchedly sick.

When his stomach was empty, he stumbled outside. Weak and dizzy, he sank down beneath an oak and laid his head against its broad rough bole.

He stared down at the wedge of gray foot-scraped dirt between two thick snaking roots. Suddenly the earth bulged and cracked, and something small began to move just below the surface in a curving subterranean path.

A mole, he thought. He had seen the tracks before in his mother's garden. They ate bulbs and stuff. His mother hated them.

He reached for a stick to spear it with and his fingers closed over a soggy half-rotten branch.

Then he blinked.

The patch of dirt was smooth. Perfectly smooth. There was nothing there. No mole. Nothing there at all.

ONE

Twenty-two Years Later

The dream again. It crawled from a crevice in his brain and quickened his pulse. He ran, legs pumping in agonizing slow motion, eyes straining against a stark twilight that drained color from the swamp.

He ran through a thick gray mist pierced with blackened tree limbs. The thing was closer now. All around him. He had to get out, get to higher ground.

He ran. But each step plunged him deeper into the sucking mud. His heart pounded with exertion—and cold fear. He knew what came next.

Suddenly, muck, thick as glue, swallowed his legs and crept toward his hips. Panicked, he snatched at a half-drowned branch. It fell apart in his hands and he sank deeper. Mud pinioned his arms. He took a shuddering breath, but his lungs would not fill, and the rotten smell of the swamp clogged his nostrils.

He could not move now. Numbing cold seeped into his bones, crawled up his spine, closed over his throat. He gave a final cry then, knowing as he did that the strangling mud would flow into his open mouth.

The taste of death.

Blackness.

He hung suspended in a void drained of sound and sensation. Gradually a thin gray light penetrated the dark and he looked down from a height. A drowning lock of his hair, black as ink in the twilight, floated for a moment on the mire. Then it was gone without a ripple and there was nothing left.

The swamp was a flat, imageless mirror. But underneath its surface, something moved.

The swamp convulsed and vomited up a huge clot of mud. The mass erupted and began to rotate, draining slime and rotten sticks and detritus until its surface was as smooth as tar. It spun faster now, drying, contracting, folding in upon itself in deep coils that glistened like a tortuous mass of thick-bodied snakes.

The clot slowed. Stopped. Fissures opened on its surface, and he saw that it was a giant brain made of earth.

Fascinated, he stared.

The brain bulged and cracked as something moved beneath its crust—something small, tunneling just below the surface. A blind thing creeping in buried patterns, leaving the curving subterranean track of a mole on the smooth dark convolutions.

Gasping, he realized it was his. His brain. He could feel it, cold as night, inside his head.

And locked within the bony plates of his skull, something moved and burrowed through the lobes and fissures of his mind. Something hidden. Something that was not him. . . .

Tim Monahan woke with a start and gulped a breath to slow the pounding of his heart. Just the nightmare, he told himself. That was all.

Ever since he was eleven or twelve years old, the dream

had recurred with dismal regularity. Each time he had tried to analyze it, tried to remember if it came from a movie or maybe a horror comic he had read back then, he drew a blank. He had finally decided that he was getting flashbacks of a parochial school notion of hell. The nightmare faded quickly and he focused blearily on his watch. Nearly eleven-thirty. Time to get up anyway.

Grimacing at the dark morning taste in his mouth, he sat up and a tangle of blanket slid to the floor. Stepping over it, he opened the window shade and blinked. Sunlight flashed through the crimson leaves of the old maple and flooded the room. Below his garage apartment, the wooded ravine plunged and leveled before it rose sharply to the road and the perpetual parade of cars headed for Lenox Square and Georgia 400.

Oblivious to the traffic just beyond her yard, Coralee Hamilton was kneeling beneath the red oak that shaded the back porch. Shifting to adjust the stack of burlap bags cushioning her bulging knees, she selected a jonquil bulb from a broken-down wicker basket and poked it into the hole she had made. Sensing Tim's presence, she looked up and waggled a dirt-daubed glove at her tenant.

Tim hesitated, then waved back. His landlady doted on him like a son, plying him with the peanut butter cookies he loved and the fruit cake he politely accepted and pitched into the garbage when she was gone. She meant well, but God, how she loved to talk—much of the time, unfortunately, to him. He had even thought of moving because of it, but the rent was cheap, cheaper than anyone could expect in this part of Atlanta. But he was more than just a tenant; to her, he was an "insurance policy," someone to protect her from "robbers and drug fiends." And from *those people* too, he thought with a grin. Coralee Hamilton spoke fluent italics, underlining her meaning with sharp darting eyes, translating *those people* into blacks or teenagers, Vietnamese immigrants or land developers, as the occasion demanded. Hoping to discourage a visit, he pulled down the shade and headed for the bathroom.

He found the toothpaste beneath a wadded, sour-smelling washcloth and tried to brush away the dark remains of tobacco and last night's beer. Absently poking the washcloth in the direction of the overflowing hamper, he stripped and got into the shower that he shared with a layer of musty towels and a green rubber tyrannosaurus rex.

The dinosaur had been a gag gift from Linda for his thirty-fourth birthday. They had celebrated with lasagna and Chianti Classico. Afterward, they lay in bed, and, for the first time, he talked of marriage. Two days later, he had come home to an empty apartment. All that was left of Linda Jean Montgomery was a discarded pair of sandalfoot pantyhose and the dinosaur. Not quite all. A week later, when he pulled out the last of the clean towels, her diaphragm rolled out and careened across the tile floor like B. C.'s wheel. He gave it to the dinosaur, who clutched it to its scaly chest as if it were a shield. That had been nearly two months ago. He wondered if she had missed the diaphragm yet and decided that she had.

He pulled on a pair of jeans and a sweatshirt. In the living room, the darkened computer screen stared at him like a blank accusing eye. Skirting it, he went into the tiny kitchenette, found a cup in the sink, and rinsed it out. There was enough Taster's Choice left in the jar for one strong cup, or two weak ones. Shaking out what appeared to be half the coffee, he ran water into the kettle and set it on the stove.

When the kettle chirped, he poured boiling water into the cup, searched for a spoon to stir it with, and found one in the sink. A film of dried chili darkened its bowl. Staring at it for a moment, he used the handle. He'd have to wash up some dishes again. It didn't take long to run out.

Balancing the coffee cup on his knee, he settled back on the couch, lit a cigarette, and stared at the computer. His novel had a bad hole in chapter seven. He wanted to fill it in, but it had to go on the back burner if he planned to eat this month. Bill Bennett was expecting the creature feature continuity first thing tomorrow, and the Jake Gerrard book was due. Tim made a careful distinction between the Jake Gerrard series and his real books. He hated to admit to himself that the espionage thrillers by "Mike Mona" paid the rent, while Timothy M. Monahan's *A Shaft of Light* was remaindered, and *Weapon of Fury*—"a thought-provoking character study" to quote *The Atlanta Constitution*—looked less and less like a smash.

Rummaging through a stack of magazines and unopened junk mail, Tim found the videotape Bennett had sent. He had been ghosting Bill Bennett's vampire host routines for nearly eighteen months now. Not the greatest of literature, but it made the payments on the computer. A terse note fell out of the tape box: "No red stuff. I'm allergic. 4 plus!"

Tim snorted. He wondered if Lewis Grizzard would like the tidbit for his column: "Channel 44's resident Saturday night vampire allergic to blood."

The Saturday Creep Show had scheduled *Alice, Sweet Alice.* Frowning, Tim tried to remember if he'd seen it before. He flipped on the TV and stuck the tape in the VCR. A game show, then snow, and the film began to play. The music sounded eerily familiar. He stared at the credits. Brooke Shields? It rang a bell. Wasn't it her first movie? She couldn't have been more than ten or eleven. Reaching for a yellow pad and pencil he wrote, “Brooke’s first? Check.” Then, absently passing the pencil to his left hand, he began to doodle on the page. The movie was coming back to him. A few moments later, he glanced down, barely noticing the Halloween mask he had drawn; he had seldom taken notes without a half-dozen or more doodles decorating each page. Flipping the pencil back to his right hand, he wrote, “Alice—red herring?”

Before the movie was ten minutes old, the outside stairs creaked with the heavy footsteps of Coralee Hamilton. “Here comes Aunt Pittypat,” he said under his breath. Groaning, he hit the VCR pause button and went to the door.

“I brought you your mail,” she said with a bright smile and thrust a thick stack into his arms.

“Oh, thanks.” Tim paused. “I must have lost track of the time. I do that when I’m working,” he said, putting slight, but unmistakable, emphasis on the last word.

“Well—” She shot an expectant look inside. “I was going to join you for a coffee break. But if you’re busy—”

“I really am,” he said quickly. A smile. “I’ve got a deadline.”

She hesitated. “I’ll just toddle off then.”

“Some other time,” he said. Another smile. “Real soon.”

“Good-bye then.”

He shut the door softly, but firmly, and flipped through the stack of mail. Coralee had stuck a Baggie full of her peanut butter cookies between *National Geographic* and *Byte.* Tim was instantly contrite, but he controlled the impulse short of calling her back upstairs.

Looking for a check, or the promise of one, he thumbed through the mail. Junk. Most of it was addressed to

Linda—or current occupant. He'd probably be getting flyers for mail order bras and genuine eelskin handbags for the next twenty years. Only one letter was addressed to him. He glanced at his name and address, assessing whether or not it was another computer-generated come-on masquerading as personal mail. No dot matrix. And no return address either. Lighting a Winston, he took a drag and opened the envelope.

The letterhead read "Institute for Psychological Studies." There was an Atlanta address.

Dear Mr. Monahan:

The Institute for Psychological Studies has recently received a grant for an important research project in the area of learning and creativity. In order for this endeavor to succeed, it is necessary to enlist the aid of appropriate subjects.

To this end, we invite you to participate in a pilot study that could influence basic theories of education for years to come. We know that you will wish to be included.

Initial evaluation will take only a week of your time. Thereafter, ongoing research should require only an occasional interview at irregular intervals. We will, of course, provide meals and lodging during the week's residency. In addition, you will receive a stipend of $500.00. This is not as much as we would like. There is the possibility of more, but we cannot commit to a larger amount at this time as the allocation for participants is, unfortunately, still enshrouded in a bureau-

cratic cloud. Net gain to you, however, will be greater than recompense alone. You will have the satisfaction of knowing that this project's success depended on your participation.

We appreciate your attention. Your cooperation is essential. Call this number at once for further information: 1-800-744-5554.

Please report to the Morgan Wing of Chandler Bryson Memorial Hospital, Atlanta, on Sunday, October 22, at 5:00 P.M. for orientation.

I look forward to meeting you in person.

Very truly yours,

Richard Barkley, M.D.

Invitation? More like a summons. Tim rolled his eyes. It had to be a pitch of some kind. "Here's your five-hundred-dollar check, Mr. Monahan. Good for a down payment on the vacation condominium of your dreams. . . ."

Scooping up the letter and the rest of the junk mail, he went into the kitchen, tossed the stack into the trash can, and reached for the last of the Taster's Choice.

As he returned to the living room, the VCR's five-minute pause button flipped off and Channel 2's noon news blared on:

". . . giving the ill-starred Underground Atlanta project a new lease on life—or at least a new lease."

The anchorwoman fixed the camera with a sober look.

"This just in: Atlanta police have found the remains of thirteen-year-old Monica Jeffers in a wooded area near her home. The seventh grader, who had been missing since Saturday, was strangled with what Police Chief Mallory Corn described as a wire garrote."

A pause as a school photograph of a freckled child superimposed on the screen. "Monica Jeffers. Dead. The fourth 'D-string' murder victim since August."

Tim blinked at the screen. His inclination was to watch the rest of the news. Instead, he reached for the remote and started the movie again, but a sudden uneasiness brought him to his feet.

A step. Another. Turning, he ran to the kitchen and began to dig through the overflowing trash can. The discarded mail slid to the floor in a cascade of garbage. Oblivious to it, he went through the stack of paper, tossing advertising circulars away with nervous movements of thumb and forefinger. It was money, wasn't it? They were paying. "Five hundred dollars," he said aloud, as if to emphasize the thought, as if to somehow make it relevant.

The gummy lid of a Hormel chili can had left a rusty streak across the letter. Smoothing the page, he went to the living room, sank back on the couch, and stared at it without knowing quite why.

A minute passed. Two. Then his left hand crept for the pencil again, and he scrawled two words on the yellow pad.

Cloud Net

Still staring at the letter, he rolled the stubby pencil between thumb and fingers and began to write again.

One more word:

Attention:

It wouldn't hurt to call, would it? Just find out more. He reached for the phone, dialing the 800 number with the end of the pencil. A ring. Another. Then a recorded voice: "Thank you for calling 1-800-744-5554. Please hold."

Music began to play, doctor's office stuff—soft, lush, and imminently forgettable, but calming, somehow. Almost narcotic.

The recorded voice again: "Thank you for your call. You may hang up now."

He placed the receiver on the hook and stared down at the silent phone . . .

By the time Tim looked up again, *Alice, Sweet Alice* had run through its closing credits and the screen was blurred with snow.

TWO

The supergrade cradled the snifter in his palm. The city lights moved on the curved surface of the glass in glittering pinpoints like fireflies captured in amber. "How many respondents?"

Oliver Pointer shifted in the wingback chair. "Five, sir."

Only five. Hal Gulliver's gaze moved across the room and settled on a picture of stylized flowers. Something the hotel decorator would call *très chic,* he thought with contempt. Buff-colored tulips that looked like they were cut out of wallpaper.

Pointer shifted his haunches again. He was doing a lot of that—each time with a faint pained look as if he had sandpaper in his pants. Hemorrhoids, Gulliver decided. He glanced covertly at his watch. Sessions was late. Nothing new there. Sessions with his Rolex, bought and paid for with Agency funds, yet he never bothered to check the time with it.

Gulliver hated having to deal with contract scientists, and the doctors were the worst, stuck in their narrow little world, condescending as hell. God's anointed and appointed. He sipped the cognac, rolling it over his tongue as if it could wash away the bad taste in his mouth.

Pointer opened his mouth to speak, then closed it.

Gulliver watched the younger man from under hooded lids, knowing the look would register.

At the prompt, Pointer said, "Five is all. Five more than we expected. Once."

Gulliver gave a short nod. He looked away, his gaze settling on the blank, dark eye of the console television, but he saw only the old images that began to move in his mind.

The project had been promising. So promising, in fact, that from the beginning ORD had tried to appropriate it as its own. A faint smile quirked at one corner of Gulliver's lips. Promising? He was playing bullshit games with semantics again. HALFLIFE had been solid gold. There was no way it could have missed. But it had. Without any warning at all, HALFLIFE had turned to shit—not once, but three times. Something they had flushed away and forgotten, until now.

Now the plumbing was backing up.

HALFLIFE had begun in the late sixties as a gleam in the eye of a neurologist attached to MKSEARCH, Subproject 6. Within months, implementation began, and the project was named XANADU. For two years, XANADU had been the star in the crown of a rival department: Technical Services. A supernova, Gulliver thought. A big bang, then nothing. In 1972, just two years before Gulliver's appointment as director of the Office of Research and Development, MKSEARCH came to an end.

Following the Watergate break-in and Nixon's sudden purge of the Agency, seven boxes of MKSEARCH records were shredded, and XANADU went further underground. But it was not enough. XANADU had, of necessity, used children as subjects. If any hint of that came to light, the flap would surely, and efficiently, destroy the Agency for all time.

The search took eight days, with no rest on the seventh, until all traces of XANADU were expunged from TSD files. Reclassified, retitled HALFLIFE, it had lodged in the Office of Research and Development. Where it should have been to begin with, thought Gulliver. If ORD had headed the project, things might have turned out differently.

Technical Services had botched the camp operation from the beginning. They had trotted in career trainees, claiming that their youth would make them believable as camp counselors. CTs right off the Company farm. Young, serious, green as new hay. Boy Scouts sent to do a man's job. Gulliver's lip curled. No wonder one of them had cracked.

He looked up sharply as a knock on the door propelled Pointer to his feet. "Pour him a double." The drug of choice, he thought, relishing the medical term. Nothing like a little booze to loosen up tight-assed old maids.

Pointer nodded and, checking the peephole, released the chain and opened the door.

Dr. Phillip Sessions stooped slightly as he came in. Except for a sagging paunch, he was thin and towered well over six feet, but his stoop was not the automatic duck that very tall men employ in doorways; it crossed the room with him.

Gulliver gestured toward a chair.

Sessions perched on its edge, his knees touching, his neck jutting forward turtle-fashion.

"Scotch, isn't it?"

Sessions bobbed his head in assent.

Pointer chinked ice into the glass, followed it with three inches of Cutty Sark, and handed him the glass.

Sessions took a generous swallow, and slid the napkin-swathed glass onto the polished coffee table. Tucking his hands between his knees, he gazed expectantly at Gulliver through ill-fitting contact lenses that gave him a wet, startled look.

The cheat sheets called him "brilliant." Translate that to read oddball, Gulliver thought. He was wearing the Rolex turned face-in on his bony wrist. His suit was expensive but out of style—and the knees were shiny. Gulliver had a sudden image of Sessions shining his knees in prayer, outsized hands clasped together, turtle neck stuck out in supplication. It was enough to make God long for an atheist. He wondered if the man did pray. He was a lapsed something-or-other. Methodist. Or was it Lutheran?

He tried to imagine Sessions at the bedside of a patient and found it impossible. But he must have done that once, back in medical school, before neurophysiology claimed him. The man was a loner—and no wonder. He had all the charisma of a cardboard cutout, thought Gulliver, visualizing a two-dimensional infant Sessions, his mother dressing him in paper clothes, folding little paper tabs over his shoulders. His mother had been the only woman in his life. Sessions was forty-two, never married, not gay. That left asexual or autoerotic. Just which, the files didn't say. Barring that, the Agency's dossier on the man was exhaustive. They knew what he ate and where; they knew how he voted and how he thought. They knew a lot about him. They had to.

Sessions was ORD's double check. TSD had made the mistake of putting all their eggs in one basket. They had reason, of course: the fewer the links, the stronger the chain. But Gulliver didn't buy it. Not in this case. Too much was riding on it. ORD simply could not take the word of one man, expert or not. One man calling all the medical shots could be a time bomb—a possible nut case.

It wouldn't be the first time the Agency had followed a certifiable medic down the garden path to the bear trap.

Sessions took another swallow and slid the glass back onto the table, his fingertips leaving damp indentations on the clinging napkin.

"You've been briefed in general," said Gulliver. "Now we'd like your opinion on a few particulars."

That was Pointer's cue to unlock his briefcase. He brought out the abbreviated file, pausing for a moment as if he were reluctant to hand it over, even though Sessions's security check had been impeccable.

"We'd like you to turn your attention to C.7." Gulliver leaned back and sipped his cognac while Sessions hunched over the papers. The file had been expertly doctored for the occasion. There was no need for the man to know HALF-LIFE really existed. All Sessions needed to know was that a scenario needed dissection. And if he suspected otherwise, so be it.

The doctor began to read, pausing only once to cock his bony wrist and, irrelevantly, check the time. At last he set the papers on the table, straightening them precisely before he raised his pale, watery eyes to Gulliver's. "Interesting."

Gulliver did not speak.

Sessions cocked a finger, tapped the stack of papers. "I'm going to need a little time on this before I proffer an opinion."

Proffer an opinion? Good God. "How much time?"

The man's gaze flickered, moved upward, fixed somewhere on the wall behind Gulliver's left ear. "A week. Maybe two. I won't need to take the file."

Gulliver blinked. He knew Sessions had a trick memory. What did they call it? Eidetic. But it was beyond belief that the man had memorized twenty-two pages of single-spaced script in the time it took him to read them.

Sessions's wet eyes tracked back to the file. "Most interesting project." His hands bracketed the papers, his thumbs brushing the top sheet in a rhythmic, circular caress that made Gulliver's skin crawl. "This, uh, Wada test . . . page C.9, section 2, I believe it was. The test originated in the fifties. Are you aware that medical science pretty much discarded it in the early seventies?"

Gulliver chose not to answer.

"The procedure might well be effective, I can tell you more on that later, but you need to consider the risks," he said. "The Wada is dangerous. There's a three percent mortality factor."

Gulliver nodded curtly. He wondered if TSD had known about that three percent. When the kid died they had covered pretty well. To give them credit, they'd had wit enough to call the death what it was: anaphylactic shock. The bee sting story explained the puncture on the kid's neck just over his carotid artery. His parents bought it. They'd even conveniently remembered a bad reaction to a yellow jacket bite the year before. TSD had managed to pull that one off, but the CT's breakdown had been harder to cover up. He'd gone off the deep end, wanted to go to the police, turn himself in as an accomplice to murder. It had taken three and a half years in a contract psychiatric hospital in upstate New York before they got him under control.

The child's death twenty-two years ago was unfortunate. When Gulliver thought of it, he saw the boy as a casualty in a war that had to be fought. The CT was another. But it didn't pay to dwell on the past. The past was something to learn from, that was all.

The trick was to find out why HALFLIFE had succeeded so well at first—and why it had failed.

Or seemed to until a month ago.

It was not until the report came from their agent in the Atlanta police that they realized HALFLIFE had not failed at all.

THREE

The deep moonshadow of the old stone church bent its spire against the brick wall of the alley. Beyond the darkened side door of the sandwich shop, a smaller shadow crept on the wall, froze, shrank back as voices came from the tree-lined sidewalk fifteen yards away.

A young couple, caught in the glow of the street lamp, passed by hand in hand.

He did not move until they had gone, their distant voices blurring with the sound of traffic, then fading altogether. He did not move because it was his custom not to move at times like this. But it was only a precaution. He was perfectly safe. No one would ever find him.

Not with the others around to step in when he needed them.

The others had their uses. But they were stupid—all of them. And stubborn. The thought brought a vague uneasiness. They had made it harder for him this time. The prim-faced girl had wanted to stay in control and the rest had taken her side. He had had to force her out. He could hear her now, talking in a whisper with the others, plotting against him again. "Stupid," he whispered under his breath, and his voice mimicked the rustle of dry leaves. Too stupid to realize that he knew what they were doing.

His distaste for the girl was exactly the same as his distaste for the blond man and the child with the face of a cherub and the smooth sexless body of a doll—impersonal. Annoyances, nothing more. They were not worth his hate.

His hate he reserved for the woman.

For days now he had sensed her, moving like a shadow in his mind, laughing softly when she caught him unawares. Her features were always blurred except for her eyes. Though she tried, she could never completely disguise them. Even when she changed their color or their shape, she could not hide the glint of mockery in them.

He glanced at the darkened door of the sandwich shop. The woman was in there now, hiding, disguising herself as the waitress named Kay. There was no doubt of it. He had found her out a week ago.

It had been by accident. He had not paid much attention to the waitress when she took his order. But when she brought his sandwich, he had looked deep into her eyes and had known her for what she was.

He had stalked her every night since then. He knew that minutes from now the yellow light would flash on above the door. The busboy was always the first to leave.

After the busboy, the waitress would come out. She would go through the alley to the tiny back parking lot and the old tan Dodge she drove. This time, he'd be ready.

The owner of the sandwich shop and his fat wife would cause him no trouble. They always stayed an extra fifteen minutes, counting the money, locking up, but they had no car in the lot. Each time he had watched them leave, they had turned toward the street. Toward a nearby apartment, he supposed.

Sharp, thin laughter invaded his head. Shards and splinters of glass.

Careful! She'd know.

Quickly, so the woman would not hear, he masked his thoughts, hiding them with singsong doggerel:

A B C D . . . E F G . . . H I J K . . . El-em-en-oh-pee . . .

A sharp breeze scattered fallen leaves across the pavement. Chilled, he drew the long plaid wool scarf around his neck, and thrust his hands deep into the pockets of his shapeless jacket. The pocket knife he had used to slash her tire was cold against his fingers.

The light at the side door flared on. The door opened, and the busboy, one hand groping for the sleeve of his jacket, came out. The door rattled shut behind him and he went to the back lot. A minute later an engine roared and the busboy turned his old Can-Am into the alley and headed for the street.

Shrinking back into the shadows, he watched the Can-Am pass, pause at the street, then turn right. His heart quickened. She would be next. He reached into his breast pocket and pulled out the long, dull-gold wire. It coiled in his palm like a live thing. A wood dowel grip was attached to each end of the wire.

Scarcely breathing, he stared at the door.

Finally, it opened. The yellow light faded the waitress's red coat to rust. A quick "good night," and the door clicked shut behind her.

When she reached the back of the building and turned into the little parking lot, he waited a moment more, then followed, whistling softly under his breath.

A faint "damn" came from the lot. Then the sound of a car trunk opening.

He was whistling louder now, advertising his presence.

"Mr. Bellamy?" called the waitress, doubt in her voice.

He rounded the back corner of the building. Tree shadows tossed in the wind, jet-black against the pale moonlit pavement. The moon was bright enough to pick out the flattened rear tire.

The waitress froze, one hand high on the gaping trunk lid, the other palm-outward as if to ward him off.

His heart raced at the surge of adrenaline. "Trouble?" The waitress's face was illuminated by the dim trunk light. He could see her eyes. Wide and pale with a glint of fear in them.

A moment. "Yeah." Then recognition. "Oh. You're the chicken salad on pita bread." A self-conscious laugh. "I mean the person that had the chicken salad."

He came closer. "You got a flat?"

"Yeah." Suspicion. "What are you doing back here?"

"Shortcut." He nodded toward the back of the neighboring church at a four-story building just beyond. "I live over there."

"If it was me, I'd stick to the streets. At least in this part of town." She reached for the jack. "Do you know how to work these?"

"Yes." His fingers were damp; the coil of wire in his palm slithered beneath them. He came up to her side. "The handle should be over there." He pointed to a shadowy recess deep in the trunk.

"Where?"

"There." He pointed again. Excitement stole his breath.

Her back was to him now. She leaned over the trunk, one hand reaching deep into the recess, the other clamped to the door surround for balance.

He held a stubby dowel in each fist now. His hands were crossed, making a loop of the wire.

He raised his hands.

"I don't see—"

The dull-gold loop whipped over her head, circled her throat. His hands jerked apart and he spun away, using his shoulders as a lever, taking the weight of her.

Spurts of warm arterial blood, black in the moonlight.

The waitress convulsed once against him, her arms flailing, legs kicking like a puppet. Then she was still.

He let her slide, lowering her body, bracing it against the car until he could see her face in the light from the trunk.

The woman's head lolled back and her gashed throat splayed open. Her pale eyes were dark now, the pupils huge and fixed.

"Bitch," he whispered. A strange exultation shuddered down his spine and twisted in his belly. Dead. She was dead this time. Dead.

He laid her on the ground and retrieved the garrote, wiping it carefully on the lining of her coat, replacing it in his pocket. Then he reached for the pocket knife.

Its blades were very sharp. He opened the larger of the two and peeled back her coat. With a quick motion, he slit her uniform. Half tearing, half cutting, he ripped open the thin fabric and slashed through her bra and panties.

Her skin was smooth. A blank canvas.

He stared down at her for a long moment. Then he folded the large knife blade and opened the smaller.

He leaned over her body, working with great concentration. When he was done, he stood and caught his breath.

Dead, he thought. Dead now. Gone.

But a tiny noise began to tinkle in his head. The sound of wind chimes rippling. Glass touching glass.

No.

The sound grew and became a laugh, mocking him, turning his bones to ice.

He clasped his hands, laced his fingers together like a child. "No."

He could hear the woman then, calling him, imitating his mother's voice: "Look what you did. Mother is not pleased with you. Mother is not pleased at all. . . ."

He whimpered, and his whimper was echoed by the cherub-faced sexless child.

The blond man in his head whispered something.

"My turn," said the prim-faced girl.

He felt her pushing in, pushing him away. He did not have the strength to fight her this time. . . .

The girl stared down at the cooling body at her feet. It was time to go home. Time to get everyone home now.

The jacket she wore was covered with blood. She stripped it off, turned it inside out, and put it on again, its silky black lining rustling with the movement. Unfolding the plaid wool scarf, she wrapped it around her head kerchief-style, and, turning toward the old church, followed its side wall to the back gate that had rusted open and to the street beyond where she had parked the car.

FOUR

The sign on the gate to the Chandler Bryson Memorial parking area read HOSPITAL EMPLOYEES ONLY. And not very many of those, Tim thought. The tiny lot was jammed, and even though it was Sunday afternoon, the overflow parking garage across the street had a chain across the entrance. He maneuvered the Maverick over a steaming manhole cover and turned right onto a one-way street. Three blocks down, past a pawn shop with rusting burglar bars, he found a parking lot.

Tim wrestled his patched brown canvas tote and chunky computer bag out of the trunk and glanced at his watch. 4:25. Time enough to stash his stuff and get a cup of coffee before the fun began. Shouldering the bag, he headed west toward a sinking sun streaked with dark clouds. It was going to rain. Rain and turn colder. He pulled out a cigarette, lit it, and wondered again why he had decided to come here.

The money, of course. Five hundred bucks and no groceries to buy for a week. Bonus: it was a chance to get some work done without having to deal with sweet little landladies bearing gifts.

Wasn't it?

A sudden chill rippled through his gut, and he blinked at its intensity. For God's sake. They weren't going to inject him with AIDS or anything. Not this guinea pig. This little pig was going to take the money and run.

Moving more briskly, he turned the corner. Chandler Bryson Memorial was a megalith of adjoining buildings of indeterminate age and architecture. The hospital had once been painted a unifying tan. Now it had a faded, sallow look as if it had caught a touch of jaundice from one of its inmates. Shifting the computer, Tim crossed the street, found the main lobby, and went inside.

An industrial-sized ashtray sat inside the door. Above it was a familiar sign: a circle with a diagonal slash across the cigarette inside. Super. The Führer had spoken; no smoking in the bunker. A week of this and he'd be ready for a jacket with straps. He took a final drag and stubbed out the Winston.

Bryson, or at least this part of it, looked newer than he had expected. A half acre or so of dun-colored carpet and three beige plastic couch groupings separated him from the elevators and a wide hallway beyond.

He passed two dark-eyed little girls wearing fluffy white dresses and huge hair bows, gave them a wink, and went up to the information desk.

A young black woman looked up. "Can I help you?"

Tim caught the scent of her perfume. Musk and spice. "Which way to Morgan Wing?"

A tiny frown line creased her brow. "Morgan?"

"That's it."

She opened a thin looseleaf notebook and traced down the page with a manicured fingertip. A puzzled look. "I don't have any Morgan here. Are you sure you've got the right name?"

Now that she mentioned it, he wasn't. Pulling the rumpled letter out, he checked, and showed it to her.

She glanced at the page, her nose wrinkling delicately at the chili stain that streaked it. "Look, I'm new here. Let me ask somebody," she said, and disappeared into a connecting office.

The somebody turned out to be a heavy-set woman with severe gray eyes and matching bangs that marched across her forehead with military precision. "You asked about Morgan." It was more an accusation than a question.

Tim nodded.

She set her lips primly together and looked him up and down. "No one goes to Morgan."

He quirked an eyebrow. "I beg your pardon?"

"Morgan Wing is closed. It's been closed for years."

And so, he suspected, was her mind. "Maybe so, but I'm supposed to be there." He handed her the letter.

The woman eyed it suspiciously. Retreating to a back wall, she picked up a telephone, and dialed an extension. After several minutes of conversation punctuated with sharp glances first at the paper, then at Tim, she hung up and said, "If people are going to be coming and going up there, it seems to me I could have been notified."

He gave her what he thought was a soothing look, but she didn't notice. She was examining the letter again. "You *are* Timothy Michael Monahan?"

No, lady. Actually, I'm a dangerous criminal. I have a knife; I collect gray scalps with bangs. The soothing look again. "That's what Mommy called me," he said seriously. "But only when I was bad."

She thrust the letter at him and produced a nose-stretching frown that deepened the furrows around her lips. "I've been told to let you go up."

Tim suppressed the urge to laugh. "Up where? Where is it?"

"I don't suppose you'd ever find it by yourself." A faint sniff. "I'll have to get someone to take you. Wait here." Picking up the phone again, she spoke briefly, and then retreated into the inner office.

The wait stretched into five minutes, then ten. Time to get out the cobwebs. If he ever decided to make his fortune as an inventor, that was the way to go: cobwebs in a can. Spray them on and strike remorse in the hearts of tardy waitresses and laggard grocery clerks: "Sorry to keep you waiting, but . . . Ohmigod, it hasn't been that long. Has it?"

One old man looked like he'd been there long enough to grow the real thing. He was staring at a television set anchored to a high shelf, but he might as well be watching a test pattern. There was a lost, vacant look on his face that reminded Tim of his grandfather—waiting to see the woman he had married forty-seven years ago, wondering if she'd make it through the night.

The balding man on the next couch had dozed off behind the business page. Bored silly. The guy was probably waiting for his wife. Up visiting her mother, who was in for female trouble, he decided.

"You the one for Morgan?"

Tim spun around at the man's voice and nodded.

The old orderly's starched whites sagged over his bony shoulders. "This way." He turned abruptly and stalked off.

Heel, boy. Hoisting his luggage, Tim caught up with the man near the bank of elevators. Instead of going up, they entered a wide corridor. They seemed to be following an array of color-coded stripes painted on the wall. At the end of a rat's maze of turns, the orderly opened a door. "Watch your step."

Two of them. Two steps down into a narrow windowed passage that led to another building, this one noticeably older. Its high-ceilinged echoing lobby, studded with scarred wooden benches, reminded Tim of a rundown train station.

"You can't get there from here, I guess," said Tim by way of conversation.

"This here's Rutledge. We want Hines. Rutledge is Peds." With this incomprehensible remark, the man quickened his pace.

They passed a large alcove where a half-dozen families waited under a sign that read PEDIATRIC OUTPATIENT. From behind a closed door, a child wailed. A dark-eyed toddler, balancing on chubby widespread legs, started at the sound, plopped down on his diapered rear, and began to cry.

The orderly hooked a thumb to the right where another passage led to the next building. "Hines is that way. Medical Records is over there. On the ground floor anyway." Unaccountably, he turned left, and, with a thrust of a gnarled index finger, called an ancient elevator that opened with a wheeze. Inside, it smelled faintly of urine overlaid with disinfectant.

"No elevators in Hines, I guess," said Tim, as the door creaked shut and the car began its uncertain rise.

"Oh, they got one, all right."

"Yeah?"

"Not much good. You want to stay away from it."

Might be sound advice.

The Rutledge elevator lurched to a stop and the door opened. A large 4 WEST was painted in black on the opposite wall just above a battered old pay phone chained to its worn directory. The old man planted a foot against the door, leaned out, and pointed to the right. "You want to go that way. That'll take you to Morgan Wing."

Tim stepped into the empty hallway and stared at the double doors at the end of the hall. They had been painted a dull institutional green that failed to obliterate the underlying stenciled words: CONTAGION WARD.

He spun back to the elevator. But the door clanged shut, and car and orderly were gone.

A connecting corridor, this one windowless. The only light came from a naked bulb dangling from a dark green metal fixture. It was enough to illuminate the wide double doors at the end of the passage. Again, the painted-over warning of contagion. Hesitating a moment, he reached out, and the tarnished brass bar across the right-hand door dropped at his touch with a sharp click.

His next step took him backward in time, into a building at least forty years older than its neighbor. He stood in a wide, chilly hallway studded with dim alcoves. The trickle of gray light through pale transoms barely reached the high crown moldings that edged the ceiling. The hall was flanked with closed doors. Like Hill House, he thought. Doors sensibly shut.

Morgan Wing had stood for ninety years, and might stand for ninety more.

He eyed the heavy, closed doors. To your left, ladies and gentlemen, in room 501, the Elephant Man. And to your right, just past the linen closet—mummy wrappings in there—we have 502 and an eclectic assortment of lepers, consumptives, and syphilitics. Several seconds passed before Tim realized he had been holding his breath.

Brilliant. Give this boy the gold star. The place had been closed for years. Any leftover killer germs were probably dead of old age. Senile, anyway, he thought, composing the scenario: "Remember the Dub-yuh Dub-yuh Two epidemic, Harry? You and me, we wuz the best damned germs in the outfit. Something to sneeze at." Infectious grin. "Remember the Normandy invasion? Ole Archie Normandy, he never had a chance." Sudden confusion. "Or was that Willard Normandy?" Blank look. "George?" Tim clucked and shook his head. That's what came of being strepto-cocky.

Past the first pair of rooms, a large alcove opened up to his left. An old waiting room? He looked across the wide hall at a dark, closed door with the numbers 504. Great view. Its transom gave him back a cyclops stare through a milky eye.

The back wall of the alcove harbored a long gray-green table with a teetering floor lamp next to it. He switched it on. Yellow light bled through its dingy pleated shade and puddled on the chipped green arm of an ancient rattan couch set at right angles to the table. Three mismatched arm chairs near the couch faced an indentation in the opposite wall where an antique Philco television set squatted, its round screen dwarfed by its massive cabinet. Cozy. On top of the TV sat a stained checkerboard with three checkers, two reds and a black. In case the Philco palled, he supposed.

He stashed his luggage and the computer bag under the table. According to the sign painted on the wall above it, this was 5 EAST. Interesting. When he got off the elevator, hadn't the sign said 4? Morgan—or Hines, or whatever it was—was either built in a hole, or this was the cue for Rod Serling's voice-over.

Behind him, a woman laughed. "Welcome to the Twilight Zone."

Startled, he spun toward the hall. The woman standing there was forty-fivish, dark-haired, and skinny as a sixteen-year-old. Tim managed a smile. "You're reading my mind."

"I do have my moments."

He stared in amazement at her outfit. She was wearing some sort of jumpsuit, skintight, and bright red, covered over with a crocheted ankle-length khaki thing that he decided must be a dress. It looked old, like something out of the sixties.

She studied him intently for a moment, then thrust out a hand and grinned disarmingly. "I'm Maureen Dorcas."

He took her outstretched hand. Three rings, one of them a silver dragon with its tail circling her finger.

"You can call me the Dragon Lady, if you like." Another grin. "What would you like me to call you?"

He was not quite sure how to take her. A little off-the-wall maybe, but she had nice eyes: frank and blue, with a glint of fun in them. He decided he liked her. "Tim," he said. "Tim Monahan."

"All right then, Tim Monahan. Over the past half hour, Morgan has revealed itself to me. I can show you wonders the likes of which you have never seen." She batted her lashes and a look of pure mischief came into her eyes. "Follow me."

Mystified, he did.

They passed what seemed to be two utility rooms on the left and another closed door to the right marked 506. "I haven't finished my explorations, you understand," said Maureen, "but there's something at the end of the hall you shouldn't miss."

"Let me guess," he said. "A rabbit hole, right? And a wafer that says, 'Eat Me.' How did you find Morgan Wing, anyway?" He was sure she hadn't dealt with the iron lady at the information desk.

"We came up the back way." She swept a hand toward the EXIT sign ahead. It was at the end of the hall nearly a city block away.

The hall was empty. "We?"

"Me and my buddy. Paul—co-author and cohort. There's a street entrance down there. More of an alley entrance, really. I wanted to take the elevator, but he talked me into the stairs." She rolled her eyes. "All five flights of them."

"So you're a writer too." He wondered what she had written. The name Maureen Dorcas wasn't ringing any bells. "Fiction?"

"Some people think so."

They passed a small alcove on the right just big enough for the wide, battered desk that almost filled it. A nurse's desk, he decided. The door behind the desk was marked MEDICINE ROOM.

Suddenly Maureen stopped and turned to him. "Give me one of your business cards."

Startled, he reached for his wallet, and after a moment's consideration pulled out one of his "Mike Mona" cards, black and white except for the red drops of blood that dripped from the knife in the upper right corner and splashed across the name. "How did you know I had any?"

"All writers do." She scrutinized the card. "Ah. A good one—and a pseudonym, too." She took out one of her own from a small black case tucked in her cigarette pouch and handed it to him. Black letters on paper bag brown, just her name and address, and centered at the top a single word: Connections.

"Now, may I have one of your real ones?"

He raised an eyebrow, found a card with Timothy M. Monahan in plain block letters, and gave it to her.

Obviously relishing the puzzled look on his face, Maureen grinned. "Thanks. I collect them."

"Yeah?"

"I have nearly a thousand. I mount them in albums."

She was watching him keenly. "You haven't done this sort of thing before, have you?"

"Done what?" Out of the corner of his eye he saw something scuttle away and disappear beneath a radiator. Mouse. Or king-sized roach.

"You know, the study."

He shook his head. "Have you?"

"I think we'll find it interesting." She tucked the cards away in the pouch and pulled out a pack of Ultra Thins.

"Can we smoke up here?" he asked.

"Honey, you just watch me." She leaned back against the desk and lit up.

He looked around. Nothing much. A door across the hall from the nurses station marked RESIDENT, and just beyond it another marked TREATMENT ROOM. "Is this it?"

Smoke curled from her nostrils. "Is this what?"

"What you wanted to show me?"

"Heavens no. Come on." She marched off briskly down the hall.

Like Teddy Roosevelt storming San Juan Hill, he thought.

Without breaking stride, she waggled her hand toward another small alcove on the right. "You'll want to take a look in there later if you're interested in antiquities. That is, if the men's room is anything like the ladies'." A grin. "Actually, it is. But don't tell anybody I peeked."

A faded stencil on a door to the left said STORAGE ROOM. Just past it was an elevator, and on the other side of the hall, room 508. "Another ward," said Maureen. "All the rooms have five or six beds in them."

At the end of the corridor she threw open the last door on the right. "Here we are. The first of Morgan's seven wonders."

It was an enormous bathroom. White tile striped with black crept halfway up the walls and met yellowing enameled plaster. A half-dozen dusty antique tubs, three to a side, bordered the room. Ordinary enough. But in the middle, precisely placed like a bizarre centerpiece, stood the biggest bathtub Tim had ever seen. Big enough for three or four Wilt the Stilts—Wilts the Stilt?—to stretch out in, and plenty of room left over.

Maureen laughed. "Isn't it something?" The tub's claw feet clung to the floor like the talons of a giant predator. "If it grows wings, we'll be airborne."

The primordial hot tub? It was hip high. Tim ran his fingers along the rim and wondered what it had been used for. Group gropes? You'd have to tread water.

At the other end of the hall a door clanged open, and a clatter of footsteps mingled with voices. "Looks like we're starting," said Tim. "I think we'd better save the other wonders for later."

She flicked ash into the tub. "You've got it, honey." A slow blue-eyed wink. "Your place or mine?"

"Better mine," he said, trying not to laugh at the impish look on her face. He waggled a thumb toward the hall door. "We don't want your, uh, buddy to get jealous, do we?"

"Ah, yes. Paul," said Maureen. Then, as if the thought had just occurred to her, "My live-in." A chuckle started deep in her throat and grew into a rich laugh. Tim stared, wondering what the joke was, but her laugh bubbled up so irresistibly that in moments he was laughing too.

They joined the small group gathered in the first alcove where Tim had left his luggage. Maureen hitched up her khaki overdress and sat down on a wicker stool in the corner. There were five other people already seated. The sixth, a pretty young woman in a lab coat, stood at the front and passed out name tags.

She was about twenty-eight or so, Tim guessed. The thick dark hair at her temple had a startling, and somehow sexy, streak of white. His gaze slid to her breasts, then down to her legs: slim, and encased in silky hose. Narrow ankles, curving calves. Dancer's legs, he thought, remembering a brief, but intense, liaison with a certain aerobics instructor who had an amazing and gratifying talent for gymnastics. A speculative look came into his eyes. Maybe the week would be more interesting than he thought.

She was saying: ". . . might as well get started. I'll fill in the others when they get here."

With a quick glance to be sure his luggage was where he had left it, Tim plopped into the only empty seat, a rattan armchair, and quickly discovered why no one else had chosen it. The chair, minus part of a right rear leg, tipped sharply, its precipitous plunge stopped only by a collision with the couch next to it. A tall blond man sitting at his left grabbed the chair arm and steadied it until Tim could extricate himself.

The woman in the lab coat looked up in dismay. "Are you all right?"

"Fine. Just fine," he muttered in chagrin. Someone produced a scarred wooden wedge that had skittered across the floor. It apparently had been intended for the chair; when he slid it under the offending leg, the fix held with only a slight lean to the right. Cautiously, Tim sat down again.

The woman consulted a list, then looked up. "Are you Mr. Corsica? Or Mr. Monahan?"

She had wide gray eyes edged with dark lashes. Smoke and soot. "Monahan," he said.

She pulled off a sticky-backed convention tag and gave it to him. White with a banal blue-printed smiley face: Hi, my name is . . . His had been typed in with a large font and a not-too-new ribbon. He covertly checked out her name tag. Plastic with black letters. Jody Henson. *Miss* Jody Henson.

She handed him a Manila envelope with his name on it. Holding up another, she glanced at Maureen. "Mrs. Dorcas?"

"Just Maureen, please."

Jody gave her the envelope, added a name tag, and turned to the others. "You'll find your room assignments inside. Some of you will be staying on this floor. The rest will be on six. If you're on six, please use the stairs at the other end of the hall. I'm told there's trouble with the Hines elevator and the Rutledge elevators don't go that high."

A groan came from a young freckled woman with a weight problem.

"I'm sorry, Carla," Jody added, "but we couldn't put everyone on five. A lot of the rooms on this floor are used for storage. We could have doubled you up, but we thought it would be better if each of you had a private room.

"After hours, everyone is free to come and go, of course. But if you're out at night, you need to know that security locks up when visiting hours are over. No one except staff can use the elevators after lock-up, but if you show your ID to one of the guards in the Hines lobby, he'll let you use the stairs." She held up a slim coupon book. "In your envelopes you'll also find meal tickets. Please hang on to those."

Digging into her envelope with pudgy fingers, Carla examined the meal tickets and groaned again. "The hospital cafeteria! I thought this project was supposed to be a class act." She flapped the pink coupon book at the others. "Let's hear it for Peptic Plaza, folks. Give your all for science."

A heavy-lidded young man across the room drawled, "In your case, Carla baby, that's a lot."

Carla shot a poisonous look in his direction. "Put it in a can, Al."

Next to Al, a thin man with kinky red hair snickered.

The fleeting look of embarrassment on Jody Henson's face quickly resolved into composure. "Let's go on, shall we? There are two permission forms in your envelopes. We'll need your signature on these right away. The first is the standard permission for . . ." She was interrupted when the double doors at the end of the hall clanged open and a round-faced girl in a shapeless tan dress wrestled a large suitcase and matching tote inside.

A look of confusion came over the girl's face when she saw the group. Her round eyes darted to her watch, rose hesitantly to meet Jody Henson's, then skittered away. "I thought I was early," she said in a voice almost too low to be heard.

Jody appraised the girl with a quick, searching look. Then she said, "It's okay, Beth. We started sooner than we'd planned."

Had they? Tim checked the time. It was five-eighteen. The girl awkwardly tugged the suitcase into the alcove, and then slid into a niche in the wall as if it offered her protection. A little brown mouse in the shadows, he thought. Jody obviously knew the girl; Beth, she'd called her. In fact, everyone here seemed to know everyone else. He wondered why he and Maureen were odd men out.

"We're still missing one person," said Jody. "But since everyone else is here, I think we ought to introduce ourselves. Let's go around the room. I'm Jody Henson." She nodded to the heavy-set girl.

"Carla Hagen."

Tim watched as one by one they gave their names. The man with the overgrown eyelids was Al Cole; the skinny redhead in jeans sitting next to him identified himself only as "Memphis." A young black guy with hornrims and a soft voice said, "I'm Tyrone Hayes." They seemed to be a trio: in their early twenties from the looks of it, and obviously friends. A quartet, actually, if you added in Carla.

The tall blond man who had caught Tim's tipping chair was Dayton Satterfield. Tim envied his mustache. Thick and theatrical. If he were dark instead of blond, Satterfield would have made the perfect villain in an old-time melodrama.

The last one to give her name was the latecomer, the brown mouse. He could barely hear her say, "Beth Quaig." Terminally shy, he decided.

Tim examined the two permission forms. The first one seemed straightforward enough, but the second was three pages of fine print. He furrowed his brow at the wording: *Selected invasive procedures.* What the hell did that mean? They seemed to be asking permission for everything short of surgery—electroencephalograms, CAT scans. And why? The study was supposed to be about education, wasn't it? Creativity? "I don't know about signing these," he said to Jody. "Just what have they got planned for us here?"

"Every test known to man," said Memphis Red.

The heavy-lidded man—Al—snorted. "Afraid the family jewels will end up on the cutting-room floor?"

Tim looked up sharply. "Only a fool would give carte blanche without knowing just what he's signing."

"Let's all draw pictures for the slower ones," said Al, exaggerating his words in an apparent attempt at comedy.

At the man's smirk, Tim narrowed his eyes. If the asshole worked at it, he was going to get a lip to match his eyelids. "Just let the lady answer, okay?"

Jody Henson shot a disapproving glance in Al's direction and said quickly, "I'll try to explain. This pilot study is not associated with Chandler Bryson. Dr. Barkley—that is, the Institute for Psychological Studies—has contracted for the use of the facility, but the institute is completely independent. That's why there are two forms. The white sheet is a hospital permission slip for routine admission tests—urinalysis, chest X ray, blood work. It seems silly, I know. You're not really patients, but since Dr. Barkley will be using Bryson's lab and radiology department for his own tests, the hospital's insurance carriers won't cover the use of the facility without them.

"On the second form—the blue one—you're agreeing to participate in Dr. Barkley's project. This is your informed consent waiver. Your signature gives permission for any medical tests associated with the study. It's an intimidating list, I'm afraid." She paused. "These things are written by lawyers, and they scare the pants off people. Basically, it spells out everything that could possibly go wrong, even if the possibility is one in ten thousand."

And it released the Institute for Psychological Studies and Bryson Memorial from any and all liability, Tim noted. He scanned the sheet again. There was no way in hell he was going to sign unless he got a few answers. "Why does this study call for"—he glanced down at the form and quoted—"'various radiological studies that may include Computerized Axial Tomography (CAT) and/or Positron Emission Tomography (PET) scans'?" Weren't these tests for serious conditions? Cancer, things like that? "Are we supposed to glow green when we get through here, or what?"

Jody Henson put up her hand to quell the laugh that followed. "There's no danger of that," she said evenly. "But to tell you the truth, I'm not sure the study will even include those tests."

"You don't know?" Unbelievable. This whole act was getting more half-assed by the moment. If he had any sense—"the sense God gave a goose," to quote Aunt Pittypat—he ought to leave now, walk out, forget the whole thing.

"I'm afraid not," she admitted. "I don't work for Dr. Barkley; I'm the hospital liaison, and I came late to the project. Only yesterday, in fact. The original assistant came down with the flu, so I was chosen to take over. Unfortunately, I haven't had an opportunity to talk with Dr. Barkley about details yet. But he'll be here first thing tomorrow, and I'm sure he can clear up any questions you have then." She hesitated a moment. "Look, if you don't want to sign the blue form until you talk with him, it's okay. But please sign the white sheet now. The lab people will be coming around at eight tonight for the blood and urine samples, and the chest X rays are supposed to be done in the morning."

Tim was still tempted to walk out. Every instinct told him to. But another look at Jody Henson put the impulse on hold. The lady and her legs were well worth getting to know better, he told himself. He glanced at the white sheet again. Routine tests, that was all. It wouldn't be fatal to pee in a cup and it wouldn't hurt to have a chest X ray. He hadn't had one done in years. Pulling out a pen, he hesitated for a moment, then signed his name. As for the informed consent—when, and if, the alleged Dr. Barkley came up with a reasonable explanation about what was going on, he'd think about it.

Jody glanced at her watch. "I'll let you get settled. Your

room assignments are in your envelopes, and you'll find a schedule in there too. The cafeteria is open now. You can eat whenever you like, but if you want the guided tour, be back here in half an hour and someone will show you the way."

With a quick "Thanks, but no thanks," Carla got heavily to her feet and the tired rattan couch rebounded with a creak. Taking the cue, the rest stood up, shouldered luggage, and ambled off to find their rooms.

Tim waited until they had left before handing the white sheet and the unsigned blue one to Jody Henson. "I don't think I can find my room," he began. "Suppose you show me."

She looked at his assignment card. "504? It's right there." She indicated the room across the hall just opposite the alcove.

"I don't know. Maybe you ought to take me there," he said innocently. "I have an awful sense of direction."

Her eyes widened slightly. Then a tiny smile. "That bad, Mr. Monahan?"

"Tim," he said and shook his head. "It's terrible. When I was a kid I got lost at recess every single day for six years."

"Oh?" The smile widened just a bit. "And what happened then?"

"Junior high." He leaned closer. "It took me two years to find the place."

"Well . . ." She tipped her head to one side and gave him a slow speculative look. "In that case, Tim, you'd better come with me."

"It's big," said Tim. "I'll say that for it." The room had been a six-bed ward. Four of the high beds were still there, thin-mattressed and dark brown, whether from paint or rust he could not be sure. The other two were ghosts, the gray-green outline of their curved iron headboards still visible against the darker green of the walls. Bedspreads covered each bed. He suspected they had been blue once, but now they were a watery-looking gray. The only chair was a heavy oak job with a hinged seat and a white enameled bucket underneath.

He shook his head in mock dismay. "How did a girl like you . . ."

"End up in a place like this?" Jody Henson laughed. "It wasn't easy. I went the long way around. I started out as a nurse."

"Ah. Nurse Henson."

A faint, pained look furrowed her brow. "Please don't call me that. Nurses hate it."

"Why?"

"Because 'nurse' is a professional designation, not a title." A sigh. "Everybody thinks it is, though. That's because 'doctor' *is* a title."

"But all the books say so. All the movies."

"All the books and the movies are wrong. You wouldn't say Lawyer Jones or Teacher Smith, would you?"

He tried to remember if he had committed the offense in a book of his own. "So what are you called?"

"Miss Henson. Or Miz with a Z. Or plain old Henson. 'Hey you' in a pinch." A smile. "But Jody will do just fine."

He peered at the plastic badge she wore and the letters trailing after her name. "What's the rest of it? Are you a psychiatrist?"

She shook her head. "Clinical psychology. I'm not licensed yet, though. I'm still an intern. But soon . . ."

She brushed a lock of hair from her eyes and Tim was struck again by that thick dark strand streaked with white.

Wild creatures with markings like that were off limits. Mother Nature's danger sign. Suddenly, he wanted to touch it, feel it trail between his fingers.

"Soon you'll be able to head up your own projects in abandoned contagion wards," he said with a wry grin. "You can use all your skills: first psychology, and then you can nurse your guinea pigs back to health when they come down with a dread disease."

Another easy laugh. "You won't catch anything."

Her short upper lip gave her a nice smile. Pretty teeth too, he thought.

"This used to be a polio ward back in the forties." Jody glanced at the high windows darkening with the early night. "It's hard to imagine what it must have been like. Polio was a summer disease. Summer heat and humidity. And the only treatment worth anything was hot packs." She shook her head. "Those poor kids must have gone through hell. But that was then, and this is now," she added quickly. "It's not the Hilton, but it's clean. And it's only for a week."

He met her eyes thoughtfully. "It could be longer."

The smile again. He caught it fleetingly as she turned away and indicated a sink on the wall between two of the beds. Its porcelain was rust-stained, but it looked clean enough.

"Plumbing and everything," she said. "Nothing that flushes or sprays though. The showers and toilets are down the hall on the right. You'll find towels and soap in your locker." She ran her hand over the thin bedspread. "You'll have to check the beds to see which has sheets and blankets. I'm afraid Bryson is chronically short of linens, so the maids were told to make up just one bed to a room."

Tim pushed back a metal folding screen of bleached cloth that looked old and yellowed. This one was still fairly sturdy, but then mummy wrappings always were. A half-dozen more screens of similar age stood in the corner across the room. "All this, and privacy too." The screen creaked away on wobbling wheels and exposed a brown overbed table. "Ah. A place for the word processor." Hoisting the computer bag onto the bed next to the table, he zipped open the case.

"That's right," said Jody. "You're the author."

"Writer," Tim corrected, hating the pretentious sound of the word. "Authors are usually dead. Or at least out on acid-free paper."

"I never met anyone who wrote books before. And now two of you at once. You and Maureen Dorcas."

"Three," he said, remembering Maureen's remark about her co-author Paul. "Which one was he, anyway?"

"Who?"

"Paul."

A blank look widened her gray eyes.

"You know. The guy Maureen said she collaborates with."

"Oh." The look on her face changed to something Tim could not read. "Maureen does call him that, doesn't she?" For a long moment Jody looked away, as if she did not know how to frame her words, or, indeed, whether she should at all. Finally, she turned to him and said slowly, "Paul is dead. He's been dead for nearly two hundred years."

FIVE

Maureen Dorcas gazed into the flecked mirror over the wall sink and affected a world-weary look. "Shall we dress for dinnah, Scarlett?"

A rapid batting of eyelashes. "Of cose, Rhett dahlin'. I believe I shall wayah mah green." Maureen batted again and grinned at the effect. Not bad for an Ohio gal. She had been born Maureen O'Boyle. O'Boyle O'Canton, as her dad used to say.

Canton had been home until she was eleven. That was the year her dad transplanted the family to Nashville over the protests of his wife, frail and crippled with the savage arthritis that had struck after her last pregnancy. He gathered them all together: Mary and his mother and the five children, none yet in their teens. "Greyhounds," he told them. "Mark my words, they're the wave of the future." He meant the buses, not the dogs. "Fix 'em up, nice and cozy. A home away from home," for Nashville's country music stars on their interminable cross-country tours. "Roll 'em out," he reasoned, "and the money can't help but roll in." He ensconced them in a rented house near the river in an old residential neighborhood turned commercial. "Just for a little while," he assured them. "Until we're on our feet." But Greyhounds, even used ones, cost a lot of money, and Kevin O'Boyle saw his dreams of fortune dribble away like the transmission fluid of the rolling stock crowding the dusty backyard. Maureen's brother Tom called it "bus poor," hissing the word, making it sound like "piss," risking the back of his father's hand each time he dared to say it.

The buses afforded them a precarious living, though the time they were "on their feet" never came. At thirteen, Maureen—"Moh-reen" as her eighth grade English teacher called her—learned to upholster, working on weekends and after school, cutting and tacking the heavy vinyls and leathers that were transformed into dinettes and couches for the rich and famous.

Remembering, Maureen grinned. Hard work, but it had been fun too, in a way. She turned to the narrow closet. Several pastel sweat suits on wire hangers nestled among vintage outfits culled from antique clothing stores and her standby, Nashville Thrift. God, how she missed that place. Four months in Atlanta, and she hadn't found a substitute yet. But yesterday back in Nashville, she had gotten her Thrift fix. Leaving her daughter Vicky's problems and cranky baby for two wonderful hours, she had browsed the familiar racks for oldie goldies.

The old clothes were a vice. Not illegal, not even fattening, but finding them and wearing them was so much fun it had to be just a little immoral. When she was a kid, she would never have worn thrift-shop dresses. Not and live, she thought with a grin. Better to be naked as a jay-bird. It was the Florida pilot study seven years ago that had started it.

The invitation had come out of the blue, and like Flora McFlimsy, she had had nothing to wear. Two whole days she had spent looking for dress-for-success suits, all of them somehow depressing. Then she had found herself in a little shop called Retrospectives, trying on a black-and-white-striped forties suit with enormous shoulder pads, loads of pizazz, and a faint rust stain on the lapel that a pin would hide. It made her feel like Rosalind Russell. And when she got back change from a ten-dollar bill, she was hooked.

To her chagrin, she later discovered that blue jeans and an old bathing suit would have done just fine. The pilot study had been held ten miles from nowhere in a tacky little Florida motel that just wasn't ready for haute couture.

Pulling out her latest acquisition, a twenty-year-old velvet jumpsuit, she held it up to her chin. "Definitely the green, Rhett sugah. It matches mah eye—the rat one, that is. The left is moh the shade of the draperies, don't you think?"

She shimmied into the green pantsuit, tied the sash around her waist with a flourish, and surveyed the result as best she could from the little mirror. Not bad, she thought, and wondered briefly if Harold would have liked it. But then Harold was probably as blind as his bats by now—and white as a toad's belly. She used to tell him that. "First the vitamin D goes, then the optic nerve." It was a joke. But there was nothing funny about playing second fiddle to a pipe dream.

Harold Dorcas was just like her father. That's why she had married him—and why she had left him. She had left him, just as her grandmother had predicted, two years to the day after he bought the cave in central Tennessee. Score one for second sight, she thought at the time. But she had known it too. From the day he bought the place, she knew she had lost her husband to a hole in the ground. When he wasn't taking the infrequent tourist through, or replacing the light bulbs that didn't last any time in the dampness, he was exploring new sections of cave with a light on his head like a coal miner. Grubbing around underground for hours—days, sometimes—while she was topside, trying to meet the bills and balance the dwindling books and pay for another goddamned carton of floodlight bulbs, trying to drive the thirty-eight miles to work and be both a mother and father to Vicky, trying to cope. She loved him still, even though she had left him buried away in his cave nearly eighteen years ago. But that was okay. It was always okay to love somebody.

Less than a year after she left Harold, Maureen had her first encounter with Paul. It happened after her Thursday night continuing ed. class, "The Philosophy of Western Thought." She told her grandmother about it when she went to pick up Vicky. They talked until nearly four A.M. when, exhausted, and full of equal doses of Grandma's ginger cookies and advice, she fell into a dreamless sleep on the old flowered couch. Maureen had never thought about writing books until then. Oh, maybe once or twice—but not seriously. Now five of them were out. Five books that were, in a strange way, as much her children as Vicky was. Vicky and the quints, she thought with a grin and went to the door.

It was almost time to meet for supper, but no one was there yet. She saw no point in sitting around, and impulsively decided to explore the rest of Morgan Wing while there was still light.

Her foray earlier this afternoon had taken her down one side of the hall and only partway back before the others showed up. Crossing the hall, veering past the empty alcove, she opened a door marked UTILITY and found herself inside a large square room tiled in the inevitable hospital white. It reminded her of a huge turn-of-the-century kitchen. Sinks and cabinets lined the walls; old cardboard cartons and wooden crates filled almost all the floor space, leaving only a narrow walkway between them that culminated in a narrow pantrylike passage lined with glass-windowed cabinets. It led to a room that was the twin of the first, but instead of the boxes, this one had an old steel desk in the center.

Out in the hall again, she opened the door marked RESIDENT. The room was outfitted with a large desk, a telephone, and a gray steel file cabinet. Dr. Berkeley's office, she decided—or was that Barkley? She ran her fingers over the steel desktop and slid open the top drawer. It *was* Barkley. Several drug company prescription pads with his name on them were inside. In an exploring mood, she went through the drawer. Nothing much. More drug company stuff: plastic paper clips marked CIBA, notepads— She stopped, intrigued, at the little stack of business cards. Bonanza. There were two kinds. The first, obviously for patients, gave an Atlanta office address and phone number. The second had to be for other doctors. This one, headed Neurology Consultations, gave two phone numbers: office and home.

Without a qualm, she tucked one of each into her cigarette pouch. After all, business cards were meant to be given away, and she had no intention of bothering the good doctor at home. These weren't on a par with her treasured Clint Eastwood or Dolly Parton, but they were still worth collecting.

Closing the drawer, she turned her attention to the gray four-drawer file cabinet against one wall. Locked, she discovered when she gave a little tug to the top drawer. At the back right, a door opened into a connecting corridor that led first to a small examining room, then beyond to a large storage room crammed with equipment.

Wooden crutches with crumbling rubber tips hung from the pegboard that covered most of one wall, some of the crutches so tiny that she blinked at the thought of the children who had had to use them. A tangle of braces filled a large wooden crate. Maureen pulled one out. It was steel with thick leather straps, dark and stiffened with age; it was small enough for a three-year-old. She could almost see the thin little leg it had encased, almost feel the pain. Shuddering, she thrust the brace back into the box when suddenly a dark sense of foreboding took away her breath. Gasping, she whirled around.

Nothing. Nothing but crutches, wheelchairs, boxes. Nothing but pale light bleeding through dull white window glass.

And that was it. The nothingness. The abrupt unwelcome feeling that she was utterly alone.

She managed a faint grin. Calm down, Maureen. Cool it. But the panicky feeling intensified.

Her heart began to pound in her throat. Get out. She had to get out. A dozen metal-framed hospital screens clattered out of her way as she ran.

A sharp metallic click brought her to a stop and her chin jerked in the direction of the sound.

The screen was resting against something. A thick silver tube as long as a coffin . . .

Maureen sucked at a breath, squeezed her eyes shut, opened them again. She had been no more than five or six years old when Uncle Joe took her to the fair. Five or six, and eating cotton candy for the first time. It was pink and warm, melting to nothing in her mouth, streaking her tongue with red. They were on their way back to the merry-go-round for one last ride, taking a short cut, winding through a maze of tents and ropes and stakes at the edge of the midway, when she heard a funny noise coming from a trailer just ahead. A sound that hovered somewhere between a hiss and a sigh.

She was old enough to read some of the ornate red and white words on the sign; she said them out loud: "The girl in the—"

She turned questioning eyes to Uncle Joe.

"The girl in the iron lung," he read. "Completely paralyzed for eleven years."

"Lungs aren't iron," she protested. Lungs were squishy like the ones Mommy pulled out of the chickens she cleaned. If she closed her eyes, she could almost see them, gray and speckled, oozing through Mommy's knobby fingers.

"It's a machine. When kids get infantile paralysis it makes them so they can't breathe, so a machine has to do it for them."

Doubt flickered in her eyes. Uncle Joe teased her sometimes, told her things that weren't so, and then laughed about it.

"It's all right," he said. "Want to see?"

She nodded and clutched the paper cone of cotton candy tighter.

He fished in his pocket for coins, and together they climbed the steps into the trailer.

The sighing was louder inside, and the heat from the press of bodies intense. Grown-ups towered over her, shoving as if she were not there. A hard belt buckle mashed against her cheek and her nose filled with cigar smoke and *Evening in Paris* perfume and sour crotch smells.

"Move over, folks. Let the little girl take a look,"

bellowed Uncle Joe. "She paid to see, just like you." Then he was scooping her up, hoisting her over the crowd.

The girl in the iron lung had red hair and a bright red lipstick smile. Just a head and a painted smile staring up at her, and a long silver tube that groaned and hissed like an animal. It was the smile that was so terrible. It wasn't real; it was thin and sly, like she knew a secret.

"Want to crawl in the lung with her, sweetie-pie?" asked the man with the cigar.

Mute with terror, she shook her head.

A fat man in overalls put his face close to Maureen and grinned. "Sure she does. I think we need a new girl, don't you?" A bubble of saliva slithered on his tongue. His teeth were loose; she heard them click, saw them bob up and down. "Time to put a new girl in the iron lung."

Somebody laughed, and someone else said, "Pop her in. I'll help." Then a woman's angry voice: "Cut it out. You're making her cry. She's just a little kid."

Maureen stared at the dull silver tube, half hidden by the hospital screen. "Cut it out," she whispered. It was just an iron lung. An antiquated iron lung in a storage room.

But her heart swelled and jittered in her throat, choking off her breath, making her dizzy and sick, and she knew it was more than the old childish panic, more than the sudden feeling of isolation. She wasn't alone—she could cope with that if she had to—she wasn't alone at all. Something was there. She could feel it, dark and cold as death, skittering along the edges of her mind.

Grabbing for the door, she stumbled through, slammed it behind her, and with the sound echoing like thunder in her head, she ran down the hall.

SIX

Tim stared at Jody Henson and tried to decide whether she was pulling his leg. Her level gaze said she was not. "What do you mean 'dead two hundred years'? Are you telling me Maureen Dorcas is nuts?"

She shook her head and lightly traced the top of his computer with a fingertip. "I'm not saying that at all. Do you know her books? She wrote *The Paul Chronicles.*"

"Should I be impressed?"

"They're very popular in some circles."

He thought he detected a slightly defensive tone in her voice. "Not in mine, I'm afraid. What does she write? No, let me guess. Historical romances cobbled from a stack of eighteenth-century love letters, right? From a dead man named Paul." He was looking at her eyes, partly checking the effect of his words, partly analyzing the color: first blue-gray smoke, then pale mist touched with flecks of gold. Funny how he had never used gray eyes for a woman in his books. At least he didn't think he had. Only blue or brown.

"Not at all. I guess you could call her books philosophy."

"Oh?"

"Some people think so," she said. "Anyway, Maureen channels them."

He felt vaguely uncomfortable. "What do you mean 'channels'?"

Jody seemed faintly surprised, as if she did not quite believe the term was unfamiliar to him. "Paul speaks through her. He dictates the books." She hesitated a moment. "Maureen is a trance medium."

"Good God." Tim sat down on the bed and felt its springs bulge dangerously through the thin mattress. Just when you thought it was safe to lie down . . . He eyed the next bed and wondered whether another layer of mattress might help. "You're kidding, right?"

"She's not crazy, Tim."

"Of course not. People collaborate with dead guys every day in the week. It's me that's nuts. I believed her when she said the two of them were here together." He snorted. "She even called him her 'live-in.' "

Jody's hand covered her mouth, but not her giggle. "I guess in a way he is."

Tim tried to frown, but her giggle was too delicious for that. It occurred to him that the hole in the Mike Mona book might be nicely filled with a touch of strange. "Tell me," he said half seriously, "what happens first? Does she go in for eye-rolling? Heavy breathing?"

"I really don't know."

"Oh, come on. Don't disappoint the fans. Tell me there's a midnight seance tonight. Ghostly apparitions. Poltergeists. Can we take notes?"

She sniffed.

"You don't really believe that stuff, do you?" He gave her a close look. "Or maybe you do. Maybe you think we can raise the dead with a little hyperventilation."

"I think we can learn a lot by studying the unconscious mind," she said carefully.

"That's a psychologist's answer."

"I *am* a psychologist."

"Not yet, you aren't," he said, wondering why he was sparring with her. What he really wanted to do, he realized in surprise, was to nuzzle her ear. "What do you really think?"

"I think we need to keep an open mind about things we don't understand."

He nodded. "Just like Aunt Bertie used to say. When her husband died she paid a fortune teller to act as a long distance operator. Only it was the fortune teller who reached out and touched someone—Aunt Bertie, for nearly ten thousand dollars."

"Uh-huh."

"What does that mean?"

"What?"

"That clinical 'uh-huh,'" he said, realizing that the defensiveness was not all on Jody's side. He had no idea why he had brought up the family cornflake. Aunt Bertie's bizarre expense account had nothing to do with what he believed or didn't believe.

"How would I know?" she asked innocently. "I'm not a psychologist yet."

He licked a finger and drew a "1" in midair. "Your point." He gave her what he hoped was a disarming smile. "So, you think Maureen Dorcas's books—what did you call them? *The Paul Papers*?—are written by a dead man."

"Chronicles," she corrected. "To answer your question,

I'm not sure what I believe. I don't know much about her, or how she works. But I do know that there's more to the human mind than what's in textbooks."

"Mind with a capital M, right? Unknowable, unfathomable. The, uh, science of psychology?" He was not sure why he had supplied the ironic emphasis; he had little, if any, empathy with the other side of the coin, the behaviorists, who were always trying to reduce people to a set of predictable conditioned responses.

"You're an expert?"

"In some things. Writing books, for instance. What comes out of Maureen Dorcas's head was there all along, things she saw, things she read. What's new is the synthesis."

Jody looked away, studying a spiderlike crack in the plaster for a moment before she turned back. "You think she's a fake then."

"You said that, not me. I like the lady. She may believe all this completely. But if she does, she's playing head games."

"Aren't we all," she observed lightly. Glancing down at the computer, Jody ran her fingers across the keyboard. "Since you're an expert, maybe you can give me some expert advice. I need to buy one of these. To write my thesis on. I'm afraid I don't know much about them. Is this an Apple? It looks different."

He nodded, admiring the deft way she had defused the conversation. "It is different." He flipped up the flat computer screen. "The Byte Fairy turned it into a portable. Power pack and everything." He reached for a small package of disks. "I'll show you my word processor."

"Great. But not now." Jody tapped her watch. "It's suppertime."

* * *

Except for the hospital employees in white uniforms or faded green scrub suits, the cafeteria could have passed for its counterpart in a bus terminal. Its two-tone walls, bottomed with industrial green and topped with tan, were relieved at intervals by yellowing posters touting the Heimlich Maneuver and a sagging bulletin board declaring that the institution was an Equal Opportunity Employer. Decor by the Blues Brothers, Cross and Shield, thought Tim. Tray in hand, he examined the offerings: an array of chilled sandwiches flattened with Saran Wrap, some boiled eggs, and a small variety of salads in throwaway bowls. For crunch, there were chips and Fritos pinioned to a wire rack; for hot, you could microwave a selection of canned soups and stews.

"Sunday night is self-serve, I'm afraid," said Jody, selecting a shrink-wrapped salad with tired-looking egg-slice eyes and a pale tomato smile.

"Looks yummy," said Tim disparagingly.

"It'll be better tomorrow, I promise you."

"The salad?" He tapped the rim of her bowl and nodded gravely. "It's not getting older; it's getting better."

"Vintage year," said Jody. "Do you think we should lay some away for later?" Her smile was full of mischief.

Dangerous, he thought. A smile like that might be addictive.

Jody ran Diet Coke into a paper cup and headed for a cluster of tables where the rest of the group was sitting. That is, most of the group. The fat woman, Carla, was conspicuously absent. Probably having a pizza, Tim thought. A large pizza with pepperoni and black olives, he amended grimly and settled for a drooping corned beef on rye and a can of beef stew. While the stew microwaved, he scooped up a handful of Saltines and found the coffee machine. The little brown mouse was there, agitating a cup of cocoa with a wooden stir stick.

"Hi," he said. Trying to remember her name, he took a sidelong look at her name tag. One edge of the smiley face had curled loose from her blouse. The faint type said BETH QUAIG.

Startled, the girl backed away so abruptly that her cocoa slopped over the sides of the foam hot cup. Avoiding his gaze, she dabbed at the puddle with a paper napkin that rapidly turned into a sodden mess.

He pulled out a half-inch wad of napkins from a dispenser and handed them to her. "Here."

Instead of wiping up the cocoa, she stared at the napkins with a strange blank look on her face. Then she blinked and gave Tim a self-conscious smile. Her gaze slid down to the puddled tray. "I get so flustrated I could just die."

"Frustrated," he said without thinking, and instantly regretted the rudeness. He had no idea why he had corrected her; it had been years since he had done anything like that. Not since his teaching days. Rudeness aside, it was a waste of breath; if a kid was violating the language past junior high, he was probably going to keep on screwing it up the rest of his life.

Astonishingly, Beth giggled.

A giggle? From the mouse? On closer look, he realized that she was a lot younger than his first assessment. He had put her age somewhere in the middle twenties, but now he saw that she was just a kid. Barely out of her teens, if that. "Better fill up again," he said with a nod to her half-empty cup.

"Right." Another giggle, coupled with a sidelong look. "Don't you just love marshmallows? In cocoa, I mean. They don't have any."

Nineteen going on fourteen, he thought. "Why don't you lighten up?" Tim grinned at the sudden consternation on her face. "With this," he said and tossed a couple of packets of coffee creamer onto her tray.

She picked one up and caressed the package between thumb and fingers as if she were touching something of great value. Then raising her eyes, she gave him a tremulous smile so full of frank expectation that Tim nearly winced. "Try it, you'll like it," he said, for lack of a better exit line, and left to retrieve his stew from the microwave.

Jody had chosen an empty table near the others. He slid into a chair next to her and was unwrapping his sandwich when someone caressed the nape of his neck. Beth.

The girl leaned closer and nodded at the empty chair to his left. "Is this seat taken?"

Her breath tickled his ear. Tim shook his head, sure that the girl had contrived to wait until he had sat down before coming up to the table. Not wanting to encourage her, he gave her a bland noncommittal smile—a checkout counter special—and turned slightly away. Not enough to be a snub, he told himself, but he wanted some body language on his side. A schoolgirl crush was probably better than a stick in the eye, but not a whole lot. With a shudder, he remembered the nymphette ninth grader in his second period English class who had turned in mash notes instead of her homework. Suki or Saki—she had a silly name like that—had dotted her "i"s with circles and doused her purple stationery with whorehouse perfume. She couldn't spell either.

Jody was watching Beth with that same intent look she had had before. Wondering why, he stole a quick look at the girl. Beth's eyes caught his—gotcha—and she gave him another ardent smile. "It's good," she murmured over her cup. "The cream, I mean." Another giggle.

Good God. Saki—or Suki—had had a giggle like that. Somehow she had managed to get his phone number. She had called him in the middle of the night. He could never forget that adolescent giggle punctuating her description of the baby doll nightie she had on: pink, like her nipples, she said, which, according to her, were plainly visible through the nylon. He had wanted to kill her. To get rid of her, he threatened to call her father and recommend granny gowns and a convent school. "Great," he muttered.

Maureen Dorcas came up. "Join you people?" Without waiting for an answer, she set down her tray.

Tim looked her over thoughtfully, as if he half expected to find something different about her, some little quirk of mannerism or expression that he might have missed, but all he saw were lines of fatigue around her eyes and a preoccupied look that he had not noticed before. His knowledge of mediums was limited to the Hollywood version. Now was his chance to see the real thing in action—that is, if he could figure out a graceful way to ask for a demonstration.

Maureen had changed into a dated-looking green velvet pantsuit. She caught him eyeing it, and her quick smile banished the tired, distracted expression. "Like it?" She struck a pose. "It's probably older than this sweet young thing," she said with a nod to Beth Quaig.

"Really?" asked the girl.

"Beautiful fabric," said Jody. "Where in the world did you find it?"

Maureen whispered sotto voce, "Nashville Thrift. Two ninety-eight plus tax."

Tickled at the conspiratorial look on her face, Tim affected an unbelieving "No." And what did he expect a medium to wear, anyway? "Are these your working clothes?"

Maureen sat down and glanced from side to side to be sure no one was listening before she said in a low voice, "Don't tell anybody, but it's all a shtik. When you're in my line of work, people expect you to be a little weird. At home I wear sweat suits."

"Do you jog?"

"Never. To tell you the truth, I don't sweat either." She gave him a demure southern belle smile punctuated with exaggerated eyelash batting. "Ladies glow, sugah. But I like sweat suits. I've got eleven or twelve. Pink, yellow, blue, you name it."

He wanted to say "Psyche in a Nike," but "psyche" didn't quite make sense, and "psychic" didn't rhyme. Instead, he said, "Jody told me what you write. I haven't read any of your books yet, but I'd like to."

"Would you, now?" Maureen began to unload clam chowder, tomato juice, and two boiled eggs from her tray. "Aren't you sweet."

They were interrupted by a breathy little shriek from Beth. She was pointing at a corner of the table. "Kill it!"

A large wasp was crawling along the edge.

Hysteria touched her voice. "Kill it!"

Tim wadded a napkin and crushed the insect. When he cautiously opened it, the wasp tried to crawl away.

"It's still alive."

He swept it off the table and crushed it underfoot.

Beth looked down at the dead wasp and caught her lip between her teeth. "I didn't mean to get crazy. I'm allergic. I got stung on the neck once and you talk about sick—"

"Well, you want to be careful about that," he said. "This is the time of year they get inside."

"The doctor said I was lucky to be alive. That close to my brain and all."

A tiny moan from Maureen. Her fingertips explored her throat along the angle of her jaw.

A welt was rising on her throat while Tim watched. "It got you."

"No."

"Of course it did."

She waved him away. "I'm all right. Really. Sympathetic reaction, I guess."

He stared. How was it possible for anyone to be that suggestible? But even as he questioned it, he felt a tingling on his own throat.

Concern crossed Jody's face. "Are you sure you're all right?"

Maureen grinned a little sheepishly. "I'm okay. It itches like blue blazes though."

"Do things like this happen to you a lot?" Tim asked.

"No." She rubbed the welt gingerly. "Thank God. Who could live like that?"

He could not keep his eyes off Maureen's throat. He had encountered something like this only once before, years ago in college, when he saw a hypnotist raise a welt on the arm of his subject with a feather. "I meant what I was saying before about your books," he said impulsively. "I'd like to know more about the process. You know, you and Paul. The, uh—"

"Foreplay?" Maureen asked with a wicked grin. Then with mock seriousness she said, "I think I know research when I see it. Am I going to be in your next book?"

Beth Quaig touched Tim's arm, running her fingers back and forth. "Research about what?"

"Could be," he said to Maureen, hitching his arm away from Beth's persistent touch as unobtrusively as possible.

Beth found his arm again. "Research about what?"

Unobtrusive wasn't going to cut it, Tim decided.

Before he could answer, Jody leaned forward and said to the girl, "Tim is interested in the way Mrs. Dorcas writes her books."

He turned to Maureen. "Very interested. Would you consider giving me a little demonstration?"

Maureen seemed startled. "Tonight?"

"If that's all right," he said, eyeing her curiously. The thick welt on her throat looked smaller now.

"Chile, I is plumb wore out. I didn't get to bed until after two." She gave a short weary laugh. "That's what happens when your daughter decides to have a marital crisis. Then I had the four-hour drive from Nashville." Her clear blue eyes narrowed and she gave him a close look. "You're really intent on this, aren't you?"

He nodded.

A sigh. "Well . . . Maybe a short session—in the name of research. But I'll need a nap first, so not until nine o'clock." She glanced at her watch. "Let's make that nine-thirty. My room. I'm in 502."

"Thanks." Tim nodded toward Jody. "Is it okay to bring a friend?"

"Why not? One or a dozen. It makes no difference to me. You can come too, if you like," she said to Beth.

"What kind of demonstration is it?" asked the girl. "What are you going to do?"

"A psychic demonstration," said Jody. "Mrs. Dorcas is a medium."

Maureen looked up from her chowder and said, "Psychic is as psychic does. I'm not really that good. Paul's the one with the batting average."

Tim swallowed a spoonful of stew. "What do you mean?"

"I've been tested several times. On my own, I don't

seem to score higher than chance, but when Paul comes through the score goes way up."

"Who's Paul?" asked Beth.

"He's my control." Maureen leveled a gaze at Beth. "I go into trance," she told the girl. "It's a little like a deep sleep. Then Paul takes over and begins to speak. When he's in charge, not much gets by him."

Beth blinked. For a moment she studied her spoon, staring down at it with a rapt look. Then she said in a low voice, "Does anybody else come?"

"No. So far, only Paul."

Beth's answering "oh" was a wispy half sound nearly lost in the clatter of silverware and the talk from the adjacent table.

Maureen searched the girl's face. As she did, her eyes softened. "It's not anything to be afraid of," she said. "You don't have to be afraid."

"I'm not," Beth said abruptly. She stared down at her tray for a long moment, and then began to dab at the drying stains of cocoa streaking her cup. She looked up again, her pupils dark against the irises, dark and closed as if an inner door had shut. Pushing away her half-eaten meal, the girl rose and, without a word, turned and scurried away.

Tim squatted in front of the old Philco and twiddled the dial. The TV's speaker responded with a puff of dust and a faint roar that might have been an adventure-show car chase, or—equally possible—electrical noise. The milky screen offered no clue. He flicked the dial to 11 and was rewarded with another roar and the acrid smell of burning insulation. Switching it off, he pulled out the plug. Judging from the gnawed cord and the suspicious little tufts of excavated mattress fluff on the floor behind the set, it looked like tonight's scheduled programming had been preempted by a mouse nest. No matter. It was nearly time for the Paul and Maureen Show, anyway.

The setting was appropriate. Night had turned Morgan Wing into something right out of Edgar Allan Poe. Tangled shadows, held at bay only by the feeble glow from the battered lamp, crept into the alcove and stretched lean fingers along every angling turn of wall.

Suddenly, unaccountably, Tim's lungs emptied. He gasped, sucking for air as if he were smothering, as if he were drowning in a sea of mud. In a moment, the feeling passed, but the echoes remained, and he recognized traces of his recurring nightmare.

It was the silence. That was all. It was getting to him. He had no idea where everybody had gone after supper. Except for Jody. She had had a "ton of paperwork to do," but she had promised—a little reluctantly, he thought—to come back in time for Maureen's demonstration.

But there was a cure for silence. Tim pressed the eject button on the little portable tape recorder slung over his shoulder. He had brought it along for seance notes, poking a blank tape into his pocket on his way out of his room. A Wynton Marsalis cassette was still inside the machine. He turned it on, congratulating himself for having the foresight to pack a little entertainment in with his socks. It wasn't stereo; in fact, the recorder's fidelity was on a par with a street hooker, but, by God, it was something.

He wondered if Jody really intended to show up. But what was the rush? There was no sign of life in Maureen's room, anyway. Across the hall, the transom above the door to 502 showed only an occasional flicker that he decided was reflected streetlight. It looked like Maureen Dorcas was either out or sleeping.

The whole evening looked like a washout. He had tried to work after dinner, but for some reason, he had not been able to concentrate. Giving up, he'd switched off the word processor and plugged in the chess game he always kept with his data disks. He had just lost his queen to the computer when a bored lab technician, wearing a tired look and a too-tight skirt, knocked and demanded an assortment of bodily fluids. Our Lady of the Lab had unwittingly provided the high point of the evening so far: on his way to the toilet—come fill the cup—he had blundered through the wrong door and found an array of shower stalls. The place was clean enough, but the rusty streaks down the tiles were obviously older and more determined than the cleaning woman. He took it as a good sign; if rust was proof of working order, it meant he could get the dust off without resorting to the bathtub from Brobdingnag.

He tweaked the recorder's volume control. The tiny speaker went from not-much to not-a-whole-lot-more, and, with alchemistic legerdemain, transmuted Wynton Marsalis's bright brass into tin and tape hiss. Halfway through "Skain's Domain," the double doors at the end of the hall swung open and Jody came in. She took off her lab coat and draped it over a chair. She had on a soft blue sweater dress that skimmed her breasts and hips. Nice. He wondered what she had on underneath.

"I'm late, aren't I?" Jody asked. "I lost track of the time."

Tim glanced at his watch again. 9:34. "Not much." Nodding toward Maureen's room, he said, "I think she's still asleep."

"Should we wake her up?"

"My mean streak says yes." He switched off the recorder and they crossed the hall.

"I don't know. Are you sure we should?"

"Why not?" he said, but in truth, he was having second thoughts. Maureen had been up late last night, he told himself. But there was more to his reluctance than that—something nibbling at his mind that would not quite come out of the shadows. Another parochial school hangover, he decided: don't mess around with the occult or God will get you. But if it was only that, why did he keep getting flashes from the nightmare? Why wasn't he able to shake the feeling that always came at the end of it?—the weird detachment, as if he had somehow been cut loose from himself.

"All right then," said Jody. "We wake her up." She raised her hand and knocked softly.

The door opened. Blue-gray light flickered in the room. "Come on in," said Maureen.

"We thought you were asleep," said Jody.

Maureen shook her head. "I couldn't drop off for some reason. I was watching TV."

"Brought your own, I see," Tim observed—inanely, it seemed to him. Across the darkened room, a misty rain beaded the tall windowpanes and reflected the red glow of a traffic light a block away.

She switched on the bedside lamp and its light puddled in one corner. The room was about the same size as Tim's, but this one had its full complement of beds, four of them placed in a soldierly row, two more shoved against the end wall.

"Like I said," Maureen explained, "I've been involved in these studies before. What you leave at home you do without."

And obviously, Maureen Dorcas wasn't planning to do without much of anything. She had changed clothes again. This time, she had on an oversized purple sweat suit and a pair of fuzzy pink bedroom slippers. Tim wondered how much luggage she had brought—and how many trips it had taken her to get everything up five flights of stairs. No wonder she was so skinny.

Maureen turned off the tiny portable television and faced Tim. "I suppose you'll want to take notes."

He held up the little recorder. "Is this all right?"

"Fine with me."

"What do we do? Sit in a circle?" asked Jody with a touch of nervousness in her voice.

Maureen laughed. "With just the three of us, it would be more of a triangle, wouldn't it?" she said. "To answer your question, you don't do much at all. I'm not into hymn singing and hand-holding like some of the fraternity. Some sitters expect it, though. I used to let people make their own music if they wanted to, but I quit doing that after one man brought his bagpipe."

"Bagpipe?" Tim gave a disbelieving smile.

"You'd better believe it. Eighteen choruses of 'Rock of Ages.' Well," she amended, "maybe not that many, but it seemed like it. Do you have any idea how loud bagpipes are?"

Tim opened the recorder, pocketed the Wynton Marsalis, and inserted the blank tape.

"You don't have a bagpipe hidden in there, I hope."

"Just an empty tape." He patted his shirt pocket. "And a little jazz in here."

"Next to your heart? Well, I could live with that." Maureen waved her arm toward a pair of armchairs. "Have a seat." One chair was covered with clothes; a tote bag and a coat occupied the other. "Have a bed instead, if you want to." Accepting her own invitation, she sat cross-legged on the bed nearest the window, propped a pillow behind her shoulders and leaned back. "It usually takes a few minutes for Paul to come through," she said. "When he does, you can ask questions if you want to. Is there anything else you want to know before we start?"

Tim shook his head and took a seat next to Jody on the bed next to Maureen's. He was switching on the recorder when a light knock came at the door.

Maureen looked up. "Come in."

The heavy door swung open a crack and Beth Quaig peeked into the room.

"Come on in. We haven't started yet."

The door opened wider and Beth slipped just inside the room. A thin lock of brown hair slid down over her eyes and she brushed it away with a nervous little swipe of an index finger. Instead of the schoolgirl-crush look she had worn at supper, the expression on her face said she was ready to run at a moment's notice.

Strange, thought Tim. But no wonder. Morgan Wing was enough to give anyone the creeps. He was surprised she had come. After the way she had reacted at supper, Beth was the last person he would have expected to show up for a seance. Maybe she figured it was better than being alone.

"Sit down," said Maureen.

The girl glanced at the bed where Tim and Jody were sitting, then hesitantly slid to a seat on the floor close to the door as if she felt safer there.

Jody flicked a look from Beth to Maureen and started to say something. Instead, she dropped her gaze, and leaned back against the steel headboard.

"See you later," said Maureen. Her eyes closed. In a few seconds her head fell back and she lay motionless.

There was only the faint sound of traffic now. Raindrops glided down the windowpanes in snail tracks of reflected green, then red.

A long, shuddering breath from Maureen broke the silence.

Silence again. Then a gasp. It was followed by rapid panting as if she fought for breath.

Suddenly Tim wanted to laugh. It was pure Hollywood corn. That, or "Paul" had a bad case of emphysema. He leaned over the recorder. Aiming the mike, he was turning up the level when he felt Jody's hand on his arm. Her grip tightened; her eyes were fixed on Maureen. He followed her gaze.

The woman's head had lolled back and to one side as if her neck were broken. The ragged breathing stopped.

As if she were dead . . .

For a blazing moment, he thought she was.

Before he could react further, Maureen's eyes slowly opened and a jolt of adrenaline coursed through Tim's chest like an electric shock.

The eyes were not hers.

Unbelieving, he stared. An unseen sculptor was at work, molding her features as if they were clay, settling them into heavier, more masculine lines.

Her face, yet not her face.

The lips pinched themselves together, opened, stretched, as if someone tested their resilience. They moved, hesitated, formed themselves into a smile: "My name is Paul. Good evening."

The voice was deeper than Maureen's, masculine, with a slight accent that Tim could not place.

She—it—repeated the "good evening," this time with more animation. Or was the word he wanted "animatronics"? The puppetlike movements seemed to rise from wax and circuits, not flesh and blood.

Maureen's upper body jerked forward. "Give us a moment to adjust to the instrument." The woman's body was moving now, struggling to a sitting position at the side of the bed. Each motion was exaggerated, almost grotesque, as if a small child had put on Maureen's skin and found it several sizes too large.

This was crazy. It reminded him of the Tin Woodman in the *Wizard of Oz.* Give this boy an oil can. Again, he felt the urge to laugh.

The head cocked; the eyes that were not Maureen's met his. "It is good to laugh. There is never enough laughter."

Tim's faint grin melted and his lips opened in astonishment. An instant later, anger flashed. It was all a con. Did Maureen think he was a complete fool? That pat line about laughter— Clever on the surface. But when you thought about it, it fell apart. Who wouldn't feel like laughing at the Tin Man act?

"Paul" seemed to gain more control. The movements of Maureen's body were more fluid now, yet still Tim had the impression of someone working the mechanism from inside.

The mouth opened, spoke: "Your skepticism is understandable to me. I was once the crown prince of skeptics. But that was a long time ago."

Tim's lip curled. He tried to remember what he might have said to give Maureen the idea for that remark. Something at dinner? Or maybe it was just a good guess. All the same, he had to admit it was a pretty convincing performance. It wasn't too hard to imagine a gullible client falling for it. He gave a sidelong look toward Jody, but he could not read the expression on her face.

Paul turned a few degrees and faced Beth Quaig. "So. You decided to come."

Flustered at the attention, Beth stared fixedly at the floor.

Paul gave the girl a benevolent smile. "The others won't be joining us, will they? No matter." He turned to Tim and Jody and gave them a quizzical look. "Oh, yes. The pilot study group. Or perhaps, if you will allow me a modest pun, I should say the *automatic* pilot group." He stabbed an index finger at them. "It is best for pilots to study their flight plans."

And what was that supposed to mean?

Paul's gaze settled on Tim. "Ah, my skeptical friend. Each of you—especially you, perhaps—has joined this group for reasons of your own. But you had better be aware of this. You had better understand the weather pattern here or you will find yourself off course."

Doubletalk. "I don't know what that means."

"I think you do," said the accented voice. "You know why you joined this pilot group; you know why you are here tonight." A pause. "You might consider that camp. . . ."

He got that one right. High camp. Tim barely suppressed a snigger. Amazing stuff. Dead two hundred years, yet able to pick up on twentieth-century slang—and only a few years out of date. For an encore, folks, a real treat: the dead man will enter the arena in his suit of lights and dazzle us with bullshit.

"You are choosing not to listen."

Tim's voice took on an edge. "Is that right?"

Paul's eyes met his, burned into his. "In the night, in the swamp, you listen."

How? How could he know that? No one did. Tim's heart swelled in his throat until it threatened to choke him—the way it had when he was fifteen. It had all started as a joke; he had only meant to scare Mary Ellen Harper, meant—literally—to scare the pants off her.

Her family had gone to her kid brother's Saturday afternoon Little League game and the house was empty. He had timed his arrival within minutes of their departure, slipping through the downstairs entrance to the Harpers' rumpus room, carrying his sister's Ouija board under his arm. It had started as a game. That was all. Just a game.

They had set up the board on the scarred oak game table where Mr. Harper played his weekly game of poker.

Mary Ellen placed both hands on the planchette. Her fingernails were pale pink lacquer. A plan came to him, and he reached out and took one of her hands in his. "You just need one hand," he said, inventing as he went along. "You're supposed to hold the other one to make it work." He caressed her fingers with thumb and forefinger. "See. It's starting."

"You're moving it," she said.

Indeed he was, exerting slight pressure with his left hand, guiding the pointer from letter to letter, spelling E-X-P-R-E-S-S Y-O-U-R L-O-V-E L-E-S-T I-T D-I-E, feeling the planchette gliding over the slick surface of the Ouija board when, suddenly, a strange current tingled through his hand.

The planchette slid to the letter J, twitched away, paused, moved back again. "You're doing that," he accused.

The planchette lurched: J-J-J.

"I'm not doing anything," she said with a nervous giggle. "It's you."

J-J-J-J-J-J-J-J. . . .

A break. A tearing sound deep inside his head. . . .

Suddenly Mary Ellen was on the other side of the room, her back to the wall, her eyes wide with fright.

He blinked in confusion. When did she get up? Why?

"Jesus and Mary." Mary Ellen's voice was a halting whisper. "Do you know what you said?"

Dazed, he stared at her. In a moment, he found his voice: "Sure." It was a lie. A shiver rippled up his spine. He had no idea what he had said. It was gone—completely—

as if someone had snipped out a tiny piece of his life and spliced the two ends together. He couldn't let her know, couldn't admit he had lost it. He licked his lips, swallowed, faked a laugh. "Sure I know." At the sudden relief in her eyes, he added, "Had you going, didn't I?"

He had come up with an excuse, something about a job to do at home, and left as quickly as possible. That night he had lain in bed sleepless, turning the incident over and over in his mind. What had he said? What was it that made her so afraid? Worse, why couldn't he remember?

And why, when finally he slept, had the dream of the swamp come again? Drowning him, until he woke in a cold sweat.

In the night, you listen. In the swamp.

Without a word, Tim looked away, staring at the rain-streaked windows, watching the sliding drops glow green, then red as blood.

Paul was speaking again: "It is always easiest to close the mind, to refuse to hear the inner voice." A faint wry laugh; the rustling of dry leaves.

"But how do you do that?" Jody asked suddenly. "Open your mind, I mean. Everything we've been taught tells us to doubt what we can't see and touch and measure."

"Your focus is narrow," said Paul. "You look at reality through a microscope. When everything beyond your tiny stage blurs and vanishes, you deny that it exists. But let me assure you, it does." A smile. "And so, what do you do about that? Set aside your ears and listen; set aside your eyes and see."

"But that's not easy to do," said Jody. "We aren't trained mediums like Maureen. We—"

Paul's smile vanished. "Even this instrument refuses to see and hear, although she believes she does. Instead, she follows an impulse that is not her own." A pause. "There is among you one you do not see, but who sees you. It would be best to watch most carefully. I will say that again: watch most carefully."

Near the door, Beth Quaig stirred. Paul turned to her abruptly. "Listen to Tabby."

Shock formed in the girl's eyes.

Paul's gaze swept the room. "There is a darkness here. A growing darkness. A red horse moves on the horizon. It carries a shadow on its back."

Beth was struggling to her feet, reaching for the doorknob, yet her eyes were fixed on Paul.

"A shadow. Growing. . . ." Paul's voice died to a whisper.

Tim stared. Paul's—Maureen's—face was changing as he watched, twisting into a grotesque snarl. And the eyes—He caught his breath. The eyes glittered, cold as stone, and so sly that a shudder coursed down his spine.

The voice grew nasal, the words mocking: "I have a little shadow that goes in and out with me. . . . In and out, in and out, in and out. . . ."

The arms twitched in an inner battle for control. Slowly they rose, wrists crossed, muscles quivering against a tension that was almost palpable, fingers curled into fists, thumbs cocked, as if they held something invisible and thin as wire.

With a sudden movement almost too fast to follow, the fists jerked apart.

Jody's hand flew to her mouth. "Oh, God," she whispered.

A horrible gurgling was coming from deep in Maureen's throat. Suddenly the woman fell back, limp as death.

No movement. Then a gasping rush of air.

The medium's eyes flew open and terror etched them. Her hands crept to her throat. "I was . . ." Another gasp.

"Someone—" Her eyes rolled up and she lost consciousness.

Jody was on her feet, running the few feet to Maureen's bed, cradling the woman in her arms. "Help me."

Jumping up, Tim bent over Maureen and lifted her to a sitting position. As he did, her head lolled back. The flesh of her throat was dough white against the narrow, indented line that circled it—a line, thin as wire, that purpled as they watched.

The door slammed and the frantic tap of Beth Quaig's retreating footsteps faded until there was no sound left but the ragged, gasping respirations of the medium.

SEVEN

Hal Gulliver stabbed the TV remote button and blipped the movie off the screen. At first, the spy thriller had been good for a few laughs; Hollywood's notion of the Agency usually was. But the wooden, oh-so-serious dialogue had quickly palled.

He tried CNN Headline, but it was all the same old stuff; not much going on in the world since he'd caught the news at supper. Switching off the set, he poured himself two fingers of cognac, and stared at the phone. Barbara had been in Florida for ten days now, and he felt vaguely ill-at-ease. He was not willing to admit to himself that he missed her. Just used to having her around, he thought, having her beside him while they watched TV, or knowing she was in the next room working with her light box and her drawings, or maybe in the kitchen fixing a bowl of popcorn.

Ten days ago, he had been sure it would be over with by now. By now, his wife should have been home and he should have been a grandfather. But the whole damn business was screwed up. That first night, Barbara had called with the cheery report. "They decided Val was in false labor," she had said. When it went on for two days, then three, Gulliver began to have murderous thoughts about Val's doctor: what in hell was he doing anyway? What kind of a doctor would let a girl suffer like that? He took a dim view of obstetricians. It seemed to him that any guy who made his living with his hand up a twat either couldn't get it up, or couldn't get it to lie down.

Barbara's spirits had been high at first, but later her calls took on a fractious air. Val was feeling like a failure, crying, saying she couldn't even have a baby without screwing up. Chip was trying, but "how much support can he be to her when he's on the road five days out of seven?" As for Barbara, she was a "mass" of sandfly bites. South Florida was infested, and she hoped to God they didn't carry AIDS. She missed the turning leaves. "Val says they have autumn in Miami. In December the poison ivy turns red."

"Come home, then," he had told her.

"And miss our first grandbaby? Are you out of your mind?"

Barbara was sure it would be a girl. When she got the call that Val was in labor, she had been working on a watercolor, a paper doll set that she planned to have framed for over the baby's crib. Taking his drink with him, Gulliver wandered into the room he called the den—Barbara called it the studio—and switched on the light. Her worktable took up most of one wall. He turned on the gooseneck lamp and looked down at the paper doll. It was a chubby baby with wings, an angel, or maybe it was a fairy, wearing gauzy-looking clothes. Its face looked like Val's when she was a baby.

Impulsively he reached for the extension phone and dialed Miami. After a few rings, Barbara answered.

"I called earlier," he said with a touch of accusation in his voice.

"We just got back."

"Out for a movie or something?"

"Not exactly." She paused. "Actually, we went for a reading." Then in a rush, she said, "Hal, this woman is marvelous. She told Val the baby would be here by Wednesday or Thursday night. She's sure it's a girl. And you'll never guess what else she said. She told me the baby was going to be gifted."

Another reading. It sounded like Barbara had picked a ringer this time. How much psychic ability did it take to tell a girl ready to pop that the baby was coming soon? As for the "gifted" business, what grandmother wouldn't be ready to believe that? "How much did all this cost?" he asked cautiously.

"Only fifty dollars for a half-hour reading." Another pause. "I treated Val to one too. It was really worth it. You should see her. She's in a wonderful mood now."

He glanced down at the table, at the paper doll with Val's baby face. "I'm glad she's feeling better," he said. Even if it cost a hundred bucks. "Can I talk to her?"

"Well, she's in the pool right now."

"The pool?" He thought of the apartment house swimming pool. When he was there last August it had been full of kids, most of them peeing in it he was sure. "Is that safe? She's pretty far along to be in swimming, isn't she?"

"It's okay. Her water hasn't broken yet, and the pool's chlorinated. Besides, she's not actually swimming. She's floating. She says it relieves the pressure. Want me to go get her?"

"No. Let it go. Tell her I called, though."

"I will."

He paused. "And tell her I love her."

"Miss you," she said.

"Miss you too."

He put the receiver on the hook, glanced down at the watercolor cherub again. Predictably, the "marvelous" fortune teller had not told Barbara that her husband had been working with psychics and mediums for years. Even if she had, he would have denied it. Security reasons aside, it wouldn't do for Barb to know. As hooked on her readings as she was, she'd never give him a moment's peace.

There wasn't much chance of the woman spilling the beans though. None of the dozens of so-called psychics Barbara had gone to had picked up on the work he did, nor did he expect them to. It had happened only once that he knew of—and not to him, but to Rudy Hollister over in Foreign Intelligence. Rudy's daughter, down in New Orleans for spring break, had had a session with a French Quarter tearoom Tarot reader. The woman turned out to be a medium who obligingly went into trance for Janie and her boyfriend in a private seance later that night. Janie got the session on tape, brought it home, and played it for Rudy. It gave him the creeps. The woman's spirit control, a little girl named Clarissa with a voice like Mister Bill, started talking about a phone tap that would have seriously interested a Senate investigating committee. Fortunately, the medium was willing to cooperate; after an appeal to her patriotism—Gulliver thought of it as a *spirited* appeal—she, and presumably Clarissa, ended up on the payroll, and Janie's tape ended up in a classified file.

A fluke, thought Gulliver. He did not believe in most of the psychic phenomena the Agency dabbled in. Oh sure, one in a hundred fortune tellers might have something, but real psychics were scarce as hen's teeth.

The Soviet Union's research on psychic phenomena couldn't be taken very seriously either. The Russians were gullible about things like that. It was the peasant mentality. Even back in their religious days, their churches had been riddled with weeping icons and fly-specked miracles. They might have given up God, but they had never lost their taste for magic.

Grudgingly, Gulliver had to admit that research parallel to the Soviet's was necessary; if the Russians were interested, it was their business to be interested too. But the cost! In the last seven years, ORD's budget for psychic research had quadrupled, and that was just one arm of the Agency. There was no way for one man to guess the total, no way of telling how much of the taxpayers' sand was being pounded down the rat hole. There were too many damn fools—inside the CIA and out—who were ready to believe the most transparent bullshit a money-grubbing charlatan could dream up.

In the last seven years, Hal Gulliver had put in thousands of hours overseeing ORD's work with psychics. But it wasn't spoon-bending, or telekinesis, or any of the rest of the mental mumbo jumbo that held his interest. What made the psychics vitally important to him—and to HALFLIFE—was the way their brains worked.

EIGHT

Maureen's eyes fluttered open. They were bloodshot. Her unsteady gaze flicked from Tim to Jody, then back again. "What is it? What's wrong?" Her voice was husky. She blinked in confusion, and her hand crept to her throat.

"Don't you remember?" asked Jody.

Maureen shook her head. "What are you staring at?"

Tim could not take his eyes from her. A tangle of hair curled around her throat and bisected the angry purpling line that circled it. He reached out and gently brushed away the strand. It felt damp. "Maybe you'd better have a look." He nodded toward the flecked mirror above the sink.

With a puzzled frown, Maureen struggled unsteadily to her feet. Tim reached out to help. Shrugging off his grasp, she swayed, then clung to the sink for balance. She stared into the mirror, her reflection pale as marble.

A quick sucking breath.

Maureen traced the thin bruise with thumb and forefinger. For a long moment she stood there, one hand grasping the sink, her knuckles white as the porcelain, the other stroking the flesh of her throat, gently, tentatively, as if to convince herself that what she saw was real. Then she turned slowly and faced them. "What happened?"

"We don't know," said Jody. "Paul was here, and then . . ." She glanced anxiously at Tim. "I don't know."

"You really don't remember?"

Maureen shook her head. "Tell me. Tell me what happened."

The urgency in her voice was real enough. And the marks on her throat—how in hell could you fake that? Tim suddenly realized that he had been thinking of the word *stigmata.* Crazy. The whole scene was crazy. "Your, uh, control," he began. "He was saying something. Then his face seemed to change. His voice—" Hesitantly, he told her what they had seen.

When Tim finished, Maureen sank down onto the bed and stared at the dark rain-glazed windows without a word.

A minute passed.

Jody touched her shoulder. "Are you okay?"

Turning back to Tim and Jody as if she had not really seen them before, she gave a short nod. "I'm fine."

"That place on your throat—" said Jody. "Let's get you down to the E.R. and let Cheryl Isaacson take a look at it. She's a friend of mine."

Maureen shook her head.

"But—"

"I said I was fine. What I need is some sleep."

Jody hesitated. "You're sure?"

"I'm sure." Grasping the pillow, Maureen lay back and closed her eyes.

It was an obvious dismissal. Exchanging a glance with Jody, Tim opened the door and they left the room. He was frankly relieved that Maureen had turned down the Emergency Room offer. What a scene that would have made:

"Well, Doctor, you see, she was attacked by an entity during the seance." Good God. They'd have been ready to lock all three of them up.

In the hall he took Jody by the arm. "Buy you a drink?"

She gave him a faint grin. "I could do without, but I'd rather not. Thanks." She turned toward the double doors.

He steered her in the opposite direction.

"But that way is out," she protested.

"We're drinking in." They came to his room. "My place." Tim opened the door, flicked on the light, and began to fish inside his luggage. He pulled out a pint of Cutty Sark wrapped in a red T-shirt. "Straight or watered down?"

"Straight, please." Jody picked up the tee shirt. On the front it read: I ARE A WRITER. Smiling, she held it up to her chest and checked the effect in the mirror.

Tim came up behind her, and, peering admiringly down at her breasts, circled her shoulders and reached for the rusty chrome paper cup dispenser on the wall by the mirror. Pulling out a pleated cup, he examined it and held it out for Jody's inspection. The exposed surface had yellowed with age. "Memento from the contagion ward?"

Her lip curled in distaste.

He tossed it into a green metal trash can under the sink where it landed with a percussive thud. The next cup looked white. He pulled out another and poured the drinks.

His tape case yielded a Bob James album. Thinking better of it, he put it back and swapped the seance tape for *Round Midnight* instead. "A little night music," he said, avoiding the word romantic. He turned on the recorder. "Booze and jazz. All the amenities."

Her smile came quickly, and just as quickly disappeared. "What in hell happened back there?"

"You're the psychologist," he said. "I was hoping you could tell me."

"I wish I could." She chewed her lip for a moment. "Self-hypnosis, maybe. That's all I can come up with. Suggestion. Like the welt she got on her throat at dinner."

"That ring around her throat wasn't a welt," he said. "It was starting to turn black and blue. Those were bruises."

"Bruises then. It could happen."

"I can't buy that. Beth talks about a wasp sting at dinner and the suggestible lady gets a hickey on her throat. But nobody suggested anything to Maureen during the seance."

"No," she admitted. "Nobody *we* heard."

"Maureen of Arc? Her voices tell her she's being strangled and so she is?"

"Have you got a better explanation? I'm open to suggestion."

"First Maureen, now you." He cupped her chin, tipped her head back, and stared at her throat. How smooth her skin was. "No welts yet."

Jody laughed and held out her empty cup. "More gruel, sir?"

"More? More!" He rolled his eyes and addressed an imaginary entourage. "She wants more." Sloshing an inch of Scotch into her cup, he handed it back. When she took it, he cupped her chin again, lifted it, and kissed her lightly on the lips. The music was compelling. "Dance?"

She nodded and he pressed her close. "You smell good." Her body was warm and slim against his. Nice. They danced for a long time, moving together naturally as if they had been partners for years. The music was drowsy jazz, coming-down jazz, just right for ending a day. Or for beginning something. His hand touched her waist, slid down, caressed tentatively. The swell of her buttocks excited him. He started to pull her closer, then suddenly stopped. Down, boy. It was too soon.

The thought surprised him. With a touch of dismay, he realized he had been looking ahead without knowing it, contemplating something long-range with a girl he barely knew.

He stopped dancing and held her at arm's length.

Her gray eyes met his. Puzzled.

Tim searched her face for a moment, and then pulled her close and kissed her. Her lips opened and he felt her body yield to his.

Suddenly Jody stiffened.

He blinked in surprise. She was staring over his shoulder. He turned his head.

The man in the doorway wore orderly's whites. He was leaning casually against the doorjamb, watching them with a frank stare that bordered on arrogance.

Tim's eyes narrowed. "What do you want?"

The man's wolfish grin exposed a row of crooked teeth. For a moment he did not move. Then straightening slowly, he gave an elaborate shrug, turned deliberately, and left.

"Someone you know?" he demanded.

Jody shook her head. "It's a big hospital."

Bristling, Tim strode to the doorway and stared up and down the wide hall. The man was gone.

"He's probably a float," said Jody. "On call for any floor that needs him."

Tim's jaw tightened. The door had been closed. He had closed it, and the son of a bitch had opened it, had stood there watching without a sound.

He jerked the door shut and looked for a lock. There was none.

Super. Suppose the jerk decided he wanted a computer while Timmy Boy was off in the can. He stared foolishly at the door. Why hadn't it occurred to him to check before now, before he waltzed off to supper with the place wide open? Stupid. Beyond stupidity. The sheer emptiness of the place had lulled him into thinking it was safe from intruders.

Jody came up to him. "It won't lock," she said. "Hospital rooms never do. A patient could bolt himself in and then pass out or something."

She nodded toward a gray steel locker near the door. "You can lock that. Did you find your key? They were in the envelopes I gave out this afternoon."

He had not bothered to look.

With a sharp click, the tape shut off and left the room in silence. "Another drink?" he asked.

Jody shook her head and glanced redundantly at her watch. "We start pretty early tomorrow." She retrieved her lab coat from the chair and slipped it on.

The tape had come to an end, and so, it seemed, had the evening.

She turned, paused at the door. "See you in the morning. Eight-thirty in the alcove."

He groaned at the hour. "Sadist."

"Eight-thirty sharp." She gave him a kiss light as a moth's wing. A final look, and she was gone.

Tim stared thoughtfully at the door that closed behind her. Whatever it was about her, it went beyond looks—although he had to admit that was what got his attention in the first place. But looks came cheap. In his randier moments, it seemed to him that at least half the girls in Atlanta were gorgeous.

There ought to be warning bells, he thought. There ought to be flashing red lights that spelled out REBOUND. But it wasn't as if he had been devastated when Linda moved out. A few bad nights, maybe. That was all.

He flipped the tape to Side B, and set his wristwatch alarm to 7:30. Thinking better of it, he reset it for 8:00. Who needed breakfast, anyway?

He poured himself another inch of Scotch and turned off the bedside light. Cradling his drink in his hand, he kicked off his shoes, leaned back against the headboard, and stared at a rain-blurred streak of light that penetrated the room and splashed its shadowed drops across the floor.

By the time *Round Midnight* finished playing, Tim had fallen asleep.

He woke with a start, his gaze darting around the darkened room as he tried to orient himself.

The rain had stopped. Water vapor haloed the city's lights, turning them to indistinct beacons in the mist. The gauzy ring of blue light circling the Hyatt Regency's roof floated in the distance like a giant electronic bug killer. Big enough to zap all the night flyers in five counties, he thought, imagining a silent rain of electrocuted insects falling endlessly over the city, smothering the streets with mounds and dunes of filmy wings and tiny, spidery limbs.

The light on his watch flashed on with a press of his finger. 3:42. He lay back and tried to decide whether to get undressed or just go back to sleep. He punched the pillow into subjection, cradled it, closed his eyes.

The sound again.

It was the sound that had wakened him. A faint high-pitched keening that might have come from a small animal or a child. He tried to identify it, but in a moment it stopped and he heard nothing more than the whisper of his own breath.

Then it came again.

He realized that he had been straining to hear, head cocked on the pillow, eyes staring as if they could filter the sound through the muffling darkness. He told himself it was nothing. Just a whistle in the air vents or the water pipes. He tried to relax, and within moments felt an overwhelming drowsiness. But as soon as he shut his eyes, another realization came: he had to pee, and he could either do it now, or do it later, but there was no getting around the fact that sooner or later he would have to get up.

Groaning, he punched the pillow again, sat up, and lit a cigarette. There wasn't much point in playing games with his bladder in the middle of the night. He knew from experience who would win. Searching for his shoes with a toe, he found them, slid them on, fumbled for the light.

Blinking at the sudden glare, he got up, paused, listened again. The sound was gone now. Half believing he had imagined it, Tim pulled open the heavy door and stepped into the hall. Just past room 506, the dim lights faded to shadows in the nurses station. Just beyond was the narrow alcove that led to the men's toilet. The painted-over light switch clicked loudly and the bathroom lights blazed on.

There were no urinals. Three wide cubicles with heavily painted doors housed the toilets. Not toilets really—water closets, with exposed pipes and tanks set high on the wall. Tim tossed the cigarette into the bowl and it hissed out.

The toilet flushed with a chain and a god-awful thundering cataract that reminded him of floods and storm tides and a clandestine junior high cherry bomb flushing that had brought the enduring wrath of Sister Mary Catherine and bodily violence from his father.

Half asleep, he stood at the sink and jabbed futilely at an empty liquid soap container. The cold water tap shuddered off with a clank and he reached for the damp loop of bird's-eye toweling cascading from a pitted chrome wall dispenser. A quick yank yielded a dry section and he began to wipe his hands. Suddenly he stopped short.

The words on the surface of the towel holder were faint, almost subliminal, as if they had been traced by a greasy fingertip:

Cloud Net.

He stared at them stupidly. Then, not knowing why, he began to scrub at the surface, smearing the words into oily illegible streaks, scrubbing again, polishing, until the smears gave way to the cold reflection of metal.

When finally he stopped, the worn toweling lay in tangled wads on the floor and his eyes reflected like dark pits from the shining surface of the dispenser.

The door from the hall wheezed open. Blinking as if he had just awakened, Tim turned toward the sound.

A tall blond man with a droopy mustache that almost disappeared against his tan walked in. He was wearing a white terry-cloth robe, the kind fitness centers issued.

Tim recognized the man who had kept his chair from tipping over that afternoon. What was his name? Dayton something. Satterfield. "Something woke me," he said by way of an opening, and immediately wondered why he had bothered; from the look on the guy's face, he obviously wasn't in the mood for small talk.

After an awkward pause punctuated by the man's hawkish stare, Tim added, "I thought I heard something down the hall."

A pained look. "So did I. You. Flushing. I'm in 508. On the other side of this wall."

"Sorry."

"Not as sorry as I am." The man's right eye twitched. "Do you know what time it is? If you decide on a return performance, hold off pulling the chain until morning." He reached for a cubicle door, opened it, looked back. "Think you can handle that, champ?"

Tim affected a short smile. "I can try."

"Do that." When the stall door slammed shut behind the man, Tim shot him a bird and stalked out.

The sound again: a muffled drawn-out wail like the whimpering of a frightened child.

He turned and stared, trying to pinpoint where it was coming from.

There. 506. The room just this side of his.

He passed the shadowy nurses station and approached the door. The low cry was louder now. It was probably somebody's TV, he thought, hesitating. But he knew it was not.

Silence. Then a muffled gasp.

He tapped on the door. Waited. Got no answer.

Bringing his mouth close to the crack, he called softly, "Anybody in there?"

Nothing.

Suddenly he felt like a fool. He was either knocking at an empty room or disturbing a stranger in the middle of the night. Any way you cut it, it looked a little weird.

He was turning away when the soft wail began again. Impulsively he reached for the doorknob.

The opening door bumped against the metal frame of a folding bedside screen. It skittered away on wobbly wheels, rolled a few inches, stopped. The faint glow from a lamp shone dimly through the yellowing cloth.

"Hello?"

Silence. Nothing but silence.

He stepped around the edge of the screen and stopped, puzzled. A second screen was just beyond it. He moved down the aisle they formed and stopped again. Two more screens were set at right angles to the first. Two more after that. He was in a narrow corridor, a twisting shadowy maze of screens. At least a dozen of them.

A chill crept along the back of his neck. This was crazy. What in hell was he doing in a Pac-Man maze in somebody else's room? He had a sudden overwhelming urge to run.

The soft wail again, coming from his right.

Unmistakable this time. It was a kid. He knew it. Somebody had left a little kid alone. In a place like this.

Tim spun toward the sound and pushed the screen aside. Wheels clacking, it rattled away into the shadows. The lamp light shone brighter through the next.

He shoved it away and stopped short.

The ghost-pale walls of cotton screens circled an iron hospital bed. And in it, partly covered with a wadded pile of thin graying blankets, lay Beth Quaig.

Unbelieving, Tim stared down at her.

The girl was wearing rumpled pink pajamas. Her legs were drawn to her chest; her round face was streaked with tears. She looked up at him with the wide-eyed gaze of a frightened baby.

"Beth? What is it? What's wrong?"

At the sound of his voice, she started and drew her knees up tighter. "Don't. Don't, Daddy. Don't." The wail ended in a shaking sob.

Jesus. Off the deep end. "It's okay. It's going to be okay." Feeling totally inadequate, he stroked her hair as if she were a small child. "It's okay. Everything's going to be all right." It seemed to calm her. In a few minutes, her sobbing abated and her eyes dropped shut. Then her thumb crept to her mouth, slid inside, and she began to suck.

God.

Uncertain of what to do next, he sat down on the edge of the bed and tried to think. She needed more help than he could give her—that much was obvious. His gaze darted to the bedside table, then to the wall. No phone.

It didn't seem like a good idea to leave her alone while he went for help, but who could he holler at to baby-sit? The half-strangled medium down the hall? Or maybe the ill-tempered asshole he'd met in the bathroom?

"Creativity pilot study, my pale ass," he said under his breath. The place was a refuge for crazies. And he was just as certifiable, he thought darkly. Signing up for this zoo was proof of it.

Beth stirred and Tim glanced down.

The girl stared at her wet thumb, and a startled look tracked across her face. "Oh, wow." She rolled her eyes and pulled the corner of the pillow over her eyes. "I'm not believing this."

Tim gave her a close look. "Are you all right?"

"Jeez." She shook her head and the pillow jiggled with the movement. "It wasn't me. It must have been Beffie."

"What?"

"Beffie," she said again. "That's what she calls herself."

"'Beffie'?" What was she talking about?

"She can't pronounce 'Bethie.'" A self-conscious giggle. "She's only two." Her hand slid off the pillow, reached out. "Just forget it, okay?" She found his arm and began to stroke it.

Forget it! It had all been a trick. The little bitch had cooked the whole thing up just to get him into her room. Outraged, Tim yanked the pillow off the girl's face and glared down at her. "Fun and games, huh? What in hell do you think you're doing?"

She recoiled as if he had struck her. "It wasn't me. I didn't do anything."

"The hell you didn't," he began. But something in her face made him stop, something that came into her eyes—a frightened, brown-mouse look that made her seem ten years older in an instant.

He caught his breath.

"What do you want?" Her voice was an anguished whisper.

God.

His anger drained away abruptly, and a hollow feeling took its place. Why hadn't he seen? Why hadn't he known? He searched the girl's face as if he could find the explanation. But all he saw was a stark, numbing terror, and suddenly he felt a pity so profound that it threatened to overwhelm him.

Beth clutched the thin pillow to her chest as if it were a shield. As if it were another flimsy cotton screen to hide behind. "Go away. Please. I don't have any money. Nothing. Please. . . ."

Eve, he thought. He was looking at Eve. He was looking at Sybil.

As gently as he could, he said, "I'm sorry." Turning, he made his way out through the maze of hospital screens, and with a soft click shut the door behind him.

NINE

When the door swung shut, Beth Quaig did not move until she was sure Tim Monahan was gone. Her pajamas were damp and sour with sweat. Shivering with a sudden chill, she pulled the thin blankets around her shoulders. Why had he come here? Why?

She thrust her wrist out of the covers and stared at her watch. It was after four. It had been eleven-thirty when she went to bed. She'd been asleep for hours.

Hadn't she?

A sick feeling crept in her belly. "Please, God," she whispered. "Don't let him know." He'd tell. She knew he would. Just like Henry had—and all the rest. Just like Mrs. Spears. Then she'd have to leave again, move, find another city, like before.

She shivered again. Dr. Schwartz was wrong. People didn't understand. They didn't care.

A stray thought slid into her mind. If Dr. Schwartz was wrong about that, then maybe he was wrong about lots of things. Nearly three years ago he had said she had multiple personality disorder. That's what he'd said, but she saw his notes when he thought she wasn't looking. "This multiple . . ." they began. Multiple. As if she had too many arms and legs. Or two heads. As if she were a freak.

She had believed him at first. But he had to be wrong. She was fine. She could function. Hadn't she been the best in the legal pool? Mrs. Martinez always counted on her to get the job done with time left over to help the new girl when she forgot how to save her files or when she couldn't even mailmerge a one-page letter without messing up. The paralegals counted on her too. Even Richard . . .

Beth's eyes squeezed shut and for a blazing moment she could see the office computer screen again. The McMartin file was gone. Nothing was left but gibberish—and the hard drive was making a terrible grinding noise.

Richard. Beth looked around in confusion. Where was he? He had wanted the printout of the McMartin brief. She felt the heat rise again to her face. She got so nervous when he was around, standing so close with his hands touching her, fingers pressing into her arms. He made her feel so strange. Like he knew what she looked like without any clothes on.

But it wasn't Richard here now. It was Mrs. Martinez standing over her, black eyes hard and cold. "Do you know what you've done? Even a high school girl knows to park the head. Thirty-eight megabytes gone, and what do you say? Nothing but garbage out of your mouth."

Mrs. Martinez's lips compressed, the flesh around them blanching, exaggerating the dark hair on her upper lip. "God knows I put up with a lot. But not this. Not gutter talk. And from you of all people! No one talks to me like that." She reached out and switched off the power supply. The red light blinked off and the drive mechanism gave an agonal sigh and stopped dead. "Clean out your desk. Then get out. You'll get your check in the mail."

After she got fired, Dr. Schwartz had tried to help. It

was Donna who had come, he said—Donna who had crashed the hard disk and destroyed years of records, sixteen-year-old Donna with her street talk and her semiliterate grasp of English. "Don't you know why, Beth? She came to help you deal with Richard."

She shook her head. It wasn't true. Richard had just wanted a printout. That's all. Just a printout.

But there had been other incidents at work. Times when the files mysteriously filled with strange typing and outrageous spelling. Times when Richard had been around, standing close behind her chair, touching her arm, the nape of her neck, his breath tickling her ear.

No! There wasn't any Donna. No Donna. No Beffie. No one else. Just Beth. There were lots of reasons a person lost time. She knew enough to know that. It could be narcolepsy. It was possible. There was that TV spot about it—about the girl who fell asleep at her mother's funeral.

She thought of the McMartin file, of the terrible grinding sound of the drive. That didn't prove it wasn't narcolepsy. People talked in their sleep and walked in their sleep, didn't they? She'd just dropped off for a moment or two. That was all.

"I could talk to Mrs. Martinez, if you want," said Dr. Schwartz.

A tumor even. It could be a brain tumor. Something to cut out, get rid of, get well from.

"Would you like me to call her?" he asked.

Beth shook her head. She knew Martinez would react like the others had. There would be shock at first, but then the questions would start, and the woman's eyes would start to glitter when she thought of all the juicy gossip. In the end, it wouldn't make any difference. Even if Martinez were to give her a reference, it would be sure to say she was a job risk.

Beth opened her eyes and stared at the maze of hospital screens around her bed. She wanted to believe that Tim Monahan had put them there, wanted to believe he had crept into her room and slid them all around her bed. She wanted very much to believe because the alternative was that another personality had done it, had taken over while she slept.

No! She was not a multiple. She was not. She was Beth Jeanette Quaig and nobody else.

She balled her fists, squeezing until her fingers were icy and stiff. Nobody else came. Nobody. She had put the screens there herself; she could almost remember it now. She had put them there because she was cold. So cold.

She tipped her head and gazed at them: metal folding stands with stretched yellowing cloth stained red with the glow of a distant traffic light. Red, now green. She blinked and her eyes widened and quite suddenly they became the eyes of a frightened two-year-old.

The basement smelled like dirt and the floor was cold and gritty against her bare skin.

"No, Daddy. No, Daddy. No."

He turned away at last and climbed the stairs. The light chain dangled at the top. The chain clicked and the light was gone.

"Bad girls have to stay in the dark," he said. But it wasn't Daddy. It was a black shadow man in the doorway and the kitchen light behind him was the sun.

The door slammed shut, the lock clacked, and the blackness came, thick and smothering like the pillow on Daddy's bed. It was cold and black and smelled like dirt. Dirt and fish.

She drew up her legs, even though it hurt, and began to whimper softly.

Cold. Black. Dirt and fish.

Maybe nobody won't come. Nobody ever.

Six minutes passed. Six minutes that to Beth Quaig were no more than a moment. Then she blinked again and tears slid down her cheeks. Surprised, she brushed them away. Sinus, she thought. Sinus trouble. She was shivering almost uncontrollably now.

Teeth chattering, she got up, dragging the blankets with her. A fierce ache started in her head at the base of her neck. A bath, she thought. A hot tub.

She opened the bedside stand, pulled out a thin towel and soap, and headed for the door. Halfway there, she stopped and went back to the bed. Her suitcase was underneath. Wrestling it out, she lifted it onto the mattress and unsnapped the lid. Inside she found a clean pair of pajamas, baby blue flannel with dark blue piping. The pants were wound around a small tape recorder, cushioning it. Unwrapping the little machine, she wedged it back into the suitcase next to a padded triangular bag. She ran her fingers over the bag, feeling the hard surface of the gun inside. It had been her father's—the only thing she had of his, and she had kept it the way he always had: loaded, but with the first chamber empty.

At the thought of him, she began to tremble though she could not have said why.

She closed the suitcase. Then, almost as an afterthought, she opened it again, and running her hand beneath a pile of panties and bras, she pulled out a large kitchen scrub brush, its worn blue nylon bristles set in a bleached wood handle.

The door sucked air as she opened it. The hallway was empty, deep shadows creeping toward dim yellow puddles of light. Trailing her blankets behind her, bare feet padding along the floor, Beth made her way to the bathroom at the far end of the wing.

The harsh ceiling light glittered on the white tile. She stood staring around uncertainly. Then, moving deliberately, she walked to the huge claw-footed tub that dominated the center of the room.

She looked down. A layer of dust grayed its interior. Dark rust streaked the white porcelain.

The hot water tap creaked and groaned, and rusty water splattered into the tub. She stood staring at the gush of fluid as it cleared and steam began to rise.

The tub was taking a long time to fill. Her fingers gripped the edge. Cold. So cold. She plunged them into the steaming water and watched in satisfaction as they reddened. But the tub was too large. Though hot vapor spewed from the gushing tap, the water was cooling fast.

She pulled off her pajamas and dropped them into a wrinkled wad on the floor.

The water was hot and deep. Deep as her crotch. Clutching one side of the huge tub, she eased herself down.

Deep. Deep enough to float.

God, she stank. Her sweat smelled of fish. Sweat and dirt.

The soap slid over her body, slithered between her legs.

The tub was so big that it made her smile. It made her seem like a midget—a doll.

It made her think of being very small, very young, in a very big tub. . . .

She was shivering again. Shivering as if her bones would fly apart from the sinews that held them.

There was only one way to be warm again, clean again. The scrub brush teetered on the edge of the tub. When she reached for it with a soapy hand, it slipped away and plunged into the water with a splash. She watched it float for a moment, then grasped it.

Her legs were pink and broken by the refraction of the water, the rust streak on the porcelain bent and rippled. She rubbed the blue nylon bristles across the soap until they were stippled with white. Then slowly, carefully, she began to scrub. First her hands and arms. Then her body. Then her feet and legs.

Then spreading her legs, she drew the bristles up and down, up and down, watching intently as a narrow ribbon deeper and redder than the rust stain widened and dispersed and tinted the water to a pale, warm pink.

TEN

Except for a half-dozen scrub-suited nurses and a few scattered housekeeping types, Chandler Bryson's cafeteria was nearly empty. Tim sat alone at a long table with his third cup of jet-black coffee and the remains of his breakfast. Each time the door opened, he looked up, hoping it was Jody.

He had learned her office location from an affable, if not too bright, woman at the information desk. Following her vague directions, he had spent twenty minutes wandering through connecting lobbies looking for the right building. When he found it, the office, like the rest of the hall, was empty, and none of the four names on the door was Jody Henson's. Hoping he was in the right place, he stuck a scribbled note in a loose corner of the door molding, and headed for the cafeteria.

He wanted some answers.

He had spent most of the night coming up with the questions. Unable to go back to sleep, he had lain in the dark for hours, staring into the mist, half mesmerized by the electric blue roof of the Regency.

There had been no more crying. Nothing but a door whispering open and the distant groan of plumbing reluctant to give up the rusty fluid that ran in its iron veins. When the first gray light of morning crept through his window, he finally dozed off, but an hour later, he had awakened again, eyes red from fatigue.

He found a clean towel and washcloth in his locker. The towel, thin as gauze in spots and not big enough to dry a wet cat, bore the black stenciled letters ERLANGER. Wasn't that a Chattanooga hospital? No telling where it had been. There was a bar of no-name soap next to the towel. Scooping it up, he headed for the door, then stopped, turned back, and stashed his computer in the locker.

The shower was just past Beth Quaig's room. He paused outside her door and listened. No sound. The shower pipes gave a groan and began to clank out a rust-flaked stream that went from cold to steaming hot.

The bathroom was drafty. Drying hastily, he threw on jeans and a sweater. Still no sound from Beth. Nice that she could sleep.

Rubbing his eyes, Tim stared glumly at his foam coffee cup. He'd give Jody five more minutes. Five minutes and then he was going to pack up and leave.

Clattering trays and silverware, the scrub nurses at the next table left. A minute later, a white-haired couple dressed in street clothes took their place. Time for visiting hours already? But it was only 8:05.

Tim took a final swig of coffee, and staring sluggishly into the dregs, he tried to decide whether to go for cup number four. Diagnosing himself as a case of the somnolent jitters, he pushed it away. A refill wasn't going to help matters. What he really could use was a couple of slugs of booze and some sleep. He took a last drag on his cigarette and dropped it into the cup. The Winston hissed and turned an instant soggy gray. He eyed it thoughtfully: he knew how it felt. Maybe another jolt of O.J. would help. Wondering if empty juice glasses were eligible for refills, he was reaching for his when Jody came up to the table.

"I got your note." She set down her cup of coffee and a clipboard crammed with forms and Manila envelopes, and took a seat. The lab coat she wore fell open. Underneath she was wearing a soft brown wool dress with a crocheted collar that reminded Tim of the ones his great-grandmother used to make. What was it she called them? Teddies? No. Dickies.

"What's up?" asked Jody.

"That's what I was going to ask you." He was aware of an edge in his voice.

"And that means?"

"That means, I want to know what this whole charade is about. I want to know why I was picked to join up with a bunch of crazies."

She gave him a close look. "What happened?"

"Well, I'll tell you," he said with a touch of belligerence. "I couldn't sleep because of the crowd next door." The dab of satisfaction he derived from the puzzled look on her face dissolved immediately. Why was he sparring with her again?

"There was a party next door to you?"

"You might say that. You might say there were several parties. And all of them looked like Beth Quaig." He caught the quick widening of her eyes before she looked away and stared noncommittally into her cup.

"Yes?"

Yes with a question mark. Yes, go on. Typical. It was a response straight out of a psychology book, he thought, wondering why he resented it. "How long have you known she was nuts?"

She hesitated. "I don't know what you mean."

"I think you do. First she comes on like Marian the Librarian, then the next thing you know, she's sucking her thumb and bawling like a two-year-old."

A look he could not read came over her face. "I think you'd better tell me exactly what happened."

As he told her, Jody's eyes grew serious, then troubled. When he finished, she said, "I'm sorry this happened. It must have been rough on you."

"You could have told me."

She shook her head. "No. I couldn't. It wouldn't be ethical. Beth isn't really my patient, but since she's part of this study, I feel responsible for her."

"Ethical? You're talking ethics? For all I know, one of her personalities might be Lizzie Borden. How do I know she won't try a hatchet job in the middle of the night?"

"That's hardly likely."

"You know her well enough to be sure of that?"

"I don't really know her at all," Jody admitted. "I saw her for the first time yesterday. When you did."

"But you called her by name."

"The process of elimination. Beth was the only woman left on my list. Who else could she be?"

"But you knew about her," he said, remembering the way Jody had almost intervened at the seance. "You knew she was psycho."

"I wish you wouldn't keep saying things like that. Multiple personalities aren't psychotic. Most of them aren't, anyway." A loud crash from across the room drew her attention. A young black man with a look of acute embarrassment on his face squatted down and began to scoop scattered silverware and broken crockery into a plastic dishpan. "It's a defense mechanism," she said. "All multiples were abused when they were tiny children. When you're two or three, and your mother or your father tortures you, you think this is normal—this is the way the world is. And it hurts. It hurts too damn much to stay there—to keep on being you. So, you fragment." She gave him a searching look. "Do you understand what I'm saying? It's the only way they have to cope. Beth probably isn't even aware of her other personalities. Not consciously, anyway."

"But last night, she talked about 'Beffie.'"

"I don't think that was Beth you were talking to. Even though the main personality may not know about the others, they know about her—and each other."

"You seem to know a lot about multiples."

"As much as I can learn. But nobody knows everything. It's too soon. The disorder wasn't even acknowledged until the early seventies."

"What about *The Three Faces of Eve?* That book was published long before that."

"Yes. But it was written for the lay public. The medical community gave it about as much credence as a fairy tale."

"I'm not sure any of this makes sense," said Tim. "Abused kids aren't new. The creeps who do that kind of thing to children have been around throughout history, so why the delay? Why did it take until the seventies to show up?"

"I didn't say it wasn't around. Just that it wasn't recognized until then." She hesitated. "Imagine that you'd never heard of multiples before. What would you think if a friend or a relative began to switch personalities?"

"About what I think now," he said. "I'd think it was pretty weird."

"And what do you suppose happened to them?"

"I guess they were locked up."

"Only the lucky ones—at least that's what I think. I think a lot of them were burned at the stake."

"As witches, you mean?"

"Devils," she said. "The possessed. The ones who harbored demons." She played with her coffee cup, running her finger along the curve of the handle. "Progress. It's a damned slow process. As a matter of fact, some psychologists and psychiatrists still don't believe multiple personalities exist. They think the patients are play-acting. Pulling the wool over the eyes of the gullible."

"But you don't," he observed.

She shook her head. "No I don't. But then I've worked with them quite a bit. Most of the skeptics haven't treated multiples. They're fairly rare, and when they do show up in private practice, a lot of them are misdiagnosed."

"This a specialty of yours, or something?"

"In a way. At least I hope it will be. Have you ever heard of Dr. Hastings Farber?"

Tim shook his head.

"He's sort of a legend. He probably knows more about multiples than anyone else alive," she said. "I told you that I used to be a nurse. I worked in a psych unit where he was Chief of Staff. He's the reason I hung up nursing and went into clinical psychology."

A stale draft from the heat register puffed toward them, ruffling their hair. "My skunk lock," said Jody, brushing away the crisp dark strand streaked with white that crept toward her eyes. "It's got a mind of its own."

"I like it," he said.

"So do I, actually," she said. "It's been that way since I was eighteen—the year I went to college. It made me feel mature. And different too, I guess."

"Different, I understand," said Tim. Different was fine

when it came at the right time in your life, when you'd grown up a little, he thought. But it had its drawbacks when you were marked with it in kindergarten. "So, tell me," he said, aiming the conversation back on track. "What have you been told about us? Why were we the ones singled out for this study?"

"Told? Nothing. I read a short summary about each of you. That's all." She glanced down at her cup, then up again. "I know you're a writer, and that you used to teach school. I know you were a gifted child, and that you were one of the kids Wallenski followed in his twelve-year study. That's about all."

"Is that the link, then? Wallenski? Were we all Wallenski kids?" But as soon as the words were out of his mouth, he realized that Maureen was too old for that, and Beth too young. Victor Wallenski, modeling his work after Terman's, had selected a group of a thousand first graders identified as gifted. Twice a year for twelve years Tim got a day off from classes—a day filled with tests and interviews. The rest of the year, he had had to deal with the fallout: the unrealistic expectations of his parents and his teachers, and the razzing from the other kids who were convinced that he was some sort of freak. Wallenski. He had hated that son of a bitch.

"No," said Jody. "No you weren't."

"What then? What's the link? And don't tell me creativity. Not unless the ability to come up with multiple personalities is a sign of it."

"It may be."

"Yeah?" He couldn't keep the suspicion out of his voice.

"Some of the studies say so. As a matter of fact, eighty percent of the people with MPD are considered highly creative."

"MPD?"

"Sorry. Multiple personality disorder." She tipped her head and the thick white-streaked lock of hair fell, engagingly, over an eyebrow. "Why are you so convinced that this study is—what did you call it?—a charade? Why can't you simply believe that it's what it's presented to be?"

Tim wasn't sure why. It wasn't anything he could put a finger on; it just didn't feel right. "Okay," he finally said. "Convince me otherwise. I'm a writer. So's Maureen. How do we know that Beth falls into the eighty percent?"

Jody thumbed through the papers on the clipboard. "She's a secretary. A typist, actually. But according to this, she's very good at macrame."

"Macrame! Tying knots is creative?"

"Well, it can be," she said, but there was a touch of doubt in her voice.

He snorted. "Give me a goddamned break."

She touched her hand to her mouth to cover the smile that twitched at the corner of her lips. "What do I know?" she said. "I haven't talked to Dr. Barkley yet."

"How about the rest of them? The bunch you stuck up on the sixth floor?"

"No pathology. They're medical students."

"Medical students?" Surprise. Then a nod. "Of course. The control group. I guess every good pilot study needs one."

"I didn't say that."

"You didn't have to."

She hesitated. "Am I that transparent?"

"Clear as Cinderella's slipper." Tim remembered his nocturnal encounter in the washroom. "What about the blond guy?"

"I don't know which 'blond guy' you're talking about."

"The one who's about seven feet tall. You know—" With his index fingers, Tim traced two downward curving lines on his upper lip. "The droopy mustache."

"Oh. You mean Dayton Satterfield."

"Yeah? What does he do? Hear voices? Speak in tongues?"

"Dayton Satterfield is a talented jewelry designer. For a living, he sells real estate."

"Yeah. Where? If he's subdividing the north forty of the funny farm, what does that make me?"

She laughed. "Paranoid. He happens to be perfectly normal."

"Then what the hell is this 'study' all about?"

Jody stood up and collected her clipboard and empty coffee cup. "It's nearly eight-thirty," she said. "I suggest we go up and find out."

"And who are those fresh-faced children?" asked Tim. "The ones dressed up in grown-up clothes?" He nodded toward the alcove to the three young people there, two girls and a guy, wearing lab coats. The oldest looked about twenty.

"That's my group," said Jody. "They're psych students."

"You their mommy?"

Jody grinned. "In a manner of speaking. They're taking their psych assessment courses this semester and this is part of their work. They're going to be administering the psychological tests. I'm supervising."

"The Boss Lady, huh?" Rubber wheels squeaked in the hallway. A young nurse with freckled arms and a freckle-free face was pushing a cart full of metal charts into the alcove. "Who's the carrot top?"

Jody looked up from her clipboard. "That must be the rent-a-nurse."

"Yeah? It's amazing what you can get from the caterer these days."

She laughed. "You're not too far wrong. She's from a temporary help agency. The pilot study is autonomous, so they can't pull Bryson's regular nursing staff to help."

"What do they need her for?"

"Charts mostly. For Bryson's medical records. Hospitals are ticky about records. Especially these days."

The rest of the group came trickling into the alcove. Dayton Satterfield, a head taller than any of the others, was impossible to overlook. Amazingly, when he spotted Tim, he smiled affably and waved.

"Psst." Tim gave Jody a gentle poke in the ribs, and whispered, "I thought you said Satterfield wasn't nuts."

"Shhhh."

Maureen Dorcas came in, wearing a red turtleneck that concealed her throat. She seemed distracted. Taking a seat across the room, she perched next to the fat girl, Carla, who plucked a raspberry Danish from a bulging white bakery bag, demolished it in three bites, and passed the bag to Memphis Red.

Although there was an empty seat between Tyrone Hayes and Al Cole, Beth Quaig was standing in the same niche she had found yesterday. Protective coloration, Tim thought; her tan skirt was topped with a shapeless green jacket that almost matched the lackluster paint on the walls. If she had noticed him, she gave no sign of it. He wondered what she remembered of last night.

The freckled rent-a-nurse parked her cart a few feet away and tapped a ballpoint pen on a chart. "May I have everyone's attention?" When the room quieted, she said,

"I need to get vital signs on everybody, and the chart cart isn't too maneuverable, so please come up here one at a time and give me your names." Picking up a blood-pressure cuff swinging over the cart handle, she nodded at Tim. "You first. Name?"

"Monahan."

The nurse ran a fingertip over the charts until she came to his and pulled it out.

She'd be cute if she had a chin, he thought. What there was of it was covered, like the rest of her face, in freckle-concealing makeup. "And your name is"—he squinted at her name tag and tried to make out the curlicued script—"Mystery Carmody?"

The nurse blinked and glanced down at her chest. "It says Ms. Terri Carmody," she said, a touch indignantly.

"Miz-tair-eee?" Tim repeated innocently. "I like your accent. French?"

The nurse, blushing at the laugh that followed, plucked a thermometer from a tray and thrust it into his mouth.

"That's the way, Mystery," said Memphis Red. "Shut him up."

Her blush deepened, and when Al Cole began to sing "Mys-tair-ree, please come and take care of me-e-ee," Tim suspected the name would stick.

While Mystery Carmody handed out thermometers and recorded blood pressures, and the baby-faced undergraduates checked their assignment sheets, Jody explained the morning's procedures. "We've divided the group into thirds," she said. "You'll be given several psychological tests and then we'll break for lunch."

A fresh-faced girl with straight brown hair claimed Tim. "Hello," she said, and launched into an obviously rehearsed introduction that began with "My name is Miss

Butterworth, a student at Georgia State University . . ." and ended with a too-bright smile.

She reminded Tim of his baby sister. He nodded at the Butterfinger candy bar poking out of her lab coat pocket. "Rot your teeth." Hers were perfect. He wondered if she had gone through junior high with braces like Kathy had.

She gave him a nervous grin and, with a quick look in Jody's direction, maneuvered her clipboard to hide the candy bar.

"I'll never tell," he whispered.

"Stay here, will you?"

"I surely will, Miss Butterfinger."

The assault on her name didn't seem to register. With a quick backward glance, as if she were afraid he would vanish, she said, "I'll be right back," and hurried off to collect Dayton Satterfield and Carla, who clutched her jelly-streaked bakery bag in one hand and a coffee cup in the other.

Satterfield, deep in conversation with Maureen, looked up at Miss Butterfinger's interruption and gave her an expansive smile. Dr. Jekyll this morning, Tim thought. He was wondering if Miss Butterfinger could cope with Satterfield in his Mr. Hyde mode when the double doors opened and a tubby little man in an expensive gray suit walked in.

Something about the man commanded attention at once. A brisk stride brought him to the center of the alcove, where he pivoted and fixed each of them with a pale stare until the room fell silent. "Good morning. I'm Dr. Barkley. I want to thank you for your participation. I'll be talking with each of you later." He scanned the room. "Miss Henson?"

"Here," said Jody.

"Come with me, please." Turning abruptly, Barkley

strode down the hall, leaving Jody to grab her clipboard and a sheaf of permission forms and hurry after him.

Miss Butterworth ensconced Tim and Dayton Satterfield on twin gray plastic chairs in the hallway and disappeared with Carla into an empty ward that had been pressed into duty as an office.

After an awkward pause, Satterfield leaned toward Tim. "I, uh, want to apologize for last night," he said. "I didn't mean to act like a sonovabitch. It's just that I was having one of my headaches, and when they come on, they get me crazy. I get supersensitive to noise."

"Migraine?"

Satterfield rolled his eyes. "I wish that's all it was. They're cluster headaches. They get you right here." He touched his temple, fingers grazing a tortuous knot of pulsing bluish veins. "It's a real bitch. They go away for a while. But about the time you think you've seen the end of them, they come back. Every goddamned night. Anyway, I'm really sorry I got on your case."

The man seemed sincere. Decent enough in the light of day, Tim thought. "They come on mostly at night, do they?"

Satterfield nodded. "Mine do, anyway," he said and launched into a detailed clinical account of his nocturnal agony.

It was more than Tim really wanted to know about cluster headaches. Though he nodded politely and interpolated sympathetic "uh-huhs" at Satterfield's "knife in the eye" and "face on fire" descriptions, he felt himself fading away.

At 9:15, Jody came to his rescue. "There you are. Dr. Barkley wants to talk to you, so here's your chance to ask him about those permission forms." She led him down the hall to the door marked RESIDENT. "Just knock," she said, and with a quick "See you later," she hurried off.

Richard Barkley reminded Tim of someone who lived in a bottle. Let him out and you get three wishes. The roundness of the man's face was accentuated by a receding hairline and pinched elfish ears with long creased lobes.

Ruffling through a Manila folder with Tim's name on it, Barkley pulled out a stapled blue form and handed it across the desk. "Your permission slip. We need your signature here," he said, indicating a penciled X on the bottom of the last page.

Tim made no move to take the ballpoint pen Barkley offered. "I don't intend to sign anything until I get a better explanation about what's going on."

"Of course you don't," Barkley said easily. "What can I help you with?"

Tim studied the man. Barkley's face was open—ingenuous, even. Why then did he feel uneasy? "First of all," he began, "I'd like to know just what it is you're after."

The desk chair creaked as Barkley leaned back. "Our research here is in the area of learning and creativity. It was all explained in the letter you received."

"Not quite." Tim rattled the permission form. "What about all these tests? These—what did you call them?—invasive procedures?"

Barkley dismissed the issue with a wave of his hand. "You'll find permission forms exaggerate everything." He gave a short laugh. "They'd make God himself afraid he'd get gangrene from having his blood pressure taken. Believe me, all of the tests mentioned are routine for a study like this."

"Routine?" Not bloody likely. "I'm not completely

uninformed about psychological testing and shrinks. I had twelve years of that when I was a kid."

Barkley's smile was not quite echoed in his eyes. "I know your history, Mr. Monahan. But obviously, you don't know mine. I'm not a 'shrink.' I'm a neurologist. An M.D. Perhaps you'll concede that I know a little more about medical procedures than you do."

A neurologist? Why? He stared at the man for a moment. "I'll concede that your 'learning and creativity study' comes on like creative bullshit. I want to know the connection between us subjects."

Barkley raised a thin eyebrow. "Connection?"

"The connection between mediums and multiple personalities. And I want to know what they have to do with me—and with the Wallenski study."

The doctor gave Tim a long quizzical stare over tented fingers. "I see," he said at last. Barkley stood up abruptly and the chair rebounded with a snap. "I'm going to show you something that I think will clear up all your doubts about this project." He pulled out a key, and unlocking a file drawer, began to flip through a series of hanging files. "Here we are. Read this." He handed a buff-colored folder to Tim. "Take your time."

Tim opened the folder. At first, he thought he was looking at nonsense. Hen scratchings on paper. Then he realized it was the bizarre type font that was giving him trouble—one of those slanted artsy-fartsy jobs that left off half of each letter.

It took all his concentration to make out the words . . .

A moment later Barkley said, "I hope I've answered your questions. I'm afraid I've bored you with all my talk about the project. I didn't intend to put you to sleep."

Tim looked at his watch and blinked. 10:35. Impossible. His gaze darted to the clock on the wall. The minute hand clicked to 10:35. An hour? Gone? A sudden rush of adrenaline quickened his heart. More than an hour. Gone. Gone in a second or two.

Concern came into Barkley's eyes. "You're feeling all right now, aren't you?"

Don't let on. Don't let him know. He took a deep breath to slow his racing pulse. "Feeling all right?" he repeated. Furtively he searched Barkley's face. Had he noticed?

"After what you said, I thought—" Barkley's voice trailed away and he shrugged.

Said? What had he said?

"Don't give it another thought." The doctor smiled. "Nice talking with you, Mr. Monahan." He stood, and reached out to shake Tim's hand. It was an obvious dismissal.

Heart racing, Tim stood up.

The blue permission form lay on the desk below him, just as before. Only now it bore a signature: Timothy M. Monahan.

Another warm smile. "I'll just file this away with your other papers." The doctor scooped up the form, stuck it into Tim's folder, and put it into the file drawer.

Barkley turned the key in the lock and looked up. "Time to get on with your testing. Miss Butterworth will be waiting." The doctor led him to the door, and when Tim stepped through, he shut it quietly behind him.

Tim stared down the empty hallway. What had he said? What was it? He blinked as the sudden uneasy feeling came to him that he had homework to do.

ELEVEN

Tim scanned the hallway. No one was around. The two gray plastic chairs outside the testing room were empty. Satterfield must have gone inside. Passing the vacant alcove, he went through the windowless passageway to the next building and stabbed the elevator button.

His initial confusion in Barkley's office had quickly given way to an anger that he nurtured carefully, focusing on it with all the concentration he could muster. It was the only thing holding off the cold fear that lay just underneath.

The elevator opened and he stepped inside. He wanted to leave, get in his car, take off—and to hell with the fucking project. They could take their money and stick it. He pressed the Door Open button. All his stuff was still in the room. He lowered his hand. Screw it. He'd come back for it later.

The door slid shut. Tim reached for the button marked L, then stopped. If he got off in the lobby, he might run into somebody from the study group. Instead, he pressed the button for the ground floor.

With a creak, the elevator began to drop. It stopped on

three and a lab technician got on. The tray she carried was filled with several tubes of dark, thick-looking blood. Suddenly he felt queasy. Dropping his gaze, he fixed it on the floor along a dark seam of curling linoleum.

The technician got off on the next floor and the car dropped again. It opened to a concrete-floored alcove, dark except for the single bare light bulb overhead. He stepped out into a damp, echoing basement corridor. Exposed pipes angled from the low ceiling. Thick cables snaked along the walls.

He turned right, thinking that might bring him closer to an exit below the main lobby. A naked light bulb dangled on a thick overhead cable, its yellow light puddling in the dark. The next was fifteen or twenty yards away at an intersection where three corridors converged in its feeble glow.

Undecided, he hesitated, then turned right again. The place was like a cave. Or more accurately, a mine shaft. *A Shaft of Light,* he thought. His first novel. He had based it loosely on the fate of the cave explorer, Floyd Collins. Trapped for days in a cavern with a ton of fallen rock pinning his legs, Collins's final agony had been turned into a tawdry carnival complete with cotton candy and balloons.

Ahead, the corridor turned sharply and he heard the faint sound of water dripping. The dank smell of mildew made his nose prickle. Underfoot, the floor suddenly turned to dirt. No. It was still concrete, but overlaid with decades of grime. The Augean Stables. It would take more than the greasy trickle of water creeping along the wall to clean this place out. The trickle widened to a puddle that reflected an oil-slick rainbow from the bare bulb overhead. Leaky pipes? Or had last night's rain seeped through?

Something scuttled in the shadows and he moved quickly on.

Another intersection. But the bisecting corridor was even darker. Sticking to the main hallway, he headed for the next light, hoping it would show a way out. Why in hell had he decided to prowl around in Bryson's filthy bowels? Hadn't he outgrown Dungeons and Dragons?

Pushed by a musty current of air, the overhead light bulb swung on its wire. There had to be an exit up ahead.

A sudden hiss. The light bulb flared for a fraction of a second, then blacked out.

The after-image jittered on his retinas and transformed the swinging bulb to a dancing hangman's noose. Disoriented, he spun around and tried to focus through the gray mist swirling before his eyes.

Suddenly his lungs emptied. He sucked air, but the damp earth smell of mold clogged his nostrils. Gasping, he felt his throat begin to close. He was suffocating. Drowning.

Get out. He had to get out.

For a terrible moment, he could not move. Then in mindless panic, he plunged down the corridor, turned blindly, plunged again.

He nearly ran into the man coming toward him.

Tim stopped short, sucked in a breath.

The baby-faced man wore a white resident's jacket with a stethoscope sticking out of one pocket. His shoes were filthy.

A raised eyebrow. "You okay?"

Tim found his voice. "Which way out? How do I get outside?"

The man pointed ahead. "That way. You just passed it." He gave Tim a searching look. "I guess you got turned around. That's easy enough to do down here. Follow me. It's just up here."

They came to an intersecting hallway and the man jerked a thumb to the left. "Right there." And turning briskly in the opposite direction, he strode away.

Tim pushed open the heavy door and stumbled up the half-dozen concrete steps into the sunlight. He found himself in a narrow weedy garden between two buildings, one dun-colored, one old red brick, connected with an eight-foot-high chain-link fence.

The cold front had painted the strip of sky overhead a hard blue. Dazzled by the bright morning, he sank down on a slanting concrete bench and took a deep breath.

It cleared his head. The north wind, cold and sharp with the tang of winter, blew away the panic until only the rags and tatters were left and he saw them as foolish and childish.

He remembered a scared fifteen-year-old kid clutching a contraband Ouija board. He had left Mary Ellen Harper's house that afternoon, walked out as nonchalantly as he could. But as soon as he was out of sight, he had broken into a blind run as if the devil himself were after him. When he got home, he thrust the Ouija board back into his sister's dresser drawer under a stack of sweaters.

He had never touched it again.

For months afterward, he thought he was losing his mind. He wanted to talk to somebody about it. Anybody. But he was afraid to tell his parents. What if they confirmed that he was crazy? Just the other day he had heard Hattie Farnsworth telling his mother about Joey Hathaway up on the next block. "Schizophrenic," she had said in a whisper, as if to say it louder would tempt fate. "They had to put him away—and him only seventeen years old."

Schizophrenia. It was something he associated with horror movies and chain-saw massacres, not with somebody he knew. He looked it up in an ancient psychology book he found in the school library, read in horror that "dementia praecox, an incurable disease of the mind, strikes in adolescence." He was an adolescent. It could happen.

Maybe it already had.

In desperation, he went to see Father Cavanaugh, but when he mentioned the Ouija board, the dour old priest drew himself up to his full height and knitted his bushy brows together until they were one continuous thatch of curling gray barbs. "How long have you been experimenting with the occult?" he demanded.

Terrified, his voice barely audible, he whispered, "No. It wasn't me. It was a friend. Just a guy I know—in another parish."

Father Cavanaugh's cold gray eyes knew a liar when they saw one. "Spiritism is an abomination. A sin against God." For a quarter of an hour, he railed against it, punctuating the lecture with dire predictions of demonic possession and promises of God's eternal wrath.

Tim grinned wryly at the memory. He never had told Father Cavanaugh the truth. Instead, convinced that he was crazy or damned, or both, he had nearly worn out a rosary doing private penances that he desperately hoped would count.

Okay. Today he'd had a memory lapse. But it wasn't the first time. If he could work through it at fifteen, he could work through it now.

Suddenly a thought came that brought a chill sharper than the wind. What if it had happened more than twice?

No. It just wasn't possible. He'd have to know.

Wouldn't he?

Of course he would. Only twice, he told himself. He would know it otherwise. He had lost time when he was fifteen years old—and he had lost it again this morning in Barkley's office. An hour gone from his life. Stolen. Neatly cut out as if a surgeon had excised it with a scalpel.

Twice. Two times. That was all.

Wasn't it?

Tim pulled a cigarette out of his crumpled pack and thought about the occasional lapses he'd had in the car. He'd be driving down familiar roads, listening to the radio, thinking about something else, and the next thing he knew, he'd be pulling up in his driveway without fully realizing how he got there. Just like a movie script: fade out; fade in.

But that could happen to anybody. Going into a brown study wasn't like going into the Twilight Zone.

That brown study was where most writers set up their offices, he thought. How many times had he sat down to write and later looked at his watch to find that what he had thought was a thirty-minute stint had stretched into three hours? A little dissociation seemed to go with the territory. Especially when the characters came alive and tried to run the show.

But this morning had been different. It wasn't because he'd had a couple of drinks last night, and it wasn't because of a lack of sleep. True, he'd been a little groggy listening to Satterfield's symptoms in the hall, but he'd been alert enough in Barkley's office.

He thought of the permission slip with his name on it. He had wanted to snatch it out of Barkley's hand, snatch it away, tear it up. But it had seemed more important to hide the fact that he had no memory of signing it.

And had he hidden it?

Are you all right, Mr. Monahan? . . . After what you said . . .

But if the man really knew, he would have said more than that, would have given more indication than that.

Unless Barkley not only knew about it, but had intended it to happen.

Tim rejected the thought. He was not so weak-willed that the man could have hypnotized him like some sort of Svengali. And why in hell would he want to anyway? The idea was ludicrous.

Yet in spite of that, Tim did not trust Barkley; he did not know just why. But one thing was sure: nothing about this operation felt right.

And where did he fit into the picture? He wondered if Jody really did know. She had known about Beth. But information like that would have been on the biography sheet. As for the rest of it, Jody had said she was new to the project. He wanted very much to believe that. Quite suddenly, he wanted to see her, talk to her, find out what she had learned this morning from Richard Barkley.

Tim was heading across the scraggly grass toward Chandler Bryson's lobby entrance before he realized that he had decided to go back upstairs.

He stopped short. Crazy. This was crazy. He wanted to run. He wanted to scale the chain-link fence, run out into the street, and never come back. Instead, following a compulsion that he could not understand or resist, he began to move again toward the hospital lobby and the waiting elevator. As he did, he told himself it was just for a little while. Just long enough to satisfy his curiosity, long enough to reconstruct the hour he had lost from his life this morning.

Abruptly he thought of the recurring dream. Nothing new about that; he had had it for years. Yet, why was it invading his mind while he was awake?

Coincidence, he told himself. That was the only logical

explanation. To believe anything else was to court paranoia. But a sudden image came to him of a dripping brain sculpted of mud, its surface broken by the subterranean tracks of a burrowing mole. Uneasily he realized that just beneath his rationale lay the conviction that it was not coincidence at all.

TWELVE

Jody had disappeared into Barkley's office, there, it seemed, to remain until lunch. Or so Miss Butterfinger/Butterworth said when she cornered Tim in the hall. She seemed pathetically glad to see him. "I didn't know where you were. If I don't have your MMPI done for Miss Henson by noon, it's all over."

It seemed that Barkley's project was stressful for everybody. "That bad, huh?"

She nodded. "This project counts for fifty percent of my grade."

"They say Jody Henson is a real killer," he lied.

"Really?" Alarm tracked across the girl's face. "We'd better get started."

Tim spent the rest of the morning with multiple choice tests until noon when Miss Butterworth, with a sigh of relief, scooped up her papers, pulled out her candy bar, and scurried off.

He caught up with Jody in the hallway. "Buy you lunch?"

"Sorry," she said. "No time. I've got a conference with

the students at one and I have a stack of papers to go through before then."

"Dinner, then?"

"In town?" Her brow furrowed. "I really need to get home and see about Sushi." Then, impulsively, "How about dinner with me? I make terrific spaghetti."

"Spaghetti and sushi?"

She laughed. "Sushi's my dog. She needs dinner too. I left her this morning with a tablespoon of dog chow and a promise to bring home more."

"Your place then. Spaghetti and Purina."

"Fine," she said. "I'll be through around five. I'll drop by your room then."

When she left, he consulted his schedule. Nothing until 2:30. Then another round with Miss Butterworth. He had time for a beer and a leisurely lunch—or a sandwich and a couple of hours work on the book. The work ethic won out. He settled for Bryson's cafeteria and a greasy cheeseburger with fries.

Back on Morgan Wing, he saw Beth Quaig standing outside the empty ward, waiting for Miss Butterworth, presumably. At Tim's nod, she clutched her schedule to her chest and lowered her eyes as if she could render herself invisible. Her paper name tag had rolled up along one edge, its stickum coated with brown fuzz from yesterday's outfit. Tim noticed she had fastened it to her blouse with a safety pin.

Why had she bothered? Most people would have chucked it into the trash by now. He wondered how many name tags the girl really needed. Three? Five? A dozen, maybe? A dozen curling tags with faint, typed names pinned to her chest.

Hello, my name is Lucifer . . . Belial . . . Asmodeus . . .

How many demons made their home in one small girl?

What was it like to be Beth? Did she know when a change was coming on? Was it like epilepsy? With an aura, a grisly little warning: here it comes, and you can't do a damn thing about it. Or was it abrupt? Lights out, then on again—so quickly you thought nothing had happened at all—only now you find yourself in some strange city you've never seen before.

Or you look at a clock on the wall and an hour is gone in seconds. . . .

A sharp chill rippled through his gut, and he tasted the grease from the cheeseburger. Going to be sick. He clenched a fist to hold on, to push everything else away, until his knuckles were white and his fingertips cold from the pressure.

He took a deep breath and felt it steady his stomach.

Beth was staring at him with a curious look on her face.

"Some work to do," he mumbled, and wheeled away.

THIRTEEN

Donaldson, still on duty in the glass cage, looked up as the supergrade got off the elevator and approached the turnstile. "Enjoy your lunch, sir?"

His voice came through to Hal Gulliver with a hiss of static. The speaker was about to puke again, he thought. Nodding in answer to Donaldson's question, Gulliver approached the window, presented his ID, and waited while the security man minutely inspected his badge, scanning first the photograph, then the little boxes that bordered the edges. Satisfied that the right boxes contained the correct red letters, Donaldson pressed a concealed switch and the turnstile opened.

Neither man thought the procedure odd even though each had known the other by sight for years, even though Gulliver had passed by the glass cage on his way to the executive dining room less than an hour before. Neither man thought of it at all. It was simply routine.

When he reached his office door, Gulliver punched in his code and the combination lock opened with a click. The office was austere as a monk's cell, partly from policy, partly from choice. The walls were bare of ornament except for a framed pair of yellowing Norman Rockwell *Saturday Evening Post* covers from the forties, a birthday present from his daughter, and a smaller shadow box frame that held three outstanding-performance medals that could never leave the building. He stood for a moment, staring at the Rockwell prints, remembering the time Val gave them to him, remembering her face. It had been childishly round at fourteen and full of pride mingled with anxiety when Val handed him the package. "Do you like them?"

"I love them, baby," he said.

"Mom said you would, but I wasn't sure. Do you really?"

"Really."

An indulgent look had come into her eyes then, as if he were the child and she the parent. "They're kind of frayed. They're from the old days." She touched the first, a soldier boy, uniform stiff and new, saying good-bye to his family and his girl. "Technically they're not antiques. But they're close."

He had been sixteen when that cover first came out—nearly the age of the soldier in the picture. Technically not an antique, but close. Now he was ten years closer and almost a grandpa.

Suddenly he wanted to talk to her, make sure she was all right, make sure the doctor wasn't screwing around with her health. Tonight, he thought. He'd call her this evening. But then he remembered he could not. Tonight he had the meeting with Sessions—and plenty to do before then.

He opened the wall safe and brought out an interoffice phone book, its cover marked SECRET, and the papers that had come in just before lunch. Spreading them out on the desktop, he extracted a toothpick from his pocket, applied it to a tenacious nubbin of beef caught between two molars, and turned to the sheaf of memos. The first two, memoranda for the record, he read and set aside. The third concerned his office alone.

ORD/BB 108-90

MEMORANDUM FOR: Chief, ORD
SUBJECT: HALFLIFE: Atlanta study

1. Intensified media attention focusing on the Atlanta police department increases the potential volatility of the southeastern situation.

2. Leaks to the media from unidentified sources, probably internal to the Atlanta PD, have increased.

3. It is essential that ORD identify the subject without delay. He/she has demonstrated aberrant behavior not foreseen by contract personnel. If subject is apprehended by law enforcement officers, a link to this Agency might be uncovered.

4. Revelations of this nature would seriously compromise HALFLIFE and the entire Agency. A media leak of the above-mentioned material would be almost a certainty, considering the lax security demonstrated so far, and would result in a major "flap" that would invite catastrophic public scrutiny.

5. On determination of subject's identity, all means necessary must be taken to ensure his/her cooperation.

Gulliver read the final sentence again. Cooperation. It was interoffice code. What it meant was silence.

He took up the list of respondents. Five names were there. One, George Corsica's, was neatly crossed out, checked off with certainty Saturday night. That left four. But it was too early to know much yet. The study had only begun yesterday. This morning, actually, when Barkley came on the scene. Maybe by tonight. He worked the frayed end of the toothpick into the pocket between gum and molar and tasted the faint tang of blood. He had been putting off the dental work. Nearly five thousand bucks they wanted. Five thousand for the pleasure of having his gums scraped, or the bone, or whatever it was they did these days. He tossed the toothpick into the wastebasket. Maybe tonight Pointer would have something to report.

Four names left. But they were the key. The answer to the extinction Barkley was always talking about.

Gulliver glanced at the medals in the shadow box case on the wall. He wanted a fourth; he intended to get it. A turnaround would do it. HALFLIFE back on track again. HALFLIFE revolutionizing the trade, cutting through the Soviets' impregnable intelligence defenses like a knife through warm butter.

His gaze traveled over the memo again. Find the subject. Ensure cooperation. Finding the subject, that was the trick. "Cooperation" was easy. They had already made provisions for that.

FOURTEEN

Oliver Pointer finished his fried clams, laid down his fork, and pulled the menu back out of its metal clip. He had read a book on subliminal advertising once that said Howard Johnson's menu photographs were retouched with an airbrush. If you looked closely enough at the fried clams, you were supposed to be able to see a pile of little nude bodies having an orgy. Tilting the menu, he narrowed his eyes and stared. They looked like ordinary clams to him.

He stuck the menu back in its slot and regarded what was left of his salad with distaste. A jellied blob of tomato innards on a shredded lettuce leaf. Somehow he had managed to eat half of the salad—all he could stomach.

Pointer had always hated salads. He got the trait from his father, and his father before him, who had been openly sympathetic to the eighteenth-century notion that tomatoes were poisonous. Cooked, they were tolerable as long as they were disguised in spaghetti and chili, but eating raw tomatoes, at least the gooey part in the middle, was about like eating glue. Lettuce wasn't much better, but the doctor had told him he needed more roughage. On the face of it,

Pointer found this hard to believe. It seemed to him that if you were having trouble with hemorrhoids, the thing to do was to eat soft food, but according to Doctor Kalksmith, that was exactly what he ought to avoid.

Wadding his napkin, he reached for the check, and went to the counter. The redheaded cashier gave him a smile.

Not bad, he thought. She was a few years older than he was. Thirty-five maybe. He paid for his lunch the same way he had paid for his room: in cash. Throwing in a roll of HoJo brand peppermints, he asked for a receipt.

"Here on business?" she asked.

He nodded and wondered whether she was interested, or whether this was just more southern friendliness. Sometimes it was hard to tell. "Sales," he said. "Aluminum siding."

"I thought maybe you were a salesman. The suit and all. My brother's in sales. Atlanta Automotive." She handed him the receipt. "I haven't seen you around before. Stay here often?"

He shook his head. "Just filling in until the new man takes over."

"Well, have a nice day," she chirped.

He pocketed his change and, skirting the empty pool, went back to his room. The maid had not been in yet. The morning newspaper lay on the floor where he had left it, and his wet washcloth was still wadded on the bathroom counter next to his shaving kit and a half-open jar of Preparation H. He tightened the lid and put the jar back on the counter. He had read somewhere that girls in beauty contests rubbed the stuff under their eyes. It was supposed to get rid of the bags or something, but then you couldn't believe everything you read.

The red bulb on the telephone was dark. No messages. Not surprising, but he made it a habit to check regularly.

He opened the peppermints and, popping one into his mouth, left the room. Three blocks south he found a pay phone. He pulled out change, dropped in a quarter, and dialed a number.

"Morgan Wing. Miss Terri Carmody speaking."

"Dr. Barkley, please."

"May I ask who's calling?"

"Dr. Winfield."

"Just a moment."

After a long pause, the woman came back. "I'm going to have to transfer your call, Doctor." Another pause, then the woman's voice again, this time touched with anxiety. "I'm really sorry, but I'm new here. I'm having a little trouble with this phone. Just a min—" Abruptly her voice cut off and he heard ringing and someone picked up.

"Richard Barkley."

"Pointer here. Same place tonight. Six o'clock."

"All right."

"Everything smooth?"

"So far." A low laugh. "One of the mules tried to balk, so I had to give him a carrot. It was Monahan. He—"

Pointer cut him off. "We'll talk tonight."

He hung up, fished for another coin, and dialed again.

"Atlanta Police Department."

He asked for an extension. A moment later, a woman answered. "Chief Corn's office."

"Roger Wagstead here," said Pointer. "Let me talk to the boss."

FIFTEEN

Tim wrestled his computer from the locker, set it up on the bedside table, and stuck a disk into the slot. While the word processor booted, he put a Chick Corea album in the tape recorder and turned the volume up. Music always seemed to help him write. Tim had never analyzed the process. It was enough that it worked. He was happy enough to leave composing in silence to genius types like Beethoven.

Linda Jean had hated the habit, especially when the stereo interfered with her TV watching, which was to say, most of the time. Reluctantly Tim had tried earphones. He didn't like the feeling of isolation he got from them, but it was better than having to put up with the daily videotape of *The Young and the Restless.*

Linda had hated his smoking too. He was killing himself, she said, and besides, it made her eyes burn. The night she walked out, he had turned the stereo up until his chest vibrated, ripped open a new pack of Winstons, and taken grim satisfaction in blowing stinging clouds of smoke at the TV's pale blind eye.

He lit a cigarette now, and slid a data disk into the

computer. Loading the latest chapter file, he studied the screen. Jake Gerrard was up to his cojones in shit. Kuryakan had him pinioned to a brass bedstead and was approaching with a sizzling hot wire plugged into the air conditioner's 220 wall socket. If Jake was to prevail by deadline time, it was time to start mopping up.

The knife! Gerrard's bound hands twitched. As his thumb moved toward his hip pocket, he eyed Kuryakan. The Russian had not yet missed the pencil-thin spring-loaded stiletto Jake's light fingers had whisked away.

Tim examined the last sentence. Two hyphenated words back to back seemed like overkill. After a moment's consideration, he inserted a comma between them.

A slight contortion. Kuryakan would think he was squirming. With a quick jab, Gerrard pressed the knife shaft through his pants pocket. The blade sprang open, splitting the fine Belgian wool. He grabbed it. The stiletto sliced into the flesh of his palm. Gritting his teeth, he maneuvered the business end toward the ropes that bound him.

"The map." The Russian aimed the splayed ends of the hot wire at Jake's eyes. "I dunt like Imperialist games, Gerrard. You want to play, you play with yourself."

"Mom always said it would make me blind." He was buying time. The stiletto burrowed between his wrists. One false move and he'd open an artery . . .

The drive whirred, saving the file to disk. Tim looked at the monitor. The screen had turned to milk.

"Shit." He stabbed at the Return key. Nothing. It had to be the hospital's dipshit power supply. But at least he'd saved the chapter.

Tim was reaching for the Reset button when something caught his eye.

A faint pulsing shadow.

Tilting his head, he stared at the screen.

A curling shadow pale as smoke.

The faint words grew sharper:

CLOUD NET

Tim's hands slid to the keyboard. Slowly, tentatively, he touched a key, stabbed a letter onto the screen.

Another.

Eyes wide, blank as dark pools, he stared, while his fingers plunged and stabbed and gathered speed:

You know me. My name is Jonathan. . . .

SIXTEEN

Jody Henson looked up from the student's paper. "I'm having a little trouble following your math."

"Oh." Miss Butterworth leaned closer to the chipped porcelain-clad steel table that served as Jody's desk and covertly eyed the paper. "Well, I can explain that. My battery died and I had to do it in my head. Can you imagine? I honestly don't know how people ever got along without calculators." A nervous smile twitched at her lips. "It was a real mess, but I worked it out."

"Did you?" The violence the girl had done to her raw data was appalling. She had managed to plug in the right statistical formula, but her basic arithmetic was, to put it kindly, highly creative. How did she get into college without knowing long division? For that matter, how did she get out of fifth grade? "I think it's time for a new battery."

"You do?" Doubt flickered across the girl's face.

So damned eager to please. Jody hid a smile and handed back the paper. "I'm afraid you're going to have to do this over," she said gently. "You can turn it in first thing tomorrow."

"Tomorrow? But we're supposed to be off on Tuesdays." A faint grin. "I guess you need it tomorrow, huh?"

Hell, she needed it today. "In the morning," she said firmly. "First thing."

Miss Butterworth left with a sigh and Jody, involuntarily giving a sigh of her own, looked around the depressing little temporary office that had once served as half of Morgan Wing's utility room. Judging from the setup, it had been the dirty side of the utility room, the side designated for soiled hot packs and contaminated bedpans back when the floor had been a polio ward. There was something unnerving about rattling around in an antique hospital wing. It was as if they were disturbing old ghosts.

After extensive remodeling, the ground floor had been occupied by Medical Records. But the rest of the building remained in limbo waiting for a restoration that might never come. Its antiquated plumbing and wiring could never accommodate modern hospital equipment. Or modern people either. Jody tried to imagine what it had been like to nurse dozens of tortured, paralyzed children here and shuddered. Cheryl would have thrived on it, she thought. When they were students, she was always the one to volunteer for jobs like that.

Cheryl Isaacson had been Jody's best friend through college. They had met in the registration line marked H-J their freshman year and immediately struck up a conversation. Their schedules coincided: Nursing 101, English, chemistry. Deciding to have lunch together, they began a friendship over Cokes and microwaved hot dogs. A friendship that had lasted through nursing school.

Right after graduation, Cheryl had gone to work in the

Emergency Room, a job Jody found appalling. But it took all kinds. Cheryl had wondered out loud how Jody could stand working on a psych floor.

The bright overhead light glanced off the scarred porcelain sinks that lined one wall and glared from her makeshift desk. Pushing her papers aside, she rubbed her eyes and wished for a reading lamp. She had tried to do without the overhead, but the light from the room's single window was no more than a cheerless gray dribble through milky glass embedded with octagonal wire mesh. Thank God it was just for a week.

Celie Carpenter, her assessment supervisor, had told her to think of it as a learning experience. "Frankly, Jody dear," she had said in that ever so sweetly serious way she had, "you need more experience in supervisory and administration, and this creativity study is tailor-made for you. I just know you'll benefit from it."

Tailor-made to pawn off on the underlings, Jody suspected. It seemed to her that the hospital stood to benefit the most. Without an intern handy, they would have had to assign a psych resident. She had been relieved of her other responsibilities for the duration, or so they said, but things had a way of piling up, and next week she'd have to play catch-up.

Jody couldn't wait until the study was over, and secretly, she suspected that the students wanted it to end as much as she did. But who was she to argue if God didn't intend for her to be a teacher? It would have been easier to give all the tests and work up the results herself. She glanced at her watch and quickly stuffed the papers onto the clipboard. Where did the time go? She had wanted to have a talk with Maureen Dorcas; the woman had seemed uncharacteristically withdrawn since last night's incident, but it was already 4:30. Time for that meeting with Dr. Barkley, and not even a minute to pull a comb through her hair.

The door to Barkley's office was ajar. The neurologist, feet on the steel desk, was reading a battered copy of this morning's *Atlanta Constitution.* Jody wondered if it was hers. Too rushed to read the paper, she had snatched it up from the lawn, brought it with her, and left it in the alcove, hoping to get to it while she grabbed a sandwich for lunch. But there hadn't been time for the paper—or for lunch either.

Barkley looked up at her knock. "Have a seat. I'll be with you in a moment, little lady." Engrossed in something on the financial page, he made no move to lay down the newspaper.

Was he that rude to everyone, or did he reserve it for females? Maybe he stored it up on weekends. Jody had had more than enough of Barkley for one day. He had immediately cast her in the role of handmaiden to the great physician. Her eyes narrowed slightly. Men who called women "little lady" deserved a special place in hell—and a special-duty demon with an arch smile and a penchant for pinching the bottoms of "little gentlemen" in his custody. Now here she sat, staring at a gray steel desk, gray file cabinet, and the dusty gray soles of Barkley's shoes. Oh, and don't forget the black telephone thrown in for accent. What did it take to get a little consideration? She wondered what he would do if she were to suddenly snatch the business section out of his hands and stuff it into the wastebasket.

She glanced at the front page Barkley had tossed aside. Same old stuff. More trouble in the Middle East. Since when was that news? And more on the D-string murders. Five of them were linked now, five women ranging in age from thirteen to fifty-five—the latest, a waitress about her age, killed Saturday night no more than four blocks from Chandler Bryson's parking lot. That meant another phone call from her mother warning her not to be out after dark. Another double-edged barb: "I worry so about you. Living alone like that. When you have a child of your own, you'll know about worry." Deep sigh. "But then, I don't suppose I'll live long enough to see a grandchild."

Knock it off, she told herself, recognizing the hollow feeling of low blood sugar—guaranteed to bring on a full-blown attack of the negatives. She should have eaten something. There was nothing standing between her and death except a bowl of Special K, and that was nearly ten hours ago.

Barkley dropped the paper and, folding his hands behind his head, gave her an appraising glance that lingered on her breasts. "You've turned in all the consent forms?"

"Almost all," she said briskly, trying to ignore the look. "Everyone signed except Tim Monahan. He was going to talk to you about that."

Barkley waved a pudgy hand. "That's taken care of."

"Any word from—" Jody consulted the list on her clipboard. "George Corsica? He never showed up."

"Didn't I tell you about that?"

She shook her head.

Barkley opened a slim folder, pulled out a paper, and handed it over.

Jody scanned the letter: ". . . sorry to inform you that my brother, George Corsica, died suddenly Tuesday night . . ." It was signed J. Corsica.

Dead? Jody blinked. Scratch George Corsica. She glanced down at her list. He was only thirty-four. She wondered what he had died of. A car wreck? According to statistics, probably, but he could have been wiped out by anything, even AIDS. Unclipping a Manila envelope, she gave it to Barkley. "Here's the raw data from this morning's tests. I'll have the statistics for you tomorrow, along with the new data from this afternoon."

Barkley pulled out the papers and gave them a cursory look. "Is everyone settling in all right?"

"I think so. I put the control group on six. They all know each other and I thought, with the elevator out of commission, they wouldn't mind the flight of stairs."

"Things haven't changed, I see." He gave a short laugh. "That was the mentality when I was in school—let the medical students walk. You'd better put a sign on that elevator before somebody ends up at the bottom of the shaft."

She felt a quick flash of annoyance. Was he implying she was negligent? Or maybe he'd just promoted her to janitor. "According to maintenance, it's off limits only as a precaution," she said, wanting him to know she had checked into it. "I asked them to put up a sign, but I guess it got sidetracked." Nobody was going to fall down an empty shaft anyway. Not in that elevator. It was an early hydraulic system like several others still in use in Bryson and perfectly safe as long as its hoses were intact. True, nobody had bothered to replace them for ages, but what was the point when the building wasn't used? "I'll put something up in the meantime."

He swung his feet to the floor. "It seems like you have everything in hand, so I'll see you first thing tomorrow."

"There's something else." She hesitated. "A problem."

"I'm running late. We can take that up in the morning."

"I really think we should talk about it now."

The flicker of irritation in his eyes was not quite masked with his smile. "All right, Miss Henson. What's this little problem that can't wait until tomorrow?"

Her jaw tightened at the condescension in his voice. She took a breath, and when she felt it settle the empty quiverings of her stomach, she said, "I'm concerned about Beth Quaig. According to my notes, she's supposed to be in pretty good control, but if that's true, she's lost a lot of ground since she got here. At least, that's what I heard from Tim Monahan." As she told him what Tim had seen the night before, Jody kept her eyes on Barkley's and tried to gauge his reaction to what she was saying.

"So," he said when she finished, "do you always base your opinion on what lay people tell you, Miss Henson?"

"Of course not. I only meant that she bears close watching."

Amusement came into his eyes. "By you, little lady? Or by Mr. Monahan?"

"By all of us. All the professional staff," she added, giving faint, but unmistakable, emphasis to "professional." She would not let him get her goat. That's exactly what he wanted; he wanted her to lose her temper, fall apart, reinforce his chauvinism. Well, she wouldn't. "There's an ethical question here. We need to consider whether Beth Quaig is well enough to sign informed consent papers."

Barkley's eyes hardened. "Are you questioning my ethics?"

She blinked. "Not at all." But was she? Was she letting personal animosity color what she thought about him professionally? "I'm simply saying that the stress of being here may have made her worse. I've had a lot of experience with multiples. I was a nurse before I went into clinical psychology. I spent nearly three years with Dr. Hastings Farber, and I—"

"I am not interested in your life's history, Miss Henson. Nor am I particularly interested in your opinion. I did not ask for you. I did not solicit your help in this project. Correct me if I'm wrong"—his lips twisted into a belittling smile—"but as I recall, your name does not appear on the payroll of the Institute for Psychological Studies. It might be well for you to remember that you are here only because of my agreement with the hospital."

The man was impossible. "I'm only suggesting that Beth Quaig may be worse."

"Oh?" An ingenuous look came into his eyes. "You've studied her complete file?"

Jody felt her lips compress. He knew damn well she hadn't. She glanced at Barkley's file cabinet. "I'd be happy to review her history."

"I'm sure you're much too busy with—" An almost imperceptible pause. "—your other work."

How trivial he made everything sound. "Not at all." She took a breath. "And I'd like to review Maureen Dorcas's history too."

He raised an eyebrow.

"I'm worried about her." She began to tell him about last night's episode with Maureen. Halfway through, she regretted bringing it up.

Another belittling smile. "Let me understand this. You went to a seance, and you were frightened by a ghost?"

"It wasn't like that. There was a definite personality change, marks on her throat." Oh, what was the use. She might as well talk to Max Headroom. "It's all on tape," she finished lamely.

He leaned forward slightly. "You taped it?"

"I didn't. No. But Tim Monahan did. He was taking notes."

Barkley glanced at his watch and stood. "I certainly understand your concern. It's very laudable."

Dismissed. Her gaze darted back to the file cabinet. It was locked. "I'd be happy to review the records tonight. I'd have them back by morning, of course."

"Let them go out of the building?" His incredulous smile implied that she was a hopeless idiot. "Why, I couldn't do that. You understand. But we'll have a nice chat about all this again." He threw an arm around her shoulder. "You're a compassionate girl. I like that. But you mustn't worry about my patients." Barkley gave her shoulder a parting squeeze. "You just see to your tests and leave the practice of medicine to me." Steering her gently, but firmly, into the hall, he shut the office door and with a final nod strode away.

She shot an angry look at the retreating doctor. The back of his neck was creased like a fat baby's. Appropriate. He was behaving like one. A self-centered baby who didn't give a diaper-load about Maureen or Beth.

Calm down, Jody, she told herself. Give it a rest.

Still, it rankled. She used to think behavior like his was unconscious, an insensitivity born of cultural conditioning. But more and more, she saw it as a weapon aimed with great deliberation. Maddeningly, there wasn't any way to fight it. If you tried, you were labeled either as a hysteric or a ball-busting female. But his type was dying out, thank God. Most of the Barkleys of the world were somewhere between forty-five and senility. The thing to do was to outlive them.

The utility-room door next to Barkley's office opened and a wiry man dressed in white came out. He stared at Jody and the flicker of surprise in his black eyes changed to amusement.

With a start, Jody recognized the orderly who had spied on her and Tim the night before. What the hell was he doing in her office? She started to challenge him, then kept her mouth shut; the utility room was the place she was hanging her hat this week, but it was also used for storage.

The man's lips split into a knowing grin, exposing uneven teeth. He was wearing a plastic name tag: B. Wiesner.

Creep. She gave him an icy stare.

Wiesner met it without a flinch. Slowly, his gaze swiveled away and paused for a long moment at the nurses station. Barkley was there, scribbling on a chart Mystery Carmody handed him. Without a word, the orderly turned and headed for the connecting hallway that led to the next building.

His walk reminded Jody of a bantam rooster. Cocky little son of a bitch. A wadded stethoscope snaked out of the man's hip pocket and she wondered why. Orderlies didn't use them. He wasn't a medical student picking up extra cash, or a nursing student either, she was sure—not working day shift; he'd have classes or clinical now if he were a student. The stethoscope was for effect, she decided, just like everything else about him. Something to impress patients with, to make them think B. Wiesner was a doctor.

She watched the orderly until the door at the end of the hall closed behind him with a clang and then deliberately dismissed him from her mind. The clock over the nurses station said 4:47. Nearly time to meet Tim, and her paperwork wasn't done yet. She'd have to make it for six or later. That or cut the evening short and do the work tonight.

No. The work came first, so she might as well get on it.

Jody grinned faintly when she realized that she was

playing games. The truth was, if the work didn't come first, the rest of her evening with Tim Monahan was shot. She remembered the way his lips had felt on hers, and the sharp sweet twist of physical excitement made her catch her breath.

Last night had bothered her a little. She had never let herself get involved with a patient before. And she hadn't now. Not really. Tim was a subject in a pilot study, not a patient. Even if he were, she was one step removed. It wasn't up to her to interpret the test results—only to oversee the students' interpretations and pass them on to Barkley.

Just like she was passing the buck right now? Rationalizing her involvement with an attractive man? Well, maybe she was. But, damn it, so what? It had been a long time since her breakup with Larry. Nearly eight months. And since Larry, there had been nobody to write home about. Nobody but Carl—and he didn't count. Not that her mother wouldn't have approved of her close encounter with the insurance underwriter. Everybody did at first. Carl Edwin Moore was good-looking and charming and intelligent. Unfortunately, he had another attribute: he held his liquor well—about a fifth of it a day.

The chilly feeling that preceded nausea rippled in her stomach. Smart, Jody. No lunch and no snack either. Better get something to eat before you pass out.

Barkley had picked up the phone in the nurses station and was deep in conversation. The redheaded nurse took the opportunity to slip out for a break.

Jody eyed her thoughtfully. The girl had been snacking all day long. Maybe her supply of junk food was holding out. She followed her to the alcove. "Do you have anything to eat, Terri?" she said, resisting the temptation to call her Mystery. "I've got the jitters."

"Hypoglycemia?"

She nodded.

The nurse fished in the pocket of her uniform and produced a crumpled package of cheese crackers.

Jody took them gratefully. "Thanks. I'll pay you for these."

"Forget it. Chalk it up to humanitarian aid." She plopped down on the wicker couch and rubbed her calf with a freckled hand, wincing as she did. Jody noticed she was wearing heavy white support hose.

"Varicose veins," she explained. "Occupational hazard. I used to be a scrub nurse before I signed up with the temp agency. When the veins went, I had to quit. That, or go to work in a wheelchair. I ought to have them stripped, but who can take the time off?"

Nodding in sympathy, Jody sat down across from her, tore open the cheese cracker package, and took a bite. "It's been a day."

"You got that right. I ran into a lot of superegos when I worked O.R., but Barkley— You want to watch out for the ones who look like they belong on a valentine. Who can figure him? Take the phone, for instance. Half the time he trots out here to call out, so a while ago I told him he had a telephone call at the nurses station. What does he do? He gives me hell for not transferring it to his office phone. Like I was going to listen in or something." She rolled her eyes. "Thank God it's only for a week. But maybe he doesn't bother you."

Jody shrugged. "We get along okay." Like cats and dogs, she thought. Why had she bothered to lie? Misplaced sense of professionalism, maybe. Or was it more pernicious? A way to build up her ego? A way to show the world that she was in control? But the day was too far gone and she was too tired to do the self-analysis bit. "You're working late. Aren't you supposed to get off at four?"

"You don't know the half of it. I've been drafted for a double."

"A double shift? Why?"

The nurse glanced toward the desk where Barkley, hand cupping the mouthpiece, was still on the phone. "In his infinite wisdom, the grand high Poohbah has decided to carry on into the night." She pulled out a pack of Teaberry gum and popped a piece into her mouth. "I had plans too." She eyed Jody thoughtfully. "You were a nurse. Do you still have an active license?"

Jody licked a crumb off her lip and nodded. Even though she did not practice anymore, she would probably be paying that license renewal fee for the next thirty years. It was a matter of values; she had worked too hard for it to let it go completely.

"I don't suppose you'd want to fill in for me tonight."

"Sorry. Tim and I are having dinner at my place."

"Tim Monahan?" A knowing little smile crept onto Carmody's lips.

Damn. Why had she told Carmody it was Tim? She changed the subject. "What did you mean by 'Barkley carrying on into the night'?"

"Didn't he tell you? His Highness wants to do some more tests tonight."

"What tests?"

"I guess it's tests he wants," she amended. "I don't know yet. He told me he was going to write some orders on Beth Quaig and Maureen Dorcas. But he said he had to cancel a dinner meeting with somebody or other first. Anyway, there went the evening."

Beth and Maureen? Wonder of wonders. Barkley must

have been listening to her after all. But who could have told? "Keep an eye on those two, will you?" she said. "Especially Beth. I'm a little worried about her."

Mystery Carmody looked up. "Why? She's not going to flip out or anything, is she? They told me I'd be passing pills and keeping charts, not running a psych ward." The rattan couch creaked as she leaned forward. "I mean, I'm not a psych nurse." She glanced toward Beth Quaig's room. "I've never been around multiples. They can be dangerous, can't they?"

"That's not what I meant," said Jody quickly. "I'm just concerned about the stress. The study might be too much for her."

"I don't know about this. I haven't been around psych patients since I was a student." Carmody's jaws worked on the gum. "Thank God."

Jody tried not to smile at the nurse's anxious look. Nobody was neutral. You either loved psych or you hated it. "You'll do fine."

Doubt crossed her face. "You're handing out guarantees?"

"Look," said Jody, "she's not going to get violent or anything like that. All multiples have a lot of hostility, but the women usually turn it inward. If they do, one of the personalities is almost invariably suicidal. But I don't think you have to worry about violence."

Mystery Carmody rolled her eyes. "Wonderful. All I have to worry about is a suicide on my floor. Should she be on precautions?"

"I didn't say that. The dominant personality usually keeps the suicidal one in check. I haven't read Beth's complete history, but nothing I've seen tells me she's sick enough to try and kill herself."

"Let's hope you're right," she said uncertainly. "I'm glad you told me, though. I didn't know multiples came with built-in snuff factors."

"All of them don't. Just the women."

"And the men?"

"They tend to turn their hostility outward," Jody said carefully. She was remembering Hastings Farber's words: "Never—never—undertake the treatment of a male multiple outside of an institutional setting. And never take the security within an institution for granted." Words that he delivered to the staff six hours after an attack on a nurse, six hours after a male multiple had broken an IV bottle and laid open the woman's carotid artery with the jagged edge.

"You're saying that unless Beth Quaig turns out to be a transvestite, we're in good shape?"

Jody smiled. "I guess you could say that." She looked up as Richard Barkley walked by and, without a parting glance, opened the door to the connecting hallway.

Someone was there. The orderly.

With a smile to Barkley, B. Wiesner turned and fell into step beside the neurologist. A moment later, the door swung shut behind them.

Mystery Carmody wrapped her gum in a wad of foil and tossed it into the metal wastebasket with a hollow thunk. "Guess I'd better have a look at His Majesty's orders." With a quick "see you," she headed back for the nurses desk.

Jody finished the cheese crackers and glanced across the hall toward 504. She hoped Tim wouldn't mind putting off dinner. Clipboard in hand, she was crossing the hall to his room when the door to 502 opened.

Maureen Dorcas stood in the doorway, staring past Jody at something far away.

The look on the woman's face made Jody stop. "Everything okay?"

The medium's gaze slid toward Jody. Her eyes did not seem focused.

Jody went up to her. "You okay?" she repeated.

For a moment longer Maureen stared at her blankly. Then her hand stretched out and closed on Jody's arm. "Please—" The woman's grip tightened, transmitting little shock waves of pain. "Please," she said again. "You've got to help me."

Jody steered Maureen back to her room and sat her down on the rumpled bed. "It's all right. Everything's okay now." She hoped it was true; Maureen seemed to be in some sort of fugue state.

The medium huddled on the edge of the bed and stared past Jody as if she were not there. Alarm etched her eyes. A moment later, it gave way to shock, then confusion.

"Maureen, look at me."

The woman did not respond.

Jody's voice grew more intense. "It's all right now." Then sternly, "Look at me."

Blinking several times, Maureen turned her face toward Jody and shook her head as if to clear it.

"You okay?"

She leaned back on her elbows and stared at the wall for nearly half a minute. Then she muttered something unintelligible.

"What?" Jody leaned closer.

"A bitch. I said, it was a bitch." The confused lost look began to fade from Maureen's eyes. As it did, she focused on Jody, staring as if she had never really looked at her before. "Yeah," she whispered to herself and twin furrows creased her brow.

"Yeah what?"

The corner of Maureen's lip began to twitch.

Was it a smile or consternation? "What happened?"

A low chuckle. Maureen shook her head again.

"Something's funny?"

"I asked you to help, didn't I? Amazing. I was asking *you."* Her smile vanished abruptly. "God."

What was she talking about? "Help do what?" Jody prompted.

Maureen stood up abruptly and began to rummage through the bedside table drawer. She found a pack of Ultra Thins, lit one, and took a long drag. "I was lying down. But I wasn't asleep," she said. "Just relaxed. I want you to understand that." She stared at the glowing end of the cigarette before she went on. "There was something out there." She fluttered a hand in the air as if to imply that "out there" was not a concrete place. "Something—" She hesitated. When she spoke again, her voice was low. "It was incredibly evil." The woman searched Jody's face. "I suppose that sounds medieval to you. Superstitious."

"Go on," Jody said quietly, deliberately avoiding any comment.

"You've read *The Paul Chronicles?"*

"Yes."

"Then you know what he teaches. He says we each create our own reality." She leaned back against a cluster of pillows. "I believe that. But we don't live in a vacuum. Other realities impinge on ours. And some of us are more sensitive than others." Her brow furrowed. "Do you follow what I'm saying?"

Not sure where this was leading, Jody shook her head.

"Let me give you an example. Let's say I just had lunch and you haven't eaten. In fact, you're starved and not too happy about it. My own reality tells me I'm full. But if my antenna's up, I pick up on your feelings, and all of a sudden I'm feeling out of sorts and irritable." She tapped her cigarette on the edge of an empty peanut brittle can pressed into service as an ashtray. "I don't know of any studies on this, but I'll tell you what I think. I think my body is reacting to yours. I believe blood sugar tests would prove it."

Strange that she would choose that particular example, thought Jody. "Are you saying psychics read bodies instead of minds?"

Maureen laughed. "Sounds like something Agatha Christie would have been interested in, doesn't it?" She tapped the cigarette again and took another drag. "No. What I mean is, I believe we tune in to all of it indiscriminately. Mind and body. Past, present, and future. All of it. That's why it hit me like it did. Physically."

"Hit you?"

"Almost literally," she said. "I was lying here, and all of a sudden I felt a pain in my head. Right there." Maureen fingered the back of her head gingerly. An intent look came into her eyes. "Have you ever been really frightened?"

"Sure. Everybody has."

"I don't mean being startled, or the kind of rush you get from a horror movie or a roller coaster. I mean the real thing."

Jody glanced away. Only once. One time for real. She had been working late. It was past midnight, and though she knew better, she had been too tired to go all the way to the lobby exit. Instead, she had taken a short cut down a dim stairwell that opened to a narrow alley and then to the street. As soon as she reached the door she knew she was not alone. Whirling, she spun to meet the glint of a knife blade, blood red in the wash of the Exit light. He had wanted money, that was all. But in that moment she had been sure she was going to die. Her gaze slid back to Maureen. "Once," she said.

"Then you know how I felt." Maureen stubbed out the cigarette. "It was evil. There isn't any other word for it. There was something utterly evil here and I was afraid."

"A person?"

"I don't know." Maureen fixed her gaze on a featureless stretch of wall. "Everything got confused. The room was spinning. I felt sick. Dizzy. Then the pictures started to come."

Pictures? "What did you see?"

"A bell. A little silver bell. It didn't have a clapper, but it made a sound." Maureen picked up a pencil and began to tap the peanut brittle can, cocking her head as she listened. "Like that. Only sharper." She dropped the pencil and it began to roll, gathering momentum, until it reached the edge of the table, hesitated, and then fell to the floor.

Maureen was silent for a moment. When she spoke again, her voice dropped until it was so low that Jody had to strain to hear.

"It was dark. Very dark. And oppressive. I couldn't get my breath. Then a faint little streak of light came and I saw something else." She leaned forward. "Do you know what a bell jar is?"

Puzzled, Jody nodded. "Curved glass," she said. "Like one of those domes to store cheese in."

"It was like that," said Maureen. "But different. More like—" She glanced around the room, her gaze moving from one object to another. Then she closed her eyes for a moment. "I know—" She gave a low, nervous laugh. "Like

Robbie the Robot. You know, the thing over his head."

"You mean a helmet? Like on a spacesuit?"

"Yes. More like that." Maureen picked up the pencil. "I could see inside." Her hands were trembling.

Maureen gazed at the pencil as if it helped her remember. "There was somebody in there," she said. "Somebody who needed help desperately. But there was nothing I could do."

She stood abruptly, walked to the window, and stood there, staring out in silence before she turned back to Jody. "It was you," she said finally. "It was you I saw."

Jody's eyes widened. "Me?" In a bell jar? The stunned feeling gave way to the urge to laugh. There wasn't much in the literature about psychics; they seemed to range from well-adjusted to around-the-bend. Up to now, she would have put Maureen in the first category without hesitation. But this? Silver bells and bell jars. Bell jars that looked like spacesuits.

But Maureen said she had been lying down. "Relaxed," she had said. More than relaxed, Jody suspected. That would explain the fugue state. She had been sleepwalking. "I think I know what happened," she said carefully, not wanting to make light of the woman's anxiety. "Sometimes dreams can seem very real."

"Until you wake up."

"Even then. When you first wake up it can take a while to get going. Sort of like starting a car on a cold morning. If you happen to wake up while you're in the middle of a dream, things can get confusing," said Jody. "There's a whole assortment of sleep aberrations that can complicate matters too. Most of them are benign, but they can be pretty bizarre. In fact, if you don't realize what's going on, they can scare the hell out of you."

"No."

Something in Maureen's tone made Jody search her face.

"I want you to know that it wasn't a dream," the medium said. "I wasn't asleep. It wasn't a dream at all."

SEVENTEEN

When the motel phone rang, Oliver Pointer was asleep, his face covered with Section A of *The Atlanta Journal.* Startled, he threw off the newspaper with a rattle and, blinking at the lowering sun, wrestled the receiver off the hook. "Yes?"

"It's Barkley. I can't meet you. We've got a problem."

Pointer was instantly alert. "What's up?"

"One of the subjects—it was Monahan—and that psychology intern talked the Dorcas woman into staging a seance last night, and something happened. Some kind of psychic attack. I think it might be a bleed-through. It might be—"

"Later," Pointer said sharply. Barkley knew damn well the line wasn't secure. Worse, the motel calls went through the switchboard. "I'll call you back." He hung up and, grabbing a jacket, headed for the pay phone three blocks away. Any phone was risky, but he had no choice; he had to report to Gulliver in less than an hour. At least there was a direct line into the nurses station on Morgan Wing.

Twelve minutes later, the nurse transferred his call and Barkley picked up.

"Start over," Pointer said abruptly. "Who were you talking about? Who was attacked?"

"The medium. The Dorcas woman. According to the intern, she was nearly strangled."

Pointer took a slow breath. "Who did it?"

"I'm not sure. I told you it was a psychic attack. I'm going to run a couple of EEGs tonight. Take a look and see if I can elicit a rerun."

"You said 'a couple.' A couple of EEGs."

"Henson—she's the intern—Henson said the Quaig girl had some problems last night. She said Monahan found out. He went to her room. Found her stuck in an infantile personality. Maybe it's stress. Maybe not. I'm going to test her too."

Shit. First day out of the box and already two screwups.

"Pointer? You still there?"

"I'm here."

"There's something else. Monahan had a tape recorder. He taped the seance."

"Taped it?" A bleed-through and he got it on a fucking tape?

"That's right."

"Do you have it?"

"No."

"Where is it, then?"

"Monahan's room. It's got to be there."

"It better be," said Pointer. His grip tightened on the phone. It was Barkley's ass—and his—if it wasn't.

EIGHTEEN

The lowering sun angled into the room and bleached Tim's computer screen to an unreadable gray. Giving the overbed table a yank, he pulled it closer and flipped on the wall light. The aging fluorescent tube flickered at one end like a dying firefly before it came on.

He surveyed the screen, immensely pleased with what he had written. It was good. Better, the writing had been effortless. He reached for the can of Coke he had extracted from a recalcitrant lobby machine after his afternoon session with Miss Butterfinger and took a swallow. It was flat and lukewarm. Making a face, he set it down.

He skimmed to the beginning of the file and began to reread it, changing a word here and there, inserting a comma. But by and large, it was finished material. Funny how the mind worked. He wondered how long his subconscious had been laboring over this character, polishing it, working out little nuances and quirks without his knowledge.

But there was no doubt in his mind. Jonathan was

real—as real as any living, breathing human he had ever known.

He had not consciously contemplated a book like this. Not at all. But who was he to look a gift horse? Of course, there was no story yet, only seven pages of stream of consciousness. Magic pages, though. A trip into a labyrinthine mind with enough twists to excite a Minotaur to orgasm. No story yet, but he was sure Jonathan would take care of that. All he had to do was follow.

It was great when a character took on a life of his own. It was like being Ben Hur in the chariot race. All he had to do was steer. He barely remembered the writing—only the dim feeling of dissociation, a floating feeling as if his body were anchored to the world by nothing more than his fingertips on the keyboard.

The last time something like this had happened was when he wrote *A Shaft of Light,* but it wasn't quite the same. The dissociation then was not as marked, not as complete. He grinned when he remembered a quote on inspiration from one of the dozens of writing manuals he had devoured years before: "This morning, I got a sonnet from an angel. When it's polished, I think I can sell it to *Harper's.*"

He was happy to let Jonathan write his own book. Go with the flow. All too often it was a dribble. When that happened, when he felt it drying up, the urge to prime the pump with booze was almost overwhelming. Only the knowledge that he would be deluding himself kept him from it. The only words that came with a bottle were on the label.

A tap at the door.

Tim looked up from the computer. "It's open." He smiled at the absurdity. He couldn't lock it if he tried.

It was Jody.

"Am I interrupting?"

He shook his head. "All done."

"Are you too hungry to put off dinner for a while?" Without waiting for him to answer, she said, "I got sidetracked. I still have a pile of papers to go through. It'll be another hour or so."

"I'll survive."

Her brow furrowed. "Do you believe in predictions?" She looked away.

"That depends," he said. "Sometimes."

Jody gave a distracted nod as if his answer had not registered.

Gone away, he thought with amusement. Just like his little brother. But with Peter it was chronic; from the time he was a baby he had spent most of his life shuttling between brown studies and blue funks, and, in the process, driving everybody else to exasperation. At family dinners he would simply go away until a stray bit of conversation brought him back again. When that happened, everyone had to backtrack and fill him in on the last twenty minutes. That, or suffer hurt looks and indignant you-don't-love-me lip quiverings.

Jody's eyes lost their distant look.

"Back again?"

"What?" Her lips looked especially enticing when they formed the word.

He grinned. "Nothing."

"You have a car in town, right?"

"Some might call it that."

Jody scribbled something on a sheet of paper, pulled it off the clipboard, and handed it to him. "Here's the address. Think you can find it?"

He glanced at the paper. An Inman Park address. How could she afford to live there? Fledgling psychologists must have a leg up on the upwardly mobile scene. Unlike struggling writers, he thought wryly. The way the cards usually fell, writers' economic legs seemed to be permanently pinned in the Hanged Man position. "No problem," he said.

"You're sure? I wouldn't want you to get lost." Her mock frown gave way to a grin. "Like you did back in elementary school at recess—"

"Every day for six years," he finished solemnly. "It's a hazard. I got stuck on an I-85 cloverleaf for six months once. But that was before I installed the automatic pilot in my car."

"Seven-thirty, then?"

"Fine." Then as she turned to leave, he said impulsively, "Come take a look at this before you go."

She leaned close to the screen, her breasts brushing against his shoulder, her body radiating warm scents of soap and spice.

"It's only a character sketch," he said, skimming to the beginning of the file, "but I think it's going to fly."

Jody began to read, her brow furrowing from time to time, smoothing, then furrowing again.

Tim's exhilaration evaporated. He had never liked to show anyone a work in progress, not since his college writing classes. Not until it was complete, polished, reexamined in the cold light of objectivity. So, why was he doing it now? As he scrolled the screen downward to keep pace with her reading he began to feel like an ass. Maybe he was wrong. Maybe it stunk. He should have stuck it in the freezer for a few days and checked for off odors before he offered anybody slices.

She finished. Her gaze met his, then slid away. For a long moment, she was silent. Then she said, "You taught English. Right?"

"Junior high." He scanned the screen for gaffes. Had he misspelled something? Screwed up his tenses?

"No psychology in college? Nothing like that?"

"The obligatory Psych 101. Growth and Development. That's all. Why?"

"It always amazes me how writers without any training can sometimes come up with things intuitively that it takes a professional years to learn." She hesitated. "I mean, reading this, you'd almost think it was a clinical profile."

What was she driving at? He waited for her to go on.

"It's fascinating. This man, Jonathan—" Her fingertip skimmed the screen, paused, moved on again. "He's almost a perfect textbook antisocial personality."

"Antisocial personality?"

"Current wisdom calls them that. The official designation used to be sociopath. Before that, psychopath."

He looked up sharply. But Jody, with a quick glance at her watch, said, "Got to run," and headed for the door.

NINETEEN

Hal Gulliver turned off the isolated road and the car bottomed with a jolt, its tires crunching gravel as he maneuvered the long potholed driveway. Even in the fading light, it was obvious the isolated farmhouse needed a paint job. Browning weeds struggled against its foundation and pine straw littered its roof. He pulled into the ramshackle garage, narrowly missing the black Ford with government plates that was hogging most of the space.

He glared at the Ford and flung his door open against it. The result was a satisfying thud and about ten inches of space to get through. He struggled out, cursing himself for eschewing a driver. But he had wanted the time alone to think, and a driver, even a silent one, was an unnecessary distraction. Gulliver did not look forward to spending another evening with Phillip Sessions, but it was unavoidable; he had to be sure Barkley was on track.

He had inherited Barkley along with HALFLIFE. Security considerations and the man's credentials had kept him on the job so far, but Gulliver had more than a few doubts, and the phone call from Pointer an hour ago hadn't helped put them to rest. What the hell was Barkley up to? Those people needed supervision; that much was obvious. Although Gulliver took most psychic claims with a large grain of salt, the Dorcas woman was an exception. Uneasily, he remembered a page out of her file: a crude picture of an office that she had drawn in trance. On the face of it, not particularly interesting—except that it happened to be his own.

The idea that they were playing around with seances down there gave him the creeps. Who knew what she might have said?

Irritated, Gulliver slammed the car door shut. He was out of the garage and on his way to the back door when a low voice behind him said, "Good evening, sir."

Horribly startled, he spun around and stared at a young man wearing a gray suit. Shit. Another fucking CT.

"Henderson is waiting inside. I'm Knowlton, sir."

And proud as hell of the Midnight Skulker routine. A sour smile crept over Gulliver's lips. "Securing the area, are you?"

The Career Trainee snapped to attention. "Yes, sir."

"Next time, wait until you're fucking told to."

A blink. "Yes, sir."

"I suppose you drive, Knowlton?"

A puzzled nod. "I do, sir."

He jerked his chin toward the garage and the offending Ford. "You drove here tonight?"

"No, sir. Henderson drove."

Two goddamned jewels, then, and both of them CTs. He had no doubt of that at all; they came in pairs, like nuns. Wondering what evil he had done to cause God to afflict him with two idiots in one night, Gulliver turned away without a word and trudged to the back door.

The white lace curtain at the window moved slightly.

Another spy. Jesus. With a silent prayer to God to let up, Gulliver raised a fist to the door and pounded it.

The door opened quickly to a second "Good evening, sir."

Henderson was blond and square-faced, but otherwise a Knowlton clone. Recruitment must be down. They were growing them in the lab these days.

He followed Henderson through the back porch into a large kitchen filled with antiquated appliances and a new-looking microwave squatting next to the drainboard. A wooden table in the center of the room was set with thick white pottery mugs and plates for two.

"We have dinner waiting, sir," said Henderson. "If you'll come this way."

The front room led to a narrow dining room with a dark, carved oak table. Sears Roebuck, 1925, thought Gulliver. Again, the table was set for two. The loud flush of primitive plumbing told him Dr. Phillip Sessions was in the can.

"We got take-out food. From The Bangkok Gourmet," said Henderson. "I hope that's all right with you."

Thai food? It was almost always hamburgers or Chinese. Henderson needed a lot of work, but there might be some promise there.

Another flush exploded from the farmhouse toilet. A moment later, Sessions came out, stooping as if he feared impact with the top of the door, consternation written on his bland face. "There seems to be a problem with the plumbing." He aimed a turtlelike thrust of his chin toward the bathroom. "It seems to be backing up."

The sound of water trickling onto the floor sent Knowlton racing into the toilet, while Gulliver sourly regarded the neurophysiologist. Sessions's alleged genius didn't seem to extend to a basic knowledge of plumbing.

"Nice evening," Sessions observed.

"Great," said Gulliver flatly.

The trickling slowed to a drip, and Knowlton emerged for a quick conference with Henderson in the kitchen. A long minute passed before they came back, Henderson armed with two glasses of bourbon, Knowlton with a plumber's friend.

When three beeps came from the microwave, Henderson steered Gulliver and Sessions into the dining room. "I'll bring dinner in now." He headed for the kitchen and came back a minute later with a tray full of white take-out containers and an array of serving spoons. "They're hot, sir. I'm afraid they're a little hard to get hold of. I had to take off the wire handles because of the microwave."

"Fine." Gulliver waved him away and nodded to Sessions. "Help yourself."

Sessions flipped open a tall container and stared at it dubiously. "What is it?"

Gulliver took a look. A dark, spicy smell struck his nose. "Gang Musselman, I think."

"Gang what?"

"Musselman. It means Muslim man."

Sessions recoiled.

Holding back a smirk, Gulliver ladled out a generous serving for himself and followed it with a blob of something unknown, but mostly peanuts.

Vigorous plunging sounds, followed by half-strangled gurglings, came from the toilet. Shooting a narrow-eyed glance in the direction of the bathroom, Gulliver took a stiff slug of his drink. He hated bourbon; he found it tolerable now. He took another swallow and wondered if he had ever thought the work he did was glamorous; he must have once, back when he was starting out.

A final flush, and Knowlton emerged carrying the

plumber's friend. A wet blob of toilet paper pasted to its bulb left a dripping trail all the way to the kitchen.

Sessions hunched over his plate and picked at his food, leaving most of it except for the rice.

Gulliver ate with a good appetite, polishing off what was left of the Gang Musselman, before he brought up business. "You've had time enough to go over the, uh, scenario?"

Sessions laid down his fork, lining it up precisely with the top of the dish, and turned his moist gaze to Gulliver. "I believe so." Wadding one end of his paper napkin, he stuck it under the edge of the plate. "I believe I mentioned my reservations about the Wada test last time—the three percent mortality."

Gulliver nodded.

"But the Wada will work. I believe the risk is justifiable."

"You said 'justifiable'?" Gulliver's remark was a way to mask his astonishment. He had expected a complete condemnation of the test on ethical grounds.

Sessions folded his bony hands and focused on them as if he were meditating. "The possibilities go a lot further than you may realize, but there's a big 'if' attached. I can explain this better with an example. First of all, you have to visualize the brain," he said, cupping his hands as if he held one between them. "The left half—in our culture, at any rate—is the logical side, the side involved with language. It controls the right side of the body. The function of the right half is spatial and intuitive—" He stopped as the door to the kitchen opened and Henderson came in carrying the bottle of bourbon.

"Would you like some coffee to go with this? We made a pot."

Gulliver nodded. Coffee might improve the stuff.

Henderson turned to Sessions. "More bourbon?"

The doctor thrust out his empty glass with alacrity. "Nothing like a snort of good old corn liquor, I always say." He followed this with a rasping chuckle that seemed to originate in his nose.

In appreciation of his remarkable wit, Gulliver supposed. The alien burst of conviviality made him shudder. Good old corn liquor, good old Scotch, good old rotgut—it was all the same to good old Sessions.

The CT refilled the glasses, left the bourbon bottle, and, stacking the dirty plates on the tray, disappeared with them into the kitchen.

Suddenly lost in thought, Sessions stared into his glass.

"You were saying—" Gulliver prompted.

Sessions raised his eyes and gave him an even look. "I wasn't saying anything."

Well, wasn't that the fucking point? "Before. You were talking about the brain before. The two halves."

"Yes, I was." Sessions stared into his glass again.

Jesus. Alice at the mad tea party.

But Sessions had apparently gone away to sort his mental database. After a moment, a sudden animated look came over his face. "What do you know about epilepsy?"

Gulliver's lips tightened. "Apropos of what?"

"That's what the Wada test was designed for. For other purposes too, but you understand I have to simplify."

For the halfwits, thought Gulliver.

"When an epileptic presents with uncontrollable seizures, sometimes surgery is the only answer. What that means is, the neurosurgeon has to selectively destroy certain areas of the brain to stop the seizure activity. That's where the Wada test comes in. It gives the surgeon a way to be sure that the half of the brain that should be dominant for language really is, before he starts cutting. Otherwise, the patient might be mute for the rest of his life. And that's not what you're after here." With this understatement, Sessions paused to gulp the rest of his bourbon. He eyed the bottle thoughtfully for a moment, then reached for it, and splashed more into his glass. "I'm not driving tonight," he said by way of explanation.

And a good thing. Gulliver was not convinced that the world would be safe with Sessions behind the wheel. Ever. Not the way he drifted into mental funks.

"When you want to anesthetize the left brain, you inject the medication into the right carotid artery in the neck. Right here." Sessions laid a bony finger at the angle of his jaw. "The right carotid feeds the drug directly to the left brain. Remember, that's the side that normally controls language. But now, we've put that side to sleep, shut off the language faculty, so to speak." A pause, then another rasping chuckle at his inadvertent pun.

Gulliver nodded, pasted a phony smile on his face, and tried to look as if he had not heard all this before. But of course, Sessions had no way of knowing that he had, no way of knowing that HALFLIFE was more than a tentative proposal on a sheaf of papers.

Sessions fell silent again and shot a wary glance toward the kitchen as Knowlton came in with a pot of coffee. He deposited it on the table and went back to the kitchen. Gulliver poured some into his mug and offered the pot to Sessions.

The doctor waggled a hand in refusal and grasped his bourbon glass. "This is the point where the Wada gets interesting. The aphasic stage, where no speech is possible. That's where the psychologists came into the picture. They teamed up with the neurosurgeons and started to run a few tests of their own.

"Remember, the right brain controls the left side of the

body. When the left brain is asleep, you can put an object into the patient's left hand, a key, for example, and tell him to remember it. When he wakes up, and you ask him what it was, he's going to deny that you handed anything to him. As far as his conscious memory is concerned, you didn't give him a thing. But the information is still there. Locked away. We can prove it by showing the patient a group of objects with the key among them. He'll pick the key every time."

Sessions swallowed more bourbon. It glistened on his lips. "What all this means is that the Wada allows us to slip information into the brain without the language system knowing it." His gaze drifted away from Gulliver and came to rest somewhere beyond. A moment later, the strange animation came back. "I've given a lot of thought to your scenario here. First of all, you can only keep the brain hemisphere anesthetized for a few minutes. That means you'll have to act fast. But I see a way to do that."

Gulliver leaned forward.

"You precede the Wada with a hypnotic. Quaaludes would do the trick. You have to bear in mind the visual orientation of the right brain. Visuals are the best way to go here, I think. Visuals with voice-overs. What you're trying to do is get a large amount of information tucked away in the shortest period of time." He waggled a hand. "Film. Videotape. You'd need to speed it up. But that's no problem." He paused. "You're undoubtedly aware of subliminals, how they work. The brain can absorb an incredible amount of information in a surprisingly short time."

Gulliver nodded. Subliminals did indeed work. Even the unsophisticated experimental techniques available twenty-two years ago.

"Then to prevent any bleed-through from the right

brain to the left, you follow the subliminals with a hypnotic command to forget—until you want him to remember. You'll need a post-hypnotic trigger for that." A glazed, sensual look came into Sessions's wet eyes. "The possibilities are incredible. Modules of information tucked away where the conscious mind can't reach. But that's just the beginning. . . ." Slowly, he focused on Gulliver. "I believe it's possible to create a construct—an artificial personality." With a glance toward the kitchen, Sessions leaned closer. "Suppose it was Joe Citizen. Joe Citizen on his summer vacation to Europe, or Central America, or even the Soviet Union. Do you know what you've got?"

Gulliver did not speak.

"The perfect courier." Sessions's voice dropped. "Don't you see? I'm talking about a courier who could withstand interrogation, torture—anything—without revealing a word to the enemy. He can't. Because it's not there. There's nothing in his conscious mind."

Gulliver had expected Sessions's work to parallel Barkley's, but not this closely. He hoped his uneasiness didn't show.

Sessions drained the last of his bourbon and leaned back. "I told you there was a problem, though."

"Yes?"

"I'm afraid we're talking about a long-term project. The right brain is normally mute; it has no language. You can stuff it full of information, but the problem is how to get it out again." Sessions tented bony fingers, and gave Gulliver a sharp look. "Right brain language is possible, but there's a catch. It has to be learned before adolescence or it can't develop." The fingertips clamped together, relaxed, tightened again. "Your subjects have got to be children. Kids."

So here it was. Gulliver took a long time to phrase his

answer. Finally he said, "We're talking about a serious matter."

A tense nod.

"There are a lot of ramifications here. We have to consider the children, of course. . . ." Gulliver leaned back and took a swallow of coffee. The bourbon it was laced with slid harshly down his throat. "It comes down to a question of whether the end justifies the means, doesn't it? But there's another consideration. We have to think about what this nation's enemies would do if they were armed with this technique. We have to think about the repercussions of that." A long pause. "So we *are* talking about the lives and safety of our children, aren't we? *All* of our children."

Sessions searched Gulliver's face. As he did, the tension in the doctor's body glided away like oil. "I see your point," he said. A faint smile bent his lips. "When do we start?"

TWENTY

Tim spotted Manuel's Tavern, his landmark. Angling right onto the road just beyond it, he passed a series of old row houses and turned left. A few blocks later he found the street he was looking for.

It was getting dark. Squinting at street numbers in the dim yellow glow of porch lights, he finally came to Jody's.

He parked on the street, blocking an old Volkswagen halfway up the driveway. Her car, he guessed. Grabbing his tape case and a bottle of wine wrapped in a brown liquor-store bag, he got out. He was in a neighborhood of old houses that had been bargains fifteen or sixteen years ago, but now they carried a price tag to match their extensive renovations.

The house was large, its second story shadowed by the inky silhouette of an old oak. Three broad steps led up to a wide porch. Next to the front door a regal old green metal glider leaned against the wall beneath a pair of tall windows.

The doorbell wobbled at his touch. Not sure if it had rung, he pressed it again. A series of excited barks came in answer and a black muzzle pushed aside a curtain. Two round eyes full of curiosity peered out.

When Jody opened the door, the barks intensified. "Hush, Sushi."

Tim eyed the dog. Its round, baby-shaped head made it look like a husky designed by Walt Disney. The frantic barks were mitigated by animated waggings of a pom-pom tail. "I think he's faking." He stuck out a hand. The dog inspected it gravely, gave it a lick, and with another flurry of barks retreated behind its mistress.

"She," Jody corrected. "But you're right. Give her five minutes and she'll want to sit in your lap." Her eyes met his, flicked away, then back again. She replaced the door chain, and turned toward him, an uncertain smile on her face. He felt it echoed on his own lips. Ridiculous. Why was he feeling like a kid on a first date? He looked around the foyer. It was empty except for a little table by the door and a reed-filled basket near the narrow staircase. Framed prints of stylized toy soldiers in stiff red uniforms marched across the wall. "Nice place," he said with a sideways look at the girl he had felt so comfortable with earlier that day. She had changed into jeans and a soft pink sweater. Her index finger plucked at the cuff, pulling, smoothing, pulling again.

"Come on back," she said. "I'm right in the middle of spaghetti sauce."

He followed her into a large high-ceilinged living room. White woodwork set off its Williamsburg-blue walls. A white rattan couch, old, but freshly painted and cushioned with blue and white mattress ticking, was heaped with half a dozen red pillows. A red stained glass lamp splashed its rosy light onto a curved glass and mahogany etagere holding a collection of books. A New Age instrumental, lush with harp glissandos, was playing on the stereo, and in the fireplace across the room a little pile of pressed logs smoked and flickered and threatened to go out at any moment.

Tim dropped the tape case onto the couch and handed Jody the bottle of wine, a Zinfandel red as blood. "Something to go with the living room."

"Thanks." She examined the label, then glanced around the room as if she were seeing it for the first time. "My mother was startled by a flag before I was born."

He concealed a smile. "I can see that. Have you lived here long?"

"Since my grandmother died. Nearly two years now. This used to be her house. She left it to me."

Grandma either lived an ascetic life, or most of her furniture had gone to somebody else, Tim thought. The dining room was empty except for several rolls of red and white pin-striped wallpaper heaped against one wall next to a built-in corner cabinet.

The kitchen was next, square and white, with a scarred porcelain drainboard and an old gas stove with six burners. Sushi went to her water bowl, drank, and then pressed her wet muzzle against Tim's knee. "What kind of dog is she?" he asked.

"A Keeshond." Jody stirred a pot of spaghetti sauce with a large wooden spoon. "Want to uncork the wine?" She pulled open a drawer, fished out a corkscrew from the jumble of utensils, and handed it to him. "We can have a glass before supper."

Plopping a lid on the spaghetti sauce, she turned to the salad she had started, adding green onions to the crisp romaine, while Tim opened the wine. "Glasses are over there." She nodded toward a half-open cabinet above the sink.

He found wine glasses, poured the Zinfandel, and set Jody's on the cutting board next to a freshly sliced pile of mushrooms. Taking a sip, he watched her covertly, liking the way the light played on her hair, and the way her lips pouted slightly as she searched the spice rack. Pulling out a jar of dill, she tossed a little into the salad and added the mushrooms. Giving her hands a quick swipe with a paper towel, Jody took a sip of wine, then another.

"Good," she said. Suddenly a dismayed look crossed her face. The paper towel had fluttered to the floor and Sushi, spotting it, centered her hindquarters precisely over the paper, and squatted.

Tim looked down at the widening puddle, then back at Jody, who was earnestly studying a blank place on the wall.

Sushi, obviously pleased with herself, wagged her tail.

Jody's gaze slid furtively toward Tim, then dropped to the little dog. "Good girl." There wasn't much conviction in her voice. She began to pull paper towels off the roll—enough, it seemed, to stop a major spill at Boulder Dam.

"Paper-trained, I see," said Tim with a wicked grin.

"I'll say." She sighed. "Big bad dog." Dropping the towels onto the offense, she opened the back door. "Want to go out?" Lured by her inviting tone, Sushi dashed into the yard. "That's the trouble," Jody went on. "None of the books tells you how to unpaper-train them." Kneeling, she stuffed the enormous pile of paper towels into a plastic bag, and with a final swipe turned a grieved look to Tim. "The Sunday paper, napkins, you name it. You have to be on guard all the time."

"Maybe her own subscription?"

"God forbid." Squirting liquid detergent on her hands, she washed them under the tap, and studiously ignored the determined thumps and scratchings at the back door. "I love that woolly booger, but sometimes I could wring her neck." She pulled out a wooden tray and arranged thin rice crackers along one side, then turned to a glass-domed cheese container. One hand on the lid, she stared at it as if it were a crystal ball.

Gone away, again, he thought. He waved a hand in front of her face.

"Sorry," she said. "I was just thinking of something." She plucked off the lid and added Gruyere to the tray. "Let's go sit in front of the fire while dinner cooks."

Tim scooped up their wine glasses and followed.

"I thought we'd eat in the living room," she said.

"Fine." He glanced at the dining room's bare oak floor. "Unless you have a checkered cloth. I could go out and dig up a few ants."

She laughed. "Okay for you. People who make snide comments get to sit on packing crates."

"Do that again."

"Do what?"

"Laugh. I like it."

She smiled again. "You're making me self-conscious. Oh, darn." The pressed-log fire had degenerated into wispy curls of smoke.

"Needs some help," said Tim. "Do you have any newspaper?"

"No. It took all I had to get this going. Wait." She rummaged through a basket and handed him a stack of thin catalogues. "Will these do?" she asked, retrieving a fall L. L. Bean. "They're out of date."

With the help of two wadded Sears supplements and a Publishers Central, Tim got the little fire going again. They settled back on the couch to sip wine and listen to his Alex de Grassi tape. The scent of smoke permeated the room.

Tim sniffed thoughtfully. Not your regular hardwood fire. A strange foreign odor overlaid the whole.

"Oh, God." Jody jumped to her feet and raced to the kitchen with Tim in pursuit. She snatched the pot off the burner. A sharp scorched odor mingled with the rich tomato and basil smell. "Damn. I meant to turn it down."

Tim poked the wooden spoon into the sauce and dragged it experimentally across the bottom. A thick gummy layer was stuck to the pot, but the rest of it seemed all right. "It's okay, I think. If you don't scrape."

Jody stared doubtfully at the spoon. An inch of blackened sauce coated the bowl.

"Really. It's okay," he said. "It's a deep pot." Deep pots were best. You could almost always rescue an inch or so of stew or whatever from them.

"Well," she said. "I guess I'd better get the spaghetti on." She rummaged through the pantry and stared at the assortment of cereal boxes and cake mixes in disbelief. "This can't be happening. I'm out." She looked again. "I really am. I'm out of noodles." Incongruously, she began to giggle. In moments the giggle grew into a rich, irresistible laugh and she flourished a can of kidney beans under his nose. "Are you game for some experimental Italian chili?"

"Well," he began with what he hoped was a grave look. "In the name of international relations—"

"Mother would die," said Jody, transferring the unruined portion of spaghetti sauce to another pot. She stirred in the kidney beans along with a generous shake of chili powder. "All she ever wanted was for me to be elegant." Brow furrowed, she held out a spoonful to Tim. "What do you think?"

He took a taste. "Needs something." He found a jar of cocktail onions on the pantry shelf and pried off the lid.

"Here we go." The onions slid into the sauce with a plop. Tim seized the spoon, scooped up a pale glutinous blob, and waved it under her nose. "Eye of newt."

Jody stared into the pot, doubt creasing her forehead.

A speculative look at the spice rack. "And toe of frog." He shook in a generous sprinkle of red pepper flakes, and, as inspiration struck, followed it with a blood-curdling witch's cackle and a mist of garlic powder. "Wool of bat and tongue of dog."

"It was actually edible," Jody observed.

"Beats Chandler Bryson anyway," said Tim with a grin. He leaned back and stared at the little fire, which was rapidly turning to embers.

Jody scooped up plates and bowls and headed for the kitchen. "Stay put," she said. "I'm not going to wash, just soak."

While she was gone, he put on another tape and paused in front of the etagere. The curved top shelves were full of opened pop-up books held in place by plate holders. The bottom shelves were full of more pop-ups, arranged library fashion.

"You've found my collection," said Jody. She brought coffee and Kahlua on a lacquered tray and set it down on the round table in front of the couch. "I loved pop-ups when I was a kid. Then a couple of years ago I found *Halley's Comet* in a used book store." She waved a hand at the shelf. "I guess you can see what that led to."

Tim reached for the cabinet door. "Mind if I take a look?"

"No," she said. Then suddenly, "Yes."

She was staring at the cabinet, embarrassment written on her face. "Go ahead," she said finally. "It's all right."

Curious, he opened the case. He found the source of her

discomfort between *The Little Tin Soldier* and *The Beatles Pop-Up Book* and pulled it out with a grin. Plopping down beside her on the couch, he flourished the book. *"The Pop-Up Kama Sutra,* eh?" He opened the book and a sloe-eyed couple locked in a naked embrace rose off the page. Grasping the covers, he slowly opened and closed. "Look at that. Animation and everything."

Grinning at the twin spots of red on Jody's cheeks, he began to read out loud:

". . . Enlarging the penis, or lingam. First rub your lingam with wasp stings and massage it with sweet oils. When it swells, let it hang for ten nights through a hole in your bed, going to sleep each night on your stomach.

"After this period, use a cool ointment to remove the pain and swelling. By this method, men like Vithas, of insatiable sexual appetite, manage to keep their lingams enlarged throughout their lives. . . ."

Tim whistled softly. "You've got to be really dedicated to your lingam." He slid an arm around her shoulder and nuzzled her nose with his. "Huh?"

She did not quite meet his eyes. "I guess so."

"Fortunately," he said, pulling her closer, "there are those of us whose lingams are more, uh, forthcoming than poor old Vithas." Another nuzzle. "Huh?"

"Uh-oh," she whispered. "Here we go."

"Hmmm," he said with his lips against hers. "Yes. Yes, indeedy."

When the phone rang, Tim opened groggy eyes and fumbled for the receiver. Before he could answer, Jody plucked it out of his hand. "Hello."

Frowning, she sat up, clutching sheet and quilt to her chest. "When? When did it start?" She listened, then said, "No, it's okay." She glanced at her watch, holding her wrist at an angle to catch the light coming from the hall. "Twenty minutes," she said and hung up.

"What's up?" He reached for his pants.

"It was the hospital." She pulled on the pink sweater and picked up her jeans from the floor. "Beth Quaig has been crying for over an hour. She's stuck in an infant personality and the nurse doesn't know what to do. It's time for her to go home, but she doesn't want to leave with Beth in that kind of shape."

Tim put on his shoes and checked his watch. It was nearly midnight. "Want me to drive you?"

Jody shook her head. "We'd better take both cars. But when we get there you need to meet me in the Rutledge lobby unless you don't mind walking up five flights of stairs. This late at night nobody except staff can use the elevators." She pulled on shoes and they headed down the stairs. Pausing to scoop up car keys from a pottery bowl, Jody checked the chain on the front door and turned toward the kitchen. "We'll go out the back way."

When Jody opened the kitchen door, Sushi rushed out from under the back porch and barked at Tim. She barred the dog's entry with a leg stretched across the door. "Can you step over?" she asked. "If I let her in, she'll hide and it'll take me ten minutes to get her out again."

He stepped partway, feigned loss of balance, and caught her shoulders lightly. Nuzzling her ear, he whispered, "Hate to eat and run."

Sushi, sensing something was up, gave a nervous yawn and planted a paw on her mistress's outstretched leg.

Jody laughed. "Between the two of you, I'll be stuck in the door until morning."

"Want company?"

She rolled her eyes, and with one hand reached down

and caught the dog's collar. With the other, she slammed the door after Tim and checked the lock. "You go first," she said, "while I hold her. I have nightmares about her getting out in traffic."

He nodded and crossed the dark lawn, half feeling his way toward a dim pool of light that splashed from under the eaves onto the chain-link fence flanking the driveway. The cold metal gate latch stung his hands.

He was closing the gate when Jody called out softly to him: "When we get there, I'd like you to look at Beth too. I want to know if this is what you saw last night."

The freckles on Mystery Carmody's nose had popped through their layer of makeup and the nurse's red hair clung to her forehead in damp little curls. The front of her uniform was wet.

"Am I glad to see you. None of this was in the job description, believe me." She headed for Beth Quaig's room and Tim and Jody followed.

The door to the dimly lit room swung open and bumped into a bedside screen. Carmody rolled her eyes. "She's got at least a dozen of those around her bed. It's like a storeroom. I tried to move them away, but she panicked, so I left them."

Muffled sobs were coming from across the room.

"I'm really sorry to call you in like this," Carmody whispered to Jody, "but Dr. Barkley disappeared after the EEG. I couldn't reach him for over an hour and when I finally got him on the phone, he said to call you."

"EEG?" Jody looked startled. "He ordered an EEG?"

"Ordered!" The nurse gave a short laugh. "He ran them himself. On Beth and Maureen Dorcas both." Carmody turned to Tim. "By the way, Barkley asked where you were earlier, but I don't know what he wanted. I told him you were with Jody." A sudden look of consternation crossed her face. "I hope you don't mind. I wasn't thinking."

"I guess you didn't break any laws," said Tim. But a look at Jody's face made him wonder.

Carmody's voice dropped as they approached the bed. "For a little while after the EEG, Beth was okay. Then this." She pushed the last screen aside, rolling it between the bed and the light fixture. The blue-white fluorescent bulb glowing through the yellowed cloth faded Beth Quaig's skin to a sickly ivory. "I was going to call her family, but I couldn't find any next of kin on her chart and there aren't any Quaigs in the phone book."

"Beth doesn't live here," said Jody. "She's from Alabama."

"I know. But she must have somebody here. When I was looking for an address, I found a bunch of Greyhound ticket stubs in her handbag. Half a dozen at least. A couple were to New Orleans, but the rest were for Atlanta. It looks like she does a lot of shuttling back and forth."

Tim looked down at the girl. It was an instant replay. She was wearing the same wrinkled pink pajamas from last night, and her thumb was in her mouth. Her eyes, round and blank with fear, stared past them, darting from side to side as they followed a horror only she could see. Gummy streaks of EEG paste streaked her temples.

Jody touched Tim's arm. "Was this the way you found her last night?"

He nodded slowly. But something was different. He couldn't put his finger on just what.

"I asked her if she wanted to shower, you know, wash her hair, get rid of that gunk, but she said she was tired. She wanted to go to bed, so I brought in a basin." Carmody glanced at the bedside table. A limp washcloth was submerged in a yellow plastic washbasin. Several sopping wet towels were wadded next to it. Tim suspected that most of the water had ended up on the floor.

"She's strong. You wouldn't believe."

"She fought you?" Jody was staring at Beth.

"More of a panic reaction, I think. It was the strangest thing. She was in bed when I brought in the basin. I'd turned my back, just for a moment, when I heard this guttural noise—it was almost like an animal—and she grabbed my collar. From behind." The nurse's hand moved toward her throat. "I thought I'd choke before she let go. And water all over.

"Then she went limp, and the next thing you knew, she was like this. Like a baby." Fatigue creased Carmody's brow and widened her eyes. "I couldn't stop her from crying."

"You're worn out," said Jody. "Go home, okay? I'll take care of this."

The relief on Mystery Carmody's face was quickly replaced with doubt. "You sure? I don't want to run out or anything."

"You're not running out. Have you signed off your charts?"

The nurse nodded.

"Then scoot."

"Okay, then. I'm gone." Grabbing the basin and towels, Carmody left.

Jody pulled a chair close to the bed and watched Beth for half a minute. Then she touched the girl's shoulder. "Beth. Bethie."

Tim remembered something. "It's 'Beffie,'" he said. "The other one, the teenager, called her that. She said she couldn't pronounce 'Bethie.'"

Jody nodded and leaned toward the girl. "Beffie, listen

to me. I want to talk to somebody else now. I'm going to count backward from ten. Very slowly. Do you understand? When I get to one, if anyone else is here, they can come in. Okay?" She smoothed the girl's hair. "Go to sleep now. Everything's all right."

A muffled sob.

"I'm going to begin now, Beffie. Just lie still and go to sleep. Ten . . . nine . . ."

The girl blinked and drew up her legs.

"Eight . . . seven . . . six . . . five . . ."

Beth's thumb slipped from her lips and her eyelids fluttered, then dragged shut.

"Four . . . three . . ."

Tim stared down at the girl. It was like watching a wax figure melt in the sun. Her body was limp now. Like a little kid's rag doll, he thought.

"Two . . . one. . . ." A moment passed. "I'd like to talk to Beth now," said Jody. "Will you talk to me, Beth?"

The eyes opened, glittered darkly, slid toward Tim.

He felt a sudden chill. Not Beth. It wasn't Beth.

"Talk to me," Jody prodded.

A mirthless smile parted the lips. "You know me." The voice was harsh and unmistakably masculine: "My name is Jonathan. . . ."

TWENTY-ONE

The startling change that came over Beth made Jody draw back involuntarily. Stay cool, she told herself. She had seen transformations like this before. Often, in fact. But she had expected a woman, and Beth Quaig's round face had transmuted into the hard angular features of a man.

It was an illusion, she knew, but a good one. The kind of illusion that professional impressionists conjure: one moment, John Wayne, the next, Richard Nixon, and as you watch, the face changes—or seems to change—to match the voice.

"Talk to me," she said.

Light from the bedside lamp etched the brow; shadows darkened the eyes. The voice was deep and male: "You know me. My name is Jonathan."

Jonathan! The same words she had seen on Tim's computer screen only a few hours ago.

Jody's eyes widened, then darted to Tim. He was staring at Beth, his face suddenly white.

"Did you talk to her?" she whispered. "Tell her about your work?"

Tim shook his head.

A chill crept up the nape of her neck. Coincidence. That was all. It had to be. But she took no comfort from the thought. She didn't believe it for a moment.

A sound from the bed. A low, childish giggle.

The harsh male features abruptly molded themselves into the face of a little girl. But she wasn't the thumb-sucking toddler of a few minutes ago. This one was older. Five or six, Jody guessed.

Blinking, the eyes oriented, widened.

"Hello," said Jody, making her voice soft.

The voice of a child: "You're not my doctor."

"No. I'm not. But I talk to people just like your doctor does." Scarcely able to conceal the sudden trembling of her hands, Jody pulled her chair close to the bed. How? How could this happen? Was it proof of her unspoken, off-the-wall theory? Her half-facetious, half-serious notion that multiples—some of them, anyway—were psychic. She suddenly thought of Robert, thin, fourteen years old and no larger than a child of seven, scarred body and soul from juvenile diabetes—and from the little wires and tweezers his mother had brought to his room each night since he was a baby. Robert, who could, impossibly, read her mind and peer into the dark corners of her soul.

Jody stole another quick look at Tim. Pale. Jaw set. She turned to the child-woman huddled on the bed. "I'd like to talk to you. Is that all right?"

Her face was round and ingenuous. "Okay, I guess."

"Can you tell me your name?"

The lip-curled scorn of a kindergartner. "Course I can. I can do lots of things."

"I'll bet you can," said Jody. "What's your name?"

"Tabby. Tabby for short."

Tabby? She'd heard that before. Where?

"Wanna know what I can do?"

"Tell me."

Cupping her hands around her mouth, the girl leaned close. Her whisper was a tickling little gust in Jody's ear. "Magic."

Jody blinked. There was no way Robert could have known, no way at all, but he did. It had been a soft spring day, a day for green buds and jonquils yellow as the sun. At dawn they had put her father on the respirator. She could never forget his eyes. Alert. Intelligent. Bright with fear. Live things trapped in a used-up body that needed tubes to feed it, tubes to drain away its waste—and now a tube in his throat, rusty with blood, glistening with mucus. Lou Gehrig's disease. Amyotrophic lateral sclerosis. A prison. A cell that shrank day by day, until it was no larger than a pair of eyes. Quite suddenly she imagined them growing dim, glazing with death. Dimming, closing, never opening again.

No. She couldn't think that. Wouldn't.

Not until later. Not until Robert had raised his head and met her eyes. "You want him to die, don't you? You want him dead." And shockingly, she knew it was true.

With an effort, Jody concentrated on the girl in the bed. "Magic," she repeated.

A nod, eager, excited. "Wanna see me?"

"Sure."

"I do it like this." Tabby's fingers crept to her stubby nose and grasped it between thumb and forefinger.

The girl was wiggling her nose, pushing it back and forth. Puzzled, Jody stared, until a sudden memory nearly made her laugh. Tabby-for-short was Tabitha. The child from the television show—what was the name of it?—*Bewitched.*

"What kind of magic can you do, Tabby?"

"Lots of things. I can make people go away. Stuff like that."

"Did you make Jonathan go away."

A giggle. "Uh-huh."

Interesting. Was Tabby the gatekeeper? "Can you make other people come and go too? Beth maybe?"

The girl glanced warily at Tim, then back at Jody and nodded. Her voice dropped to a whisper again. "There's lots of people in here. Sometimes they get real mad. But I don't care."

Jody gave her a grave look. "How old are you?"

"Five and a half." A moment's thought. "Almost."

"You're a big girl then." Five and a half. A forever child, frozen in time. She wondered how old Beth had been when she created Tabby. The same age? Younger? Beth had created a little girl no bigger than she was, and on the surface just as vulnerable. But Tabby was magic. Powerful. She could make Beth go away, disappear—hide from the grown-ups who wanted to hurt her. Suddenly Jody's heart clenched at the thought of a snub-nosed child who had needed magic to survive.

She wanted to ask, "Who hurt you? Your mother? Your father? Both of them? Did they both come at night to your crib?" Instead, she clasped her hands and squeezed until her fingers were cold. Her voice when it came was low. "Why was Beffie crying?"

"Losted. She got losted again."

"Does that happen a lot?"

Tabby nodded. "She's scared 'cause she's in the cellar and it's dark in there. She can't get the door open 'cause she's bad."

"Bad?"

"Daddy said."

"Has Beffie been in the cellar before?"

A nod. "She's scared. Maybe nobody won't come get her out this time."

God.

"She gets nightmares down there."

"What nightmares? What happens?"

Tabby stroked an index finger, stroked, pulled. "There's a big gun." She stared at her finger intently. "It's stuck in her mouth." She looked up, cocked her finger at Jody. "Click." She blinked solemnly. "There isn't any bullet. But she knows the next time there will be."

Nausea crept in Jody's stomach. "Who's in the dream, Tabby? Who's holding the gun?"

Tabby's gaze dropped to her finger again.

"Who's holding the gun?"

Brow furrowed, Tabby thought for a moment. A shrug. "I don't know."

Oh yes you do, thought Jody. Only it's just too dangerous to talk about, isn't it? And what about Jonathan? Is he dangerous too? Is that why you pushed him out so quickly? She eyed the girl speculatively. Barkley's sketchy data sheet had told her that Beth had been under a doctor's care for several years. It had referred to a couple of hospitalizations, but there had been no dates, no names, no places.

"Do you know your doctor's name?" she asked impulsively.

"Uh-huh."

"Can you tell me?"

"He's—" A giggle, then a finger to her lips, a whisper. "—Dr. Sh-hh."

A nickname? "What's his whole name?" Jody urged.

"Warts," she said. Another giggle. "Dr. Sh-hh Warts."

Sh-hh? Warts? Schwartz? "Dr. Schwartz?"

Tabby nodded.

"Can you tell me his first name?"

Tabby shook her head.

"Does he see you every week?"

"Sort of." Tabby tented two fingers and stared at them intently. "Mostly, he sees the other ones."

"I'll bet Dr. Schwartz thinks you're a good girl," said Jody, toying with a sudden notion. "Does he know you're here? In Atlanta?"

"Huh-uh."

Unbelievable. Had Barkley really brought Beth here without her doctor's permission?

"Are you sure?"

Tabby twisted away and began to chew her lower lip.

The question was obviously causing her a lot of stress. "It's okay," said Jody quickly. But an idea was growing, and she couldn't let it go. According to Barkley's cheat sheet, Beth lived in Birmingham. A big enough town, but it wouldn't be hard to track her doctor down. How many psychiatrists or psychologists named Schwartz could there be?

There you go, idiot, she thought. Jody Henson, Super Girl. Able to leap tall ground rules at a single bound. But she knew she was going to do it—she was going to contact Schwartz, and the hell with Barkley. What choice was there, anyway? Was she supposed to stand by and watch Beth deteriorate while Barkley sanctimoniously preserved his sacred pilot study?

A quick thought undermined her hastily constructed rationale: she had been asking Tabby questions that Beth could have answered in a moment, awkward questions that Beth might repeat to Dr. Barkley. But—clever girl—she had known that five-year-old Tabby wouldn't do that.

The truth then. The truth was she wanted to ask Schwartz if he knew about Jonathan. If he didn't, then maybe Beth had really somehow read Tim's thoughts.

And if Schwartz did know?

Jody stole a sidelong look at Tim. He was staring at the girl, tension in every line of his body.

She turned back to Tabby. "You know, it's way past Beth's bedtime. Why don't you let her come back so she can go to sleep?"

Tabby pulled up a leg and thoughtfully scratched her knee. "He better go then." Her eyes slid toward Tim. "He scared her last time."

Jody and Tim exchanged glances, then he turned abruptly and went to the door.

"We'll both go," said Jody. "Okay?"

When Tabby nodded, Jody switched off the bedside lamp and the room plunged into darkness except for a yellow rectangle of light from the open hallway door.

Jody joined Tim in the dimly lit hall. When she touched his arm, he turned sharply toward her. "Any explanations? Any theories as to why one of my fictional characters decided to move in with Beth Quaig?"

The edge in his voice made Jody uneasy. Was the girl psychic, like Maureen? Or was it something else? "Maybe she saw what you wrote."

Shadows darkened his eyes. "Impossible."

"She could have gone to your room, looked at your computer screen."

"No. The computer was off. I put it in the locker before I left."

Schwartz, then. Maybe he could shed a little light. First thing in the morning she intended to call him and find out what he knew about Jonathan. She frowned at the half-formed thought hovering in the back of her mind. Something about the seance—something Paul had said. "That tape you made in Maureen's room—where is it?"

Tim patted the tape case slung over his shoulder.

"I want to hear it again."

His eyes grew suddenly tired.

He's worn out, she thought. No sleep last night. Now this. "Never mind. It can wait."

"It's all right. The tape recorder's in my room. Come on."

When they came to his room, he pushed open the door and switched on the lights. Halfway to his locker, he stopped short.

"What is it?"

"Look. Look at this." He pointed to the metal locker. It stood ajar. "Son of a bitch." He reached it in two strides and yanked the door wide open.

"Is anything missing?" She could see the tape recorder propped next to a pair of boots.

Squatting beside the locker, he pulled out the computer case and unzipped it. The machine was still there. "Thank God," he whispered. Snapping open his disk box, he looked inside. The disks made little clicking sounds as he checked them. "It's all here." He looked up at her. "I don't know what the fucker was after, but it wasn't a computer."

"Maybe the door wasn't locked," she said. "Maybe you left it open."

He shook his head. "No way. I know I locked it."

"But you could have—" she began.

"Yeah?" he said harshly. "I could be stupid. I could have lapses of memory too. Is that what you're saying?"

"No. Just lapses in common sense," she said sharply. "I'll see that you get another padlock in the morning." Turning stiffly, she headed for the door.

He caught up with her before she had tugged it open. "I'm sorry." Taking her shoulders in his hands, he turned her around and brushed her forehead with his lips. Almost against her will, she felt her annoyance begin to drain away.

"I'm a little paranoid about that computer. I didn't mean to take it out on you. Come on back," he said softly. "We'll play that tape."

Jody stared at him for a long moment without speaking. He looked as contrite as a child caught with a fist full of contraband cookies.

He cupped her chin in his hand. "Hate me?"

How could she?

"Will I make it better if I eat worms?" he asked. "I can make my chin quiver if I try real hard."

She tried not to smile. "You're playing on my sympathy."

"Would I do that?"

"Uh-huh."

He grinned. "Tape time?"

The tension slid away, leaving her fatigued. "I wasn't thinking. It's really too late. We can play it tomorrow, okay?" She started to turn toward the door again. Instead, she ended up in his arms.

"You can't leave now," he whispered. "Something's come up. Just like in the pop-up book."

"You're incorrigible," she said, laughing.

"Not so very." His kiss teased the corner of her lips.

"It's much too late for bedtime stories," she said with more resolve than she felt. "It's time to close the book and get some sleep."

"Do I have to, Mommy?"

"Uh-hum." Extricating herself from his grasp, she gave him a warm, but final, good-night kiss and reached for the doorknob.

When the elevator door slid open on the ground floor, any thoughts of sleep Jody harbored had vanished and she decided abruptly not to go home. Not yet. There was no way she'd get any sleep. Not with so many questions churning around in her head.

She wanted a cup of coffee and some light conversation. Anything to get her mind off the thoughts she kept pushing away. Funny how coffee never kept her awake. For a wake-up, she needed the sweet jolt that orange juice carried—or else something to prey on her mind.

Impulsively she turned right and headed for the Emergency Room hoping that Cheryl was on duty.

The E.R. waiting room was nearly empty. A middle-aged ward secretary, a woman Jody did not recognize, was at the desk.

"Is Cheryl Isaacson on tonight?" Jody asked. "If she is, I'd like to speak to her."

The woman glanced up from an admittance form and gave her a suspicious look. "Are you with a patient?"

"I'm on staff here," she said, wishing she had worn a lab coat. If she had, she could have walked right in without anyone noticing. "I'm an old friend." A long lost friend, she thought with a twinge of guilt. They had been as close as sisters all through nursing school, but since graduation, except for a few early evening movie dates, and a drunken weekend spent dredging up war stories and lolling on a houseboat on Lake Chatuge, they had scarcely seen each other. Their big plans to work together had gone out the window when Cheryl, night owl that she was, decided the graveyard shift was the quickest way for a brand-new graduate to advance. She was a nursing supervisor now, and a part of Jody's past that seemed to grow more vague every year.

The ward secretary's dubious look took in Jody's jeans and sweater. "Your name?"

"Jody Henson."

With a faint groan, the woman got to her feet. "I'll see if she's available." She disappeared through one of the doors leading back to the E.R.'s inner sanctum.

Jody looked around the waiting room. Not much business tonight from the looks of it. A black mother was doling out vending machine cheese crackers to a toddler in faded He-Man pajamas. Across the aisle a bleary-eyed young man with the shakes was hunched between two buddies. Hoping for a bed on the detox unit, she guessed. Half a dozen others were scattered on benches throughout the large room. Probably waiting for someone inside, she decided. None of them looked sick to her.

The door opened and the ward secretary came back to her desk and sat down heavily before she looked at Jody. "Miss Isaacson says for you to go on in." She nodded toward the door marked MEDICAL.

Inside, the broad tiled hallway was studded with treatment rooms down its length. A door on the left opened and a young nurse pushing an empty wheelchair gave Jody a curious stare. "Do you have a slip?"

A voice from behind the girl said, "It's okay, Morris," and Cheryl Isaacson stepped out. "Hi, stranger." Her smile lit up brown eyes behind a pair of round tortoise-shell glasses so large they seemed to cover half her small face. She reached into a pocket of a green scrub suit defaced with overlapping black-stenciled CHANDLER BRYSONS, and pulled out a pack of cigarettes and a lighter. "Let's go hide while I have a cigarette," she said.

"Only if we stop at the coffee pot on the way."

"You're on."

They went into a tiny nurses lounge furnished with a once-white plastic couch and a sagging card table that held a coffee pot and foam cups. Lighting a cigarette, Cheryl balanced it on the battered lip of a purple aluminum ashtray and snagged a paper napkin. She pulled off her glasses, misted the lenses with a breath, and began to polish. "Every night about now I need a guide dog," she said, holding them up to the light, surveying for streaks and specks. "Look at that," she said, rubbing again. "Benzoin all over."

"There's no telling where they've been," said Jody.

Cheryl laughed suddenly. "Remember the culture?"

Jody looked blank for a second, then grinned. Back in nursing school, just before their senior finals, Cheryl had solemnly streaked an agar plate with glasses swabbings and sent it to the lab with a slip made out in the name of Mr. I. M. Sikh-Azahdawg. The lab report had come back positive for pseudomonas.

She settled the glasses on her nose. "So, what made you decide to come down to the inner sanctum? Homesick for bedpans and emesis basins?"

Before Jody could answer, Cheryl glanced at the door and jumped up. A tall police officer was leaning against the doorjamb, grinning at them both. Cheryl caught his hand in hers. "Well, hi. What brings you back in tonight?"

"Another DUI. Karen's down the hall drawing a blood alcohol," said the man. "The guy's a real jewel. He says if she leaves a bruise, he'll sue."

"She can handle him." Cheryl pulled him into the room and said to Jody, "I want you to meet somebody." Her eyes slid toward his, then back, and a self-conscious smile quirked her lips. "We're going to be married."

"Married! The two of you?" Jody flushed. Why couldn't she dial in her brain before she opened her mouth? "I mean that's great. When?"

"The Saturday after Thanksgiving. You'll come, won't you?"

"Of course." She hadn't even known that Cheryl was going with anyone. "Of course I will."

The policeman took Jody's hand. "I'll bet you have a name."

"Jody." She stared down blankly at the hand that covered hers. Little black hairs studded the backs of his fingers. "Jody Henson." Suddenly she wondered if Tim was still awake.

"God, I'm sorry," said Cheryl. "Jody, this is James." Then with a touch of pride, "James D. Young, the second."

So, Cheryl was going to be Mrs. James D. Young, the second. It sounded like royalty. What would their son be? James the third? James the Younger?

"Are you a nurse?" asked James the Elder, releasing her hand. "I haven't seen you around the E.R."

"I used to be." She tentatively decided she liked his smile and his big woolly mustache.

"Jody and I went to school together," Cheryl explained. "But she's a psychologist now."

"Almost," Jody corrected.

"She's slumming tonight."

"Actually, it's research. I'm doing a paper for *The Journal of Irreproducible Results:* 'The Emergency Room Considered as a Cure for Insomnia.'"

"Yeah?" James grinned. "I've got a project of my own that can't wait: *Work Considered as a Cure for Starvation."* He gave Cheryl a quick peck on the cheek. "See you in the morning," he said, and went off to collect his DUI.

"He's nice," Jody said when he had gone, and wondered whether they were living together.

"I may be prejudiced, but I think you're right." The plastic couch cushion wheezed as Cheryl sat down. "You must think I'm out of my mind to marry a cop."

"No," said Jody, but she was wondering how anyone

could. How could you watch your husband go off to work knowing this might be the last day, the last time, you'd see him alive?

"At least, working here, if something happens to him, I'll probably be the first to know."

"That's not funny," Jody blurted.

"You're damn right it isn't." Cheryl sucked deeply on her cigarette and watched the smoke curl in a lazy spiral toward the ceiling. "I almost decided not to go through with it, thinking about that. I probably should have hooked up with a stockbroker or an insurance salesman. But you don't meet many of those in the E.R."

No, thought Jody. You meet cops. And you meet interns and residents. Lots of those—and all of them married.

"Anyway, for better or worse, I'm stuck with it. I love that big dude." Cheryl put her feet up and wriggled a heel out of her white loafer. "God, I'm beat. I'm still used up from last week."

"Rough weekend?" Jody took a swallow of coffee and grimaced. The stuff tasted like it was left over from breakfast.

"Weekend? It's been a zoo for the last ten days."

"It's quiet enough now," Jody observed.

"Sh-hh," hissed Cheryl. "You know better than that."

"Sorry," whispered Jody with a wicked grin. "I didn't mean to attract the evil eye." Raising her voice to normal, she addressed the walls: "It's been hell tonight. It really has. One thing after another—drunks, car wrecks, crazed murderers . . ."

"Drunks, yes." Cheryl sighed. "We can't get through the night without them. But I sure as hell can get along without another killing."

"Another?" What was it she was hearing in Cheryl's tone?

She stubbed out her cigarette and turned to Jody. "The kid last week. You must have seen it on the news."

"You mean that little girl?"

Cheryl nodded. "D-string killer four, police nothing. Five now—the waitress Saturday night. But I was off, thank God." She was silent for a moment. "You know me. I've assisted the medical examiner before; I can take things in my stride, right?" Her gaze slid away. "Did you ever see a garrote victim?"

"No."

"You don't ever want to, believe me. It sliced through that kid's trachea like a knife. It nearly took her head off." Her eyes came back to Jody's. "She was only thirteen. Thirteen years old." Cheryl fished in the scrub suit pocket for another cigarette and lit it. "You know, I didn't think anything could get to me anymore. You work here, you see everything. But this—" She bit her lip. "I thought about quitting. I really did. I mean, a wreck, a heart attack—you can do something. But this—" Her eyes hardened. "When they catch that bastard, I hope they cut his balls off."

"That might not be feasible. That is, if the killer turns out to be a woman," said Jody lightly, hoping to defuse the conversation.

"No way," said Cheryl.

"You can't be sure of that. Not really."

"I'm sure."

"How?" They weren't sex crimes; none of the victims were raped. "It doesn't take a lot of strength to strangle somebody with a wire." Especially when the somebody was a child or a small woman.

"You didn't see that kid," said Cheryl. "I did."

"Then it *was* rape," Jody whispered.

"I didn't say that."

"What then?"

"You don't always get the whole story on the evening news, you know. When you go with a cop, you find out the police don't let the media in on everything." Cheryl did not speak for nearly half a minute. Then she said, "I shouldn't be telling you this, so keep it quiet, but they found something near each victim. It looked like this—" She pulled out a pen and drew something in red ink on the paper napkin.

Jody tried to make it out. It looked like a fluffy cloud, but it was covered with crisscrossed markings as if a fish net had been pulled over its surface. "What do they think it means?"

"Nobody knows. What we do know is the killer left a signature."

"You mean the cloud you just drew."

"No. I mean a signature. He carved his fucking name on her body." Cheryl stabbed her cigarette into the ashtray and stared at the dying wisp of smoke. "She was naked when they brought her in. A skinny little kid. And there it was.

"That's how I knew." Cheryl's lips tightened to a thin, bloodless line. "It's a man, all right," she said. "His name is Jonathan."

TWENTY-TWO

As soon as Jody left his room, Tim went through his locker again, checking and double-checking everything inside. He was sure he had locked it, but the lock was old; even a ten-year-old could break in. Yet, nothing made sense. Why would somebody go through his stuff and then leave without taking anything?

His jaw tightened. When he found out who had done it, he was going to flatten the son of a bitch. It could have been anyone, but the most likely candidate in his book was the creep orderly hanging around the hall last night. Somebody had probably spotted the guy, scared him away before he had a chance to rip off anything.

Resolving to ask around in the morning, Tim pulled out his tape recorder and put on the Bob James. He ran a stream of water in the sink and was brushing his teeth when a knock came at the door. It was probably Dayton Satterfield with another one of his headaches. If he'd come to complain about the music, he had damn good ears. When the knock came again, Tim spit out toothpaste and, tipping his head, sucked a quick rinse from the tap. "All right. I'm coming," he muttered, his tongue exploring a dab of toothpaste still clinging to a molar.

But it was not Satterfield at the door. It was Maureen Dorcas.

"I know it's almost one o'clock," she said, "but I saw your light." She crossed her arms over her chest and began to pluck the fuzzy pink sleeves of her sweat suit as if she were cold, or nervous.

"Really?" he said. Maureen's room was on the same side of the hall as his; how could she have seen?

"That's not exactly true," she amended. "I heard you come in a while ago. I wanted to catch you alone."

Was this some sort of bizarre seduction scene? Lonely middle-aged psychic comes on to insomniac novelist? A joke, maybe? He searched her face for some sign of it, but the clear blue eyes that had been so full of mischief when they first met were guarded. "What can I do for you?" he asked cautiously.

"Last night when you were in my room you made a tape. I need to hear it."

Though her voice was low, it was urgent. Quite suddenly he remembered his mother's voice coming to him in the middle of a winter's night when he was eighteen. "I need you," she had said. "I need you now." Galvanized by her tone, he had leaped out of bed and stared dumbly at his watch the way people did when they were disoriented. Three A.M. Three A.M. on Christmas Eve—and his father had just died.

"I have to hear it," Maureen repeated.

He stared at her for a moment, then stepped away from the door. "Come on in."

She pulled out a half-dozen folded sheets of notepaper from a pocket and sat down on the nearest bed.

He turned off the jazz tape and the room fell quiet. "Going to take notes?" he asked.

She shook her head, and he saw that something was already written on the pages. Something in a thin, spidery script.

Tim opened his cassette case and found the tape he had made of the seance. It needed labeling. He started to slide it into the machine, then pulled it out and broke the safety tabs off as a precaution. No need to take a chance with it, he thought, remembering the time he had inadvertently recorded an hour of radio jazz over a tape full of notes. Two months research down the drain.

The little speaker hissed and the tape began to play. The sound of Maureen's ragged breathing came from it, faint and hollow, as if she were a great distance away.

She leaned forward. "Can you make it louder?"

He shook his head. "That's it. Sorry."

The volume rose abruptly of its own accord, and he remembered that he had moved the machine closer.

Silence. Then the accented voice: "My name is Paul."

The tape somehow emphasized the alienness of the voice.

Tim studied Maureen's face. She was staring intently at the slowly moving tape as it played. What was she listening for?

Paul's voice again: . . . *You had better understand the weather pattern here or you will find yourself off course* . . . .

Tim stirred uneasily.

. . . *you are choosing not to listen.* . . .

He could almost feel the smooth thin wood of the Ouija board again.

. . . *In the night, in the swamp, you listen.* . . .

A chill crept up his spine, and his fingers twitched as if a planchette moved beneath them.

J-J-J-J-J-J-J-J . . .

. . . *Even this instrument refuses to see and hear, although she believes she does. Instead, she follows an impulse that is not her own.* . . .

Maureen's fingers tensed, worked the folded papers, creased, smoothed, creased again.

. . . *There is among you one you do not see, but who sees you.* . . .

Eyes glittering from a fissure of mud . . .

Tim blinked at the sudden image that had invaded his mind. His lungs felt empty.

. . . *A shadow. Growing.* . . .

The hoarse sound startled him. His gaze darted involuntarily to Maureen, but the sound was coming from the tape recorder.

"Shut it off," she said.

He stared at her dumbly.

Her hand groped outward. "Shut it off."

He reached for the switch.

"He's gone," she said.

Tim stared at her without comprehension.

"Paul. He's gone." Maureen's eyes darkened. "That's never happened before. He's always been around—ever since he first came." Her hand fluttered toward him like a small bird. "I could always sense him out there somewhere. But now he's gone."

Unsure of how to respond, Tim was silent.

"Do you understand?" she asked. "Something's happening here. And I don't like it." Maureen's gaze slid away, hesitated, slid back. "At first I thought it was me. I felt a little off center, so I tried meditation, but it didn't help. Then I tried automatic writing. It always put me in touch with Paul before," she said. "That's the way a lot of the book material came to me. But instead, this is what came." She thrust out the blue-lined notepapers.

Tim took them, unfolded them, read the first line: *You know me. My name is Jonathan.*

He caught his breath.

Maureen's hand moved to her throat again. "This Jonathan. He's the one who came during the seance," she said. Her voice dropped. "He's the one who tried to strangle me."

. . . *My name is Jonathan.* . . . it began.

He scanned the spidery lines. As he read, a chill grew in his belly. It was his story, his character sketch—paraphrased, but still his. The one he had written that afternoon. "How did you know this?" he demanded.

Maureen shook her head. "Finish reading it first."

Tim reached for a Winston, his fingers cold as he lit it. He took a deep drag, balanced the cigarette on the edge of the ashtray, and looked down at the paper again.

The second page began:

Cloud Net. . . .

He blinked. Looked up. Tried to read the look on Maureen's face.

"It's happening to you, too, isn't it?" she said.

"What do you mean?" He followed her gaze to the ashtray, where a moment before he had laid his freshly lit cigarette.

The Winston's filter was smoldering. Its unbroken ash was over two inches long.

TWENTY-THREE

Jody's fingers were stiff and cold even though the Volkswagen's heater was blowing warm air. There was something eerie about driving late at night. The streets were unnaturally quiet as if they were waiting for something. She loosened her grip on the steering wheel and took a long breath. Uneasily, she realized that somehow she had been waiting too.

Ridiculous. The car doors were locked, and she'd be home in a few minutes. But without conscious awareness, she tightened her fingers again.

Cheryl's talk of the D-string murders had shaken her. Until then, the killer who prowled the streets of Atlanta had had no more substance than a shadow—nameless, faceless, a dark fantasy sealed in a picture tube and trotted out on the evening news. But the name had made him real.

Jonathan. It was just a word, she told herself—a name on a computer screen, a name on the lips of a disturbed patient. A name carved on the dead body of a little girl. The coincidence made her shiver. Think warm, she told herself, trying to banish the cold jitters that crept across her arms and chest.

She turned onto her street. How dark it seemed. When she pulled into the driveway, the dim yellow glow of the light at the corner of the house seemed almost cheerful.

The Volkswagen's engine shuddered to a stop and she got out. What light there was dribbled away to almost nothing by the time it reached the gate. Lifting the latch, Jody stepped inside quickly, the way she always did, to keep Sushi from running out. But the little dog was not there.

Odd. She was always at the gate. "Sushi," she called softly. "Lazy thing. Where are you?"

There was no answer except the faint rustle of dry leaves in the wind.

She called again, and followed it with a low, summoning whistle.

Nothing.

"Sushi?"

Again, nothing.

A thin, sharp fear. Had she dug out? Run away? Jody's pupils were huge in the darkness as she scanned the fence. Please let her be here. Please.

She fumbled in the back pocket of her jeans for the penlight she always carried, switched it on, aimed it along the edges of the fence.

There. Something there. A dark mound, motionless beneath the oak.

Heart pounding, she ran to it. But it was only a pile of windblown leaves captured by the surface roots of the tree.

Jody tried to whistle again, but her mouth was too dry. "Sushi? Where are you?" She was only a puppy. A dumb little puppy. She didn't know about traffic.

The penlight flickered along the fence, skimmed the ground, came to rest on a chewed-up rubber bone. "Come back, puppy," she whispered. "Come back."

She walked the boundaries of the fence. Nothing. No hole. Nothing.

Under the back porch. She had to be there. Sound asleep, that was it. On hands and knees, she aimed the light beneath the porch. Only packed gray dirt and basement wall.

Shivering, Jody made another circuit of the yard, shining her light beneath every bush. Hiding, she tried to tell herself. Sushi was hiding the way she hid in the house when she didn't want to go out. Playing a game. A dumb puppy game. But a hollow feeling clutched at her belly and she knew it was not so.

She made her way to the back door, and though the kitchen light spilled through the window, sudden tears blurred her vision and she had trouble finding the lock. At last she got the key in, turned it, pushed open the door—and caught her breath. "Sushi!"

The little dog launched herself into Jody's arms.

Half falling, Jody knelt and clutched the dog. "Why didn't you bark? Why didn't you tell me you were here?" She stroked velvet ears with a hand that trembled from relief.

Sushi responded with a slurping dog kiss.

"Big bad thing. You were hiding again, weren't you?" But as soon as she said it, Jody knew it could not be true. She'd left Sushi in the back. In the yard.

A long, slow breath. "How did you get in?" she whispered. There was no way she could unless someone had opened the door.

Had they?

Had someone broken in while she was gone?

Her eyes darted around the kitchen. Just as she left it. Dishes still in the sink. Chili pot left to soak. But burglars didn't steal dirty dishes.

Holding the little dog close, she stared through the open door into the dining room. It was dark. Beyond it, a narrow ribbon of light from the entry hall lay on the living-room floor.

Someone had broken in. She knew it. Someone had come through the back door and Sushi had darted inside. She must have been hiding under the bed when he left.

If he left.

A cold shiver jittered along her spine. He could still be here. In the house. In the dark.

She had to call. Get the police. But the closest telephone was in the living room.

Sushi wriggled away and went to her water bowl. Not daring to move, Jody listened, straining to hear the slightest sound. All she heard was the pounding of her heart and the dog lapping.

Come on, she told herself sternly. Sushi might be a puppy, but she wasn't stupid. If anybody was here she'd react. She'd bark, run around, do something to show it.

Jody moved silently to the drainboard. The knife rack held half a dozen kitchen knives. She pulled out the largest. Clutching it, she moved along the wall as quietly as she could. At the door, she reached out and flashed on the dining-room lights.

Nothing. No one.

The light spilled into the living room beyond. She switched on the lamp and stared around the empty room. The TV was still there. Her grandmother's blue Wedgewood vase filled with dried Queen Anne's Lace still sat on the mantel. Her books were still here, and the stereo.

The cassette door on the tape deck was open. She was reaching over to close it when she saw the basket that held her stereo tapes. It lay on its side, a dozen cassettes spilling onto the floor.

She hadn't left them like that.

Still holding the knife, she knelt down and looked quickly through them. Nothing was missing, nothing she could see.

In the entry hall, red-uniformed paper soldiers still marched in their frame on the wall, and the security chain still clung to its hasp on the door.

Throwing on all the lights, she called the dog and together they went up the stairway.

Upstairs was quite empty. Nothing missing. Nothing at all. And yet she knew without the slightest doubt that someone had come into her house that night while she was gone.

Twice she reached for the phone to call the police, but each time she put the receiver back in its cradle without dialing. What could she tell them? What would they think? A hysterical woman forgot to put out the dog. And the spilled basket of tapes? Easy. Knocked over by a bored puppy left alone in the house.

She pulled off her clothes, put out the lights and got into bed, snuggling up to Sushi. The puppy curled up and fell asleep at once. But sleep did not come easily to Jody. Alert for any sound, she stared around the darkened room and reached out more than once to touch the little sleeping dog.

Someone had been here. She knew it. The empty violated feeling in her gut told her that.

TWENTY-FOUR

It was quite late when Hal Gulliver pulled up to his house. The shadowy ranch seemed bigger with Barbara gone. Too big for one person. He stabbed the remote control and the garage light flashed on, glowing yellow as the door cracked open and began to rise like the lid of an eye—the robot from *The Day the Earth Stood Still,* so Val had said when they first moved in twelve years ago. "Watch out!" she had screeched in mock terror. "Here comes the deadly laser beam." Rolling her eyes, she yelled, "Don't get me, Gort! *Klaatu, marenga nicto!"*

The thought of his daughter warmed him, and at the same time brought a furrow to his brow. She was barely twenty-four. A baby having a baby. The grandchild itself was an abstraction, no more real to him than the pink teddy bear Barbara had bought for it the day she left for Miami.

The garage door slid down, enclosing him in a yellow cocoon. He got out, climbed the four steps to the back door, and fumbled with the array of keys. There were three locks on each of the outside doors now. Val lived in Miami among the drug dealers and the crazies. How many locks would it take to make her safe when she was his age?

The fluorescent kitchen light gave off a dim blue-white glow that enhanced the shadows. The trashmasher was overflowing with newspapers, junk mail, and foam and cardboard containers from the take-out food that had sustained him while Barbara was gone. He thought of carrying the bag out, but the cleaning woman was due in the morning. No point in coddling her. Not at the rates she charged. He poured himself what was left of the cognac, deposited the empty on top of the overflowing trash, and frowned. It was Barbara's job to restock the liquor. She should have seen to it before she took off for Florida.

Carrying his cognac, he went into the living room. The aquarium light was still glowing. "They won't eat if the light is turned off," Barbara had said. He had solved that problem by leaving it on all the time. The water level had dropped an inch since she had left, and a thick scum of green algae had begun to creep up the glass. Good for them, he thought. Didn't it give off oxygen? Ignoring Barbara's written instructions and the measuring spoon she had left on top of the tank, he opened the lid and shook in a quantity of fish food, startling the big Angel, whose stripes had dimmed in sleep. Closing the lid, he polished off the rest of the cognac and left the glass on top of the tank.

The message light by the bedside phone was flashing. He rewound the tape and a computerized voice began a pitch for aluminum siding. He pressed the forward button and Barbara's voice came on: "Out with the mistress again, I see . . ." Gulliver smiled. "The mistress" was her term for the Agency. ". . . Val's in the hospital. She's not in labor, but they put her in as a precaution. Her water broke while she was sitting in the tub. Wouldn't you know it? A tub full of dirty bath water. Anyway, there's a chance of infection so they're giving her antibiotics. The doctor said if she doesn't do something pretty soon they're going to induce her. I got him to swear he'd phone me if she starts in tonight." A pause. "Well, that's all, I guess. Good-bye."

He stared at the phone. He wanted to call her back, find out what was happening, but it was much too late for that. She'd be asleep—unless Val had gone into labor. But he knew Barbara would have called again if that had happened. That is, if the hospital had bothered to let her know. Gulliver had no faith that the doctor would phone her. He narrowed his eyes. The guy was young, no doubt about that; they always were. After they built up a practice, raked in a little money, they gave up obstetrics and concentrated on female trouble. The hours were better, and the patients were older and more affluent. The idea of Val at the mercy of a faceless stud who was in it for the money made him set his jaw so hard that he jarred a tooth that was already loose.

Ignoring the dental plaque washes that Barbara had set out on the bathroom counter, he smeared toothpaste on his brush and took a few listless swipes at his teeth. When he spit into the sink, a pink streak dribbled toward the drain. Jesus. Blood again. Although he knew it was inevitable, he resisted going to the dentist. No time, he told himself, but in truth, he knew it was the vulnerability he dreaded, the instruments in his mouth, the extractions, the aftermath. He viewed his body exactly the same way he viewed everything else in his life: control it, or it controls you.

Stripping down to his underwear, Gulliver stared at the unmade bed with distaste, and haphazardly arranged the covers. At least the cleaning woman would take care of it tomorrow. Before she left, Barbara had tried to get her to come in every day while she was gone, instead of twice a week, but the woman had been too damned independent for that, even though her only other job was on Saturdays. Typical. That's what came of paying them too much.

He crawled into bed, and tried to relax, but the sheets felt gritty from the cheese and crackers he had eaten last night. He gave the bottom sheet a savage swipe and managed to brush most of the crumbs onto the floor. Switching off the bedside lamp, he closed his eyes, but he was too keyed up to sleep; his thoughts kept going back to Val and the faceless doctor she had so much faith in. The obstetrician had become a green youth in Gulliver's mind. A punk—practicing medicine until he got it right. His jaw tightened when he thought of her in labor—frightened, in pain. He did not like the idea of the doctor playing around with her body, as if she were an animal in a lab. He wondered how they brought on a baby. Drugs. Needles. What else? The image came to him of glittering vicious instruments and he pushed the thought away abruptly. If Val went into labor in the morning, it could mean a baby by this time tomorrow. Maybe sooner.

So much for the Wednesday child that Barbara's fortune teller had prophesied.

A hundred dollars thrown away on bullshit. His lip curled. But jarringly, he thought of Pointer's phone call about the Dorcas woman. A seance. A fucking seance. Barkley should have been on the scene when they showed up. He should have kept them busy—with shit work, if necessary. Anything to keep them from getting together and playing mind games.

Barkley was too goddamned independent. Like the cleaning woman, he thought suddenly, playing with the analogy. When you got right down to it, the work they did wasn't much different. Both of them were paid, and paid dear, to tuck things away, out of sight—like the summer camp fiasco.

The Agency had had to play C.Y.A for years to cover that one.

To be fair, it had not been Barkley's responsibility alone, even though he had been in charge of Camp Challenge in the Smokies—or at least in charge of the medical end of the operation. Dr. Clifford Montgomery, a man Gulliver had never known, had been running the show back then, back when Barkley was a green young doc barely out of his residency. It was ultimately Montgomery's responsibility, but he had been a thousand miles away at the camp in the Adirondacks when the kid died of anaphylaxis.

Ironically, Montgomery had barely outlived the boy. Only hours after the child's death, Montgomery had flown in to Camp Challenge to investigate. Before morning, the neurologist was dead of a massive heart attack, and Richard Barkley, by default, was the new medical director of HALFLIFE.

By the time Gulliver had inherited the operation, Barkley had contrived to make himself indispensable. No one could make sense of his cryptic notes without a translation. Like a computer programmer creating a program nobody else could run, he presented himself as an initiate in an arcane science far too deep for a mere layman like Gulliver to comprehend. From God's mouth to Barkley's ear. But the neurologist hadn't figured Phillip Sessions into the equation; he hadn't figured on another high priest who knew the same tricks. Tonight's meeting with Sessions had settled the issue in Gulliver's mind. Push or shove, by the end of the week Barkley would be out.

The thought of Sessions made Gulliver's skin crawl. But

the man came with a big plus: he was controllable. And he was already close enough to Barkley's game plan to take over HALFLIFE without too much lag time. With nothing much to go on except an artfully edited scenario, Sessions had come up with a hypothesis that paralleled Barkley's almost point for point.

It had been eerie, sitting there, listening to the man. For a fleeting moment, Gulliver had had the feeling he was being duped, that somehow Sessions knew about HALFLIFE and was playing head games. When that moment passed, a more disturbing one came: the notion that HALFLIFE was transparent somehow, evident to anyone who thought about mind control, an open book to any neurologist who knew the language. For the rest of the evening the idea had nagged at him, bringing an urgency to the meeting that he had not foreseen.

They had anticipated parallel enemy activity long ago, of course, but it had been an intellectual exercise, a series of what-ifs: what if the Soviets come up with a home-brewed version of HALFLIFE? What if they score a breakthrough first? What-ifs and what-thens; that was how you played the game. But the feeling tonight was different. It had gripped him in the gut.

The game wasn't a new one. They had been playing it for almost forty years, starting back when the cold war heated up and brainwashing was the new toy out of the box. It had led to MKULTRA and the LSD experiments. From there it had branched into dozens of different directions: the amnesia research with prisoners; the behavioral work at the Scientific Engineering Institute near Boston; the contracts with Parke, Davis and the other drug companies; the parapsychology research that ORD pioneered . . . The list went on and on. But none of them had shown the promise of HALFLIFE.

Sessions had known intuitively how it worked, how to program the construct, how to sequester it in secret parts of the brain. He had known how it could lie hidden, latent, out of reach, until it was needed. He had even known about the need for right brain language . . .

Twenty-two children at Camp Challenge had developed it—a phenomenally high percentage, but one they had meticulously calculated. Another nineteen had shown up at Camp Spirit in the Adirondacks. The kids were gifted, among the brightest in the country. Quick learners. Over two hundred and fifty constructs had been implanted—forty-one of them useful. Or so they had thought.

Then extinction.

They had not factored in that possibility, and when it came, it was the proverbial bolt out of the blue. There had been no reason to expect it; HALFLIFE was more than a conditioned response, more than Pavlov's dogs and bells. But random tests bore out the initial suspicion: after a few months, a year at most, their carefully engineered construct vanished without a trace.

Barkley had blamed adolescence as the cause—an immature brain made more unpredictable by a barrage of hormones. The HALFLIFE files gathered dust while the research veered off into the blind alley of brain electrode technology.

Then Calhoun's paper was published. It was only a half-dozen pages in an obscure British psychology journal eight years ago, but it brought HALFLIFE back into sharp focus:

Dissociative States and the Spontaneous Development of Right Brain Language in Adolescence: An Observation of Three Patients.

Three patients: two of them hospitalized with severe multiple personality disorder; the other an elderly outpatient in an alcohol treatment center—a woman who made her living as a trance medium.

Spontaneous development of right brain language. Their chance to work with adult subjects.

Again hope rose and HALFLIFE under Barkley's aegis was revived, first in Florida with a half-dozen so-called psychics, later in a proprietary hospital in north Georgia's Blue Ridge Mountains with three patients diagnosed as multiple personality syndrome. But after a promising start, within a few months the new constructs vanished. Extinction again—or so they believed—and two more open doors slammed shut. HALFLIFE was dead.

Until a month ago. Until it rose like a moldering Lazarus to haunt them.

Jonathan: the code name of the Camp Challenge construct, and the code name of Barkley's studies with multiples and psychics. Jonathan: the code name of the Atlanta D-string killer.

Sessions had immediately seen the covert possibilities: the construct as courier. One more step, thought Gulliver, and he'd have the rest of it.

Designed as a courier—and as the consummate agent. An agent who would never defect, never sell out, never be deviled by inconvenient memories.

But there was one thing more:

Though untrained, undifferentiated, even awkward in its raw form, the construct was exactly what it was meant to be. Jonathan did not carry the normal human baggage of conscience; he was not hampered by remorse. In short, he was a psychopath.

Jonathan was intended, by nature and design, to be an assassin.

TWENTY-FIVE

It was nearly two in the morning when Maureen left Tim's room. When the door closed behind her, he played the seance tape again, pausing it, backing up, listening.

Paul, speaking to Beth: "The others won't be joining us, will they?"

The others. The rest of the study group, he told himself. That's what Paul meant. A gray curl of smoke from his cigarette vanished into the shadows of the darkened room. That's all it meant. It felt like a lie. And yet, he could not quite admit to himself that the spirit of a dead man had known about Beth, had known about the shadowy group that lived in her head. To do that would give credence to everything else he had said.

There is a darkness here. A growing darkness.

Tim had turned to Maureen abruptly—as if he were a prosecutor. "You've done this before. Other studies like this. Tell me about them."

But a look he could not fathom shadowed her eyes, and she sidestepped the question. "The others were different. That's all."

"How?" he persisted, wondering why she was being evasive.

"For one thing, Paul was there," Maureen said. "I hate it when he's not around. It's like he died or something." She laughed at her little joke and rolled her eyes comically, the way she had when they first met. It came across as self-mockery.

A burlesque, Tim thought. She was trying to coax it all back, trying to play a part as if the playing would make it real.

"Who am I kidding?" Her voice trailed away, and she fell silent for a long time, leaning back against the thin bed pillow that served as a backrest, staring at the featureless wall as if it were a window to another world. Finally she said, "You've got to understand. In a way, he's my crutch. I mean, when Paul's around, nothing much ever bothers me. If something weird happens, something bad, then that's okay. It's like I saw it coming, sensed it somehow. The handwriting on the wall. So now it's here. That's all. Do you understand?"

"You mean *déjà vu?"*

"In a way. Only it's more than that. What's happening is familiar, scary a little, but you know you'll get through it okay, because you can feel what's up ahead. And what's up ahead feels safe. Only now—" Her hand fluttered out, dropped, plucked at the faded bedspread. "It doesn't feel safe anymore," she said. "It feels empty."

The way it felt to him now, in the darkened room.

The tape droned, but he no longer heard it. The distant traffic light flashed green, then red. He stabbed out the cigarette, smearing the dead end through the pile of ashes as if he could obliterate the awful moment when Maureen had known.

"It's happening to you too, isn't it?" she had said.

To you too.

He had wanted to admit it, wanted to talk about it, wanted to ask her a dozen questions, but he couldn't. Instead, he had masked his anxiety with a carefully bland look and a quick lie: "You been trying to give up cigarettes, too?" A dismissing gesture at the ashtray and the damning two-inch-long ash. "Most of the time they just burn up. Expensive way to quit, I guess." His laugh sounded unconvincing to him.

Mercifully, she did not pursue it. Perversely, he wished she had. He wanted her to explain. He wanted her to admit that she had lost time, so he could cluck his tongue, and distance himself, and deny once more that it had happened to him.

Then he had tossed the papers with their spidery script onto the bed as if they were of no consequence. When she picked them up, folded them, thrust them into her pocket, he wanted them back again.

Cloud net.

There had been at least a page that followed, a page he knew he had read. He could not remember a single word of it.

A sudden idea almost made him laugh. They were coming down with it. All of them. Quaig Fever, he thought.

CONTAGION
Quaigitis Ward
Asafetida required beyond this point

Or else something begins to grow inside your head.

Something with a life of its own.

Jonathan.

J-J-J-J-J-J-J-J . . .

A vestige of the dream shivered through his mind. A blind mole, tunneling through a glistening brain of mud.

Another hour passed before he could sleep.

TWENTY-SIX

Shoulders moved beneath the thin blanket, turned, and the shadowing pillow fell away. A security light mounted high on an adjacent building flared through the window and danced on closed eyes. Muttering, the sleeper threw up a hand, palm out, to ward off the light. Then the eyes opened.

Jonathan was awake.

For over a minute he lay very still, listening, straining to hear the slightest movement, but no sound came from Morgan Wing. Nothing.

He maneuvered his wrist into the light and read the time: 4:23.

The others would be sleeping now.

Silently he got to his feet, moved into the shadows, made his way to the door. It whispered open, closed behind him with a sigh.

Night lights set low on the walls displaced the darkness with dingy yellow puddles. The wide hallway was empty. He felt its chill ripple up his spine.

She was back then.

It was the woman who brought the cold; he knew the

signs of her. Cocking his head, he stood very still. There. He could feel her moving inside his mind just out of reach. He could hear her now—faintly—taunting him, disguising her voice, making it sound like his mother's.

The bitch was clever. She liked to cast her net from a safe distance. Pull the strings. Manipulate. But he was clever too. The thing to do was to ignore her, lull her into stupid carelessness, until she dared to look him in the face again.

It would be soon now. His fingers began to move, caressing his empty palm in a curving motion. He could almost feel the thin coil of wire, the wood dowels at each end. This time, he would be quick. Quicker than the woman. Quick enough to capture the black soul behind her eyes before it dimmed and flickered away and hid again.

Pushing the thoughts of her away, Jonathan crept down the hall and paused at Barkley's office door. Fool. Barkley could look and look and never find him. A thin smile. Never.

Except for the woman . . .

The realization brought a sharp chill, and the smile vanished. The woman would tell. He could hear her, whispering from the dark place, gloating. Listening to his thoughts.

A B C D . . . E F G . . . H I J K . . . El-em-en-oh-pee . . .

He had reached the utility-room door now; he pushed it open. The white light from outside the window cast a thin finger of light across the room, across the desk in its center.

It was cluttered with papers. Tests, graphs, folders. He ran his hands over them, felt them under his fingertips. Smooth. Like skin.

They belonged to Jody Henson.

Remembering what he had heard her say, he frowned.

Henson had not known he was listening. Listening,

outside the door while she told Barkley about the seance, about what had happened to the medium. He'd seen that she meant to control Barkley . . . just as the dark, nameless woman in his own mind meant to control him.

The thought was a sharp electric pulse that echoed in his groin. He could trap them both. . . .

A B C D . . . E F G . . .

The time was coming. . . .

H I J K . . . El-em-en-oh-pee . . .

The time when the bitch would grow careless again.

It would be soon, he knew. Soon she would grow reckless, come too close. A half smile skittered on his lips. The bitch was coming for him—and this time she would look out of Jody Henson's eyes.

A B C D . . . E F G . . .

Jonathan turned, went to the hall door, opened it.

H I J K . . . El-em-en-oh-pee . . .

His excitement grew, throbbed, quickened his breath. Hurrying now, Jonathan raced on tiptoe back to his room. And with each step came a faint metallic click—a sharp tic-tic-ticking sound.

The sound of a silver bell without a clapper.

TWENTY-SEVEN

Tim took a final swallow of coffee and grimaced. Grounds streaked the foam cup and gritted against his teeth. He wiped his incisors with a fingertip and examined the residue. He never drank anything but instant at home. For good reason, he thought.

The troops had trickled into the alcove—one by one from the fifth floor, in a clump from six. The medical students had made it an Egg McMuffin morning he noticed. He felt ragged, as if he were trying to come down with a stomach flu, and the determined chomping of Carla, who had supplemented her sandwich with fries bloody with ketchup, wasn't helping. He stared at her rear end: bulging rump wadded into faded jeans, jagged letters embroidered in red yarn spelling out WIDE LOAD. Bloody fries and self-abasing cynicism for breakfast. God.

Jody looked a little ragged too. There were dark traces under her eyes and a strained look at their corners, as if she had not slept. So join the club, he thought darkly, and scanned the hall. Barkley hadn't showed yet. When he did, Tim intended to have it out with the man. And, by God, he meant to get some answers this time.

"Where are the young'ns?" he asked Jody.

"You mean my psych students? They're Monday, Wednesday, and Friday. We've got other tests scheduled today."

He started to make a flip reference to Monday Butterworth, but dropped it. "What kind of tests?"

She checked her clipboard. "Some of you are for EEGs. You're down for eleven. Then, there's the old-fashioned kind—a written test. It measures creativity." She smiled. "You might even enjoy that one." Her smile vanished, and the strained look came back.

"Something wrong?"

"No." She bit her lip. "Yes. When we left my place last night do you remember where I left Sushi?"

"Sure."

"Tell me."

He raised an eyebrow. "In the yard. You left her in the yard."

"When I got home last night, she was inside."

He stared at her blankly.

"Don't you see what I'm saying? The door was locked. Somebody let her in."

"The neighbors?"

She shook her head and hugged the clipboard to her chest. "I don't know who. I don't know how. The door was locked."

"Did you call the police?"

"No. Nothing was missing." She shrugged, and somehow the movement was almost apologetic. "I didn't think they'd believe me. Oh—" Sliding her hand into the lab coat pocket, she pulled out a padlock and key. "Here. Your replacement."

Tim ran his fingers over the padlock. The metal surface felt greasy. "Nothing missing," he repeated. Slowly he met her eyes. "So, you tell *me* what's happening."

"Coincidence, I guess." There was no conviction in her tone.

What in the fuck was going on? He reached for her arm. "Let's run away to Tahiti," he said. "At least down the hall. We need to talk."

"Maybe. Maybe we do. But not now." She glanced over her shoulder. The doors at the end of the hall clanged and Barkley walked in.

A cherub's smile creased the neurologist's lips as he surveyed the group in the alcove. "I have a surprise for everyone." Opening a Manila folder, he pulled out a stack of envelopes and began to pass them out.

Carla shot Barkley a poisonous look. Then she whispered something to Memphis Red, who answered with a snicker.

Tim looked at his: a Chandler Bryson Memorial envelope. A bill for services? When he opened it, a peach-colored ticket fell out. Puzzled, he turned it over. It was for a revival of *A Chorus Line* at the Fox. For tonight's performance.

Barkley rose up on his toes. Up, down, up again. Like Daytona Beach, Tim thought irrelevantly, almost feeling the surf over his bare feet again, almost feeling the red-brown sand. There was a rhythm to it: the wash of tide suddenly dissolving the sand beneath his heels. Up on your toes or you lost your balance. Then the sea sucked back and the sand firmed again.

"Just a little 'thank you' from the institute," said Barkley. "All work and no play makes Jack a dull boy." He beamed at Jody, who fingered her ticket as if it were not real. "That goes for Jills too."

"That's very nice," she said.

"Enjoy it. But enough of that now," he said briskly.

"Let's get to work." And turning, veering around Mystery Carmody's rattling chart cart, Barkley strode away to his office.

Tim watched for a moment. Then he stood up and followed.

Tim knocked on the office door, and without waiting for a reply pushed it open and walked in.

Barkley slammed the file drawer shut abruptly and turned the key. Surprise coupled with annoyance flickered in his eyes. "What can I do for you, Mr. Monahan?"

Tim was suddenly uncertain. "Just a few questions," he began.

Again the quick flash of annoyance. It was masked almost at once with a smile. "We want to keep everyone happy here." A glance at his watch. "Go on, Tim."

Tim, was it? Barkley's voice had assumed the tone a busy father took with a little boy's tiresome questions. Get it on, and then get out. Although the doctor's demeanor was calm, his thumb and forefinger played ceaselessly with the file cabinet key, turning it over and over, stroking it, turning it again.

Tim stared at the man. What in hell was it he intended to say? The questions were blurring in his mind. He cleared his throat. "I'm thinking about dropping out."

Barkley waited.

"I have a lot of work. I'm backed up. I thought I could get some of it done here, but—" He stopped.

"You're finding it hard to work," prompted the doctor.

Tim nodded. "So, I'll just be packing up. You understand," he ended lamely.

"Of course," said Barkley, absently fingering the key, stroking it between thumb and forefinger. "First thing in the morning, then. We've got a light schedule today. You can get in a few hours work this afternoon, I'm sure, before the play." Barkley was watching him intently.

Tim stared at the man in amazement. Did Barkley think he was a child? Somebody to manipulate? Who the hell did the sonuvabitch think he was? His lip curled. "Well, gee, Daddy," he started to say. "I thought I'd just split right now." But something stopped him: a faint, almost inaudible click as Barkley's hand absently moved beneath the desk.

At once the hand was back, pudgy fingers stroking the metal desktop, reaching out, straightening a stack of papers with military precision.

And the key was gone.

The key to the locked file.

Tim's gaze slid to the file cabinet, then back. "Tomorrow will be fine," he said. "Just fine."

TWENTY-EIGHT

Jody Henson got off the elevator on 4 Clayborne, Chandler Bryson's psychiatric wing. Locked doors to the left led to the acute ward. To the right, past a shabby waiting room, offices flanked the hallway. As she approached the first, its glass-topped door rattled open and Bill King, one of the clinical psychologists on staff, came out.

"Well, hi, stranger," he said. "Enjoying your vacation?"

"Don't I wish?"

He laughed and held the door for her.

She hesitated a second, wanting to talk with him about Beth. "Have you got a minute?"

"Just." He nodded down the hall at a thin, middle-aged woman emerging from the elevator. "Here comes my ten o'clock appointment."

"Later then," she said, and watched him greet the patient and steer her toward consultation room B. Then she went into the office.

Waving at the secretary the group shared, Jody went to the cubicle she called her office. It wasn't much, but it beat the utility room on Morgan. There was a stack of mail and memos on her desk. She thumbed through it guiltily. Should have checked yesterday, she thought. But who had time?

She glanced at her watch. It was a few minutes past ten. Birmingham was on Central Time. If Beth Quaig's doctor kept normal hours, he ought to be in the office by now. Reaching for the phone, she got an outside line.

Birmingham information could find no one by the name of Schwartz listed under psychiatrists, but an A. David Schwartz was listed under clinical psychologists.

After three rings, a woman answered. "Drs. Schwartz and Mannheim."

"Dr. Schwartz, please. I'm calling from Chandler Bryson Memorial Hospital in Atlanta."

"Doctor is on another line now. May I ask what the call is in reference to?"

"It's about one of his patients. Beth Quaig."

"Will you hold?"

"Yes."

Generic music began to play over the phone. Jody skimmed an idiotic memo from Personnel, and threw it into the wastebasket. What if he wouldn't talk to her? He might not. Schwartz didn't know her. Even if he did, it would be skirting ethics for him to tell her anything about a patient. A minute stretched to three. She read the rest of the memos. Nit-picking. Unimportant. The wastebasket was filling up.

A click, and a cheerful, "Doctor Schwartz here."

"Uh, hi," she began. "This is Jody Henson calling."

"What's this about Beth?"

"Look," she said abruptly, "I know it's a little out of order for me to be calling, but I hope you'll talk to me." Briefly she told him about the study and her background. "I've had a fair amount of experience with MPD patients," she said, hoping he would believe her. "Frankly, I'm very concerned about her."

"Then she's not really a patient." Schwartz sounded relieved.

"No," Jody admitted. "But I'm worried about her."

"That makes two of us," he said. "Beth never mentioned the study to me. Two weeks ago she canceled her appointment—or rather Anne did. This week she didn't bother to call at all."

"Anne?"

A pause. "This is all in confidence, you understand."

"Of course."

"Anne is one of Beth's more difficult personalities. You said you were worried about Beth. What's up?"

Anne. How many were there? She told him what she had seen.

There was a long pause before Schwartz responded. "Jonathan, you say?"

"Yes."

"He never seemed to fit."

"Then he's shown up before?"

"As the mystery books say, under rather strange circumstances. It was about three years ago."

Three years ago! What did it mean? A chill scurried up her spine. "You said, 'strange circumstances'?"

"How much of Beth's history do you know?"

"Not much, I'm afraid."

"Then, maybe we'd better go back a few years. . . ."

The study group had just started the written creativity test when Barkley showed up in the alcove. Waggling a dismissing hand at Jody, he went up to the long table against the back wall which the medical students had appropriated. Carla Hagen was leaning over her test paper.

Barkley tapped her on the shoulder and said something in a low voice to the students. All four got up and followed him down the hall.

Jody wondered what was up. They were almost out of sight, standing in a little clump outside Beth Quaig's room, and Barkley was saying something. Whatever it was, the students weren't too pleased about it. From the looks of things, it was degenerating into an argument. Al was waving his hands, Carla and Memphis were frowning, and Tyrone Hayes, usually even-tempered, wore a grim look.

Barkley gave them a thin smile and walked away. Heading for his office, Jody supposed. The students grumbled among themselves for a few minutes, and then broke up and straggled back to the alcove.

Tim looked up from his paper, glanced first at the students, then at Jody.

Reading the question on his face, she shrugged.

Carla scribbled something on her paper, then pushed it away. Picking up a medical text from a pile of books on the floor, she began to read.

Jody was annoyed. Carla had no right to slough off the test. She was being paid good money to participate. Resolving to talk to her about it later, Jody scanned the room. Dayton Satterfield was leaning back in a wicker armchair, using an old magazine for a lap desk. Maureen was writing furiously.

Jody eyed Beth Quaig. Brow furrowed, the girl played with her pencil. Her paper seemed to be blank.

Stress? Or maybe Beth just couldn't figure out twenty things to do with a razor blade. It was only a simple test of creative thinking. Surely the girl could come up with something.

But then, maybe she could. Maybe that was the problem.

Jody winced. Why in hell hadn't she picked a brick for the test? Or a paper clip? Anything except a razor blade. Brilliant. She'd probably managed to trigger God-knew-what self-destructive ideas in the girl's head. But even as the thought came, she knew she was overreacting.

She looked down at her clipboard and tried to decipher the notes she had scribbled when she talked with Dr. Schwartz.

"So, who have you met, so far?" he had asked, and Jody had told him—the teenager, little Beffie, Jonathan, and Tabby, the magic child. Schwartz called the teenager Donna.

"You work fast," he'd said with a wry laugh. "It took me months to ferret out that many." Then seriously, "If she's shown half of them to you this soon, then I'd say she's pretty close to the edge."

"Half?" Only half?

Surreptitiously, Jody glanced at Beth again. Why in hell had she thought it was such a good idea to call Schwartz? Muddy the water, that's what she'd done. If word got back to Barkley, she'd be looking for a new career. Yet ethically, she knew she ought to tell him. The girl *was* ultimately Barkley's responsibility.

Beth was still bent over the paper, brown hair sliding across her eyes. But now her pen was flying across the page. Uneasily, Jody wondered who was taking the test.

There were eight of them, Schwartz had said. Eight fragmented personalities, not counting Beth herself.

Tommy lived in her head too, eleven years old, and his father's favorite. Tommy, the Little League pitcher.

And Michelle. Michelle was twenty-five, studious and intelligent. When she took over, Beth's allergies got better —and her vision worse. Michelle needed glasses.

The Paper Doll was a shadowy little figure who never

spoke and seldom moved. Curled in a fetal position, The Paper Doll could only cry softly and soil herself. She was the one who came when Tabby whisked Beth away to safety. The only one who really knew what Beth's father had done in the night.

Then there was Anne. Anne, the dark girl, full of rage. It had been Anne who had opened Beth's wrist with a pair of nail clippers, carefully snipping away bits of flesh until she had reached the thick, pulsing arteries. Beth had nearly died that time.

"It was probably Anne," Schwartz had said, "who got Beth in trouble over in Georgia."

"What kind of trouble?"

"She simply disappeared. Didn't go to work, didn't keep her appointments, didn't answer the phone. She was gone for nearly three weeks. When I finally heard from her, she had just been released from a private hospital in north Georgia and was on her way home by bus."

"Which hospital? Woodridge?"

A pause. She heard him riffling through papers. "No. It was Oakmont."

"Oakmont!" Oakmont was a proprietary psychiatric treatment center in the mountains. In Union County, if memory served. "But how?" she asked. Beth was a typist. You didn't enter Oakmont on a typist's salary; it was a hospital for the rich, for celebrities. "How could she afford it?"

"I don't know," he admitted. "It never was clear how she got there, and Beth doesn't remember. Oakmont listed her as a transfer from one of the county hospitals up there. Just a minute . . ." The rattle of papers again, then he was back on the line. "It was Union General Hospital. Only Union had no record of Beth as a patient. Nothing in the Emergency Room records either."

"Strange."

"I'll say. Oakmont said it was a phone referral. Said she arrived in a private car. Anyway, that's when Jonathan showed up. While she was there."

"From the stress?" Jody asked. Multiple personalities didn't do well in hospitals. Most psychiatric institutions didn't know how to handle them.

"Probably. Only I've never been able to figure Jonathan out," he said. "The others were adaptive reactions to her childhood. But he doesn't seem to fit the picture." A pause. "To tell you the truth," he said, "there's something about him that sets my teeth on edge."

She blinked. "Would you call Jonathan an antisocial personality?" she asked cautiously.

"Possibly." Then, more firmly, "It's more than possible. I think he's dangerous."

She started to tell him about what Tim had written. Instead, she said, "Do you mind if I ask you an off-the-wall question?"

"Go ahead."

"Has Beth ever shown any signs of being psychic?"

"Psychic?" Schwartz laughed. "I don't hold with mental telepathy or any of that stuff. Why are you asking? Has Beth come down with some sort of wild talent over in Hotlanta?"

"Possibly," Jody hedged, sorry she had asked. Feeling she had to explain, she reluctantly told him about what Tim had written. "So when Beth came up with Jonathan later, I just had to talk to you."

"Interesting," he said. "I want you to keep me posted on all this, okay? Don't tell Beth I know she's there, though. I'll let her tell me herself in her own way."

"Okay."

Schwartz seemed reluctant to hang up. "About that

psychic business . . ." A long pause, a note of caution in his voice. "You don't admit these things to everybody, but there was something . . . . I was talking to Beth, and all of a sudden, Tabby came." Another pause. "There was a letter on my desk. Tabby knew what was in it."

A letter? What did that prove? Letters could be picked up and read. "Maybe she saw it while you were out of the room."

"Maybe," he said. "But the thing is, I hadn't opened it yet. . . ."

TWENTY-NINE

Tim had filled both sides of his test sheet with nonsensical things to do with a razor blade. He had taken a few artistic liberties, his blade variously double- or single-edged, dull or sharp, as invention demanded. He had long ago come up with "letter opener," "registered trademark for cocaine cartel," and "tool for refinishing furniture." Now into miniaturization, he wrote, "Scrape blade for toy bulldozer."

He scratched the end of his nose with the eraser, then absently taking the pencil in his left hand, he doodled a small figure eight while he looked over his paper. Flipping the pencil back to his right hand, he put down, "Ice skates for Lilliputian." But that was plural. Scratching it out, he substituted, "Ice skate for one-legged Lilliputian."

"Time," said Jody. Her wicker chair rebounded with a creak as she got up and began to collect the papers.

As chairs scraped around him, he scribbled "hair splitter" and "Lilliputian meat cleaver (with broken handle)." When Jody paused at his chair, hand out, he added, "French onion soup cheese-string cutter" and then scrawled in large letters, "Dinner tonight?"

Jody chuckled softly. "Before or after *A Chorus Line?*"

"Early," he said. "I have plans for later." He was thinking about Barkley's key, about the click he had heard when it disappeared beneath the neurologist's steel desktop. It was still there, he was sure, held in place by a magnet.

"Oh?" Her voice was velvet.

He put on a quick smile. "A workout," he said. "Thought I'd try out this new fitness routine—" His voice dropped to a whisper. "Something I picked up from *The Pop-Up Kama Sutra.*"

A self-conscious smile crinkled the corners of her eyes. They were gray mist this morning, like the fog that had crept into Atlanta before dawn and shrouded the city. "Six tonight?" he asked. "In town." The Fox theater was within walking distance from Chandler Bryson, and there were several restaurants close by. No need to fool with cars and parking lots.

"Better make it six-thirty, okay?"

He nodded.

"Back to work, then." Jody added his test paper to the stack and headed down the hall, passing Mystery Carmody, who came into the alcove.

The nurse looked around, spotted Tim, headed his way. She was carrying a single chart sheathed in hinged silver metal.

"Dr. Barkley is ready for you now, Mr. Monahan. It's time for your EEG."

Something jittered abruptly in his stomach. Just the ragged feeling he got up with, Tim thought. An electroencephalogram wasn't anything to get worked up over. He smiled to mask the breath he took. "Don't I get a last meal?"

She leaned closer. "A last what?" She smelled of lemon soap.

"Meal," he repeated. "Before my electrocution."

Her faint smile told him she had heard all the EEG jokes she could stand, thank you. With the authority that seemed to be second nature to nurses, she fixed him with a pleasant, but unrelenting, gaze. "This way, Mr. Monahan."

His cue to jump up and run alongside.

"There's no need to be nervous," she said briskly. "EEGs are perfectly harmless."

"Who's nervous?" He got to his feet slowly, feeling the jitter in his belly again. Japanimation Syndrome, he thought—Mothra, taking flight. Suddenly he felt very tired.

Carmody gave him an appraising glance, then said evenly, "I tell everyone that. You'd be surprised how many people think EEGs send electricity to the brain. But that's not what happens at all. We simply measure the electrical activity that's already there."

Grateful for her tact, Tim followed Carmody down the hall to a swinging door stenciled TREATMENT ROOM in dull black letters. It was dark inside, and windowless, the only light coming from a half-opened doorway in the back. A steel examining table stood near the front wall.

Carmody flipped a metal lever and raised the head of the table. "Lean back and make yourself comfortable."

He shot a wry look at the table, then at Carmody. "You did say comfortable?"

She handed him a folded blanket. "In case you feel chilly."

Tim got up on the table. Using the blanket to pillow his head, he leaned back self-consciously and eyed the nurse. "Why is it so dark in here?"

Carmody opened the chart and pulled out a pen. A pinpoint of light came from its tip. "To help you relax."

"That my chart?"

"Uh-huh." She wrote something, then snapped the chart shut with a little click and laid it on a table next to the wall. "Doctor Barkley likes to run these tests himself." She turned to the hall door. "He'll be along in a few minutes."

"I thought you said he was ready for me?" Tim began. But the door closed and Mystery Carmody was gone.

When a minute passed with no sign of Barkley, Tim swung to the edge of the table. A dim ribbon of light streaked the battered metal chart. On impulse, he crossed the room and picked it up. Squinting, he opened it to the last page, but he couldn't make out the words. He moved into the light from the open door when something caught his eye—a squat piece of equipment facing the back of the room. He eyed it suspiciously. Colored lights blinked on its face. Like the control panel of a 747, he thought. A single swivel chair faced the console.

His gaze moved to the chart again. Carmody's handwriting was a neat backslant: "11:00 A. To treatment room for EEG. Pt. seems anxious." Then her name followed by "RN."

Pt. seems anxious.

He was obviously the "pt." Patient, he decided. And who the hell was anxious? He flipped back a page. Another note: "10:30 A. To alcove for psych. test."

Nothing he didn't know already. He thought again of the locked file cabinet in Barkley's office.

Tim slid the chart back onto the table and checked out the back room. But it wasn't a room at all, just a tiny hallway, light spilling from its single overhead fixture. There was a door at each end. Calculating directions, sure that Barkley's office was on the left, he turned right and pushed open the door.

Misty white light dribbled through tall streaked windows. It was a ward about the size of the room they had given him, but this one was crammed with stretchers and odd-looking equipment meant for God knew what. A real junk shop. Leftovers from the forties, he decided, spotting what looked like a steel coffin on wheels. Somehow, he knew it was an iron lung, though he couldn't remember ever seeing one before. Across the room a pair of wood and wicker child-sized wheelchairs squatted next to the wall. Real antiques.

Pulling the door shut, he went back to the dim little treatment room. He was fingering his chart again when footsteps in the main hall catapulted him back onto the examining table.

By the time the door opened, he was leaning back, eyes closed.

With a nod in Tim's direction, Barkley crossed the room, pulled a small extension lamp from the wall, and switched it on. "Good morning." He wheeled a metal stand toward the table.

Tim eyed the tray. Jars and tubes, and a small black box bristling with wires.

"You'll be tied up here for a while," said Barkley.

Tied up.

A split second of panic, a faint grin. Figure of speech.

"It's going to take a little time. About an hour." A cherubic smile from the neurologist. "No need to be anxious. I do this all the time." As he spoke, his hands moved quickly, attaching electrodes to Tim's scalp.

He could feel paste oozing from them into his hair, and suddenly he remembered being a little kid, no more than four years old, out with his grandmother. She had taken him along on her trip to the beauty parlor and promised him lunch at Morrison's Cafeteria afterward. The beauty parlor was full of odd smells that tingled his nose. A half-dozen women, heads shrouded with thick silver metal hoods, sat along the wall and stared at magazines. Then he saw something else.

He tugged at his grandmother's arm, but his eyes were fixed on the woman across the room. She was old, older than Grandma even. Wires snaked from her head, dozens of them, twisting up like coiling black snakes.

Out of the corner of her eye, the old lady saw Tim watching. She smiled, turned her head toward him, nodded, and he was stricken with stomach-clutching alarm. The black snakes were moving. They were alive!

His whisper trembled against his lips. "What's that?"

Grandma hoisted her silver hood and followed his gaze. "Heat wave," she said and went back to her *Ladies' Home Journal.*

He began to cry then, and his grandmother abandoned her magazine and took him onto her lap. "What on earth?"

Through shaking sobs, he managed to tell her.

"What an imagination," she said.

It gave him no relief at all, and that night he dreamed of serpents crawling out of his head. He woke up crying. Clucking softly, his mother called it indigestion, and gave him a spoonful of Pepto Bismol. But it wasn't a stomach-ache. It was something infinitely worse, something he could not quite put into words. "Not indian-jest-chin," he had protested. But he had no words to explain the horrible sense of violation he had felt.

Tim grinned at the memory. It had added a whole new element of horror to his young life, especially when he saw

Medusa on Saturday Matinee a few years later. But the smile faded. What he had been really afraid of wasn't old ladies or snakes growing out of his head. The real horror had been being helpless, violated, out of control.

"Something funny?" asked Barkley.

"Not really," he said. But he was wondering why a buried memory like that had surfaced so abruptly.

The cold image of the earthen brain slid behind his eyes and he shivered.

Barkley was humming in a low-pitched monotone that jittered Tim's nerves. He wanted to tell him to stop, to knock it off. Instead, he closed his eyes as if the act would shut out the sound.

"I want you to try and relax."

Play along, Tim told himself. But the relaxation part was hard to come by. Play the game, he thought. It was just for today. By five, Barkley would be gone. By seven-thirty or so, Morgan Wing would be empty. They'd be playing with a new deck then—and a new set of rules.

"It's important that you lie very still. Don't move any part of your body."

He could hear Barkley moving away, crossing the room. To the 747 control panel, he guessed. Fasten your seat belts, ladies and gentlemen. Here we go.

"Try not to fidget," said Barkley. "When you move, we get artifact."

"Artifact?" What the hell was this? An archaeological dig? Pot shards from the kitchen midden of his brain?

"Electrical spikes. The machine reads extraneous muscle movement as well as brain waves. Close your eyes and lie still please."

Tim's right eyelid began to twitch, and a gob of paste crept down his temple.

"Take slow deep breaths." A pause. "That's right."

The doctor fell silent.

Within a few minutes, Tim's muscles loosened in spite of himself. Whether it was boredom, or simply lack of sleep, he did not know, but suddenly he felt very drowsy.

"Good." Barkley's voice was quiet. "Now, Tim, I want to try a little word association. When I give you a word, I want you to say the first thing that pops into your mind. All right?"

"All right."

"Black."

"White."

"Water."

"Drink."

"Sleep."

"Dream."

"Dream," repeated Barkley.

Tim hesitated.

"Dream," Barkley said again.

"Image." *Earth. Mole. Brain.*

"Image."

"Swamp."

"Swamp," echoed Barkley.

"Mud." *Mole.*

"Mud."

"Brain."

A beat, then Barkley said, "Cloud."

"Sky."

"Cloud."

"Storm."

"Cloud."

Net. Net. The word pulsed in Tim's brain.

"Cloud."

"Net."

"Attention. . . ."

The lamp flared, and Tim blinked.

"Thank you, Mr. Monahan," said Barkley.

Tim shook his head stupidly. "Wha—?"

"You fell asleep. That's common enough during an EEG. It happens all the time. The room's dark. You're relaxed." A smile. "You can get up now."

Tim focused on his watch. Just past noon. His hand moved to his scalp, felt gummy paste. The electrodes were gone. And so, with a wave of a pudgy hand, was Barkley.

Tim stood up. Still half asleep, he was staring at his watch again when Mystery Carmody came through the door.

"All done," she observed, whisking away the blanket, tearing off the wrinkled paper lining from the examining table, pulling a fresh one from the roll at its foot. "You'll feel better if you wash your hair now." She plucked a folded towel from a stack on the table and added a sample-sized bottle of shampoo. "In case you didn't bring any of your own."

He touched his temple, grimaced at the paste that transferred to his fingers, and glanced down at the little bottle. "Industrial strength?"

Carmody grinned. "Better living through chemistry." Jotting something in the chart, she snapped it shut, and headed back to the nurses station.

By 12:30, Tim was out of the shower, dressed, and wide awake. The queasy feeling that he had had all morning translated itself into a sudden, ravenous hunger.

He found Jody at her desk. "Jeet chet?"

"No. And I'm starved."

"Let's go get lunch."

She hesitated, then shook her head. "I really can't leave. Bring me back a sandwich?"

"Sure."

She reached for her wallet. "The egg salad here isn't so bad."

He waved away her offer of money. "I've got a better idea."

Half an hour later, Tim was back with several big white deli bags. He headed for his room. Then an idea came to him, and he veered across the hall.

A few minutes later, he popped his head into Jody's office. "Madam, dinner is served. Today we picnic at Warm Springs." He offered her his arm.

Mystified, she took it.

"Warm Springs" proved to be the storage room down the hall. He opened the door with a flourish.

After a startled look around the room, Jody began to laugh. The hastily cleared center of the room was laid with blankets and pillows around a low wooden crate that served as a table. In the middle stood an enormous clear plastic bowl partly filled with potato chips and flanked with two bottles of imported beer and crisp half-sour pickles. "Pastrami? Or corned beef?"

"Pastrami." She pointed to the bowl. "Where did you find that?"

"The bowl from Brobdingnag?" He grinned. "I borrowed it from the guy in the bathtub down the hall. Big fellow. About twelve foot eight, I'd say." He took a handful of potato chips and began to chew.

She shook her head in amazement. "Do you know what that is? I haven't seen one of those since I was in school."

"I told you. The bowl from Brobdingnag." He was

reaching for another handful of chips, when his hand dropped. "What? What is it?"

"It's part of an iron lung."

He shot her a startled look.

At the consternation on his face, Jody stifled a giggle. "It's the head piece. The dome."

"You're kidding. Right?"

"No. I'm not. When I was in nursing school, our med-surg instructor used to take us to the hospital basement and drag out all the rusty junk they had down there. She called it 'Orientation to Equipment and Procedures.' We called it Antiques 101." She chuckled softly. "Walker was convinced we needed to know how to use every medical device known to early man. But then, you had to consider where she was coming from. She was an ex-nun from a medical mission in Haiti. The hospital's cast-offs would have saved a lot of lives down there, I guess." Jody touched a strip of rusty metal at one edge of the bowl. It matched another on the opposite side. "See. That's the latch."

"But all the pictures— They never showed anything like that. They always showed somebody's head sticking out in the open."

"That's the way it was most of the time. But if the nurses had to open the main carriage to give a shot or something, the iron lung depressurized. That's why they had to hook up the dome." She touched the latch again. "When you press, it makes an airtight seal."

"Sure," Tim said wryly. "The polio victim can't breathe, so to fix things, you seal him up in a can, right?"

"You have a point." A tiny smile quirked the corners of her lips. "Extensive scientific research revealed that it was helpful to plug in the lung first.

"It's a positive pressure device," she added. "A fairly handy one at that. It let the patient go on breathing while he got a bath."

"You mean that thing really did cover somebody's face?"

"That's right."

Tim stared at the makeshift bowl and felt his appetite slip away. Not just anybody's face. A sick face breathing—who knew what?—all over his potato chips.

Jody took pity on him. "It's all right. You won't catch anything."

Was that a guarantee? Uneasily, he remembered reading something about an island—off Scotland, he thought it was—where the ground had been poisoned by disease, where the infection was supposed to linger for a hundred years. "What about spores?"

"Spores? You mean like anthrax or something?"

Anthrax. That was it.

"There aren't any spores. Polio's caused by a virus. Believe me, you won't catch anything."

Spores. Viruses. They were all germs, weren't they? He gave her a suspicious look. "I don't see you eating any potato chips."

"They're fattening." She cocked her head, selected a large one, and crunched. "Look. I'm eating. See?"

Tim's appetite came back enough for him to demolish his corned beef and pickle. But he found the potato chips lacking in appeal.

Jody fed him the last of her pastrami sandwich, and brushed away a lock of hair that had crept down his forehead. "Soft," she said. "Just washed?"

"Gunk removal."

"Oh. You mean the EEG. How did it go?"

"The first part was okay. After that, I'm not sure. I fell asleep."

"You're not supposed to do that, you know."

"What do you mean? Barkley said it happens all the time."

"He said that? What else did he say?"

"Nothing. Not much, anyway. Just the word association stuff."

"What?"

"Word association. You know. He says 'black,' you say 'white.' "

Two parallel lines creased her brow. "He did this during the EEG?"

"Yeah. Why?"

Jody looked away, then back. "Nothing. It's just a little unusual. That's all." She put down her empty beer bottle. "I shouldn't have drunk that. It was great, but it made me sleepy." She lay back on the pile of pillows and blankets and yawned. "Nice of you to raid the linen closet."

"What linen closet?"

"The one at the end of the hall. Across from the alcove."

He shrugged. "I found these in the corner. No telling how long they've been there, I guess." A wicked grin crossed his face. "But you don't have to worry. No spores."

Gaze fixed on the plastic dome, Jody blinked, and a strange look tracked over her face.

Tim looked at her closely. "Just kidding."

"What?"

"I said I was just kidding. About the spores, I mean. Are you okay?"

"Sure. I'm okay. It's just that for a moment there it looked like—" Her eyes flicked back to the dome. "Like something else."

"Like what?"

She sat up, tipped the bowl over an open deli bag, and slid the leftover potato chips into it. "I don't know," she said, setting the bowl down, touching the latch again. "A big cheese dome, I guess."

Tim nodded solemnly. "For the cheddar from Brobdingnag."

The strange look again, fleeting. Then a smile accentuated her short upper lip. "Rat cheese for the aristocrats of Brobdingnag?" An exaggerated head shake. "I say it's Brie."

THIRTY

Phillip Sessions looked up at last from the thick files he had been reading since nine A.M. "Interesting." The neurophysiologist's gaze skittered past Hal Gulliver and settled on the framed Norman Rockwell prints on the office wall.

"Yes?" Gulliver prompted.

Sessions turned wet eyes toward the supergrade. "Interesting," he said again with a hint of petulance. The subtext was obvious: pay attention and I won't have to repeat myself.

The annoyance Gulliver had tried to keep in check all day pinched his lips into a tight line. He drew a long whistling breath through compressed nostrils before he said, "How so?"

Sessions's tongue slid across his lips. "A few minutes to gather my thoughts—"

Gulliver eyed him through slitted lids. "Certainly. Take all the time you need." Only, please God, let him make it quick. Let him say his piece and get the fuck out.

He was heartily sick of Sessions. The man had been

there all day, planted like a toadstool at the table across from his desk, turning the pages of top secret documents with a tongue-dampened index finger, sucking his teeth every ten pages or so. The first time it had happened, Gulliver was sure Sessions had come across something startling in Barkley's records. After the fifth or sixth time, he realized the tooth sucking was no more than a disgusting habit.

He stole a look at the words he had scrawled on his desk memo pad, each of them followed with a question mark. Ripping off the top sheet, and, through habit, the half-dozen underlying pages that might hold faint impressions of his pen, he fed them into the shredder. He was settling back behind his desk when the phone rang.

"Yes."

"Mrs. Gulliver on the line."

It had to be about Val; Barbara would never call him at work about anything trivial. "Put her through."

A pause. Then his wife's voice: "Hi, Granddaddy."

He blinked. "Really?"

"Really." Another pause, then Barbara's voice came distantly as if she spoke through a muffling hand. "I just got on." Something followed that he couldn't make out, then she said, "Honestly! What is it about pay phones that brings out the worst in people?"

"Val? How is she?"

"She's fine. Tired, but fine. Chip's here. He made it just in time for the delivery." A short laugh. "Aren't you going to ask if it's a boy or a girl?"

"What? Of course. What is it?"

"A darling little girl. Eight pounds, twelve ounces. They're naming her Melissa. Isn't that sweet? She's got a heart-shaped face like Val's, only . . ." Barbara hesitated.

Then her voice dropped, the way it always did when she had bad news. "Right now she's a little lopsided."

Lopsided? "What do you mean?"

"She's got a lump on her head as big as my fist. It scared the pie out of me when I saw it, but the doctor says it's fairly common. He called it a cepho— Wait a minute; I wrote it down—"

He pushed away what she had said and concentrated on the sounds he heard: the snap of her handbag opening, the rustle of foil. A gum wrapper again. Barbara never could remember notepads. Dozens all over the house, but never one in her handbag.

"Are you still there?"

"I'm here."

"He called it a cephalhematoma." She pronounced it carefully, breaking the word into discrete syllables. "It sounds awful, doesn't it? I had to ask one of the nurses what it meant. She said the 'cephal' part means head. The rest of it means a blood tumor."

He was suddenly aware of his heart beating: short, sharp taps against his breastbone—a stubby finger drumming. "The baby's got a tumor?"

"More of a lump. It's on the right side of her head."

A tumor. Jesus Christ. "Will it grow? Is it going to grow?"

"That's what I wanted to know. But it's not that kind of thing. It's more of a blood clot between her skull and her scalp."

A blood clot? "The baby's bleeding?"

"No. Not anymore, anyway. The doctor says it'll go away in about six weeks. He says it was caused by molding during labor. Val's small down there, and the baby was nearly nine pounds."

Labor the doctor brought on. Gulliver clenched his jaw and blinked at the sudden jolt of pain from a loose tooth. "Does Val know?"

"Not yet. She's sleeping now, and if they do things the way they used to, they won't bring her the baby for hours. But the doctor says everything is fine."

Fine? Easy enough for him to say. Only it wasn't *his* fucking grandbaby that had the tumor. An image from years ago kept coming back: Val, no more than six years old, crying, holding a baby doll with a broken head. The doctor must have known all along that something like this could happen. Didn't they do measurements? Figure the size of the baby? He had to have known. But not a word. Not a fucking word.

"You still there?"

"I'm here."

"Just a minute—" She said something, but he couldn't understand. Then a sigh. "Somebody's really antsy to use the phone. I'd better get off, okay? I'll call you tonight."

"Right." He cradled the phone, stared at it a second, then directed a hooded glance at Sessions. Doctors. Fucking incompetents. All of them. In his mind, he could see his daughter, see the lost-little-girl look in her eyes as she cuddled her damaged baby. His hand curled, made a fist; his nails bit his palm. Jesus. She was a human being. A human being. Didn't anyone give a shit?

Sessions took Gulliver's look as an invitation to speak. "After the extinction of the conditioning noted here," he said, tapping the stack of documents for emphasis, "I was a little surprised by the Atlanta development. I realized that a cursory look wasn't enough, so I had to go back. Rather minutely, I'd say." He cocked his wrist and checked his watch. "Or maybe I should say 'minute-ly.' *Tempus* does *fugit* when you're having fun."

Gulliver winced at the donkey bray that passed for a laugh. When it died away, he said, "I'd like your opinion about a couple of things. You mentioned extinction . . ." *Extinction*—the first word on his shredded list. "Is it, uh, ever reversible?"

Sessions's lips gaped into a broad smile. "That would be a contradiction of terms, wouldn't it?"

Gulliver's eyes hardened. "You tell me."

"You mean the Atlanta phenomena, of course. The murders." Sessions's fingertips perched on his knees, spiders ready to pounce. "You have five suspects, I believe."

"Four."

"Five," corrected Sessions. "The dead man, George Corsica, is still a suspect, is he not?"

"Not unless you believe in spirit possession," said Gulliver. "He's been dead ten days. The last D-string murder was Saturday night—three days ago."

"Four suspects, then." Sessions's tone was unruffled. "You want to know why these four exhibited extinction of the directive, when, obviously, no extinction had occurred."

"I want to know why these four fell through the cracks."

Sessions chuckled softly. "The cracks? I'd call it more of a trapdoor."

"What's that supposed to mean?"

"I told you a cursory look wasn't enough. So I went through all of this again. That's when I noticed several discrepancies."

Gulliver leaned back in his chair and stared at Sessions from under hooded lids. "Such as?"

"Such as the fact that your Dr. Barkley's official reports didn't always reflect the content of his records." Sessions hitched forward, and thumbing through the stack of documents, he pulled out two, the first no more than twenty pages long, the second, thick as a phone book. "Of course the *Reader's Digest* version is handier, I'll admit. And quite clever, really. I'd guess quite a few of my colleagues would be misled by it. But the knack of reading between the lines helps." His pale eyes shone with an ill-disguised gleam of pride. "It puts things back in context, so to speak."

"Just what are you trying to say?"

"Well, you people are handicapped by not being familiar with scientific nomenclature, but it seems that your Dr. Barkley tried to handicap his medical readers too." He tossed the files back onto the table. "It looks like your man discovered the key some time ago. One that puts the model back in working order."

Gulliver's chair snapped to the upright position. "Cut the bullshit, Sessions. Say what you're trying to say. And say it in English."

Sessions blinked, centered an errant contact lens with index finger to eyelid, blinked wetly again. "Barkley found out what caused the extinction. It's all in here if you know what to look for."

"What is? What are you saying?"

"The right brain. It's the key. That's where Jonathan was sequestered. You knew that. And you knew right brain language was necessary to communicate with the construct. But what nobody knew was how well hidden Jonathan was." He drew a tongue across his lips. "Jonathan lives in a special place," he said. "The place where hypnogogic images come from. They're related to dreams, but hypnogogic images are different; they don't show up in REM sleep. Instead, they occur when the brain hovers between waking and sleeping. They're different in kind, too: they're more vivid. Visual. People often say that it's like looking at a rapid film montage. And the images are accompanied with a feeling of detachment, a depersonalization. Sometimes they come with sickness: the fever-dreams of literature. The important thing is, not everyone sees them. The potential is there. In all of us. But not everyone sees them."

Sessions put his fists together and linked his thumbs. "The point is," he went on, "the images act as a psychological channel between the brain's hemispheres." He stopped, then said, "No. That's not quite right. The images are a *result* of a psychological channel between the hemispheres. Socrates's daemons, Pascal's 'mystic hexagram,' William Blake's angels—they all came from the same place." He looked up at Gulliver. "Do you understand what I'm saying? Jonathan is sequestered at the spring head—the place where creativity wells up."

Creativity? Gulliver looked blank. All he could think of was the creativity study, the cover for the Agency's search for a killer.

"That's why Jonathan manifested in so many of the children," said Sessions. "Children are born creative. But it's bred out of them. By the time a child reaches puberty we've taught them not to trust hunches and intuition, not to see what isn't there, not to hear what isn't there. If it doesn't register on the five senses, then it doesn't exist. We teach them to turn off the tap, dam up the channel."

"The extinction," said Gulliver. "That's when it stopped. When they got older—"

"Exactly. Except for a few. The creative ones. The ones who weren't afraid to use their minds for play the way children do."

"Barkley knew all this?" But Gulliver knew the answer. Barkley had known—just as Val's obstetrician had known that he would deliver a damaged child. His thumb played over a tightened fist. Intuition. Turn it off; it doesn't exist. It had been intuition that had plagued him. Intuition that had told him to hire Sessions, take a closer look at Barkley. An intuition he had come within a hair of ignoring.

Sessions nodded. "He knew. He just didn't bother to put it in his reports."

Creativity study—calling it that had been Barkley's idea. The son of a bitch had been so sure of himself he hadn't even bothered to call a spade a shovel. But why? Why hide it from the agency that paid him?

Sessions cleared his throat. "There were other discrepancies too. Back at the beginning of the project, for instance." He paused to stare at the wall again, but just as Gulliver opened his mouth to prompt the man, he went on. " 'Cause of death: myocardial infarction.' "

It took Gulliver a moment to realize what he was talking about. The death of the first HALFLIFE medical director back in the sixties. The heart attack.

Sessions pulled out a thin folder and opened it. The pages were browning at the edges from twenty-two years of aging. He slid his hand over the report, caressing it, as if he drew in information through his fingers. "Barkley did an EKG on the spot. His clinical notes sound right," he said, "but the EKG tracing doesn't bear them out." He flipped forward several pages, and beckoned at Gulliver to take a look. "See here?" He pointed to an incomprehensible array of fading squiggly lines. "No Q-wave. You can't have an MI without a Q-wave, can you? The Q-wave can disappear temporarily from a strip, but not this early." The fingertip moved toward the end of the strip, stopped, tapped commandingly. "See this?"

Gulliver stared, understanding nothing.

"Cardiology isn't my field, you understand, but I do have a nodding acquaintance with EKGs," he said with a touch of pride. "They're not so different in concept from electroencephalograms, are they now? I'd say, from the look of this, that your man's heart stopped in systole." Sessions paused and looked expectantly at Gulliver.

"What do you mean?"

"I mean your man's heart stopped like this—" Sessions held out his hand and clenched it into a tight fist. "In tetany." He gazed at his outstretched fist intently for a moment, then dropped it to his lap. "A bolus of potassium would do it."

"What is it you're trying to say?"

"Your man here didn't have a heart attack. It wasn't an MI that took this fellow out." He glanced at the strip again and shook his head. "I'd say he was murdered."

Gulliver stared at the closed door after Sessions left. Twenty-two years. Jesus Christ. Twenty-two years. And how many before that? How long had Barkley been waiting in the wings for his chance to take over HALFLIFE? How long had he been groomed for the part?

Gulliver's jaw clenched, worked, jarred a loose tooth. Scarcely aware of the stab of pain, he reached for the phone, dialed a motel in Atlanta, asked for extension 146.

Half a minute later, Oliver Pointer picked up. "Roger Wagstead here."

"I understand you do land surveys for your company."

A moment's silence. "That's right."

"I have a client who needs a survey. Can you start right away?"

"Yes, sir."

"That's a survey only. Do you understand? I'll be sending you more details by messenger."

"Yes, sir. And the name of the client, sir?"

"Richard Barkley."

THIRTY-ONE

The double doors clanged open and loud laughter advertised the return of the control group. Jody threw down the test papers, got up from her desk, and strode to the alcove. The four medical students had already littered the room with textbooks and fast-food containers. "Where have you guys been?" she demanded. "Isn't an hour long enough for lunch?"

Carla Hagen looked up from her bag of French fries. "Obviously not."

Al Cole plopped down on the wicker couch beside Carla and gave Jody a flat stare.

Angered, Jody returned the look. "You want to be doctors, don't you? I think it's time you developed a professional attitude."

Carla curled her lip. "Like Barkley, maybe?"

Memphis Red snickered and Tyrone Hayes barely concealed his smirk.

Jody narrowed her eyes. "I don't see the joke."

Al grinned. "Well, he's not here right now."

"Knock it off," she said fiercely. "You're getting paid to

participate in this study. That means finishing tests I give you and showing up on time. You ought to know enough science to realize how important this is to Dr. Barkley's study."

The generalized laughter that followed unnerved her. "All right. What's going on?"

Carla crumpled the greasy French fry bag. "Wouldn't we love to know?"

"What's that supposed to mean?"

The girl threw the wadded bag down, and glared at Jody. "I've tried to cooperate with that son of a bitch. But I've had it."

Tyrone Hayes nodded. "That goes for all of us."

Jody looked from one to the other. "What's happened?"

"For one thing, Barkley's been treating Carla like a galley slave," said Tyrone.

In a credible imitation of Barkley, Al laid his hand on Carla's shoulder and beamed angelically. "I'd like you to do something for me, little lady. Just run these packages over to my office, drop off my laundry, and pick up a birthday present for my great aunt Sally. Oh, and don't forget to water the dog and clean the canary cage. You don't mind, do you, dear?"

Carla smirked back. "Not at all, you old fart." The smile vanished. "He thinks women were put on earth to serve his every fucking need."

"What did he want you to do?"

Carla picked up her Coke and dabbed at the wet ring on the table. "Look, I don't mind running an errand or two. But, Jesus. Doesn't he know that girl was killed just three blocks away from here?"

"What are you talking about?"

"The Fox. It's not in the best neighborhood, you know."

"Barkley sent her out alone last night to get the theater tickets," said Tyrone.

"I was scared shitless," said Carla. "I had to go right by the sandwich shop where that waitress was killed. For all I knew, the goddamned murderer was still hanging around."

Typical, thought Jody. Three men in the control group, and Barkley picked the woman to do the scut work. "I'm sorry that happened," she said. "But that's no reason to slack off. You never finished the test this morning, and you're half an hour late." She looked at the others. "You're all being paid for a week's work."

"Oh, are we?" drawled Memphis.

"Well, aren't you?"

"You really don't know?" asked Carla.

"Know what?" asked Jody.

"We got canned."

"He fired you?" Impossible.

Imitating Barkley again, Al said, "Thanks so much for your assistance. But I won't be needing you students after today."

"We're only getting two hundred dollars, instead of the five hundred he promised," said Carla.

"I really needed the money," added Tyrone. "That's the only reason I signed up."

Why would Barkley fire them? What good was his study without a control group? And why in hell hadn't he told her? "Did he say why?"

"Ours not to reason why," said Carla tartly.

Tyrone stood up. "Any reason for us to hang around until five?"

"You have EEGs scheduled."

"Canceled," said Al.

Canceled? Jody looked at him blankly for a moment. Something else Barkley hadn't bothered to let her know. Something else to make her look like a fool in front of the others. Well, screw him. "I guess you can go then," she said. Jaw set, she watched in silence as the four students gathered up their books and walked out.

At a quarter of two, Jody found Mystery Carmody in the nurses station, red-faced and near tears. "What's wrong?"

"Nothing." The girl tried a shrug, but it looked more like a nervous little twitch.

"Can I help?"

Carmody shook her head. "I'm okay." She wiped her nose with a crumpled tissue. "It's just that I'm so damned mad, I could— I could— Oh, shit." She wadded the tissue and began to cry.

Jody slipped an arm around her shoulder. "Rough day?"

"I've had it. I'm not going to put up with any more of this crap."

"Barkley?"

A short nod.

"What happened?"

"He just called me incompetent." She blew her nose. "To be absolutely precise, he said, 'If you had the proficiency of a beginning nurse's aide, Miss Carmody, you might be able to do your job.' " Her eyes narrowed. "The old fart was smiling when he said it, too. That goddamned sarcastic smile of his. I wanted to slap it right off his face."

"What was he so stirred up about?"

"Dayton Satterfield. Like it was my fault or something." Carmody fumbled for another tissue and the little gray box fell to the floor.

Jody retrieved it, pulled one out, and handed it to her.

"Thanks." Carmody wiped her eyes and brown mascara smudged the tissue. "Satterfield was scheduled for an EEG at one-thirty, but he refused. He said he felt sick—one of those cluster headaches he gets—"

The phone at the nurses desk shrilled.

Giving her eyes a final swipe, Carmody picked up. "Morgan Wing. Miss Carmody speaking." She shot a glance toward Barkley's door. "Let me connect you." Punching a button, she held the receiver to her ear. "Damn thing," she whispered, and punched again. A faint ringing came from the office across the hall. "Mallory Corn's office on the line," she said stiffly, and hung up.

"Mallory Corn!" Jody blurted. A month ago, Corn's name might not have registered, but now it was a household word—at least in Atlanta. Mallory Corn was Chief of the Atlanta Police Department.

Carmody shrugged. "He called yesterday, too. Old drinking buddy or something, I guess. Anyway, like I was saying, Barkley was out to lunch, so I couldn't tell him about Satterfield's headache. Well, he shows up a few minutes later, trots right by me like I was furniture or something, and goes into the treatment room expecting Satterfield to be there." Her lip curled. "The Great God Barkley. Thy will be done.

"So out he comes and wants to know where his patient is. I told him Satterfield refused; he had a headache. And Barkley says, 'Well, you just march right down there and *get* him.' Like I was a five-year-old or something."

"Did you?" asked Jody.

"I tried. By then, Satterfield was getting pissed about

the whole thing—not that I blame him. But Barkley wouldn't take no for an answer; he wanted me to go back and hogtie him, I guess." Carmody's eyes flashed. "So, I refused. I mean the patient has rights, you know? That's when Barkley called me incompetent. And what's the big deal, anyway?" she said indignantly. "He's got all week. He can run the EEG tomorrow."

A door swung open across the hall. "Well, shit," Carmody muttered under her breath. "Here he comes again."

"Short conversation," said Jody. Why was Mallory Corn calling Barkley, anyway? She was puzzled by the phone call. It wasn't likely that Corn was calling about a psychological profile of the killer. Not from Barkley. He didn't qualify as an expert; he was a neurologist, not a psychiatrist.

Not to fret, my dear Miss Henson, she told herself. Who said it was police business, anyway? It could be anything—a mutual investment, a mutual girlfriend. Maybe Carmody was right; maybe Barkley and Corn really were old drinking buddies.

But Cheryl Isaacson's words from last night kept coming back to her:

The killer left a signature. His name is Jonathan. . . .

Coincidence, she told herself. It had to be.

Barkley strode up to the desk.

Jody eyed him with distaste. She was tempted to confront him about the control group. Put him on the spot. Demand to know why he had dismissed them without a word to her. But what was the point? He was going to do exactly as he pleased, anyway. It just wasn't worth getting into hot water over it.

Ignoring Carmody, Barkley turned to Jody. "Miss

Henson, would you please tell Mr. Satterfield it's time for his EEG?"

Jody gave him a steady look. "Mr. Satterfield doesn't feel well. He's refused the test; he has that right, you know. But I'll be happy to try." Wondering if her voice sounded as wooden to Barkley as it did to her, she turned, and, without waiting for a response, walked briskly to Dayton Satterfield's closed door and knocked.

An unintelligible mumble.

Taking it as an invitation, Jody opened the door and went in.

She had expected to find Satterfield in bed, or at least showing some sign of discomfort. Instead, he was sitting calmly in front of an overbed table covered with shiny little pliers and tweezers and several spools of fourteen-karat gold wire in varying gauges. Head bent over his work, he twisted a length of gold around a notched wooden dowel. Once. Twice. Once more.

He gave her an even look. "You the second team?" There was an edge to his voice.

No point in antagonizing him. She fell back on a neutral opening. "How are you feeling, Mr. Satterfield?"

A drop of acid. "Now, how do you suppose I'm feeling?"

Why was he so hostile? The neutral tone again. "I don't know."

He continued to work the gold wire, looping, making intricate twists and whorls, transforming the wire into a delicate filigree.

"Oh," she said in surprise. "You're making a ring." She leaned closer. "It's a butterfly!"

"Close, but no cigar." He held out the dowel. "Take another look."

Relieved that some of the hostility had gone out of his

voice, Jody took the dowel and held it up. Tiny outstretched wings caught the light. "It's a bird."

"A dove."

"It's beautiful." She handed back the dowel.

Taking it, Satterfield looked at it as if he were seeing it for the first time. "It is, isn't it?"

"I didn't know filigree was done that way."

"It isn't. This is a technique I worked out myself. I don't suppose I'd have thought of it, if I'd had formal training."

She nodded. "I think I know what you mean." It worked that way in singing, she thought. The voice that everyone had called "different" when she was sixteen turned out to sound like everybody else's after two years of lessons. "Do you always do birds?"

"No." He leaned over, picked up a cigar box from the floor, and handed it to her. "Take a look."

She opened the box. Inside, half a dozen delicate rings shimmered in the light from the tall windows. Slipping one over the tip of a finger, she held it up. A bumblebee, fat body balanced by thin veined wings. One by one, she examined the others: a golden egg in a nest, a spidery daisy, a tiny snake gliding across a twig—and something else . . .

Curious, Jody picked it up and felt a sudden disquiet. The ring had been twisted beyond recognition, as if heavy pliers or a violent hammer blow had crushed the delicate gold.

With an abrupt movement, he took it out of her hand, threw it into the box, and snapped the lid shut. "They don't all fly." A thin smile, hard and tight as twisted wire. A low voice, edged with metal. "Why don't you just run along now? And tell your Dr. Barkley to fuck off."

* * *

It was all Jody could do to keep from slamming Satterfield's door on the way out. Childish, she thought. She wanted to rattle it off its hinges.

Carmody looked up from her charts as Jody stalked up to the desk. "Bad news?"

"That depends on your point of view. I never even got around to asking about the EEG. Before I had the chance, he threw me out."

"ESP at work. That sucker can spot an ulterior motive from twenty paces." She clicked a chart shut and reached for another. "Satterfield ought to go to work for Barkley. He could handle the switchboard." She stared at the neurologist's closed door and shook her head. "He doesn't want a nurse; he wants a mind reader. Preferably one from AT&T."

"Maybe he does," said Jody absently. Then she blinked.

Maybe that was exactly what Barkley wanted.

Moments later, Jody was knocking at Maureen Dorcas's door. But though she tapped, waited, tapped again, there was no answer. She hesitated, then went inside.

The closet stood empty. A scarred leather suitcase on the bed was heaped with clothes, fuzzy slippers, a thin pillow in a blue satin case, and Maureen's tiny portable television, cushioned in a nest of underwear, its blind, gray eye filmed with a cataract of panty hose.

"Maureen?"

It was a futile question. The medium was gone.

Puzzled, she headed back toward the nurses station, intending to ask Carmody why Maureen had packed up. On the way, she passed Beth Quaig's half-open door and stopped.

A child was singing. A slow rhythmic chant in a minor key that sent a chill skittering down Jody's spine:

"It's raining . . .
It's pouring . . .
The old man . . .
Is snoring . . ."

Beth, sitting cross-legged on the bed, staring intently at the length of twine looped around her hands.

"Beth?" But she knew it wasn't Beth. It wasn't Beth at all.

Fingers moving in a pattern.

"Bumped his head . . .
And he went to bed . . ."

Fingers catching loops of string, lifting, twisting.

"And he didn't get up . . .
In the morning . . ."

Hands spread, the girl held up a cat's cradle. "You have to do it right or it doesn't work."

"What?" Jody moved closer to the bed. "What doesn't work?"

"The magic."

"What magic?"

An exasperated sigh. "Don't you know anything?"

"A few things. You're Tabby, aren't you?"

"Course I am. I told you before." Carefully, the girl lifted the string off her fingers and wadded it in the palm of her hand.

"What kind of magic does the cat's cradle do?"

Scorn. "It's not a cat's cradle."

"What is it then?"

"Something." She stretched the string to its length, wadded it again. "Something people can't go through."

A fence? Or a wall.

"What people, Tabby?"

"Just people." She stretched the string again. "They don't like it here."

"Why not?"

A tilt of the head. An arch look. "Because."

Who was behind the wall?

The loop of string pulled taut between two open palms. Old dead-white scars crisscrossed the girl's wrists.

The question came on impulse: "Is the magic for Anne?"

"Maybe."

Anne, the angry one. "Who else, Tabby?"

She tipped her head and stared at the string. "Somebody."

"Somebody scary?"

A head shake. "I'm not scared. I'm not scared of nothing." Tabby grasped her nose, wiggled it, stretched the ellipse of twine.

"It's raining . . .
It's pouring . . ."

The web of a cat's cradle growing.

"The old man . . .
Is snoring . . ."

Beth and Maureen. Tim and Dayton Satterfield. All of them building a wall. Why? she wondered. Why?

"Bumped his head . . .
And he went to bed . . .
And he couldn't get up . . .
In the morning. . . ."

THIRTY-TWO

The rest of the afternoon, Jody worked with her door open and one eye on the room down the hall. She was hoping to catch Maureen when she came back for her luggage, but it was four-thirty now, and still no sign of the medium.

"If she's going to opt out of Barkley's little party, that's fine with me," Mystery Carmody had said. "Just as long as she does it after I get off." The nurse had signed off her charts in record time, and at the stroke of four, she scooped up her coat with a sigh of relief and was out the door.

Beth Quaig had shown up a moment later, asking for change for a dollar, giving no sign that she remembered seeing Jody in her room earlier. Within fifteen minutes, she was back with a fountain Coke from the coffee shop. "I thought you might be thirsty," she said shyly and, thrusting the paper cup into Jody's hand, scurried back to her room.

The stack of file folders cascaded across the desk, and only quick action kept them from sliding to the floor. Sighing, Jody anchored them with a metal emesis basin filled with paper clips that served as a paperweight, sucked on a chip of Coke-flavored ice, and went back to the pile of test papers from that morning. She gave a final glance at Tim's. Three pages of what to do with a razor blade, and no sign of running out of ideas. She smiled at the scrawled, "Dinner tonight?" He had been shut away in his room all afternoon, working on his book.

She wondered what her mother would think of Tim, and decided that, with reservations, she would approve. The reservations would be because of his work, she thought, imagining the response:

"But, dear, will he be able to support you?"

Margaret Henson had grown up with the belief that a girl worked only until she could get a man to bring in the money for her, and thirty years of marriage and a substantial life insurance check at the end of it had done nothing to change her mind. "A man brings home the bacon, Jody, and the woman cooks it."

The ice rattled in the paper cup and another big chunk slid into her mouth. Her mother always told her eating ice would break her teeth. Well, it hadn't yet. She held up the cup. "Cheers, Mom." Then she blinked as an inadvertent swallow mechanism sent the ice down her throat.

God. A mother's revenge.

The headache came on instantaneously as she knew it would. Wincing at the excruciating pain, she took deep breaths and counted the slow seconds until it was over. When it finally stopped, she leaned back in her chair and panted with relief. It had to be the worst agony known to man. The only thing that made it bearable was its brevity; if it went on for very long, it would lead to suicide, she thought, imagining the coroner's report. Cause of death: ice-cream headache. Wondering if the *New England Journal of Medicine* had ever published a paper on the syndrome, she threw the cup and the rest of the ice in the trash, put Tim's test paper aside, and picked up Beth Quaig's.

The first few lines were in a large childish hand:

> *1. Shave with it.*
> *2. Cut things out like paper.*
> *3. Notch baseball bats and things with.*

Who had been taking the test? Tabby? Or one of the others? Maybe the boy, the Little League pitcher.

Abruptly the handwriting changed to an adult's, and the ideas had began to tumble out. Fifteen or twenty of them.

Jody skimmed the page:

> *18. Cold meat slicer for party sandwiches.*
> *19. Texture tool for clay sculpture.*
> *20. High-pitched musical saw.*

Then the last, in writing so small and crabbed that she had to squint to make out the one word repeated over and over:

> *Cut . . . cut . . . cut, cut, cut. . . .*

And how about that, Dr. Barkley? Or maybe you still think Beth Quaig is doing fine.

Jody was debating whether to knock on Barkley's door, test paper in hand, and tilt with windmills again when the phone in the nurses station began to ring. He'd probably heard it; his office was next to hers. Unless his door was closed. Well by God, she could close hers too, deny she'd heard it if he asked. If he wanted a goddamned switchboard operator, he could hire one.

She was on her feet, reaching for the doorknob, when she was struck by how ridiculous her reaction was. Who said the phone was for Barkley? It might even be for her.

The telephone's shrill ring cut off as she picked up and gave an automatic floor-nurse response: "Morgan Wing, Miss Henson speaking."

A man's voice. "Barkley, please."

"May I ask who's calling?"

"Jones."

"One moment." She stared at the faded script on the old switchboard set. Was Barkley "Doctors Lounge"? Or "Resident"? Resident, probably. That's what it said on the door, anyway. She punched four.

No response.

"Doctors Lounge," then. The button wobbled. When she released it, a faint ringing came from across the hall.

"Barkley."

"Mr. Jones is on the line."

A pause. "Put him on."

She pressed number one and, hoping she really had made the connection, held the phone to her ear.

"Hello."

"Pointer here. One hour."

"Same place?"

"Right."

The phone disconnected with a loud click. Startled, she hung up and stared across the hall, half expecting Barkley to come roaring out and accuse her of eavesdropping. But she had only meant to check the damned connection.

A dozen questions popped into her mind. Pointer. Was it a first name? Possibly. But she had never heard of it before. Or was "Jones" really "Pointer"? What the hell was going on here? Her gaze moved speculatively to Barkley's door, and she picked up the phone again.

She got an outside line and called information. "Cheryl Isaacson, please."

The operator checked. No number listed.

"It's a La Vista Road address." At least, it used to be.

"I have a C. L. Isaacson on La Vista."

"That's it."

She dialed the number. When it began to ring, she tried to remember if Cheryl slept mornings or afternoons.

On the fourth ring, Cheryl answered.

"Hi. This is Jody. I hope I didn't get you up."

A laugh. "If that was your plan, you're half an hour too late. What's up?"

"I was just wondering something. Your fiancé . . ." What was his name?

"Yeah?"

"Would you happen to know if the police department ever uses psychics?"

"Psychics?"

"You know, to help solve crimes."

"I don't know. Hang on a minute and I'll ask."

So they *were* living together.

Two minutes later, Cheryl came back on the line. "James said to keep it under your hat, but once in a while they do. It's not the kind of thing that they like to have get out, though. The newspapers have a lot of fun with that sort of thing." A pause. "Why do you want to know?"

"Just wondering. I was thinking about the D-string murders."

"Hard not to, I guess. You can't turn on the news without hearing about it."

The double doors at the end of the hall swung open and Jody glanced up. Maureen Dorcas came in. "I've got to run. Are you working tonight?"

A sigh. "Uh-huh. Drop by if you're around."

"I will. And thanks."

Jody caught up with Maureen just outside her door. The medium was carrying a brown shopping bag with something white and fuzzy inside.

"I need to talk to you," said Jody. "I knocked earlier, and when no one answered I opened your door."

An ingenuous smile. "And saw my packed bags."

"Well, yes."

"I made up my mind this morning." She clutched her bag closer and several inches of pale downy feathers crept out.

Jody stared.

"It's not alive. Not anymore, anyway," said Maureen, grinning. "I've been shopping. Like it?" She pulled out an antique feather boa. "Only two dollars. Of course, it needs work." The boa, delicate feathers yellow with age, was in two pieces.

A door clicked open down the hall and Jody turned toward the sound. It was Barkley.

"Miss Henson." A cherubic smile. "I need you."

"I'll be right there." She turned back to Maureen. "If you want to leave, I won't stop you. But I need to talk to you." She glanced back toward Barkley. "I'm having dinner with Tim at six-thirty. Will you stay 'til then and join us?"

"Actually, I was planning on staying over until tomorrow morning. It's against my religion to pass up anything free—especially theater tickets, but I wasn't crazy about driving home late at night. It's a forty-five-minute trip."

"Then you'll meet us for dinner?"

Maureen batted her lashes. "Of cose, dahlin'." She glanced at her watch. "Just as long as I have time to splice mah boa and put on mah theater clothes."

THIRTY-THREE

The inevitable red lamps with gold tassels dangled from the Mandarin Temple's ceiling, and cliché pan-sized goldfish raced in the hundred-gallon tank by the cash register. Scooping up three menus, the hostess said, "You follow, please," and led them to a round, teetery-looking table in the corner.

Tim tweaked Jody's elbow. "*Déjà vu?* Do you feel like you've been in fifty-seven places just like this?"

"Fifty-eight, if you count past lives," she said.

"It's a package deal. You call Yin Yang Gottlieb of Oriental Eateries, Inc., and for a flat fee, he sends you the lamps, the fish, the folding screens, and a year's supply of pineapple."

Jody took a seat across from Maureen, and, when the hostess was gone, said in a conspiratorial tone, "How about the gong?"

"Gongs are optional." This one was suspended from a black-lacquered frame near Tim's right elbow. He reached out, drummed his fingers on the rippled brass, and was rewarded with a deep shimmer of sound. The gong was missing its mallet, but it sported a long tassel of dragon-breath red with black and gold wrappings. If he wanted to make his financial mark, that was the way to go: Tacky Tassels, Ltd., suppliers to kings and Yin Yang Gottlieb. He fingered its synthetic strands. God-awful. Still, he reflected, if God liked Char Su Ding half as much as he did, He forgave the Mandarin Temple its excesses.

Tim was not so sure how God felt about Maureen's. At the stroke of six-thirty, she had emerged from her room, struck a pose, and peered at him through a pair of opera glasses inlaid with chipped mother-of-pearl. "My theater clothes."

The dress she wore was red silk, skintight to just below the knee, then flaring out in a kind of ruffled thing that reminded him of a Spanish dancer. The limited action it afforded her legs, and the thin spiky heels she had on, made him wonder how she managed to walk. She had topped off the outfit with a white feather boa that had a pinched place in it, and to Jody's delight flirted it in his face.

He had inadvertently inhaled an inch or so, and it was like breathing in cobwebs. "Breathtaking," he managed to say.

He cast a sidelong glance at the medium and hid a smile behind his outsized menu. She had pulled out a long cigarette holder and the narrow-gauge Ultra Thin she poked into it immediately fell out. Undaunted, she shimmed it with a little wad of Kleenex and lit up. Vintage Busby Berkeley—and just as innocent. Like a little girl dressing up in Mommy's clothes. He wondered why Jody had been so determined for Maureen to come along. From the speculative looks she'd been giving the medium, it was obvious there was something on her mind.

The black menu featured a gold pagoda on its cover and, inside, a special on dinner for two, four, or six. They settled on the dinner for four, and ordered drinks: white wine for Jody, Kirin beer for Tim, and the specialty of the house for Maureen, a pink and potent concoction that came in a hollowed-out pineapple topped with a little paper parasol.

Jody played with her drink, fingering the wine glass, turning it in her hand. "I was wondering," she began. "Is it possible for someone to be psychic and not know it?"

Maureen balanced her cigarette holder on the ashtray. "Certainly."

Tim snorted.

Maureen gave him a sidelong look. "Everyone's psychic. Our brains are hard-wired for it."

"Oh, come on," he said with a vehemence that surprised him. "What about those so-called 'study groups' you were involved in before?"

"What about them?"

"Why don't you admit it? They weren't study groups at all. You were involved in government-funded psychic research, weren't you?"

She blinked. "You may be proving my point."

"Baloney. I'm a writer. Writers read books. There've been several that mention the Russians' psychic research and our own parallel studies."

"So?"

"So if everyone's psychic, why did they pick you instead of the guy off the street? If everyone's psychic, why the research in the first place?"

"Good question," she said. "Because there's a catch."

"I thought there would be."

"The catch is, you have to believe in it. You have to let yourself see and feel beyond the senses, and our culture doesn't allow that." She plucked the little parasol out of her drink, twirled it, and stuck it in her hair.

A metamorphosis, he thought. Spanish dancer hatches into Madame Butterfly.

"In a sense," Maureen went on, "you have to allow yourself to believe in magic, to be a small child again. Most people can't do that. If you see something, or sense something that you've been told all your life isn't there, you don't trust it, so you look for an explanation, and you rationalize it away."

Jody leaned forward. "What if a person, an adult, believed she was a child—a little girl with magical powers? If she really believed that, then she'd have to be psychic. Isn't that what you're saying?"

"Interesting," said Maureen. "I guess I am." The waiter interrupted with a sizzling platter of pork ribs, egg rolls, and crisp fried won tons. She selected a rib and drizzled it with Chinese mustard.

Jody knitted her brow. "There's something I don't understand, though. In your book, you didn't mention any childhood psychic ability. You said Paul came when you were in college."

"That's right. He did. Right in the middle of a philosophy class." She laughed. "And he came as quite a surprise, too. We were looking at a film about Martin Luther—not King, the first one—and there he was. All of a sudden, I could see him. He was standing by the screen, big as life, using his cane as a pointer. And when he disagreed with Dr. Costanzas, he'd shake his head and scowl like this—" Maureen pulled down her lip in an exaggerated frown. "When I realized no one else saw him, it was a bad moment. I thought I'd gone crazy.

"That was the Western culture asserting itself. Fortunately, I had a grandmother who was not only sympathetic, but psychic too. She couldn't actually see him, but she could sense him. When she told me the impressions she was getting and they jibed with mine, I felt okay about it; I wasn't sure about my own sanity at that point, but I knew damned well that Grandma wasn't nuts.

"Bless her. She helped me keep my balance through all of it—the channeling, the first book, the psychic research . . ."

"The government study," said Jody. "What was it like?"

"Trying. But when you care about your country, you do what you can. They had me go into trance several times, so the work involved Paul." She paused to sip her drink. "I can't tell you any more than that."

"Why not?" asked Jody.

"I took an oath." A pause. "And to tell you the truth, I don't remember much about it anymore."

The silence that followed was broken by the anxious-to-please waiter bringing more food and asking if everything was all right. "Just some more of this." Maureen held up a nearly empty bottle of soy sauce, and the waiter hurried off with it. She watched him go, then suddenly laughed. "There is one thing I can tell you. We went to Florida. You know, palm trees, surf, sun. But the place turned out to be forty miles inland on one of those highways nobody uses anymore. We're talking first-class dump.

"I still have the bathing suit I took down there. On the Monday I arrived, it was navy blue, but by Wednesday it was the color of Plochman's mustard from all the chlorine in the pool. I wore it Thursday and had to go back to my room in a towel. The seat split right down the middle."

Tim trapped a pea pod with his chopsticks. "I call that cheeky of you."

Maureen grinned. "But never again. When I got it home, I put it back together with reinforcements and a flat-felled seam. A package of Rit and it looked almost like new."

"So they were interested in Paul," said Tim. "Isn't he Catch Number Two in your 'everybody's psychic' theory? The other night, you said your scores are no better than chance without him."

"Touché, love," she said, opening the new bottle of soy the waiter brought, and dousing her fried rice with it. "I'm not sure just why that's so, but part of it at least is probably ego. It's a matter of nerve, the fear of losing control. I trust Paul. More than I trust myself, I think. If I let him take over, I know I'll be safe, but it's scary when I'm on my own, so I shut it off."

"Convenient." Tim did not try to mask the skepticism in his voice.

"Very." Maureen nibbled a won ton. "Some people call Paul a guide. It's not a bad term. My ex-husband owned a cave. When he took me down there, he was my guide and I wasn't afraid. Without him, I could have been lost." She looked away, remembering. "I could have died down there alone in the dark."

Jody helped herself to the cashew shrimp. "In your book, you said Paul was an aspect of yourself."

"Yes. But a bigger and better one than I am, I think. He knows more, and sees more, and he isn't afraid of it. Maybe it would be more accurate to say that I'm an aspect of Paul."

"Then what do you think happened during the seance in your room the other night? I mean, Paul was there, but you got hurt."

The medium's hand went to her throat. As her fingers traced the flesh, Tim saw the thin line that circled her neck. It was only slightly darker than her skin, but when he looked closely, he could see the shadowy discoloration of old bruises. Startled, he realized she had covered them with makeup. He suddenly felt ill at ease, as if he had blundered into her room while she was dressing.

Instead of letting up, the feeling intensified. He remembered Maureen had worn turtlenecks yesterday and this morning, but he had thought nothing of it. "Why didn't Paul warn you?" he blurted.

A pause. Fingers tracing flesh. "Maybe he did."

He met her stare, then blinked as Paul's voice came back to him:

Even this instrument refuses to see and hear, although she believes she does. Instead, she follows an impulse that is not her own.

A sense of foreboding came and shadowed his eyes.

Maureen pushed away the plate of food and, not bothering to use the holder, lit a cigarette. "It's all a play, you see. A drama of probabilities. We may not understand what part we're playing, but we always know our lines—and sometimes we need to change the script." A curl of blue-gray smoke took ghostly form, then dissipated in a faint current of air. "I told you last night that Paul was gone," she said. "He still is. That's why I packed up." A short laugh, followed by a cough. "Maybe they ought to put up a sign: Morgan Wing may be hazardous to your mental health."

"Don't you have an inconsistency of logic there?" Tim said, aware of the edge to his voice, but unable to control it. "If Paul is a part of you, an alter ego—"

"Her greater self," Jody put in.

"Whatever you call it. If he's a part of you, then he can't be gone, can he?"

Maureen fixed him with solemn eyes. "Haven't you ever felt out of touch with yourself?"

He looked down at his plate; he felt that way now.

Jody crumpled her napkin, folding it, smoothing it, crumpling it again. "You've been reading the papers, watching the news," she began. "This . . . person who came during the seance. The man who attacked you—"

"The entity," said Maureen in a low, suddenly harsh voice.

"The entity," said Jody. "Is there a connection? Is he part of the Atlanta murders?"

The medium's head jerked back. Although her gaze was fixed on Jody, she did not seem to see her. Instead, her eyes began to shift from side to side as if they followed a shadow show that only she could see. "The dark thing," she whispered. "The thing in the storeroom . . ."

Slowly, Maureen focused on the girl across from her. "Yes," she said at last. "I think he is."

THIRTY-FOUR

It was a quarter to eight by the time the fortune cookies arrived. Tim cracked his open:

One whose head is in the clouds will turn his attention to business.

He found it vaguely disturbing, though he could not say why.

They paid the bill and Maureen, with a glance at her watch, said to Jody, "Sure you won't change your mind?"

Jody nodded. "I'm sure."

"Well then, thanks for the company." With a parting wave, Maureen hurried off to the Fox Theater, spindly heels clicking on the sidewalk, feather boa streaming behind her.

"You'll miss the curtain," Tim said to Jody.

A night breeze ruffled the crisp hair on her brow and caused her to shiver after the warmth of the restaurant. "I told Maureen to go on without me."

"Why?"

"I've seen *A Chorus Line* twice. Besides, I want to talk."

"I'm going to be busy." As soon as the words were out of his mouth, he regretted them.

Jody blinked. "Oh. I don't want to interrupt." She glanced quickly away, fixing her gaze on the restaurant window, but he had seen the look in her eyes, half puzzled, half hurt.

God, she was beautiful. "Forget I said that. I'm not that busy." He took her arm and steered her toward the intersection that led back to the hospital.

They walked in silence the few blocks back, breaking it only when they entered the drafty Rutledge lobby. Although the Pediatric Outpatient Clinic was closed, the high-ceilinged room was full of children, minded by a handful of relatives and a harried-looking Gray Lady. "Visiting hours," said Jody. "Kids aren't allowed upstairs unless they're patients, so they have to wait down here while the rest of the family goes up."

Tim eyed a chubby two-year-old eating a candy bar. Most of the chocolate was smeared on his face. "Don't they let parents go up anytime?"

"Not anytime. We're in a high-crime area here. The parents can sleep over if they want to, but they don't let them come and go after the shift changes. Security locks up then. And a good thing too—" She stopped and glanced away. "I was robbed here once. At knife point." A crooked little smile as if she were half ashamed, as if it had somehow been her fault. "It's funny how your mind works," she said. "I could have been killed, but that didn't hit me until later. When it did, I was a wreck. I had nightmares for months. But right after it happened, the only thought in my head was, 'Don't tell Mother.'"

Tim laughed. "I suspect your mother is a lot like mine."

The elevator was crowded. When it stopped on 4 West, four other passengers got off too, but no one else turned right toward the connecting passageway to Morgan Wing and its painted-over Contagion Ward sign.

The double doors clanged shut behind them. The hollow echoes reverberated through the deserted corridor, and a startled gray mouse scurried into an inky crevice.

Morgan Wing was in its night mode. Dim lights burning low on the walls spilled yellow puddles among the shadows, and though the radiator in the dark alcove clanked, a damp chill seeped through the hallway. Tim cast a quick glance toward Barkley's office. The door was closed, the overhead transom black. He knew the key was there, under the desktop, held by a magnet against the metal. He knew it as surely as if he had seen it and touched it.

The fluorescent light in Tim's room was a cold blue-white oasis that accentuated the black-edged shadows that lay just beyond. He glanced at his watch. Barely 8:30. Curtain time. It would be at least two hours before the others got back. Silently, he poured bourbon into pleated paper cups and handed her one. "A little jazz with your juice?"

"Sure. Why not?"

He opened the locker, looked down. The tape box lay on its side next to the computer. Squatting, he opened it. One of the slots was empty. For a long moment, he did not move. Then he straightened, crossed the room, threw the open box on the bed.

"What is it?"

"The seance tape. It's gone."

"Are you sure?"

"I'm sure, all right. It was a BASF tape. The only one without a label."

"Maybe it's in the machine," said Jody.

"No."

"Your pocket, then."

He patted his shirt pocket, pulled out cigarettes and

lighter, threw them on the bed with the tape box. "Give me your ticket."

"To the play?"

At his nod, a puzzled look crossed her face, but she took it out and handed it to him.

He opened his wallet, pulled out a matching ticket, compared the two. "Take a look."

The tickets were for different sections of the theater.

"So?" She looked up. "What are you suggesting?"

"That the rest of our happy little group is scattered all over the Fox right now."

"You think someone is trying to separate us?"

He shook his head. "Just the opposite. The idea was to get everybody out of the building. But it was a last-minute plan—too late to get seats blocked together."

"You're right about that," said Jody. "Dr. Barkley sent Carla Hagen to pick them up last night."

Startled, he wondered why she hadn't told him before. But then, why should she?

A puzzled look came into her eyes. Then, a half smile. "Are you saying that someone tried to lure us out of Morgan Wing just so he could steal your tape?"

"That's why my locker was opened last night. Barkley knew we were at your place—his rent-a-nurse told him so. But the tape wasn't in my room. I had it with me. Then he told Carmody to call you back to the hospital." Tim watched her closely, gauging her reaction. "He wanted you out of the house."

Surprise widened her eyes. A whisper. "Then someone *was* there. . . ."

"You win the Kewpie doll."

"You think it was Dr. Barkley?"

"Barkley or somebody working for him." The question

was, why? Why was the tape so important? He thought of the dark office down the hall, remembered Barkley's hand beneath the desk and the click of metal on metal.

Jody leaned forward and said abruptly, "I know why you're here."

Tim stared into his cup to hide his startled look. How? How could she know about the key?

"I wasn't positive until dinner. That's why I wanted Maureen to come along. But now I'm sure. It's a double-blind experiment."

"What is?"

"This whole thing. You're not here for a creativity study. I think you're all here on police business."

Astonished, he forgot his anger enough to laugh. "You've found me out. Undercover for the vice squad."

"I'm serious," she said. "It makes sense. The tape—everything."

She wasn't making sense at all.

"They obviously didn't want you to know what the study was really about. But I can think of a couple of reasons why. First of all, there's the embarrassment to the department if any of this got out to the media."

"I don't know what you're talking about. What department?"

"The Atlanta police," she said patiently as if she were explaining to a small child. "They use psychics. Sometimes it's the only way to a breakthrough. But they didn't want it to get out because it's unorthodox; the newspapers and TV would have a field day. Then there's the decline effect. When a psychic knows he's being tested, the results fall off. After a while they're no better than chance."

"Are you saying the police are hot for my crystal ball?" Tim tried to keep a straight face, but he couldn't help smiling. "You're overlooking one little thing: there's not a psychic bone in my body."

"How can you be so sure about that? You're a writer. Creative people can dissociate without even knowing it. That's exactly what happens to Maureen when she goes into trance. It's what happens to Beth too, for that matter. It's a question of degree."

"Right. Diversified Dissociates, Inc. Call 1-800-FOR-OMEN to order your prediction today. Only nineteen ninety-five." He was grinning broadly now. "One question. How come none of us psychics figured out the police department's game?"

She looked away, then back, this time with a defensive set to her lips. "It isn't funny. There's nothing funny about what happened to those women."

"What women?"

"The victims. The D-string murders."

He studied her face. "You're really serious, aren't you?" But he did not need an answer; her expression told him that.

Jody looked down at her cup. "Last night I talked to a nurse I went to school with. Cheryl works in the E.R., and she happens to be engaged to a policeman. She was there when they brought in one of the murder victims—the little girl. The killer had carved his name on her body, and . . ." She stopped as if she had suddenly thought better of what she was saying.

"And?"

A heartbeat. "His name is Jonathan."

For a moment he could not get his breath. He closed his eyes and saw the marks on Maureen's throat, saw Beth Quaig's face, saw his own computer screen:

You know me . . . you know me . . . you know me. . . .

"At first, I thought it was coincidence, but this morning I talked to a psychologist in Birmingham about Beth, and . . ." She stopped. "Are you all right?"

His stomach twisted. "What you're saying— It's bullshit."

Her chin jerked up.

"So, we're all going to save society from a degenerate killer." The ironic smile he intended was stillborn. "You really swallowed Maureen's line, didn't you? 'Everybody's psychic.' It follows, doesn't it? All the police have to do is pick a few names out of the phone book. Presto, a mystic task force. Fucking bullshit."

Jody's lips were a thin line. "I suppose you think it's more logical to call it coincidence."

Sharp nausea rippled his stomach. He took a deep breath, and though the queasy feeling ebbed, he suddenly felt drained. For a long time, Tim studied the cup he held, traced its stiff pleats with a thumb. "There's another possibility," he said at last. "One of us could be the killer."

Jody started. "No." She reached out, touched his arm. "Is that what you think? No." She shook her head. "It isn't possible."

He searched her face, saw earnest eyes, a tentative smile meant to reassure. She had shut off what he said—click—like throwing a switch. "You don't understand," he began, and suddenly the words poured out in a flood with no way to stop them. "Beth isn't the only one who lost time. So did Maureen. So did I."

A stunned look as if he had slapped her.

Splinters of ice crept in his belly. Why had he told her? He had opened a Pandora's box of words, and they were live things, out of control. He wanted them back.

Finally, she spoke. "What time? When?"

He focused on the cup he held, set it down without drinking, shivered at the cold vulnerability he felt. "Once with Barkley. Once when Maureen was here."

"And Maureen?"

He shook his head. "I don't know. She mentioned it last night. She didn't say when."

"What about Dayton Satterfield? Has it happened to him?"

Satterfield? Satterfield and his headaches. Who knew? "Why?"

"Nothing. It's just that I saw a few of the rings he makes—he keeps them in a cigar box—and one of them made me feel a little uneasy. That's all."

He wanted to ask, do I do that? Do I make you feel that way? Instead, he said, "You think it's happening to him too, don't you?"

"There's an explanation." She reached for his hand. Her fingers were cold. "We just don't know what it is yet."

He stood abruptly, shrugging off her touch. "I'm going to find it."

"How?"

"Barkley's files. I saw him put the key under his desk. That's why I skipped the play; I was thinking about going through them while everybody was out." His lips thinned. "I don't seem to have any choice now."

The startled look on her face gave way to a frown. Then she stood. "Not you. Me. You don't know what to look for and I do."

"Both of us then."

Jody shook her head. "If Barkley finds out, I'll be hunting for a new job. You need to stay in the hall and make sure no one sees me." She retrieved the lab coat she had tossed onto Tim's bed before dinner, pulled out a thin penlight from the pocket, started to turn it on, then stopped. "Whoever took your tape—You don't think he's still here, do you?"

"No," he said. "He got what he wanted."

Heart pounding, Jody turned the knob and slipped into Barkley's office. The heavy door swung shut behind her with a gunshot-loud click. Jesus! She might as well put up a sign. Robbery in progress.

Stupid. Why was she doing this? If Barkley found out, it was all over.

The room was pitch-black. Jody thumbed the penlight on, and blinked. Its puny glow seemed bright as a floodlight. She eyed the transom uneasily. It was clear glass; someone could see. Shading the light with one hand, she aimed it toward the desktop.

Except for the telephone, it was bare. Barkley had cleared everything away before he left.

Squatting, Jody pushed away the swivel chair and aimed the light up at the smooth underside of the desktop.

Nothing. Nothing but a bare expanse of metal.

She tugged at the center drawer. Stuck. Maybe locked. Giving it a yank, she snagged a fingernail and reflexively snatched her hand away. Damn.

The nail was torn to the quick.

She stuck the fingertip in her mouth and tasted the faint salt of blood. Just great. Bleed all over everything. And what about the nail? Jody had no idea whether or not a criminal's identity could be traced to a fingernail; she suspected it could.

She played the light over the floor, looking for it, finding nothing, imagining the headlines: Barkleygate Defendant Linked to Broken Fingernail. For an encore, she could leave her name and address.

At least the drawer was open. A quick look showed nothing but paper clips, prescription pads, pens. The usual doctor's office stuff.

There were two other drawers. Except for a box of hospital tissues, the top one was empty. A deep file drawer was underneath. Metal rollers clicked and it slid open.

There was a folded newspaper inside. When she lifted it, something slid out and clattered to the bottom of the drawer: a cassette with the brand name BASF—and no label.

Tim's tape. It had to be.

She fingered it for a moment, then impulsively tucked it into a skirt pocket and pushed the drawer shut.

Her light explored the underside of the desk again. He had been so sure the key was there. Where was it?

Puzzled, she thought for a moment. Then abruptly pulling up the chair, she sat down and ran her upturned hand beneath the desk, sliding her fingers just inside the lipped edge.

The ragged margin of a key grazed her fingertips.

Her hands trembled as she tried the file cabinet lock. It turned with a click and the top drawer rolled out at her touch.

A series of plain Manila file folders. The first was stuffed with Chandler Bryson forms. Pushing it aside, she opened the next. More forms and consent slips.

A cough. Muffled, but close.

Jody doused the light and whirled toward the hall door. Tim? Was it a signal? She strained in the dark to hear.

Nothing. Nothing but the beat of her heart.

She waited half a minute. When no sound came, she grabbed the remaining files, and, feeling her way in the dark, crept to the door and opened it a crack.

No one.

Stifling a sigh of relief, Jody slipped into the shadowy hall. Tim's door stood open, the light from inside splaying into the corridor. She headed toward it. Froze.

Footsteps behind her.

Her heart flipped.

A sharp whisper: "Hurry. Don't stop."

She whirled toward the sound. Tim!

He came out from the alcove, pushed her into the room, shut the door.

A long shuddering breath. "My God! You stopped my heart." She was suddenly furious. "What in the hell were you doing out there?"

"Sorry." He glanced toward the hall. "I thought I heard something, so I ducked into the alcove. I figured if somebody showed up, I could head them varmints off at the pass." He poured her a drink. "Here. You earned it."

"You're damned right I did." She tossed the stack of files onto the bed. Taking the cup Tim offered, she drained it. "So much for scientific culling. I grabbed and ran. You better hope the right stuff was in the top drawer. All I wanted to do was get out of there."

"I should have gone," he said. "You've got too much to lose. You don't need to go in there again. I'll do it."

"Thanks. But you're too late with the offer. I've got to put everything back the way I found it. I don't know what to do about this, though." She pulled out the tape and handed it to him. "I found it in his desk."

Tim turned it over, studied it. "The son of a bitch must have hit my locker as soon as we were gone." He slipped it into his shirt pocket.

"You can't keep it. I've got to take it back or he'll know."

He thought for a moment. "Maybe not." He reached for

the tape case, flipped it open, and ran a finger over the titles. "Shit. Wouldn't you know it? Only one BASF—and it's the Bob James." He pulled it out and glanced at her hands. "You've got fingernails—some anyway. See if you can scrape the label off."

"You're going to give him a music tape?"

"Have you got a better idea?"

She worked a nail under one corner and began to pull the label up. "We could erase it."

"There isn't time. It's a ninety-minute cassette." He glanced at the door. "Did he have a tape recorder in there?"

"I didn't see one."

"Chances are he hasn't played it then."

"And if he has?"

"What can he do? Admit he stole it from me?"

Jody shot an alarmed glance toward the hall. "We have to hurry."

He studied her expression. "Barkley's got you where it hurts, doesn't he?"

"Theft of records? Unethical conduct? Breaking and entering?" She gave a short, unhappy laugh. "You bet he does. He wouldn't think twice." Jody pulled most of the label off in one piece and scratched the tiny patch that remained with a fingernail. Satisfied that it was clean enough, she stuck the tape in her skirt pocket and looked at her watch. God. It was already after nine. She reached for the stack of file folders. "Let's get on with it."

She spread them out on the bed. The medical students were lumped together in a single folder marked CG. The control group. There were six other files. The first, unlabeled, was stuffed with printed material. She set it aside. The other five bore names: Satterfield, Quaig, Dorcas,

Monahan, and the last—thinner than the others—Corsica.

Tim reached for his.

"Wait," said Jody. "Look at this." Each name was followed by a period, then a pair of letters. Satterfield.CC, Quaig.MS, Dorcas.FL, Monahan.CC, Corsica.CC. "It must mean something."

Tim pulled out a pad and pencil from the bedside table and copied them down. "Who is this Corsica?"

"He was supposed to be here," she said.

"So he opted out. The man shows uncommon intelligence."

"He's dead. It happened about a week ago."

Tim blinked. "Dead?" The off-the-wall flash came that the man had been murdered. Absurd. That's what an overdose of Saturday Creep Show scripts did to you. But irrational as it was, the notion stuck in a crevice of his mind.

He opened Corsica's file, read for a minute, then frowned and handed it to Jody. "Take a look at this."

There were only two pages: the letter telling of his death, and a brief biography. As she read, a puzzled look came over her face.

"It says he was a Wallenski kid," said Tim.

"Then, Satterfield," said Jody. "Maybe he—" She reached for his file, but Tim beat her to it.

A half minute later, he threw it down on the bed and shook his head. "We struck out. There's no mention of Wallenski."

"It's just a coincidence, then?" She meant it as a statement; it came out with a question mark.

"A damned unbelievable one." He picked up Corsica's biography again. "Charleston native. Wallenski study for twelve years. College dropout. No military—and no prospects apparently. It says here he tried acting for a while, gave it up, went in as junior man with an Atlanta ad agency. Except for a three-week sojourn with Burger King, he's been unemployed for the last five months."

Jody glanced at the file codes. "Monahan.CC., Satterfield.CC, Corsica.CC. All the men—"

"Read them again."

"Quaig.MS . . ."

"MS," he said. "Mississippi . . . Miz . . . manuscript . . . What else?"

"To medical people, MS means multiple sclerosis." She paused. Multiple? But multiple personality disorder didn't fit. She went on with the list. "Dorcas.FL."

"Florida . . . funny lady . . . Florida. Isn't that where she went for that psychic study?"

"That's what she said. Maybe MS *is* Mississippi."

"Not unless you can come up with a state that's CC."

"All I can think of is Civilian Conservation Corps."

"That's three Cs."

Conservation . . . conversation . . . concentration . . . "Concentration camp," she said. "Two 'C's."

"Give me a break." But he glanced away, and stared at the ceiling as if it held a clue. A moment later, a strange expression came into his eyes.

"What?"

"Something . . . I don't know. Something that rang a faint little bell." He turned abruptly, picked up the file with his name on it, and thumbed through it. "Do you know how to read these?"

Jody looked over his shoulder. He was holding the electroencephalogram printout. "What I know about EEGs you could put in a thimble," she said. "Most doctors can't read them either; not unless they're specialists. I might be able to figure out a little of it though." She took the strip, unfolded it, frowned in concentration. "These are alpha waves, I think. See? They're fairly low amplitude."

"What do they mean?"

"That you were relaxed. That's really all I know about them."

Tim leaned closer. "What about those? They look different."

"I don't know. Thetas, maybe." Jody scanned the strip, frowned again. At the bottom, a penciled notation: a faint J. Pushing away the thought that started to emerge, she looked up. "You said you fell asleep during the EEG?"

He nodded.

"I don't think you did."

A pause. "Why not?"

"When you're asleep, the brain generates delta waves. They're slower than alphas and the amplitude is higher. I don't see anything like that here."

He lit a cigarette, blew a stream of smoke through tightened lips. "I suppose you think I lost time again."

Her voice matched the tension in his. "I told you I didn't know how to read these." She threw down the printout. "Read it yourself." She reached for another file, opened it, pretended to concentrate, but when the silence grew she stole a look at Tim.

He took a long drag on his cigarette, and stared at it without seeming to focus. "What's happening to me, Jody?" His eyes slowly met hers, and the pain in them made her look away.

"I don't know," she whispered. "I don't know." She drew in a slow breath, then made a show of glancing at her watch. "We've got five minutes to find out," she said, making her voice light. "It's nine-twenty—and I've been nervous long enough. At exactly nine-twenty-five these little suckers go back to Barkley's office."

THIRTY-FIVE

Tim stood in the doorway of his room, watching. Jody, her arms full of files, had reached Barkley's door. A glance in his direction, a little childlike wave of her fingertips, then she was inside.

The door shut behind her.

He looked at his watch for the second time in two minutes. 9:26. She'd be okay, he told himself. It was still early. The play would run until ten at least, maybe longer. Then, it would take a while before anyone got back. She'd be okay.

He began to pace, walking up and down the hall, ten steps this way, ten that, pausing to glance sharply at every clank of radiator or creak of settling timbers, and all the while the words he had said to her played back:

. . . lost time . . . lost time . . . lost time . . .

Her stunned look had quickly changed into a carefully reassuring one. A professional face. The kind you used with a patient.

. . . lost time . . . lost time . . .

Like Maureen. Like Beth. They were all linked somehow. Beads on a string.

And Satterfield too?

Something had made Jody uneasy. A piece of jewelry she saw in Satterfield's room. A ring.

The impulse was too strong to resist. Casting a quick glance at the double doors, willing them to stay closed, Tim started up the hall. He paused at Barkley's door. An almost imperceptible flicker of light at the transom. She'll be okay, he told himself again. It would only take him a second.

Moments later, he opened Dayton Satterfield's door.

A light burned in the empty room, an ice-pale fluorescent over the sink. A small gooseneck lamp sat on the overbed table, high-intensity from the look of it, a work lamp. Tim switched it on.

Bright incandescence flooded the table and bounced off spools of glittering wire. Gold, he thought. The irony of it bothered him. Satterfield had left jeweler's gold in full view without a qualm, while he had not dared to go so far as the shower without stashing everything in his locker. Yet he was the one who had been robbed.

Pliers and clamps littered the top of the narrow table and spilled from the open cigar box. Inside, a half-dozen rings, each tucked in a tiny plastic bag, glowed in the warm lamplight.

He picked one up and tried to make out the design through the cocoon of plastic. One lay tossed in the corner of the box. This one had no bag. He held it to the light. It had been crushed beyond recognition.

Why? he wondered.

He put it back, noticed several folded sheets of paper underneath, opened one: a rough pencil sketch of a stylized bird. Work sheets. The next was a sunflower, petals curving away in rays from a cross-hatched center.

Tim opened the third.

Curving lines met intersecting curving lines.

The outline of a fluffy cloud, obscured—captured—by the taut lines of a net. . . .

Though Tim's gaze was fixed on the paper, his eyes glazed. Then, they began to move, slowly at first, then faster. Back and forth, back and forth in the jittering motion of dreams. . . .

THIRTY-SIX

Jody opened the door to Barkley's office and stepped into a dark cell that throbbed with energy. She caught her breath. It was the pulsing of her own heart, the blood rushing in her ears, the sound of her breath rustling in and out of her lungs.

Why? Why did it feel so different this time?

She clutched the files to her chest, shone her little light, trembled with the beating of her heart. For an interminable moment she stood there, unable to move. Then, the spell lifted.

Talk about wired! She managed a faint grin.

Her light played on the bottom desk drawer. Still open, the way she had left it. The newspaper was inside. Sliding the tape cassette into a fold, she shut the drawer, turned to the file cabinet, then stopped and stared helplessly at the folders.

What was the order? She knew it wasn't alphabetical.

How could she have been so stupid? Why hadn't she made a list, kept them stacked the way they belonged? She could see Barkley opening the file drawer, frowning, knowing somehow that she had been there.

Think, she told herself. You know where they go. Just let yourself remember. She laid them on the desk and scanned the first: Corsica. But Dorcas came first, didn't it? No. It was Quaig. She was suddenly sure. Quaig, then Corsica. Dorcas. Monahan. Satterfield. Almost alphabetical except for Beth's file, as if Barkley had pulled it out, then stuffed it back in haste without paying attention to where it belonged.

Angling the pencil of light, she stacked the files in order, frowning in concentration.

The faint click of metal on metal. Tic, tic.

In the hall!

With fingers suddenly numb, she switched off the light.

Tic, tic. Tic, tic.

Just outside the door.

Tim, she thought. Tim. But she knew with certainty that it was not.

Silence.

The files!

Snatching them up, she spun to the drawer, stumbled against the desk chair, felt the files slither out of her grasp and slide to the floor with the terrible rattling sound of snakes.

It had to be Barkley. She'd tell him she heard something. . . someone. . . . Someone in the office. . . . A thief.

Theft . . . theft of records . . . theft. . . .

Just straightening up . . . I was going to call . . . going to tell. . . .

A click.

Oh, God. She crouched behind the desk, pressed her body close to icy metal.

A click at the door.

He'll know. Oh, God . . . he'll know. . . .

The door swung open, and the dim light from the hall played like a searchlight across the desk.

THIRTY-SEVEN

The bone-thin teenager in the seat next to Maureen parted her lips in an unconscious parody of Marilyn Monroe and gave a little sigh. She had come in just before the curtain with two friends, all three with the stigmata of ballet, the duck walk that came from years of toeing out. Now, with the second act of *A Chorus Line* barely ten minutes old, she was head-over-heels in love. Maureen hid a smile, but she need not have bothered. The girl's luminous eyes saw nothing but the charismatic young man who played the dance captain.

Maureen had spotted Carla and Al in the lobby at intermission, but she had seen no one else from the study group—and no wonder; the theater was packed for what the reviews called the best and most energetic revival in years. She dug around in her beaded evening bag and found a single wintergreen mint in a shroud of torn foil. Brushing off the embedded tobacco crumbs, she popped it into her mouth. That was the main drawback of theatergoing, she thought. You couldn't smoke.

The florid-faced man to her left was playing King of the Armrest again. Maureen gave an answering poke, grazed her elbow on unyielding tweed, and abandoned the contest. From the row behind, someone fired a volley of coughs that triggered a return barrage from the balcony. Like dogs barking, she thought. She had a private theory that dog barks went around the world, suburb to suburb, traveling west, picked up by prairie strays and coyote packs until they finally crossed the Bering Strait on the tongues of wolves and set off a malamute in Moscow.

She fully expected to hear a chorus of coughs around the theater. In fact, she heard nothing.

Nothing at all.

Silence. Thick silence.

A silence so profound it felt like death.

Her gaze darted to the stage. A dancer jigged frenetically. A puppet dancer, feet tapping in mute rhythm, lamb's wool on cotton batting.

What is the sound of one foot tapping?

Irrationally, she wanted to laugh. The urge slid toward hysteria, and she struggled to her feet.

"Excuse me," she said. "Excuse me." But the words spilled from her throat without a sound.

She stumbled past knees and handbags, reached the aisle. In the next row a young man stared at her. His lips moved. Silence tumbled out.

What is the sound of one voice rapping?

Applause. Hands striking insubstantial hands. Moth wings clapping.

Somehow, she got to the lobby, leaned against the wall, clamped her hands to her head . . . and felt the smooth curving glass of a bell jar. . . .

Sound rushed back with the sharp rush of her breath: the foghorn bleat of a distant semi; the shriek of a hidden phone; the insistent blat of brass and throbbing drums pulsing in counterpoint to her heart.

Got to get back, got to get back, got to get back . . .

She pushed open the door and the wind caught her hair and ruffled the pale strands of the downy boa. Clutching it, wrapping it around her shoulders as if for warmth, she turned toward the hospital, the click of her stiletto heels quickening as she made her way to Morgan Wing.

THIRTY-EIGHT

The latch clicked and the office door closed, obliterating the light from the hallway. Except for a faint gleam from the transom, the room was dark.

Jody crouched behind the desk, straining to hear, praying to hear footsteps going away.

Nothing.

Was he gone? Please let him be gone. If Barkley found her here— She trembled and thought of the files littering the floor. No way to explain. No way.

A metallic sound, sharp as splintering glass:

Tic, tic . . .

Oh, God.

She pressed closer to the metal desk and ice crept into her bones. Don't let him turn on the light. Oh, don't. Her eyes darted blindly toward the sound. Don't turn on the light.

But he would. She knew he would.

Silence.

The cold black silence of a well, a cave, a cellar.

She squeezed her eyes shut and waited like a small

trapped animal for the light to blaze bright as the sun and give her away.

A breath. A faint sighing expiration.

Her eyes started open, met only blackness. And suddenly she knew, knew with utter conviction, that it was not Barkley who stood there in the darkened room.

Then who? Oh, God. Who?

Tic, tic . . .

Metal on metal.

The memory flashed: the red Exit light glinting on the knife blade, turning it to blood . . . the point pressing against her throat. . . .

Not again, not again.

But only ten days ago a nurse's aide had been raped and slashed with a razor. Three days ago, a waitress was killed just blocks away.

She choked off the scream welling in her throat. No! Quiet. Don't let him know. He could have a gun. A knife.

Tic . . . tic . . .

A roaring in her head, surf and storm tides, and faintly in the distance Maureen's voice: *a bell . . . a silver bell . . . a little silver bell without a clapper. . . .*

Get out. She had to get out.

The side door. It was only a few feet away. Just a few feet. Holding her breath, she began to crawl toward it.

Her hand touched down, touched something smooth. . . .

The sheaf of papers slid beneath her fingertips, skittered away, rustling bat wings in the dark.

Tic . . . tic . . .

She froze.

Tic . . . tic . . .

Closer. Just beyond the desk.

Her pulse swelled in her throat and squeezed off her

breath. Get away, get away. She stretched out cold fingers, groped in the dark, felt nothing. Just a few more feet . . .

The wall! Fingers touched, patted, slid over plaster, found the door. The knob . . . where was it? There. Higher. Higher than she thought. Fingers damp with cold sweat grasped it, turned it.

Tic . . . tic . . .

The door swung open.

Heart pounding, she crept into the hall, crouched, reached back to close the door. No. Go on, go on. Get to the treatment room. Then run.

She slid along the wall, rough plaster scoring her fingertips, scraping arm and shoulder. Nearly there. Oh no, oh no . . .

Light from the EEG machine. Red lights. Green. Blazing in her dilated pupils like floodlights. Not there. Go on. Get to the storeroom.

Tic . . . tic . . .

Her legs were shifting sand, buckling, threatening to crumple beneath her. She clung to the wall. One step. Two.

The storage-room door.

The knob turned in her grasp, gave with a click. A click loud as a gunshot.

White light. Blazing white light pinioned her against the door.

She spun toward it. Froze.

A flashlight, bright as a beacon, a searchlight. Behind it nothing but black, nothing but shadow.

Tic . . . tic . . .

Ohgod, oh run, ohgod.

She stumbled into the storeroom and slammed the door shut. Black haloed after-images danced on her retinas, dazzled her. She plunged blindly in the dark, collided with a heavy crate, careened away, fell to her knees on something soft. Pillows. Blankets. Wadded in a heap on the floor.

Behind her, the door opened with a sigh and cold breath from the narrow throat of the back hall puffed into the room and skittered over her body.

The flashlight blazed, played over the crate, danced on a wall of dangling crutches.

A crutch. Get one. Hit him. Kill him, kill him.

Creeping on failing legs, keeping boxes and crates between her and the probing light, she got to the wall, reached out, grabbed . . . missed.

The tip of the crutch pivoted, struck another, and the wall was alive with a dozen more—striking, clattering—eccentric swinging pendulums.

The light swung back, found her, pinned her against the wall—then suddenly went out.

Tic . . . tic . . .

Get to the door. Get to the door. But she could not move, could not make her limbs obey.

Tic . . . tic . . .

Tic . . .

Run, go, run.

The heavy paralysis lifted and she plunged away—and stopped short as something soft and thick and horrible circled her throat, tightened, squeezed.

Her hands flew to her throat; her eyes widened in a blind stare.

Then blackness . . .

THIRTY-NINE

Not pausing to catch her breath, Maureen shoved open the door to Chandler Bryson's main entry, and running through the nearly empty lobby, she made her way to Rutledge. The elevator doors opened with a creak as she arrived and a clump of passengers got out.

She pushed through them blindly, then stopped as a hand caught her arm. She turned blank eyes to the lined face of a security guard.

"Sorry, lady. You can't go up. Visiting hours are over."

"I have to."

He dropped her arm, but his voice, quiet, polite, firm as steel in velvet, held her. "It's after hours, ma'am."

"You don't understand. I have to."

"Sorry," he said again. "Nobody but staff after visiting hours."

The man's set look was a warning; she knew he would tolerate no nonsense. "But I'm part of a study group," she said. "I have a room on Morgan Wing." A silent prayer. A placating smile. "You wouldn't want me to spend the night in the lobby, would you?"

"A study group, you say?" He pulled out a small notepad from his shirt pocket and flipped it open. "I'll see if I have you down."

Please, she thought. Please hurry.

His stubby index finger traced a list. "What's your name?"

"Maureen Dorcas."

He nodded and tucked the notepad back in his pocket. "It's after hours, ma'am, but if you just go over to Hines, the security guard there will let you use the stairs."

"Please." She clutched his arm. "Oh, please."

"You all right, lady?"

She blinked, shook her head. "I don't think so."

"You look a little peaked."

She tried to look worse.

He steadied her with a meaty hand, thought for an endless moment, said kindly, "I guess it's a long walk up when you're feeling under the weather." He led her to the elevator and deposited her inside. "I'll let you use the elevator this time, but the door to Morgan may be locked. If it is, you tell the security man up there that Barney down in the lobby says it's okay to let you in."

"Thank you," she whispered. "Thank you."

The elevator door clanged shut and the car began to rise. The cold darkness was growing in her head. "Come on," she whispered, trying to hurry the balky elevator through a force of will. She had to get there, had to . . .

And what then?

She pressed her hands to her ears as if to shut out the thought, but it clamored in her brain: What then? What then?

The darkness gathered in her head. Images. A silver bell . . . a bell jar . . .

She squeezed her eyes shut and heard again the words

she had said to Jody: *There was nothing I could do . . . nothing I could do . . . nothing I could do . . .*

No. She could. She would.

The elevator clattered open. 4 East. A heavy woman in pajamas and robe, pay phone receiver at her ear, gave Maureen a curious look as she veered past and ran toward the door that led to Morgan Wing. Her hands were slick with sweat as she reached for the tarnished brass bar. Unlocked, thank God. It gave under her hand.

The walls of the dim connecting corridor closed in, thickening the air, compressing her lungs. CONTAGION WARD. The faint stenciled words jittered before her eyes and she touched the wall to steady herself.

The cold grew in her brain, a chill black tumor that dizzied her and stole her breath.

Go on, go on.

She reached the door, and with an echoing metallic clang, it opened.

Morgan Wing.

The hallway stretched ahead, empty, silent, darkness crouching in its nooks and corners, shrouding its high moldings.

She clung to the door and stared. The dark thing in her mind was alive, growing with each quick beat of her heart, swirling, projecting into the lonely corridor, touching heavy wood and crumbling plaster.

A puddle of dingy light dimmed and thickened, and from its midst, a tiny wavering pattern sharpened into the image of a child. A dark-eyed little girl, tiny tortured limbs bound with hoops of steel, tiny wooden crutches tapping.

Maureen's lips moved, echoed the child's silent plea: "Help me. Help me."

A young man, athlete's body twisted with disease . . . a girl, no more than fourteen, struggling for breath, terror in her eyes . . . a baby . . . another . . . another. A spectral host, growing until there were a dozen, two dozen—more.

Help me. Help me.

The images vanished. The dark pulsed.

Then the sound: the sound of a silver bell without a clapper.

A face, pale in the mist. Eyes staring from the gleaming prison of a bell jar.

Help me. Help me.

Maureen's lungs emptied. The air was gone, sucked up by the thick, swirling blackness.

Her pulse hammered in her skull. She could not get air, could not draw a breath. She clung to the door, nearly falling, unable to move. Then she was whirling, running back through the narrow connecting hall, thrusting open the door to Rutledge.

Air rushed into tortured lungs, rushed out, rushed in again.

Frantic, she stared down the hallway. It was empty now. The woman on the phone was gone. Muted voices came from somewhere beyond a dingy waiting room. She had to tell them, had to get help.

She started to run, stopped.

Tell them what? That she saw ghosts, heard voices? That sometimes she knew things before they happened? Tell them—and watch startled expressions turn cautious. Humor the mad woman. Call the guards, the police.

She doubled a fist, chewed a knuckle. Then she was fumbling through the little brocade handbag, emptying the cigarette pouch, pulling out a little stack of business cards.

She stared at the first: Mike Mona—knife blade dripping blood. She threw it down, threw down the next, found the one she needed.

Her change purse splayed open. Coins clattered to the floor. She snatched one up, ran to the pay phone, dialed.

One ring. Two. Two more. Then a man's voice, irritated, tired: "Barkley here."

The receiver felt clammy. "You've got to come. You've got to come now." Her gaze whipped toward the end of the hall, toward Morgan Wing. "Something terrible is happening."

FORTY

Jody's lips parted and a faint little moan escaped. Hurts . . . Head hurts . . . She tried to raise her hand, touch her throbbing temples, but something stopped her—something hard and cold.

Her hand moved again, knuckles grazing curving metal. Confused, she shifted and tried to sit up.

She could not move her head.

"Wha—" She tried to focus.

A dark blur resolved into a dim shaft of light penetrating the blackness. Disoriented, she stared. A diamond flashed and danced inches away from her eyes.

Memory flooded back with consciousness: Choking . . . Something thick around her throat, pressing, choking. An electric shock of adrenaline jolted her chest. Fire and ice.

Get away . . . get away . . .

Her body arched. Knees struck curving metal, elbows flailed confining walls, throat fought the unyielding circular embrace of a collar.

What? What was it?

Her eyes blurred, focused again, found the glittering

diamond. Hands crept upward, sought her throat, scrabbled against a thick barrier.

What? Oh, God. What?

Cold fear shuddered through her body. Dead. Was she dead?

A convulsive shiver. Her spine turned to ice, sent cold fingers into her belly, dead cold trembling through her limbs.

The diamond danced with every wracking tremor, danced and glittered, broke into spikes and needles of light.

She stared, and the horror grew. The shimmering point of light was a reflection—a reflection from the security light beyond the storeroom window, a beam of light dancing on a curving band of steel that locked a clear curved dome in place.

Dome . . . headpiece . . . bowl . . .

Bell jar . . .

No!

She was in the iron lung.

Elbows wedged against the metal wall of the iron lung, she clawed at the collar circling her throat, seeking a purchase. The thick soft rubber defeated her scrabbling fingers.

She screamed. A single drawn-out cry. She had no way of knowing if it penetrated the locked dome of the headpiece; she did not think of that.

A second scream welled in her throat, choked off, died to a strangled guttural moan. The air. She'd use it all. Use it all. Suffocate.

Lie still. She had to lie still. Save air.

Her breath rushed out, rushed in again, rushed out, fogging the dome, outlining a greasy streak on its surface that might have been left by a man's thumb.

Stay calm. She had to conserve air. Had to.

For a moment, it worked. For a moment, she concentrated on the frantic whisper of her pulse, the sound of air moving in and out of her lungs. Then she was flailing out, battering with feet, with doubled fists, striking again and again until the iron walls that trapped her were streaked with blood.

FORTY-ONE

The distant clang of the hall doors brought Tim to himself with a start. Satterfield? Coming back? He dashed for the door, then stopped and stared around the room in confusion.

He was not in Satterfield's room. It was his own.

His gaze shot to his watch. 9:50. "God," he whispered in despair. Twenty minutes. Over twenty minutes gone.

A faint sound. Footsteps in the hall.

Jody! Where was she? It didn't take twenty minutes to put back a few files. Pulse quickening, he hurried to the door.

The heavy door sighed open and bumped against the door stop. He stared toward the alcove. No one in sight.

"Looking for someone?" The voice came from behind him.

Tim whirled toward it. A white-uniformed orderly stood just outside Beth Quaig's door. The man who had spied on Jody and him the other night. "No," he said sharply.

"Well, I am. Looking for someone, that is. I got a

message here for Beth Quaig." The man brandished a long white envelope folded in half. "Know where she is?"

A faint thump. Tim's gaze darted down the hall. It was coming from the storeroom.

The orderly came closer. "I said, you know where she is?"

"No." Tim stared at the man's name tag. B. Wiesner. The sound again. Something was wrong; he had to get rid of the guy. "She's still at the play, I guess. Give it to me. I'll see she gets it."

"The envelope says Beth Quaig. That your name?" A mocking smile exposed crooked teeth. "You don't look like a Beth."

Tim narrowed his eyes. "Suit yourself." Only get the hell out now, asshole.

The orderly shrugged, moved past. At a series of faint thuds from the storeroom, he turned back, a startled look tracking across his face. "What was that?"

Tim set his jaw. "What was what?"

"That noise." The man's chin jerked toward the storeroom. "Down there."

"I didn't hear anything." The lie was barely out of his mouth when the thumping started again, this time muffled and slower. "Oh . . . that what you mean?" A dismissing grin. "It's, uh . . . the radiator. Makes a real racket sometimes."

A note of suspicion. "Yeah?"

"Kept me up half the night at first, but I got used to it. I hardly notice it anymore."

Doubt. "Well . . ." The man glanced again in the direction of the storeroom. "If you're sure . . ."

"Happens all the time, especially at night. You know . . . when it gets colder. If you think that was loud, you should have been around last night. I'm talking major noise."

"Yeah?" The orderly's dubious look gave way to a sudden insolent twist of his lips. A long look. A shrug. He turned away and headed down the hall. At the exit, he paused, looked back, waggled the white envelope over his shoulder. Then the door clanged open and he was gone.

Tim waited until he was sure the man was not coming back. Then he sprinted toward the storage room.

The room was dark. He fumbled for the light switch, found it, threw it on.

Light flooded the room, dazzling his eyes. For a moment, thick silence. Then a scraping sound. He scanned the room. No one. No one there.

A dull metallic thump.

His head jerked toward it. "Jody?"

A faint moan.

He moved closer. "Jody?"

Nothing. Nothing but pillows, wadded blankets—and beyond, the silver cylinder of an old iron lung . . .

He stared. It was moving. A crazy wobbling that sent a chill coursing up his spine.

Another moan.

Two leaping steps. He caught his breath: Jody's face, blurred through the transparent dome of the iron lung, her eyes wide with terror, her mouth open in a silent gasping scream.

"Jody! God!" His fingers scrabbled at the latch. Metal scraped the skin from his knuckles; blood oozed from a tiny wound. The latch gave way with a dull click.

Tugging frantically, he twisted. Nothing. He twisted again with all his strength and a second latch on the opposite side tore away from its frame. He yanked the dome loose and fresh air flooded the compartment.

A shuddering gasp.

"Jody! Are you all right?"

Another gasping breath. "Please. Get me out. Please."

He stared at the steel cylinder. A metal ring studded with clamps circled the large rubber diaphragm around her neck. He tore them open, shoved, and the body of the cylinder slid away.

She was lying on a stretcher, eyes wild, hands tugging at the rubber and metal collar still around her neck. Tears coursed down her cheeks. "Help me."

Five straps spread like the legs of a starfish from the thick gum rubber around her throat. He grabbed them and pulled. The rubber splayed open and Jody was free.

He grabbed her up in his arms and got her to a sitting position. "What happened?"

She began to sob.

Cradling her as if she were a child, he held her close. "What happened? Who did this?"

"I don't know. Couldn't see . . . I couldn't see."

"Do you need a doctor?"

She shook her head and the movement tossed a strand of hair across her eyes. "I tried . . . I was trying to get away." Her hand crept to her throat.

Tim caught her chin in his hand, tipped her head back gently, winced. Faint circling bruises darkened the pale flesh. "It's all right now. It's all right." He patted her shoulder with awkward little taps, stared around the room, tried to think. The orderly. It had to be him. But as quickly as the thought came, he rejected it. Would the guy who attacked her want to check out the storage room? Not bloodly likely. But who else?

He swallowed hard. Twenty minutes. Twenty minutes gone out of his life. It could have been anyone. "We've got to call the police," he said.

Panic in her voice. "No!"

"It's all right. He's gone now."

She pulled away, stared at the door. "The records. They're all over. I've got to put them back."

"Screw the records." He caught her shoulders in cupped hands. "Somebody tried to kill you. I'm calling the police."

"Oh, please! You can't. They'll know. My fingerprints are everywhere . . . my fingernail . . . They'll know." Her face was pale and tear-streaked. "Don't tell. Please. Please don't tell."

She raised wide pleading eyes and the overwhelming fear in them brought a sudden lump to his throat. "Oh, Jesus, baby," he whispered. "Let's get you out of here. Right now."

FORTY-TWO

The Volkswagen's engine was lugging. Tim dropped it a gear and turned onto Jody's street. He stole a glance at the girl beside him. Her gaze was fixed on the dark road. On the surface she seemed calm, but her pale face and trembling hands gave her away. "The next time you fill up," he said, breaking the silence, "a dose of high test gas won't hurt."

He knew he had to call the police. As soon as she'd let him. As soon as they'd talked. But they had scarcely spoken since the hospital, and not at all about anything that mattered.

Another sidelong glance. Her chin was up, lips pressed tightly together: the defiant look of a little girl trying to hide how scared she was. Why hadn't he pressed it? He should have made her talk, made her get it out. But he had not. They had hurried to her car, driven in virtual silence this far, and now the barriers were in place.

The VW's engine shuddered as he turned into Jody's driveway. He parked in back beneath the light at the corner of the house.

When they opened the gate, Sushi let out a volley of

welcoming barks and began to dance on her hind legs. Jody caught the little dog in her arms, hugged her close, buried her face in her dark fur.

Tim fumbled with her keys and finally found the right one. The moment he got the door open, Sushi leaped down and dashed inside to her food bowl.

Bright kitchen light spilled onto Jody's face. Her eyes were red again. She blinked, turned away, said to the dog, "Want to play? Where's squeaky bird?"

The waver in her voice made Tim reach for her, take her in his arms. "Do you want to talk about it?"

She shook her head, offered a too-bright smile. "I'm okay." Pulling away, she said quickly, "Coffee?" Without waiting for him to answer, she grabbed up the pot and turned on the tap.

His hand covered hers. "Forget the coffee."

She stared at the pot for a moment, then set it down.

He shut off the tap. "It's a shame to let good branch water go to waste. Got anything to go with it?"

"Up there," she said.

Tim opened the overhead cabinet, found a bottle of Maker's Mark, and poured stiff drinks. "Come on," he said, handing her the glass, steering her into the living room.

He went through her basket of tapes hoping for something calming. New Age stuff, mostly, interspersed with a few light classics. He put on a Suzanne Ciani tape, sat down beside Jody, and studied her face.

She looked away, sipped her drink, focused on the dancing row of red lights on the stereo.

He took her hand. Such a little hand. He could feel the tension in it. "It's no good to bottle it up," he said.

A tiny smile quirked her lips. "Is that your professional opinion, Doctor?"

"You know I'm right."

"Maybe you should hang your shingle next to mine." Her voice was light, but the little smile vanished and she began to tremble.

He put down his glass, pulled her close, began to knead away the tight knots in her back and neck. "You can't just pretend it didn't happen," he said. "You could have been killed."

Several seconds passed. Then she said, "Why wasn't I? I was unconscious. He could have killed me in a moment."

He squeezed her shoulder, felt her muscles tighten again. "Thank God he didn't."

Jody tried to sip her drink, but the glass trembled too much for that and she set it down. "He didn't want it to be quick, did he? He put me in that—" She took a long shuddering breath. "He wanted it to be slow. He wanted me to wake up and know I was going to die. Why?" She searched his face. "Why did he do that to me?"

"Because he's crazy. There isn't any reason."

She shook her head. "There's always a reason."

He took her hand. "Maybe the police— Let me call them."

"No. I can't. I can't do that." Her hand pulled away from his, crept to her throat.

Something about the gesture caught Tim's eye: the faint pulse at the angle of her jaw, rising and falling with each beat of her heart.

A sudden flashing image made him blink: a mud-slimed brain, swelling as something burrowed just beneath its surface . . .

. . . a welt swelling, throbbing on Maureen's throat with each heartbeat . . .

He felt his own throat tighten and close.

Bee sting . . .

The Blue . . .

He gasped, but there was nothing in his lungs.

"What is it?"

He shook his head; he couldn't breathe.

Jody gripped his arm. "What is it?"

Air flooded back. "I know what the letters mean," he managed to say.

"What letters? What are you talking about?"

"The 'CC' on Barkley's records. It stands for Camp Challenge. I was there when I was a kid—" He caught his breath, sucked in more. "Right now, I'd bet anything that Dayton Satterfield was there too—and the other one, the guy who died last week."

"George Corsica?"

"Yeah. Corsica." Tim blinked as the strange conviction came again that the man had been murdered. "Barkley's records said he was a Wallenski kid. Nearly half the kids at camp were Wallenski kids."

He could see the doubt in her eyes. "It sounds crazy. But I just realized— That's when the nightmare started."

"What nightmare?"

Half ashamed, he hesitated. He had never told anyone about it before, although he was not quite sure why. "When it starts, I'm alone," he said. "In a swamp. It's almost dark and I know I have to run . . ."

Jody listened in silence while he told her. Her eyes were shaded, and though he tried to read them, they gave no hint as to what she was thinking. When he finished, Tim lit a cigarette, dragged deeply, felt a little of his tension drain away. "I've had the dream ever since, but it's different now," he said, at a loss to explain just how. "I know there's a connection."

"How could there be? That was years ago."

"There is," he said fiercely. "I know it. They divided us

into two groups. The Grays and the Blues. One of the Blues died from a bee sting. Only it wasn't a bee sting. Remember dinner Sunday night? The wasp on the table? It threw Beth into a panic."

"Of course it did. She's allergic."

"Is she?"

"She said she almost died."

"That's what they claimed happened to the Blue—the kid at camp."

"A lot of people are allergic," she said carefully. "People get stung."

"On the throat?"

She shifted uncomfortably. "Coincidence."

"Yeah? What about Maureen's reaction? The welt? It was right there—in the same place." He touched the bruise on Jody's throat, felt the quick tap of her pulse, pulled back at her wince. "Was that coincidence too?"

"We talked about that," she said. "Suggestion."

"But I felt it too. Was *that* suggestion?"

"I didn't know you did," she said. "But yes. It could be."

"Only it wasn't," he said flatly.

"Why are you so sure?"

"Because—" He stopped. "I don't know why. Just that I am, that's all."

She looked at him closely. "Why did you stay?"

He blinked. "Stay?"

"At the hospital. With the study group."

"Simple. I—" He stopped. He had started to say it was for the money, for the chance to see more of her and get paid in the process, for the chance to go through Barkley's records. "I wanted to leave," he finally said. "I almost did."

"Why didn't you?"

He stared at the cigarette he held for a few seconds, then raised his eyes to hers. "I don't know."

Jody watched him intently for a few seconds, her eyes narrowing in thought. "Have you ever been hypnotized?"

"Me?" Surprise. "Sure. Once or twice. You know, playing around when I was in college. That sort of thing."

"I'd like to try it now," she said. "I'd like to try to regress you back to that camp you went to."

"I don't know—" he began, feeling his guard go up, wondering why. Stalling, he reached for his drink, drained it, set down the empty glass. "Okay," he said a moment later. "Why not?" Maybe it would help. Nothing else had.

Jody switched off the lamp. Except for the faint glow that came from the kitchen and the red and green flicker from the stereo, the room was dark. "Just lie back and try to get comfortable," she said.

Trying not to look as self-conscious as he felt, Tim stretched out awkwardly on the couch.

"Trust me?"

"Sure," he said uneasily, realizing that it was himself he did not trust. No telling what idiocies might come out of his mouth—especially if she turned him into an eleven-year-old again.

"Good." A smile. "I can't do this alone. I need your cooperation." She pulled out the little penlight and flicked it on, aiming it at a silver candle holder on the mantel, bobbing the light in little circles. The reflection dazzled his eyes and he blinked, remembering a clandestine late-night session his freshman year at Georgia: Hank Clement's Psych 101 term paper had been due and in lieu of library research material he had talked Tim into being his guinea pig. He made a good subject too—or so Hank had told him afterward; he remembered none of it himself.

Jody began to talk to him, telling him to relax, telling

him to watch the light. In a few minutes, her voice became a drone in the distance. The silver glitter was brighter now; it hurt his eyes. At her suggestion, he closed them, grateful of the chance to shut out the glare.

"Deeply asleep. Deeply asleep now . . ."

He was floating in rich warm darkness.

". . . going back now. Back . . ."

Her voice was no more than a hum, the faint hum of bees in summer.

Icy water smacked his belly, rushed into his nose, his ears . . .

"Where are you?"

"In the lake."

"Who else is there?"

"Everybody. Everybody's laughing."

"Why?"

"'Cause I did a belly flop." The skin on his chest and abdomen stung like fire. "Hurts . . ." He whispered it under his breath so no one would hear.

"I want you to go forward now, Tim. Forward to the time of the bee sting. Forward . . ."

The stinging pain receded, vanished.

". . . forward . . ."

The Blue!

". . . forward . . ."

Darkness.

Jody's voice, distant, faint: "Where are you?"

"In bed. I'm in bed."

The harsh beam of a flashlight struck him in the face. . . .

"This one."

"What's happening?"

"Somebody's here."

Hands grasped him. He squirmed and tried to pull away. . . .

"Come on, buddy. Lie still."

Blackness. . . .

"Where are you?"

"No place. It's dark. I'm no place."

"I want you to go forward now," she said. "Go forward fifteen minutes. It's fifteen minutes later. Fifteen minutes."

Cold. Cold splashing against his throat, the sharp smell of alcohol stinging his nostrils. . . .

"What do you see?"

The man's face was shadowed except for his lips. Tim blinked, saw them move. . . .

"He's talking."

"Who?"

"The man. I can't see his face."

"What is he saying?"

". . . Jesus! Why isn't he under?"

A mask pressed against his face, covering his mouth and nose, smothering him. Sharp cold blazed in his head. Couldn't breathe . . . couldn't breathe . . . couldn't breathe. . . .

Another voice: "Son of a bitch! Hold this kid down for Christ's sake. He's kicking the stuff out of me. . . ."

"What do you see?"

The man moved closer and the shadows fell away. . . .

"No!"

Panic. It shuddered through his body in overwhelming waves. He tried to run.

Jody's voice: "It's all right. Nothing's going to hurt you. It's all right."

Drowning. Drowning in the swamp. . . .

He whimpered, drew up his legs.

"It's all right. You're safe. You're safe now. . . ."

"No! No, no, no, no . . ."

"It's all right. Relax. Relax now and forget." A breath. "You're going to forget all this. You're going to forget everything until you're ready to remember, until it's safe to remember. You're going forward now. Forward in time. Leaving it all behind . . ."

His body grew limp, slid into darkness. . . .

". . . five . . . four . . . three . . . two . . . one . . ."

He blinked at the harsh glare from the lamp and looked up into Jody's face.

"Are you all right?" she asked.

He considered the question, then nodded.

"Remember anything?"

"No." Then, "Yes."

"What? What do you remember?"

He sat up, shook his head, looked around. "Do you have a pencil?"

"Yes. Somewhere—" She rummaged through an end-table drawer, pulled out a ballpoint pen and a sheet of stationery.

He stared at the paper for a second, then drew a dark, shaded ellipse. "There was a shadow, there," he said, "and something—" He thought for a moment, then sketched a man's chin and lips just beneath it.

Jody leaned over the paper. "Who is it?"

"I don't know." He searched his memory, shook his head. "I don't know."

They looked at each other for a moment. Then he shrugged and drew a Hitler mustache above the mouth. "Adolph the Aberration, I guess." he said. Who the hell knew? He rolled the ballpoint between his palms, shrugged again, tried to smile. "I can't remember."

"It's okay," she said. "You will. When you're ready." Jody got up, put a tape in the recorder, turned it on.

Tim flipped the pen to his left hand and scratched his head as the new one began to play. He recognized the distinctive harp sound of Andreas Vollenweider. "Compatible."

She sat back down. "What is?"

"Our taste in music," he said. Still holding the pen in his left hand, he began to draw—a slow, rhythmic doodle. "A little different, but definitely compatible."

"I think so," she said and, peering over his shoulder, leaned closer and looked at what he had drawn.

He was not sure what came first. Not sure whether it was the sudden tightening of her muscles or the sharp intake of her breath.

His gaze darted to hers.

She was staring at the sketch, staring as if she could not see anything else in the room.

Her held breath quivered out, and for a split second, her gaze caught his, locked with his.

Only for a moment, a fragment of time. Just long enough for him to see the terrible, wrenching horror growing in her eyes.

FORTY-THREE

The color drained from Jody's face. No, she thought. It couldn't be. It was only a sketch, only a doodle.

An innocent picture of a fluffy cloud trapped in the curving lines of a fish net. . . .

The killer left a signature. His name is Jonathan.

Her mouth dried. She stood on trembling legs, turned away. Don't let him know. Oh, God, don't let him know. Buying time, she twiddled the stereo controls with fingers of ice.

She wanted to run, get out of the room, out of the house, run.

No! He'd follow.

Think. She had to think, come up with a plan. Making her voice as casual as she could, she said, "Time for a potty break," and hurried to the stairs.

Out of his line of sight, she clung to the railing to keep from falling. Quick. Get to the phone. Call the police.

She crept on rubber legs to the bedroom, picked up the phone, listened. A dial tone, thank God. Call the police. 911. . . .

And tell them what? That the man sitting quietly in her living room was the D-string killer?

The sketch. It was proof. Cheryl had seen it, told her about it.

But did the cop on the beat know that? Or did they keep these things from everyone except a few?

The police chief would believe her. She could talk to him. He'd know she was telling the truth. But it was late. He'd be home now. She'd never get through.

She stared helplessly at the phone. Think.

James! Cheryl's policeman. She could call Cheryl, get help from James.

She started to dial, stopped. The phone number? What was it? She knew it like her own. It flashed into her mind and she punched it in.

"Chandler Bryson Memorial Hospital."

"Emergency Room, please."

"One moment and I'll connect you."

Hurry.

A flat voice: "Emergency Room. Mrs. Borders speaking."

"Cheryl Isaacson, please."

"Just a minute."

Hurry. Please hurry.

A minute stretched to two.

Oh, God. Hurry.

A click. "Miss Isaacson here."

"Cheryl. Thank God you're there. Where's James?"

"Who is this?"

"Jody. It's Jody."

"Jody? You sound funny. What's up? Why do you want James?"

A sound from downstairs made Jody catch her breath. What was he doing? Was he coming up?

"Hey," said Cheryl. "You okay?"

"James," she repeated. "Where is he?"

"God only knows. Out on patrol somewhere. What's wrong?"

Footsteps in the entry hall. On the stairs.

"Call me back. Right now. I have to have the phone ring here."

"Sure, but—"

"Right now. Please." Please God. The receiver rattled in the hook, and Jody rushed into the hall bathroom. She flushed the toilet, hoping he'd hear, and rattled the doorknob on her way out.

Tim was waiting outside the door.

She caught her breath.

"My turn." He reached for the door, paused, gave her a curious look. "Are you feeling all right?"

Her answer came too fast, too high-pitched. "Fine."

A long look, then he opened the bathroom door.

The bedroom phone began to shrill. She ran to it, grabbed it. "Hello."

Cheryl again. "It took me a minute. It's been a while. I had to look up your number." A pause. "Are you okay? What's up?"

"I, uh— Somebody's here. I need to leave the house. I need an excuse."

The muffled sound of the toilet flushing.

"Who's there?" Suspicion. "Are you in danger?"

A door opening.

"Yes—"

Footsteps. Coming closer.

He'd hear.

"—How long did you say she's been like this?"

"Jody? Can you talk?" Cheryl's voice dropped. "Want me to send the police?"

A quick glance. Tim standing in the doorway. "No. Not really. I guess I'll have to come in then."

"Are you coming here? To the E.R.?"

"That's right."

"Want me to get hold of James?"

"Right. You do that." She hung up and looked warily at Tim.

"Another drink?" he asked.

She shook her head. "I, uh, have to go back to the hospital. Beth Quaig is in a bad way again." Did he believe her? He was looking at her so strangely.

"You can't do that, you know."

"I don't have a choice." She began to shiver.

"Cold?" he asked.

"No." Then, "Yes. A little." Her belly filled with slivers of ice and she felt slightly nauseated.

"You can't go back there," he said. "It's too dangerous."

Dangerous! She wanted to laugh; she knew if she did, she would not be able to stop. Briskly, she pressed past him, headed for the stairs. "I'd better go now," she said over her shoulder. "Just stay here. I won't be long."

His fingers closed over her upper arm. "You're in no shape to go anywhere."

Her heart swelled in her throat and choked her. "I'll be okay," she managed to say. "I won't be long."

The telephone shrilled again. "I'll get it." Breaking loose from his grip, she ran down the stairs and snatched up the living-room phone. It had to be Cheryl calling back. "Hello."

"Miss Henson?"

The man's voice on the other end startled her horribly. Barkley. Oh, God.

"Maureen Dorcas got very upset, so I had to come back

to the hospital," he said. "She was very worried about you."

"Worried?" she said, weighing the word. Tim had followed her into the room.

"Something has happened here," he said carefully.

He knows. He knows.

A pause. "Would you know where Mr. Monahan might be?"

"Uh, yes." A glance. "I might."

"Well?"

"Uh . . ." Think, she told herself. Think. "Yes. Here."

"There? He's there?" A rising tone in his voice.

She shouldn't have told him. He'd found the files strewn all over, the cabinet open. Everyone else must be back now—except for the two of them. She shouldn't have told him.

"Miss Henson—"

A note of urgency in his voice?

"—I want you to meet me here at once. In my office."

"At once," she whispered.

"Alone," he said. "Come alone." A long pause. "I don't want to alarm you, but I'm afraid your life might be in danger." Barkley hung up.

Jody replaced the receiver with trembling fingers.

"You get a lot of calls for this time of night," said Tim.

"Another call about Beth," she said. "So, I guess I'd better get going." She snatched up her lab coat, put it on, stuck the car keys in the pocket.

He caught her arm. "If you're set on this, I'll go with you. But I think it's crazy."

She shivered at his touch, marveled at the look of concern in his eyes. He really doesn't remember, she thought.

He was a multiple. She knew it now. Why hadn't she

seen it? Why hadn't she known? She had been too damned blind, too infatuated, to realize what his memory lapses meant.

Never, ever, undertake the treatment of a male multiple outside an institutional setting.

At least half of the serial murderers out there were multiples. Maybe two-thirds. Only this one wasn't "out there" at all. He was here. In her house. Touching her. "You're right," she said, pulling away. "I won't go." To emphasize her words, she sat down, away from the couch, away from him, in the single wicker chair by the fireplace.

He sank down on the couch opposite. "What you need is rest," he said. "A good night's sleep."

"You're right." Think. "I *am* tired. But more than that, I'm starved." She jumped to her feet. "Want some popcorn? I do." She headed for the kitchen, stopped, said to keep him there, "Why don't you pick out another tape while I fix it? I'll be back in a jif."

She escaped to the kitchen and noisily banged cabinet doors so he would hear. Thrusting a bag of popcorn into the microwave, she set the timer. A few minutes. That's all she'd have. She reached for the outside door, turned the knob as noiselessly as she could, pulled it open. Then Sushi ran up and placed a paw on her leg.

"No, baby. No," she whispered. "You can't go."

She pushed the dog away. Outside, she shut the door and began to run. And as she ran, one prayer drummed over and over in her mind: Don't let him hurt her, God. Please don't let him hurt my little dog.

FORTY-FOUR

The faint smell of popcorn wafting into the living room caused Tim to wrinkle his nose in anticipation. It seemed like days since he had eaten. The Andreas Vollenweider tape came to an end and the tape deck door popped open. He was reaching for another tape, when he suddenly remembered something—something Paul had said during the seance:

"You might consider that camp. . . ."

Tim had dismissed it as out-of-date slang. But was it? Or was it a backhanded reference to Camp Challenge?

Impulsively, he took the BASF tape from his shirt pocket and thrust it into the machine. He started to press the Play button, paused, pressed Fast Forward instead; the session had been well underway before Paul made the remark. He let the tape run for a quarter inch or so, then started the playback.

". . . you feel yourself moving now. Moving aside. . . ."

Tim blinked. It wasn't the seance. It wasn't Paul's voice he was hearing at all. It was Barkley's.

". . . you move aside . . . give way to another now. . . ."

Quiet. Tape hiss.

"... I am speaking now to the construct. There is only one person here now who can hear my voice. His name is Jonathan...."

Tim's hands turned to ice.

"... only Jonathan will remember my words ... only Jonathan...."

Quiet. Tape hiss.

"Good evening, Jonathan. You are going to take a short trip. This time you will buy a bus ticket on Sunday morning. The ticket will be for New Orleans. Monday morning you will enter the French Quarter and go to the Café du Monde by the waterfront. You will not enter. Wait at the corner for a man wearing a black jacket and a red and black tie. He will arrive at ten-fifteen. He will know you. He will approach and say these words to you: 'I always have beignets for breakfast. Beignets and orange juice.' You will answer with these words: 'I prefer coffee. Beignets and coffee.'

"You will go with this man. He is a friend. When you hear him say the word 'picayune,' you will tell him these things: 'The satellite transmission code is zero-four-zero, enter, seven-zero, enter, four-one-three-zero-two, enter, eight-four-two-zero...."

Fury building, Tim stared at the tape player as Barkley's voice droned on. Dates, names, more codes. The fucking son of a bitch had some sort of pipeline to the national security system. And Jonathan—

"... I am speaking now to the construct...."

The construct.

The earthen brain bulged and cracked—and something small tunneled just below its surface. A mole....

A mask covered his face. Gas, cold and acrid, flooded his nose.

His throat closed.

"*. . . Hold this kid down. He's kicking the stuff out of me. . . .*"

He could not breathe, could not breathe.

"*. . . better. That's better. Hold him still now. . . .*"

The face moved out of the shadows. Barkley! Barkley twenty years ago.

A bee sting on his throat. The Blue, the Blue. . . .

"*. . . that takes care of the left brain. Time to plant our little mole in the other side. . . .*"

. . . My name is jonathan, my name is jonathan, my name is jonathan. . . .

It was in his head. The construct. For years in his head.

Vomit welled in his throat. Gagging, he swallowed it down, quelled the nausea with deep gasping breaths.

He stopped the tape, rewound it, started it again.

Music. Muzac stuff.

Then Barkley's voice: "Just relax now . . . relax and visualize. . . ."

Against his will, Tim felt his muscles loosen.

"It's a beautiful summer day. . . . You're looking up . . . watching the sky. . . ."

Sun on his face. . . .

No!

He sat bolt upright.

". . . watching the sky . . . watching the cloud in the sky. You see the cloud now, Beth. . . ."

Beth!

Beth Quaig.

". . . see the cloud . . . cloud . . . cloud net. . . ."

No. He wouldn't, he wouldn't, he would not . . .

"Cloud net. Attention."

Hold on. Have to hold on.

His fists tightened and he struggled up, struggled to

reach the machine, turn off the tape, before it overwhelmed him.

". . . you're moving now . . . moving aside. . . ."

His vision blurred. The switch. Where was it?

". . . you move aside . . . give way to another now. . . ."

He found the tape door, scrabbled at it, grabbed at the cassette.

". . . I am speaking now to the construct. There is only one person here now who can hear my voice. His name is . . . Jahh . . . nahh . . . thannnn. . . ."

A yard of brown tape snarled on the capstan. Brown coils cascaded down the black face of the recorder.

Silence.

Footsteps: echoing across the bare dining-room floor, echoing on old linoleum, pausing in an empty kitchen filled with the smell of cooling popcorn.

FORTY-FIVE

Chandler Bryson's impersonal lobby felt like a haven. Sanctuary, Jody thought. She felt numb.

The security guard at the Rutledge elevator eyed her lab coat. "Any ID, Miss?"

She pulled her name tag from a pocket and clipped it to her lapel. Nodding, the guard punched the Up button and the elevator door slid open.

The old car began to rise. Back to Morgan Wing. Jody shivered at the thought of it, at the thought of the storage room and the iron lung that had seemed so innocuous at their picnic lunch. God. She had practically given him instructions on how to do it. Stupid. Stupid.

The deep pain would not go away. It was worse than the fear, worse even than knowing she might have died. She had begun to believe that this was right and good, that a relationship was possible. "I trusted you," she whispered. The tears started up again and she blinked them back savagely. Good girl. You really know how to pick them, don't you? Stupid. Stupid.

Her tongue skittered dryly over her lips. She'd have

to call Cheryl when she got upstairs, tell her she was okay.

But was she? The numbness had crept through her body and permeated her brain. She felt out of it, as if she were moving through a dream. Automatic pilot, she thought. The only way to fly.

On the way over, hands clenching the wheel, foot heavy on the gas, she had planned not to go up, not to see Barkley, yet all the while, she knew she had to. If she didn't show up now, after the warning he had given her, he would know she had something to hide—and it wouldn't take a degree from the Sherlock Holmes School of Detection for him to figure out what that was.

The elevator door opened to a black stenciled 4 EAST and a deserted pay telephone across the hall. Another security guard, his straight-backed chair tipped against the wall, was drinking coffee from a foam cup. She did not recognize him.

"Will you open the door to Morgan for me, please?"

"Morgan?" The front legs of his chair came down with a sharp click.

"Yes, please."

The man got heavily to his feet, pulled out a big ring of keys, and opened the first lock. He pushed the heavy door open and she followed him down the dim connecting corridor.

"You coming back out tonight?" he asked.

"Yes." And then where? A motel? Maybe one that called itself a home away from home?

"If you want to go out this way, it'd be best to call over here to the nurses desk," he said with a nod back toward Rutledge, "and tell 'em you want out. Don't know if I'd hear you knock." He searched his keys, found another, and opened the door to Morgan Wing.

She stepped through and the door clanged shut behind her. The key turned on the other side with a metallic click, and she was locked in.

The hall was dark with only dim pools of light spilling onto its scarred floor. A faint glow came from the transom over Maureen's door, another from Beth Quaig's room.

Barkley's office was dark.

She paused outside the door, shivering, wondering what to do, when a faint noise down the hall made her look up sharply. The elevator door opening? No, she thought. The group had been told not to use it. Besides, the security guard in the Medical Records lobby was supposed to send everybody up the stairs.

The door across from the alcove opened—Tim's room—and Barkley stepped out. Without a word, he came up to her and took her by the arm into his office.

Barkley touched the switch and the lights flared on.

Jody blinked. The files were gone, the papers, everything. Where? Had he cleaned them up? It didn't make sense. Wouldn't he leave everything the way it was for the police?

Barkley pulled out a chair for her. "Sit down."

Confused, she did.

"I'm sorry I had to alarm you, but it was necessary." He sat down behind the desk. "You've been in the dark about this project, I'm afraid. That was unavoidable." He tented his fingers, stared over them, fixed her with a long look. "I've been working very closely with the police on the D-string murders."

The police. Then Mallory Corn's phone calls *were* about the murderer. "You think it's Tim Monahan," she whispered.

For a split second, a look she could not read flickered in

Barkley's eyes. "This has been very hard on you." His voice was gentle. Painfully gentle. "I'm sorry for that."

A lump that only tears could dissolve grew in Jody's throat. "He—" She wanted to say, "He tried to kill me," but the words would not come. To say them would make it more real somehow, more immediate, turn it into something she had to deal with right away—and she could not do that. Not just now.

"He what, Miss Henson?"

She tried to swallow the lump away, but her mouth was too dry. "He . . . frightened me."

Barkley gave her a curious look—the kind of look someone would give to a butterfly pinned and fluttering on a board. Then he said, "It seems that Mr. Monahan did not attend the play. Instead, he went through my files before he showed up at your place. I found a page from one of them in his room."

A page? Jody thought of the files spread out on the bed. So many papers. One of them must have slithered to the floor. Her stomach churned. It was a trap. She stole a furtive glance at Barkley, studied his face from under half-closed lids. But she saw nothing there, not even a flicker of accusation. Nothing. In surprise, she realized that he didn't know. Didn't know she'd been in his office.

"When he came to your house tonight, did he bring anything with him?"

"Bring anything?"

"An audio tape perhaps?"

The seance tape? But why? How could that be evidence?

"It's very important, Miss Henson."

"He, uh—" Think, she told herself. But she was too numb; it was too hard. "Maybe. He might have had a tape."

A sharp look. "Do you know for sure? Did he play it for you?"

"No."

A beat. "Is he there now? At your place."

"I think so."

"Monahan is a sick man." Barkley pushed the telephone toward her. "Call him. Tell him whatever you have to, but get him here."

"Here?" Not here. Not again. "But the police—Couldn't they just pick him up? I have a key. I could give them a key."

"That won't be necessary. The police will manage quite well without it."

"Then they do know."

"Of course." Barkley stood, came around his desk, laid a firm hand on her shoulder. "Call him, Miss Henson."

She picked up the phone and dialed. Her fingers had no feeling in them. A ring. Another. Six more. "No one's answering," she whispered.

Urgency in his voice. "Does he know where you are?"

"No." But he did know. He had to. "Yes. He knew I was called back here. But I slipped out. I took the car."

"You took the car?"

Jody bit her tongue. Barkley didn't connect her with the break-in. He thought Tim had showed up later with the tape—and his own car. "A cab. He came in a cab. When I came here, I took my car."

"Then we wait." Barkley opened his desk drawer, pulled something out, slipped it into his pocket. Something he didn't want her to see from the way he cupped it in his hands. "You shouldn't be alone." He took her by the arm. "Come with me. We'll wait in his room."

Five minutes, she thought numbly. That's all it took by cab. Five minutes. Five minutes.

Down the hall, the elevator door stood open. Out of sight above its antique cage, swollen hydraulic hoses strained and bulged, and a thousand fissures in the dry-rotted rubber splayed open with the pressure.

From inside the car, a shadowy figure emerged, crossed the empty corridor, ducked into the black cave of the nurses station.

In Dayton Satterfield's room, a dim yellow light bled through the transom. Across the hall, the storage room was dark. But a low-pitched scrabbling that might have been nothing more than rats in the woodwork came from inside.

At the far end of the corridor, the dull echo of footsteps came from the enclosed stairwell as Tim Monahan inexorably reached the fifth floor and pushed open the heavy door.

And at the opposite end of Morgan Wing, Maureen Dorcas sat alone in her room, bolt upright in her chair, her eyes wide and fixed and full of terror, her head throbbing with a whispered voice that only she could hear:

Help me. Help me.

Tim's room was dark except for the single fluorescent light above the sink, its glare cut by a folding screen in front of it. Ivory light streaked with rust bled through and dribbled away to gray a few feet beyond.

A distant siren grew in volume, shrieked toward Chandler Bryson's Emergency Room. "The police—" Jody's voice was a whisper, subdued like the light. "Shouldn't they be here? Shouldn't we call them?"

"The police have been notified, Miss Henson. They're close by."

Barkley took something out of his coat pocket and laid it on the table next to the bed.

A syringe. The hypodermic needle was uncapped. Its sharp tip glistened with moisture.

"What's that for?"

"Just a sedative. Valium." Barkley pulled out a flat rubber tourniquet from his pocket and dropped it in a snake's coil next to the syringe. "We're trying to handle this quietly. He doesn't belong in prison, Miss Henson. He's a very sick man. Sicker than you might imagine. He'll need tests. Treatment."

"What do you mean? What kind of tests?"

"Tim Monahan has a brain tumor. An astrocytoma."

She caught her breath.

"I'm afraid it caused extreme mental aberration."

A sudden memory of a patient shackled to his bed. Astrocytoma. "God," she whispered.

Footsteps. Footsteps in the hall.

Her throat constricted.

"He needs care, not prison. He has only a few weeks to live."

A few weeks?

The door flew open.

Tim stood on the threshold, his face molded of stone.

Jody shrank back at the look.

Barkley eyed him warily. "Jonathan?" His voice was a cat's purr. "It's Jonathan, isn't it?" A faint smile flickered across the neurologist's face. "Come here, Jonathan." He reached for the syringe.

Tim took a step. Another. He stopped, a startled look in his eyes, followed by an anguish so wrenching that Jody could not get her breath.

He stood, swaying slightly, staring at Barkley.

A blink. A sharp look. "Pay *attention,* Jonathan." Barkley's voice was oil. "Everything's going to be all right."

Jody's heart pounded. Dying? A few weeks?

A flashing memory: *The average survival time from the first symptoms of astrocytoma is sixty-seven months. . . .*

"Come here, Jonathan."

Her gaze darted to Barkley.

"He'll need tests. . . ."

. . . various radiological studies that may include Computerized Axial Tomography (CAT) and/or Positron Emission Tomography (PET) scans. . . .

Tests that required injections of dye. Dye that could kill from anaphylaxis—or something that looked like anaphylaxis. . . .

"It's all right, Jonathan."

Bastard. Lying bastard.

He skinned Tim's sleeve past his elbow, snapped on the tourniquet.

"No!" Jody grabbed Barkley's arm.

"Get back." He shook her off savagely. "It's all right, Jonathan. All right."

"Tim!"

A flicker in his eyes; they moved toward hers.

"He's trying to kill you!"

The needle flashed.

Tim jerked away. But not in time. Not before the needle grazed the swollen vein and sank into the flesh of his inner arm.

And as it did, as the pale fluid shot in, a high-pitched wailing scream ripped from Jody's throat.

The scream echoed through the chill corridor of Morgan Wing.

Maureen Dorcas scrambled to her feet, stopped short, then ran to the door.

Down the hall, a lump of metal clattered to the floor as Dayton Satterfield jumped up, his fingers tightening on a long loop of gold jeweler's wire.

In the room next to Tim's, Beth Quaig froze over her open suitcase. Then, scrabbling in the depths of the bag, she threw out clothes, pushed aside a tiny tape recorder, found the padded triangular bag that had belonged to her father. The bag fell open and her sweat-slimed hands closed over the Colt .38 revolver inside. . . .

Tim shook his head and tried to clear it. It seemed like only a moment had passed. A second or two. He had been in Jody's living room, listening to a tape. Then he was in Morgan Wing, standing in his own doorway.

Since then, consciousness had been intermittent—a circling strobe light, freezing motion, leaving dark gaps in his mind. He gazed stupidly at his arm, at the long scratch over the vein and the tiny puncture inches below it.

Jody was staring at Barkley, her face set, her eyes dark with outrage. "You planned it from the beginning. Your tests—" She spat out the word. "You were going to kill him, and then make it look like an accident. That's why you were so worried about the permission forms."

"Quite an imagination." Barkley smiled, but his eyes were stone.

"Liar. Tim was right, wasn't he? You did something to him—to his brain." She stopped short, her eyes whipping toward the open door.

The others stood there. Maureen, Satterfield—and Beth, holding a gun, clutching it as if it were alive, as if it would turn on her if she eased her grip.

Beth . . .

Memory rushed back; anger exploded in Tim's brain. "I heard the tape, Barkley. I know what you did to Beth." He spun toward the girl. "He's a spy. He used you. You've been his courier—" He winced as shock dilated her pupils. "—And you didn't even suspect."

"Oh, God. Beth too?" Jody stared at Barkley, shook her head in disbelief. "You did this to all of them, didn't you?" She strode to the door. "I'm calling the police."

"Really?" Barkley grabbed her arm, yanked it behind her back, twisted until she gasped in pain.

"Let her go," Tim yelled.

Barkley's chin jerked toward him. "Cloud. Net . . ."

The words on the tape. He caught his breath, froze.

"Attention." Barkley's eyes whipped from one to the other. "Come in. Now."

His voice was a drug. Blackness . . . Fight it.

Barkley's gaze darted across the room. "Beth . . . who's here?"

The girl raised eyes that were strangely blank. Eyes that changed in an instant to sly, glittering stone. A voice harsh and masculine: "You know me. My name is Jonathan."

You know me . . . you know me. . . .

Dayton Satterfield's lips moved. A whisper. "You know me. . . ."

Maureen Dorcas raised her face to the ceiling. "My name . . . my name is . . ." An anguished imploring wail: ". . . *Paul. . . .*"

Barkley jerked Jody's arm, shoved her away, sent her reeling into the folding screen that clattered away on impact. She tripped, spun toward him, fell back against the sink.

"Shoot her, Jonathan. Kill Miss Henson."

Beth raised the gun, leveled it at Jody.

Jody froze. Only her eyes moved, searching out Barkley. "You can't do this. The others—"

"I can control the others, Miss Henson."

A coarse intake of breath: Maureen. Her head lolled; her mouth slid open. A voice. Not hers. *"So, it has come to this."*

Paul? Tim blinked. His head pounded.

The strangely accented voice of Maureen's control: *"Listen to me. Jonathan is not you. Not you. Let him go."*

Beth Quaig cocked her head, listened.

"Shoot her."

Her finger tightened on the trigger.

Paul's voice was a command: *"Tabby! Let him go."*

The finger squeezed reflexively.

The hollow click of the hammer on the empty first chamber was loud as a shot.

Pivoting, steadying the .38 in outstretched hands, Beth turned the weapon on Barkley.

"Let him go, Tabby! Send him away."

The girl's eyes slid toward the commanding voice, and in that moment, Barkley leaped forward, grabbed the gun, knocked her to the floor.

He spun toward Jody, aimed.

"No," Tim yelled. She was only a few feet away. One leap and he was in front of her, yanking the night table out from the wall. "Get down."

Gasping, Jody ducked behind it.

"Both of you then." Barkley's finger tightened on the trigger.

"Wait." Tim faced the neurologist, but he was focusing on a point a few feet behind the man—on Dayton Satterfield, creeping up silently, gold wire in his hands.

The wire looped over Barkley's head, tightened around his throat in a glittering noose.

Barkley's shot went high. A tall window shattered; a guttural cry exploded from his lips. In a bizarre dance, he spun toward his attacker, one hand clawing at his throat, the other ramming the gun deep into Satterfield's ribs.

The door splayed open, banged against the wall. "Freeze!" The man in the doorway held a gun. "CIA."

The gold wire slithered to the floor.

Swaying, throat ringed with a narrow collar of blood, Barkley raised the pistol and aimed at the intruder.

A single shot.

The .38 clattered to the floor. Crumpling, Barkley went down, his hand scrabbling at his chest. He gazed stupidly at the blood spurting through his fingers. Shock widened his eyes. Then slowly, they began to glaze.

"Help me!" It was Jody, running to Barkley's side, thrusting fingertips over his carotid artery. "He's still got a pulse."

The man at the door ran up, knelt.

"Throw me a pillow," she yelled.

Tim grabbed one from the bed and tossed it to her.

She wadded the thin foam, pressed it to his chest.

A ragged gasp. Blood began to bubble from Barkley's lips.

"It's a major vessel," said the man at her side. "He's going."

"Hold this." Jody grabbed his hand, thrust it down onto the pillow. "Press hard." Snatching blankets from the bed, she threw them to Maureen and ran to the door. "Cover him," she yelled over her shoulder. "I'll call a code."

Tim grabbed a thin pillow, slid it under Barkley's head and stared at the man across from him. "Who are you?"

"Oliver Pointer. CIA." The pillow in his hand was bloody. He pressed harder.

"How the hell did you get here?"

"I was following him. When he headed up here, I couldn't get past the guard without broadcasting what was going on, so I had to look for another way. I ended up in the basement. I took the elevator and hid out down the hall." He stared down at Barkley. The neurologist's face was gray. "He's going."

Tim jerked his chin toward one of the beds. Dayton Satterfield sat hunched on the edge, his face expressionless. "The D-string killer?"

Pointer gave Satterfield a sharp look, then nodded. "Looks that way. Anyway, it's over now."

Across the room, Maureen looked up. Her eyes were dark. "No. It isn't. It's not over."

A whimper from beneath the bed. Beth Quaig's thumb crept to her mouth, and she curled into a fetal ball against the wall. A stream of urine spread and puddled beneath her.

Maureen's body was rigid. She stared at the door. "It isn't over at all."

"But the garrote," said Tim. "The D-string—" He reached for the length of gold wire.

Gold. Soft. Malleable.

The wire was a toy, not a weapon. The loop was stretched as thin as thread.

A toy, he thought.

Useless . . . useless . . .

Jody ran to the empty nurses station. Racing behind the desk, she flipped on a light and threw open the inner door to the med room. No crash cart. Nothing. She spun back to the desk, grabbed the phone, dialed an extension. "Ring," she commanded it. It was a direct line into the E.R. nurses station.

A click and someone picked up. "Emergency Room. Cheryl Isaacson speaking."

Cheryl. Thank God. "It's Jody—"

"Jody! Where are you? I've been worried sick—"

She cut her off. "Call a code. Morgan Wing. It's a gunshot wound."

"Gunshot! I'll get James. He's down the hall. Hold on. . . ."

Jody heard Cheryl's voice in the distance.

Stretching the phone cord as far as it would reach, she flung open the drug cabinet. No emergency meds. Nothing but Tylenol, sleeping pills, over-the-counter drugs—and something else tossed into the plastic-lined trash can. A broken ampule.

She fished it out, read the label. Valium Injectable.

"Thank God," she whispered. Valium. Only Valium, like he said.

The wall speaker crackled and an impersonal female voice said: "Code Blue. Morgan Wing. Code Blue. . . ."

"You there?"

It was Cheryl.

"Yes. I heard the code. I have to go—" Across the hall, the storeroom door clicked open.

The orderly stood a few yards away, staring at her.

"That way." She flung an arm in the direction of Tim's room.

The man did not move.

"What's the matter with you? The code's that way."

His lips split into a slow grin that chilled her blood. She had seen that look before. Yesterday. Then, he had gone out through the double doors, walking in that cocky way he had. But he hadn't left. He had waited for someone—waited for Barkley. "You're in on this!"

Cheryl's voice in her ear: "Jody? What is it?"

Her fingers tightened on the receiver. "You've been working for Barkley."

The man moved toward her, slowly, warily, the way a cat moves before it pounces.

A sound registered: sharp, metallic. Tic. Tic.

He circled to one end of the desk, blocking her way, cutting her off from the others.

Her gaze darted to his waist. She could see part of the stethoscope sticking out of his hip pocket—its metal bell clicking against the steel crosspiece.

A little silver bell without a clapper.

Adrenaline struck her chest like a lightning bolt, and her hand flew to her throat. An instant flashing memory: something thick, soft, horrible . . . choking her. . . .

The thick gum rubber tubing of a stethoscope. The bruising edge of its metal crosspiece.

"You're not an orderly."

Wadded blankets and pillows in the storeroom. . . .

He had been sleeping there. Hiding there. "You're not an orderly at all." Her whisper died in her throat.

A soft laugh. "No." The man held out his hand. Something thin looped from his fingers.

What?

He smiled again—the lip-raised grin of a predator; he opened his hand.

. . . A dull-gold wire . . . short wooden dowels at each end . . .

The receiver slid out of her hand, careened off the desk, swung in a wide arc from its cord.

An arch look. "You know who I am, don't you?"

She shook her head, felt the movement go out of control.

"You know me"—his voice was oil and silk—"My name is Jonathan."

She could hear faint voices coming from Tim's room. Run. She had to run. But he'd cut her off— If she circled the desk, went around, she'd never make it.

A low laugh. "You can't get away, you see." His tongue skittered over his lower lip. "Not this time."

Out of the corner of her eye, she saw the elevator. Its door stood open. Run. Get inside. Slam the door.

She darted out from behind the desk, raced toward the open car. His footsteps pounded behind her like the beat of a heart.

Suddenly he stopped. She whirled around, faced him.

He grinned. The cat. Ready to pounce. "Try it."

Jody stared at him wildly. He was right. The elevator was a trap. She'd never get the door closed in time, never get out alive.

She tried to scream then. But her parched lips and dry throat would not obey her, and all that came out was a harsh guttural cry. Then she was running, running with the zigzag gait of a hunted animal, toward the stairs at the end of the hall.

FORTY-SIX

A hoarse cry from down the hall.

Tim's head shot up.

"Jody," whispered Maureen. "It's Jody."

Heart pounding, he raced into the hall in time to see a man disappear through the stairwell door.

"Come on," he yelled over his shoulder. "Somebody's after her."

Oliver Pointer's chin jerked toward the door.

"Go on." Maureen's voice was urgent. "I'll do that." She pressed the bloody pillow to Barkley's chest and Pointer jumped up. By the time he got to the door, Tim had reached the stairs.

Racing after the footsteps echoing below, Tim plunged down the steps. He got to the first landing, swung around the sharp turn, when an overwhelming dizziness struck. Grabbing the rail to keep from falling, he stared at his arm.

The drug.

He clenched his jaw, tightened it, tried to banish the half-drunk feeling. Hang on, he thought.

But overhead, the stairwell light bobbed and swayed and jittered in his vision.

Jody's footsteps pounded like drumbeats on the metal stairs. Her breath came in short gasps. The second-floor exit was just ahead, but she did not dare stop and try the door. Locked, for sure. Like three and four. No one there.

She had to make it to one, to the lobby.

The orderly was only a half flight behind, pacing her easily, making no attempt to gain ground. Playing with her. She wanted to scream, but she had no breath. She had to get to one. Had to. Had to.

Just one more flight. Hurry.

The lobby door.

She grabbed the slick brass knob. It would not turn.

It couldn't be locked, she thought wildly. It couldn't. Doubling both fists, she pounded on the metal door. The guard! Where was he?

The orderly swung around the landing just above. The garrote looped from his hand; a slow grin split his face.

Oh, God. Run.

She spun away from the door and raced down the final flight of stairs. Only the basement was left.

Let it be unlocked, she prayed. Please, God, let it be open. . . .

Barkley gave a final rattling gasp, then stopped breathing.

Maureen stared down at the man. His face was gray, his lips blood-streaked.

A faint gold mist rose in a thin filament from Barkley's body, thickened, hung in the air like a pale translucent cloud. Fascinated, Maureen watched it disperse and vanish like smoke before a wind.

Although she had never experienced anything quite like this before, she knew that he was dead, knew that she had seen his spirit leave his body. She knew it without the slightest doubt, yet still she clamped the wadded pillow to his chest as if her hand had grown there.

Her gaze shot around the room. Dayton Satterfield, his hands pressed to his temples, lay immobilized by one of his headaches, moving only when nausea threw him into a spasm of retching. Beth Quaig was still curled in a huddled little ball, her thumb in her mouth, her eyes wide with horrors no one else could see.

Maureen closed her eyes and a new vision flashed into her mind: a point of light streaking through the night sky, winking out. A falling star blazing for an instant. Then it was gone.

Only a falling star. Yet it brought a terrible foreboding.

A shudder coursed down her spine. "Jody," she whispered. It had something to do with Jody. But what? What did it mean?

A clanging noise came from down the hall, and the connecting door to Rutledge burst open. Footsteps.

"In here," she yelled.

A half-dozen people ran into the room and knelt at Barkley's side. A woman in a scrub gown tilted his chin up, thrust a mask over his face, rhythmically squeezed a black football-sized pump. A nurse snapped on a tourniquet and slid a large needle into the pasty flesh of his inner arm. Swearing softly, a young man in white felt for a pulse, while another in a lab coat cut away Barkley's shirt and inserted needle electrodes attached to a portable cardiac monitor.

"Got a vein yet?" demanded a woman in a white jacket.

"Got it," said the nurse.

"Let's push an amp of bicarb."

"Out of the way, lady." The man in white elbowed Maureen aside and, rummaging through a red metal case, pulled out amps and vials.

"There," yelled the nurse, pointing to a 50-milligram ampule.

Maureen watched him hand it to her.

The falling star streaked through her mind. Cold fire. She shivered, and suddenly she wanted to run, wanted to take the stairs two at a time, follow Jody and—do what?

The star shot by, and the sound of it came into her head like thin glass breaking:

Jonathan. . . .

She clutched at the young man's arm.

He shook her off.

Jonathan.

Barkley had evoked him tonight. But somehow, all along, Maureen had known that he was there, sequestered in her head, hiding, always slipping just beyond her grasp. A shadow figure elusive as smoke.

She looked at Satterfield. He lay on his back, his hands pressed to his eyes, his face taut with pain. A different, deeper pain darkened Beth's eyes.

Barkley had called up the Jonathan in all of them, she thought. And now the bullet had left the gun and there was nothing she could do to stop it.

Half dazed, Maureen stared at Barkley's body. The team worked frantically, inserting needles, pumping blood pressure cuffs, doing God knew what. As if it made a difference. "He's dead," she said.

The nurse turned on her. "Get out of here."

"Don't you understand? He's dead."

"Get her out!"

The man in white grabbed her arm, half pushed, half

pulled her to the door. Maureen stumbled into the hall. Fatigue trembled through her legs and she leaned against the wall for support.

She could hear the medical team through the half-open door, and suddenly she knew that she envied them. Barkley was dead. And deep down they all knew it, but still they went through the motions. They had that at least. The salvation of action—even when it was futile.

Tears stung her eyes. Barkley was dead. And Jody would be.

Soon. . . .

Tim clung to the rail and tried to focus on the light bulb above the landing. But it wasn't the light that dimmed, brightened, dimmed again. Not the light. It was his vision.

Gulping a breath, hoping it would clear his head, he began to run again.

He paused at the landing to four, tried the door.

Locked.

A door clanged overhead. Pointer. Following him.

The stairs angled sharply. He tilted his head and giddiness swept over him. The steps wavered, plunged.

Look at the wall. Don't look down.

Don't look down. . . .

The basement door.

Jody grabbed the brass knob, turned it. Gasping, she opened the heavy door, darted through.

It banged shut behind her, and the current of air set a naked dangling light bulb in motion.

Get away. Away from the door. . . .

She scurried around the side of the stairwell, slid behind a wide column studded with plumbing stacks. Her gaze whipped frantically around the dim basement. Which way out? Which way? Dozens of cables thick as snakes hung from the ceiling. Beyond them, a blank wall. She saw no exit.

The sudden clank of a pipe inches away nearly stopped her heart.

Get out. Get away.

She ran, stumbled over something on the floor, fell heavily to her knees.

Just around the corner of the stairwell, the door clanged open.

Oh God, oh God, oh God . . .

A footstep.

Get up, run, run. . . .

Her hands scrabbled for purchase on the damp floor, felt something cold and jagged: a piece of broken brick no more than three inches long. Clutching the puny weapon, she scrambled to her feet.

A footstep. Closer.

She crept on tiptoe behind the thick, dangling mass of cables. She could not breathe.

Tic . . . tic . . .

Oh, God! She could see him. Half hidden in the shadows only a few yards away.

Her fingers tightened around the fragment of brick. She wanted to throw it, hit him, gouge out his eyes.

She drew her arm back—and froze. Stupid, stupid. It wouldn't stop him. It wouldn't even slow him down.

She did not dare move. Not a muscle. Not an eyelid.

Seconds crawled by.

He was motionless too. He had not moved. Not an inch. Not a hair.

The realization struck like a blow: he was hiding too. Watching. Waiting for her to show herself.

He didn't know where she was!

Her gaze whipped past him, beyond the stairwell to a thick, dark cylinder behind him twenty or thirty feet away. A reel of cable. A hiding place. Away from her. And his back was to it.

Her thumb pressed into the broken piece of brick. Please. Let it work. Please. Aiming past the reel, she threw it with all her strength.

The shard whizzed through the air, glanced off the cable, skittered across the concrete floor.

His head turned, followed the noise.

A breath.

Then he was moving toward it, creeping on tiptoe toward it, moving away.

Jody circled the stairwell. Quick. Go around. Get to the other side.

The concrete wall that enclosed the stairs was cold. Moving faster, she slid around it to the back—and stopped short.

A light swung overhead, illuminated the dull gray wall that enclosed the back of the stairs—and something just beyond:

The elevator.

God! How could she have forgotten it?

She ran on tiptoe toward it, reached out for the button, stopped. No. No good. He might hear it coming. If he did, she'd never get the door open in time.

She pressed close to the wall, listened, heard him moving. Was he going away? Still going away?

A red box on the wall: FOR EMERGENCY USE ONLY.

A red, windowed box with a metal loop on the front—and inside, a long cylindrical brass key.

A key to the elevator!

Her gaze darted to the metal doors. The keyhole was round and near the center.

Praying that he would not hear, she yanked open the box, grabbed the key, stuck it into the lock.

She turned it clockwise.

Nothing.

Struggling, she pressed, then turned it in the opposite direction.

A click.

Oh, God. Don't let him hear . . .

She pressed icy palms to the metal, pushed, and the doors began to slide apart.

Jody stared inside in dismay. Idiot! She had expected the car to be there. She *knew* it was on five; she had seen it there. Yet, somehow, she had thought it would magically be here when the door opened. Instead, she saw a pit—at least three feet deep, and soaring upward from its center was a huge shiny pole flanked by two jacks.

The elevator doors splayed open. The brass key wobbled in its perch. She grabbed for it.

Too late. . . .

The key slithered out of her grasp, rolled in a slow, agonizing arc, and clattered onto the concrete floor.

No way to breathe. No air.

Footsteps.

Tic . . . tic . . .

Hide. For God's sake, hide. . . .

The overhead light bisected the pit, leaving half of it in deep shadows. Crouching, one hand on the floor, the other swinging out for balance, she jumped and came to a jarring stop in the bottom.

Tic . . . tic . . .

Eyes shut tight, she shrank into the shadows.

Silence.

Then the heart-stopping bang of the stairwell door.

"Jody!"

Tim. It was Tim.

She opened her eyes, looked up—stared into the terrible, grinning face of the orderly.

Help. Call for help. . . .

She opened her mouth, but nothing came out.

"Jody?"

Jonathan's glance whipped toward Tim's voice, then back to Jody. For a second, his eyes burned into hers. Then he grabbed the edge of the elevator door and jumped.

Jody scrambled to her feet, her back pressed to the side wall of the pit, her heart pounding in her throat.

The wire garrote was in his hands.

Get out. Get away. . . .

Not the door. Too high, too high. Her gaze darted wildly from side to side. There . . . on the back wall. Handholds.

A short, breathy shriek. Then she leaped away, ran to the back of the pit, and grabbed hold.

One foot was on the first step when the garrote whipped over her head and tightened around her throat.

"Over here," Tim yelled to Pointer. He raced around the stairwell, stared down into the elevator pit, and froze.

A crablike movement in the shadows.

The orderly turned, and Jody, her head thrown back, her eyes dark with fear, turned with him in a terrible sidling pas de deux. Her hands clutched her throat.

Oh, Jesus. Hostage at the end of a garrote. Dizziness struck again, and for a moment Tim thought he would fall.

Oliver Pointer ran around the corner, gun drawn.

Tim's warning gesture stopped him.

Hugging the wall, Pointer crept close to the pit opening.

"Let her go," said Tim.

The man's low laugh echoed from the pit. "Did you really think I'd do that?" He cocked his head, gave Tim a quizzical look. "You know who I am, don't you?"

"Yes," he said. His lips twisted. "I know you, Jonathan . . . intimately."

A blink.

Tim's head swam. He sucked a breath. "I know you had to come here. Didn't you? Just like the rest of us. You had no choice."

"I do what I want."

"Do you? That's what you want to believe, isn't it?" Tim's glance darted to Jody. Her eyes were bright with fear. Close to the edge, he thought. The wire was biting into her neck. Just enough to keep her from moving—like a choke chain on a dog.

A flash: a tangled pile of blankets and pillows in the storage room . . .

Fucking bastard.

"You've been here all along, haven't you? Watching us, listening—" Tim's eyes narrowed, then suddenly widened. "Of course— That's what the stethoscope was for. You could hear through doors and walls with it, couldn't you?"

A twitch of a smile. Condescension.

"Do you know what you are?" Tim's lip curled in disgust. "You're a puppet, Jonathan. When somebody pulls your strings, you dance."

The flesh around the man's lips turned white. "I told you. I do what I want."

Tim blinked, swayed, felt the floor begin to tilt.

Hang on. . . .

"You want to think that, don't you?" he said. "But you

had to come here. You couldn't help it. After all, you had an invitation."

A thin, sucking breath.

"I'm right," Tim said. "Aren't I?

"That's why you killed George Corsica."

Shuddering, Maureen leaned against the wall, her fist pressed to her mouth, her eyes squeezed shut.

A star. A falling star, blazing in darkness, blinking out.

The doors from Rutledge burst open and two uniformed police ran in.

Thank God.

"Jody Henson," yelled the first, a big man with a mustache. "Where is she?"

Maureen's hand fluttered toward the other end of the hall. "Down there. Down the stairs. Help her, please."

A sharp look. Then he was running to the stairwell.

The second policeman followed, veered away, ran to the open elevator. "You get the stairs, the lobby. I'll check the basement."

Maureen caught her breath, grabbed the doorjamb for support. His uniform . . . his badge . . . the star.

"Don't!" she cried. "Don't go. Not that way."

Then she was running to the elevator, watching in horror as it slid shut, clawing and tugging at the narrowing gap of the metal doors. But she was too late.

Too late, too late. . . .

Tim's jaw tightened. "You wrote to Barkley, didn't you? You said George Corsica was dead, and you signed the letter, 'J.' You had to. George was going to accept Barkley's invitation, and you were afraid. But you ended up here anyway, masquerading as an orderly right under Barkley's nose." Scorn dripped from his voice. "The failed actor's greatest role.

"You thought you were safe. You'd killed off George. Only it didn't work. He didn't die, you bastard. *He didn't die.*"

A startled look and Jonathan's grip tightened on the garrote. Jody's eyes were wild.

Gun drawn, Oliver Pointer crept closer to the door, and Tim motioned him to stop. "It was George in the hallway tonight, wasn't it? It was George who heard Jody in the storeroom. He wanted to help her, get her out."

Something sly and dark crept behind Jonathan's eyes. "I sent him away. With the others."

The others! Good Christ. . . .

The dizziness struck Tim again and he fought for balance at the edge of the pit. "How many are there, Jonathan?" How many more? "How many of your selves will you have to kill before you're safe?"

"I do what I have to do."

The thick elevator piston in the center of the shaft. His eyes were playing tricks; it seemed to be moving, sinking into the black cylindrical housing.

He blinked, fixed on a thin streak of grease on the piston, saw it sink and disappear. Jesus! It *was* moving.

His gaze shot upward. No sound. But there wouldn't be. It was hydraulic. The car on the top of the piston was coming down.

How far? All the way to the basement? How far? There were only a few feet of clearance at the back of the pit. Scarcely a yard.

Tim's horrified gaze whipped to Jody, then Jonathan. The man's back was to the piston; he didn't know; he hadn't seen.

But Jody's gaze slid upward and widened. She knew. He saw it in her eyes.

He heard her voice in his head: *He could have killed me. Why didn't he?*

Tim caught his breath. "Why didn't you kill her, Jonathan? Tonight—in the storeroom. Why didn't you?"

A tiny movement in his eyes.

The hydraulic piston crept down; Tim's words rushed out: "You tried to. But George came back and pushed you out. It was George who put her in the iron lung, wasn't it? He was trying to save her life."

Confusion.

"George isn't dead. You can't kill him!"

A blink.

Surprise, then horror flickered in the man's eyes. The garrote fell from his hands and slithered to the floor.

"Get back," yelled Tim.

But his words were masked by a giant's sigh from overhead as a rotten hose burst and hydraulic fluid spurted into the shaft.

The silent elevator fell like a stone.

"Get back!"

A scramble in the pit.

A second. No more.

The car struck the floor of the pit, and thunder reverberated through the building.

Silence.

The telescoped car filled the lower two-thirds of the opening. The policeman inside sprawled motionless, his neck at a crazy angle, his body pierced by a jack driven through the buckled floor.

"Jody?" It was a whisper. A prayer.

A tiny sound. A moan.

Tim grabbed the top edge of the car, grabbed a rail. The dizziness struck again. "Help me."

Pointer grabbed his foot, steadied, boosted.

The roof of the car was split, half of it slanting sharply upward to the left. Sticking to the high side, Tim crept to the back. "Jody!"

A whimper.

He looked down into the dim pit.

"Don't, Mommy . . . hurts. . . ."

Not her voice. Not hers.

A faint gurgling sound: "No, Mommy . . . no, Mommy . . . hurts. . . ."

Tim's eyes dilated.

George Corsica lay facedown in the pit, his head and shoulders twitching, his body crushed to pulp beneath the car.

A tiny movement in the shadows. A tiny voice: "He's dying."

"Jody?"

He saw her then, pressed against the back wall. A whisper: "I have to help him."

"You can't. Nobody can."

Clinging to handholds he felt rather than saw, Tim scrambled down, grabbed her, half pulled, half pushed her to the top of the car. Sprawling beside her, he sucked a breath. His head lolled; the giddiness was overwhelming.

"You're hurt," Jody whispered.

She was splattered from head to foot with brown hydraulic fluid.

He shook his head and groaned at the dizzy sensation. Loose. Loose as a goose. "I'm drunk," he said. A silly laugh. "And you're a mess."

Jody's eyes widened, brimmed.

Now he had done it. She was going to cry. His voice slurred and he tried to compensate with careful pronunciation. "Not a mess. I lied."

"Did you hear what he said?" she whispered. "All those women he killed. The little girl— To him, they were all his mother."

FORTY-SEVEN

It was half past three in the morning. A cold mist beaded the windows of Morgan Wing and glittered red, then green, as the traffic light changed on the deserted street below.

The fluorescent lights in Maureen's room had been dimmed by strategically placed folding screens, and the drowsy little group was subdued. Tim reached for his coffee. Cold. He glanced at Jody. It seemed like days, instead of hours, since they were in the Emergency Room.

The dead cop had been laid out in a cubicle next to theirs. Behind the curtain, Tim had heard the other cop's soft profanity, and then the sound of muffled sobs.

Cheryl had come in a few minutes later, carrying a paper. "Bobby was James's partner," she whispered. "He's taking it pretty hard."

Cheryl showed them the paper. It was a petition hastily drawn up by an E.R. "canning committee" that began: "The undersigned respectfully request the ass of Calvin Douglas Carpenter . . ."—the security guard who had locked Jody out of the lobby.

"Drunk," Cheryl said in disgust. "They found him

asleep in Medical Records." She collected their signatures, then pulled back the curtain and led them to the hallway.

Oliver Pointer had been waiting. They were to go with him back to Morgan Wing. Someone was coming. "A debriefing," he said.

There had been time though, before Hal Gulliver had arrived, owlish from his red-eye flight, to follow Cheryl's prescription: coffee—three cups of it—for Tim and brandy for Jody. Brandy and a hot bath.

Jody's thick hair, still damp from her shower, was caught up in a long twist tie salvaged from a box of plastic trash can bags, and she was wearing Maureen's yellow sweat suit.

Except for an unzipped tote bulging with the feather boa, a beaded handbag, and a green thing she had called a snood, Maureen's bags were packed and standing in a soldierly row by the door, ready for a quick getaway. Tim's luggage and the computer, salvaged from his room by Oliver Pointer before the police sealed the door, stood next to hers.

Tim was ready to leave. There was something about Hal Gulliver that did not sit well with him. He wasn't quite sure what it was, but it seemed best to trust his instincts. After all, he hadn't been wrong about Barkley.

Gulliver was standing next to the wall, frowning slightly. He had not sat down since the debriefing began. Tim recognized the tactic; he had used it himself back when he was a schoolteacher. Stay on your feet, and you have better control of the class.

Gulliver cleared his throat. His voice was hoarse, and growing rougher by the minute. He fixed the group with a hooded stare. "Richard Barkley was a mole," he said. "There is evidence that he was engaged in subversive activities as early as the sixties. Activities in connection with a Soviet operation fronting as a children's camp in the Smokies."

Mole. A word an eleven-year-old kid had concretized into a monstrous nightmare. The dark edges of it still shadowed Tim's mind and he wondered if he would ever be totally free of it.

Hal Gulliver paced back and forth in a spot he had appropriated between two tall windows. "We've been watching him for some time."

What did that mean? Two years? Two weeks? Or had they known about it twenty-two years ago? "Just how long is, 'some time'?" Tim asked.

A sharp look from Pointer. Gulliver said, "That's classified."

And so was just about everything else. Tim wondered how much of this was going to end up in the newspapers. Not much, he decided. Certainly nothing from this crowd; they had all signed official-looking forms swearing them to secrecy before Gulliver opened his mouth.

Tim glanced at the others to see if anyone else shared his doubts, but no one seemed to. Dayton Satterfield, still struggling with the dregs of his headache, leaned back against a stack of pillows and stared at the ceiling. Beth Quaig, back in her brown mouse mode, huddled at Maureen's feet with her eyes fixed on the medium's fuzzy pink slippers.

Beth seemed to be listening, but he wondered how much really registered. The advantage of being a multiple personality, he thought. If it bothers you, tune it out. But the dark gaps in his own memories were too raw, too fresh, to take so lightly and he shuddered.

Gulliver cleared his throat again. "Your government sincerely regrets any inconvenience to you."

Jesus. The man was serious. Sorry about your boy,

George, Mrs. Corsica. Sorry you were nearly wiped out, Miss Henson. And those of you who jumped out of your fucking tree for a while—well, it *was* a bit of an inconvenience, wasn't it? But it's all going to be made up to you. We want you to have, at absolutely no charge, other than the usual increase in your taxes, the finest therapy money can buy. The catch is, the therapist is our choice, not yours.

Gulliver had been preaching the government cure since he first opened his mouth, but Tim wasn't buying it. If the others wanted to take Gulliver up on it, it was their business, but he had had enough. The only therapist he wanted anything to do with was sitting across from him, with her hair caught up in a ridiculous, yet somehow endearing, twist tie from a garbage bag.

But how did she feel? Tim's heart clenched in his chest like a fist. Just a few hours ago, she thought he was a murderer.

Just a few hours ago, he had been ready to believe it too.

He stared up at Hal Gulliver and scowled, then backed off. Aren't these guys on your side? he asked himself.

Yeah, came the answer. *The same guys who gave the world LSD back in the sixties? And Noriega for dessert?*

Same team, new game, he thought. But the nagging idea that they might have prevented all this would not go away.

And neither would he.

Tim blinked. He had just made a resolution. Where it came from, or where it would lead, he had no idea. But he knew that somehow he was going to follow through.

Tim glanced at Beth Quaig and remembered Jody's whisper: "She's got to get back to her doctor in Birmingham. Right away. If she doesn't—" A head shake. He looked at Gulliver and wondered if he gave a shit about the girl.

Tim had intended to turn Barkley's tape over to the Agency. He still did—but with minor revisions; he was going to erase Beth's name. A cold chill crept in his belly when he thought about it. They'd probably call it treason if they knew. But Beth had never heard the tape, never got the conditioning. The tape had all the information the CIA needed to pick up Barkley's New Orleans contact. Did they need a live sacrifice too?

Gulliver stopped pacing, glanced at his watch, and faced the group. "Time for a break," he said.

"No." Tim stood up. "It's time to go home." He turned to the door, but Oliver Pointer neatly cut him off.

"Sorry. You can't leave."

"Then you're holding us here?"

Pointer did not move away from the door.

Tim swung around to Gulliver. "On what charge?" he demanded.

Pointer and Gulliver exchanged looks. Then the older man made a quick placating gesture. "It is late. Go home. We'll be in touch."

Put it in the bank, he thought. A final glance at Gulliver, and Tim scooped up his luggage and went to the door.

Jody followed him out and they crossed the hall to the alcove. "I guess I've gone completely paranoid," she said, "but there's something about that man I don't like."

"Yeah?" said Tim. "You'd better watch that. Next thing you know, you'll be imagining nasty little clouds of CIA germs in the subways."

"They're on our side, you know."

Where had he heard that before?

"Tell me something," she said. "How did you know it was Jonathan who said George Corsica was dead?"

Tim shrugged. "I don't know. The signature, I guess. The 'J.' Maybe it lodged somewhere in my subconscious."

But that wasn't the whole truth. After a long moment, he said, "It was because I knew Jonathan wanted to kill me too."

She gave him an earnest look. "It's over, Tim. Only one Jonathan was a killer."

He had to believe that. But a lingering, dark fear made him avoid her eyes.

Jody touched his arm, concern in her eyes. "You're not George Corsica. You're not a multiple personality."

"How do we know he was? Back when it all started he might have been fine."

She shook her head. "He wasn't fine. He probably had MPD before he started school. But no one knew it. Multiples are seldom diagnosed until they're adults. When the—what did they call it?—the construct . . . when it was introduced into his brain, he was just a little boy."

"About eleven," Tim said dryly. Like he had been. Eleven, going on twelve.

She squeezed his arm gently. "George Corsica was sick. Even then. He incorporated Jonathan as another personality."

"A killer personality."

"George was a male multiple," she said softly. "The instinct was there all along." Her gaze moved away for a moment, then back. "He never had a chance, Tim."

The look in her eyes made him catch his breath. So beautiful, he thought. So sweet and serious and beautiful.

The door to Maureen's room opened and Beth came out lugging a big brown suitcase and a tote. Maureen followed, with Oliver Pointer right behind, laden down with Maureen's luggage.

"Thanks, sugar," Maureen said lightly and poked a car key between Pointer's thumb and a suitcase handle. "You can't miss it. Lemon Drop is the only maroon '69 four-door you'll see in the parking lot—or maybe anywhere else." As he trudged off, she said, "When you get those in my car, Beth here can use some help."

Beth crossed the hall, approached Jody, stopped a few feet away. "I wanted to say good-bye."

Jody looked at the girl with concern. "When you get back, you'll see the doctor, won't you?"

Beth stared at the floor for a moment. "Tonight, watching the others—I mean, when Jonathan came, I . . ." She stopped as if it were too difficult to go on. Then she said in a low voice, "I think maybe Dr. Schwartz was right." She swallowed. "I need help, Jody."

Tears brimmed in the girl's eyes and Jody gathered her in her arms. "You're going to be okay," she whispered. "I know it. It just takes time." A hug. Then with her arms on Beth's shoulders, Jody drew back and searched her face. "You're not going all the way to Birmingham at this hour, are you? Do you want a bed for the night?"

"She's got one," said Maureen. "With me."

"One last prediction before you go," Tim said to Maureen. "Will our paths cross again?"

"For more adventures in deepest, darkest Psyche? God. I hope not." She shook her head. Then a reflective look came into her eyes. "Remember what Paul said about me on the seance tape? He said that I refused to see and hear, although I thought I did. That's why he went away for a while. On some level, I must have wanted him to. My declaration of independence, I guess." She shrugged. "Now all I have to do is figure out why I decided to create a reality for myself that included Barkley and Jonathan."

"Ask Paul," he said. "He's the only one who seems to have a handle on all this."

"No. This is something I have to do for myself." She turned to the door, then stopped and began to laugh.

"What's so funny?"

Maureen gave a rueful little grin. "It just occurred to me that that's why I got into this mess to start with. But that's okay, honey," she said to Beth. "I'm harmless most of the time." She grabbed Beth's suitcase and said, "Come on. If we hurry, we can catch up with the spy."

When the door closed behind them, Tim said, "Do you really think Beth will be all right?"

"I hope so. She's got a good chance. At least she can admit now she has a problem." Jody glanced at Dayton Satterfield who, without a word to the others, headed down the hall. "That may be more than he can do."

"What happens to the rest of us?"

"You and Maureen?"

"Yeah. Maureen and me—and everybody else." He gazed at the wall to hide the look in his eyes. "Everybody's conditioned, Jody. That's why we buy Big Macs and Reeboks. That's why four-year-old kids say things like, 'nigger' and 'gook.' It's easier than thinking, isn't it?"

Jody shook her head vehemently. "I won't believe that. It's too cynical. I believe in free will."

So did he. Once. "It isn't free, Jody," he said softly. "It comes with a price. You have to work at it."

He looked into her eyes. Gray mist. Beautiful. "You and I— We have to start over, don't we?"

Her lashes dropped and the gray eyes slid away.

He caught her chin with a fingertip and raised it. "Can we?"

A pause. Then a tiny, almost imperceptible nod.

"What are you doing for breakfast?" he asked.

"Sleeping."

"Lunch?"

"Sleeping."

"Supper, then," he said. "Pancakes? I know this intimate little I-HOP . . ."

She shook her head. "I don't think so." She tried to frown, but she couldn't completely hide the little smile that played at the edges of her lips. "I think . . . waffles."

"Waffles," he repeated solemnly. "And eggs." A grin. "Two of them, snuggled together. Sunny side up."

EPILOGUE

Eight Months Later

A wide yellow banner swung above the open gate:

WELCOME CAMPERS

The car pulled up in front of a parking area marked off by a split-rail fence. As soon as it stopped, two young men with hearty smiles came up and helped them unload, pulling duffel bag and backpack from the back seat. "The other kids are in the mess hall," said one of them with a nod toward a low wooden building twenty yards away.

"I wish we could stay," Joey's mother said. "But you know Daddy has to get back to the city. There's that banquet tonight."

"We'll take good care of him, ma'am."

She searched her son's face, then thrust a bulging paper bag into his hand. "Mars bars," she whispered. "You can share with your cabin mates." She gazed at him for a long moment, then planted a kiss on his cheek.

Joey squirmed under her hug, knowing that the two guys were watching. He wanted her to quit, wanted them to drive away. But when they did, when the car left in a cloud of road dust, he felt suddenly empty.

The first counselor shouldered Joey's duffel bag, and glanced back. "This way, sport."

With a surreptitious look back over his shoulder toward the empty road, Joey followed the two men past a small log building. The sign over the front porch said INFIRMARY.

Someone was standing there. Maybe the tallest guy he had ever seen.

The man came up to him in a strange hunching gait, and Joey blinked. He was wearing khaki shorts with knee socks and a yellow Camp Tralyta T-shirt. His legs and arms were pasty white with reddish hairs sticking out.

Creepy.

The second counselor grinned. "Say hello to Doc Sessions, Joey."

"Joey, is it?" The big man grabbed his hand, pumped it. "You can call me Dr. Phil."

Joey stared up at his face. His eyes looked wet.

"You're going to like it here, I'll bet." His laugh sounded like a donkey bray.

Really creepy. Like out of a horror movie or something. Uneasily, Joey remembered the weird priest in *The Laughing Dead.* His eyes were like that too.

Something cold crept in the boy's belly. I'm not scared, he told himself.

He wasn't scared at all. Nothing could scare him. Nothing.

He tried to pull his hand away, but the man held it

tighter, shook it, pumped it up and down.

"I know you're going to like it here," said Dr. Phil. He released Joey's hand, threw his arm around the boy's shoulder, and said in a confidential tone, "I'll bet you just love chocolate milk.

"Don't you?"